SASHAWARMAS,
AND THE DOMAIN OF THE LUST

Jorge Bandido

DEDICATION

"Gracias,
Un millón y medio por ser
Sobre todo mujer
Cada noche un Misterio"

Excerpt from Enfrentarnos de Nuevo a la Vida
by José María Cano

Contents

Sashawarmas,   by Jorge Bandido

1.   WARRIORS

The smoldering remains of the rural mission provided some light despite
of the pitch black darkness of the rainforest in the Ecuadorian Amazon. The
black woman stood petrified on the beach of the Napo River surrounded by
Waorani warriors. She towered about a foot over them but she was still
terrified of them. She had seen them moving like ghosts in the dark,
delivering death with poisoned darts, and arrows that stroke with deadly
accuracy without any sound but the death cries of their victims. Their first
reaction after seeing her was of surprised; they have never seen a black person
before, or a woman that tall. She was woman alright. There was something in
the air that intrigued the curiosity of the warriors. Her woman's scent flooded
the forest and merged seamlessly with the mist and musty smell of the river.
They spoke different languages and could not communicate speaking. But the
all spoke the language of the forest, the language of their nature. The warriors
hid the call of her nature, they all did.

She had arrived to the mission following the old priest Antonio, her
protector, who was intent in forming a mission in deep in the Amazon to work
with the Waorani Indians, who were among the few indigenous nations that
had not been contacted. By "contacted" it is understood that a western person
interacted with them and came back alive. It was well into the second half of
the 20th century, when he finally succeeded in establishing a mission into the
Waorani territory, after having made contact with one of the tribes of the
Indian nation. However, not all families and tribes were on board with
befriending the white man. The ferocious Tagerii, an especially feisty group of
Waoranis, was vehemently opposed to any contact with the western
civilization, and for a good reason. They distrusted everything about their
culture, machines, their way of living, and specially their intentions.

The black woman was a maid in the mission, having been kind of adopted
by Father Antonio since she was a teenager. At age 14 her uncle Pedro had
started to notice her developing body and had gotten on the habit of feeling
her up when he came home to visit. By 15 her mother worried she was not
going to be able to keep her daughter safe at home from her lusting older
brother and entrusted her to the church protection. She helped the old priest
with cleaning and housekeeping duties and in exchange she got room and
board, learning to read and write, and the mentoring and protection from the
priest. She had been adopted by father Antonio for about two years when he
came to the forest to start this new mission, so she came along with him. She
had been sleeping in her modest quarters the night of the raid. After the
warriors had killed every one they saw, for good measure they set fire to any

human made structure in the area.   It was not a raid to take captives, as they sometimes did on other tribes. It was not a territorial dispute among two tribes to set a precedent; it was a murderous raid to eliminate any traces of the enemy. They knew how dangerous the white man was and they did not hold their punches when dealing with them. They saw the forest being profaned by the intruders and they were cleaning it up. It is the same thing they have been doing for the last 400 years, keeping the western civilization from reaching their land.

The black woman had hidden under her bed at first but she had to escape the flames when the fire engulfed her bedroom and she ran out in the open. She would have been stabbed with several arrows, in the spot were it not for the astonishment of the men. The only reason she was spared is because they were surprised to see her black skin. At first they thought it was some deity of the forest and held their attacks. When they realized that she was a human being they thought the color of her skin was a dye and tried to scrub it off with sand. When that did not work they tried to wash it off in the river. The black woman was terrified after seen all the missionaries murdered. She had heard about the Sashawarmas, those spirits that protect the forest from invaders that want to hurt it, but the Shashawarmas were supposed to present themselves as beautiful member of the opposite sex of the person they wanted to protect the forest from; normally a woman. If the intruder was a man the Shashawarma presented herself as a gorgeous woman that lured men into the forest with promises of sex and pleasure from where the intruder never returns. Supposedly the intruder is incorporated into the forest luxuriant vegetation, a tree, an orchid, a fern growing by the river. These did not seem like Sashawarmas, and not only because they were men. These were more like spirits that floated in the air and deliver death. It did not sound nearly as romantic as the legend.

It took her a while to realize that they were surprised by her color. She has always thought that blacks and Indians were of the same group of segregated people and she always felt more at ease among Indians than among white people. But now seen how odd she was to them she felt very self aware. She did not dare to move or object the warrior's actions. It was only when they took off her sleeping gown and let her naked that she dared to move and cover herself, out of modesty. She felt the rough hands of the warriors, touching her legs and thighs. They were debating if she was human, and then if she was a woman but she could not understand their language. She felt them feeling her derriere, speaking in tongues, and exploring her breasts breathing in deeply her scent. She was paralyzed of fear. She could not see their faces in the dark but she could feel their lust developing and engulfing her body as they discovered that she was a woman and her scent told them

7

that she was in time. She took a deep breath and relaxed her body. She let them open her arms that were attempting to cover her breast. There was something familiar about their touch that made her feel more relaxed. It was the same kind of touching of her uncle Pedro. She never liked when her uncle touched her, she was always afraid when it happened but at least that experience prepared her for the encounter with the warriors. She could see the similarities with the touch of the warriors feeling the proximity of their lust, but now her mom was not around and she was about to learn what followed.

She was surprised when one warrior took her breast in his mouth and started sucking it so greedily, breathing deeply as in trying to fill up his lungs with her scent. She did not dare to move, did not dare to breathe as more hands came to fondle her body. She was brought down on her back. The warrior that was sucking her breast spread apart her legs and brought his member hurriedly inside her. She swallowed a scream feeling her insides burning as he pushed his way inside her. She was in deep pain but did not dare to scream or opposed what they were doing to her. The warrior starting thrusting inside her producing excruciating burning every time he moved his member. She looked up at the jungle's starry sky and saw the silhouette of the warriors above her on the crisp back ground. She found a particularly bright star to focus on and travel to.

The warrior continued thrusting inside her. Suddenly she could not breadth when she felt him crushing her against his chest with his powerful arms thrusting harder and deeper until he relaxed his body over her. He got up and she felt it was over for a brief moment. Yet, she quickly learned how wrong she was when another warrior took the place of the first one between her legs and took her with the same enthusiasm than the other. She found her star in the sky again and went there, for the foreseeable time. When the third warrior took her she at least knew what to expect.

2.   *UNUSUAL BABY SITTER*

José Ignacio had always had an inclination towards the ladies. At first, before he figured out all the details of his health condition, he thought that it was because of his upbringing which was very peculiar. Unlike most kids that grow up within a family and learn about women as they grow up, and mature, his case was very different. José Ignacio grew up with his mother alone in the city of Quito, Ecuador. His mother, a nurse that worked long shift to provide for her son and get along in a society that makes life very difficult for single mothers. Because she was a nurse and was all day at work, there was normally a maid that cleaned the house, cooked and took care of him and pretty much did all the parenting.

Finding a good maid that was reliable and affordable with a small budget was not easy. They often did something wrong or were not reliable to take care of a young boy. José Ignacio was about 6 when Maggy came to the house. She was a country girl, from Esmeralda, a small town in the Ecuadorian shore, where his mom had a few friends. She claimed to be 18 then, but later his mother learned that she had been really 16 at the time of hiring, but claimed to be older in order to get the job. José Ignacio got along great with her because she was the older of a long list of siblings and some of her younger siblings were his age. Her mom had passed away very young and she had been uncharged of bringing them all up being no much more than a girl herself. So for her to take care of little José Ignacio was pretty much and extension of her own family life, that also gave her money to support her real family.

They spent a lot of time together because when he returned from school she was the one that was home for him, cooked his meals and made him company during the afternoon. He did not see his mom until late at night when she came back from work and when his mom had shift at night, it was Maggy the one who would put him to sleep. As the time passed, they continued getting closer and closer. At first he did not noticed but as he was growing up it was becoming more and more obvious to him that Maggy was a very sensual woman. Mix of Quichua Indian, white, and black, her skin was cinnamon in color, she had brown, slanted eyes. Her jet black hair was long, straight and coarse, evidence of her native Indian blood.

As José Ignacio approached puberty, he started to notice things he did not notice before. Her body was well formed, well defined shoulders, muscular legs from the hard life living of the country. Her thin waist line, broad hips, a round and prominent derriere that along with her large white teeth, her thick lips and her broad nose showed her African heritage. Her breasts were large and round, barely contained by her bra since her modest means, and need to

9

support her siblings, forced her to wear the ones she had own for several years, when her body was less developed. In few words she was knock-out of a woman with a body good enough to drive any man crazy; let along a development teenager.

She was a bit of a figure mother for José Ignacio. He had his real mother that was always around in the background but the one that had most contact with him, the one that cared for him day to day, was this extremely sensual woman. As they spent so much time together, she would tell him stories from her home town, or they watched TV together, it was not unusual that their bodies would touch. At home she always wore shorts or a comfortable skirt that would show much of her voluptuous thighs producing, could it be said, an "early stimulation" in his developing adolescent mind. Frequently she would go to the balcony of the apartment to fix the plants, the only connection to her past farmer's life that she had in Quito, and José Ignacio always joined her to help and hang out with her. When he was some 11 years old, he was as tall as she was and while she was busy with the plants of the balcony he would stand behind her looking over her shoulders. As there was not a lot of room in the small balcony of a working class apartment in Quito, it was not unusual that their bodies would touch. At first by accident, but soon he grew curious of her body and started provoking those encounters where he could gently lean his curious member on her behind.

As the time passed José Ignacio felt more and more attracted to her body and sought more and more contacts and accidental touching and rubbings. His hormones were kicking into high gear and he was growing bolder. He would hold her by her waist when she went by him, touch her back when he walked behind her, or put his hand on her knee while they watched television. José Ignacio did not know if she noticed him pressing himself on her butt but she ignored it as if nothing happened. Nothing happened, perhaps to her, but for him a whole world was developing inside his head and inside his groins.

Of course, as she was so hot there was no shortage of real men who desired her too. She was attending to adult school to finish her elementary education which in the country side did not go beyond 2nd grade. It was par for the course that she would get pregnant by somebody she was dating. José Ignacio's mother, a good Christian, supported her going to school and supported her having her baby so she had her girl while living with them. Maggy was a well endowed woman and when she was pregnant her breast became downright massive. When her baby was born, Flavia, they continued their frequent contacts and close relationship. José Ignacio felt his groins exploit when she breast fed the baby, looking at her huge breast. He actually felt ill the few seconds her bare nipple was exposed between taking it out of her bra and giving it to her baby. José Ignacio would caress the girl's cheek while she was breast feeding to have an excuse to rub her bare breast with the back of his hand. He did not know what Maggy thought, perhaps she just saw him as her younger little brother or as her young son but with his hormones *in crescendo* it was difficult to keep his sanity.

By the time José Ignacio was 13 his hormones were poisoning his blood and with the constant stimulation of having such siren in the house, it is not surprising that he became obsessed with her body. As he continued developing he became bolder and dared to touch her body more directly. Now his hand would not stay put on her knee when they watched TV. Instead, it would climb up her thigh. When he held her belly when she was taking care of the plants in the balcony, his hands would move and wander towards both side of her belly bottom. Obviously when he stood behind her to look over her shoulders the contact of his pubis with her behind was far more intense, and transformative for his young mind. As he was growing taller, his member was no longer perfectly matched with her behind but he would bend his knees to match the right height and still press himself on her derriere. He could feel her buttock and she had to have felt his erect member behind her with the same intensity. However she never said anything or made any sort of reaction to this contact.

The range of movement of José Ignacio's hands over Maggy's body kept growing every time more, while she simply ignored his wandering hands on her skin. She would let him touch any part of her body that was exposed: her legs, her thighs, up to the border of her short or skirt. He would caress her arms, even her neck and cleavage were fair grounds for his hands to explore. It was simply too much for an adolescent. She would let him touch her at his leisure so long as the contacts were not too intense. As he grew bolder he would stick his hand up her skirt, below her blouse or touched her breast. In these cases she would hold his hand and bring it back to permitted grounds. She never told him not to touch her here or there, she simply impeded him from touching her under her clothing and prevented him to make too intense a contact on her breast, or behind. She allowed him to touch her softly and briefly pretty much anywhere.

The only time she told him not to do something was one time when he grabbed her from behind at her room' door and started sucking her neck and licking her ears. He was intoxicated with her woman's scent and was feeding hungrily on the smooth texture of her bare skin. She allowed him brief moments of that and then told him to stop.

"Stop, you are turning me on." She stated.

José Ignacio knew that to turn her on was exactly what he most wanted to do but he was so young and naïve that he did not know how to take her from there to where he wanted.

"Yes, I want to turn you on." He countered but she laughed kindly pushing him away.

"Ah, but I can't let you do that." She told him and pushed him out of her bedroom closing the door behind her.

Later it became obvious to him, that she liked him touching her but she did not want to be carried away seeing that she was ten years older than him and his mother trusted her so much. Clearly she was grateful with his mother for supporting her and her daughter and did not want to risk all that by betraying his mother's trust.

Maggy's body became his obsession. He did not have many friends in school. He was in classes and could not concentrate in the subject, since all that was occupying his mind was what part of her body he was going to touch and trying to guess which outfit she would be wearing when he got home. When José Ignacio was 14 he finished class and came running to his house to be with her. Flavia was in Kindergarten in the afternoons, so when he came out of school Maggy was home alone. He was not interested in having friends in school or on dating girls his age. *What for?* None of them compared with the Goddess of sensuality he had at home. He was not going to waste time inviting a girl to a movie or trying to impress a developing teenager when he had a fully formed woman at home that he could touch at his leisure. He had far more license to touch and feel Maggy than he could hope to have with any teenager and Maggy had far more to touch than all of them combined.

It came to a time that he always "played" at touching her while she played to ignored him until he got too excited and sought too intense contacts or tried to reach under her garments too intently. Then she stopped the game and went to hide in her room. He would touch her behind and she would take his hand off it and put it lower on her thigh. His hand would climb right back up to touch her buttocks and she would bring it down again. As soon as she let it go José Ignacio would move it up again. He always allowed her to reposition his hand but always brought it back up as soon as she let it go. In the meantime, they both ignored what they were doing and continued talking about any other topic that came to mind or just watching TV. Nobody said anything.

On occasions, José Ignacio would touch her breast and she would protect them blocking his hands with her forearms but trapping his hand against her immense bosom. He felt his heart racing when she did that because he had

12

the possibility to hold and grab her breast more intensely than usual. He had the other hand free, of course, to touch her elsewhere until she grabbed it which often resulted in his other hand being freed to continue carousing. If she open her arms to free her breast from his hand, he would leave it on her breast or reposition it and continue touching and feeling her, or would reach for the other one. If she used her hands to remove his hand from her breast his other hand was free to feel her buttocks or whichever part of her delicious body became available.

This normally ended up in a situation that could not be ignored but even then, they managed to ignore it. When his insistence for touching became out of control she would start laughing.

"You look like an octopus." She would declare as she placed his hands away from her body and covered herself from them.

José Ignacio would transform the game in a tickling game that would make her laugh more and granted him a lot more opportunities to fondle her. She would try to defend herself tickling him back and they both ended up in the floor where he could maximize the opportunities to rub himself with her while she continued covering herself between laughter and giggles. After a few minutes of this struggle she would end it getting up and running to her room, only to come out of the room again after his enthusiasm had subsided. There is no need to tell that in those moments she left, José Ignacio ended up masturbating. When Maggy came back out he had already masturbated and resumed chatting in calm terms where he equally would touch her but with less insistence until the time that his blood heated up again and repeated the cycle of laughter, tickles and fondling. They spent the whole afternoon that way, often with 3 or 4 cycles of touching and fondling when he masturbated in every single one of them. This game was only interrupted in the evening when she had to pick up her baby and when the girl was around, he had to go back to subtle touching but still spent the time feeling her up.

In actuality she avoided him touching her and left to her room to protect herself from her own desires. As much as he got turned on touching her she had to be turned on too. Although he was only a boy, he was tall and muscular and his caresses over her body had to count. Having more control over her sexuality that him, it was her, the one to interrupt it before it got out of hands. José Ignacio was in love with her with her gorgeous body and had no mind for anything else in the world.

3.   SASHAWARMA

The night was dark, the air was heavy with mist, the fire from the burned mission was almost out but the black woman could still smell the acrid smell of the fire. The heat was suffocating; it had nothing to do with the burned mission. It was all about the heat of the jungle. The air was of a deadly stillness without the smallest breeze. The sweat of her skin stayed there trickling down her body. She could smell the musk in the skin of the warriors as they took turns on her. She could recognize the scent of the forest and how it merged seamlessly with the smell of their sweat, the smell of their lust, as if they had a common root. The warriors were too short to penetrate her and still reach her face but one of the warriors reached down and kissed her while another warrior was thrusting inside her. The warrior had never seen lips so thick and so meaty in his life. He sucked her lips and licked them so intensely that the black woman was overwhelmed by the sensation. With one warrior penetrating her, laying on her chest and sucking her breast, and the other one gobbling down her entire mouth, so close to her nose, she could hardly breadth. Gasping for air she was poisoned by their smell. She could smell their sweat, their skin, and most importantly she could smell their Lust.

She closed her eyes and could see clearly into the night. She could see the river flowing lazily as if it had no hurry. She could see the beach where she was being raped by the group of Waoranis. She could see from outside her body the warrior between her legs and his expression of ultimate pleasure when he ejaculated inside her crushing her with his powerful arms. She could see the infinite thirst on the face of the warrior that was kissing her so greedily. The black woman had the sudden realization that she was theirs. They were not taking her by force in a momentary act of lust, she belonged to them in soul and body. She was no longer a black scared teenager from a small town in the jungle, she was part of the jungle. She was the temple of their Lust. She was part of the forest. She was a gigantic Kapok three with her canopy overlooking over the jungle. Her fingers extended into the canopies of the trees, reaching for the stars, her feet merged deep into the sand and touching the waters of the river. There were thin rootlets coming out of her toes that dug far and deep in the recesses of the jungles. Microscopic filamentous hyphae extended from her roots into other trees, throughout the forest. drinking their zap, connecting her with the every single being of the jungle in a large understory mycelium that science were still far from understanding.

The Lust, the drive to breed, the ultimate mandate of very living organism connected them all in the mega diverse rainforest and took life of its own. It was a super organism that lives in the forest, protected it, and was an essential part of it. Her body was covered by the hands of the warriors that turned into epiphytes and mosses and ferns covering her branches. She could see clearly the face of the new warrior that was taking his place between her legs and inside her. He was the most beautiful man she had ever seen. His cheek bones were high, his jaw line was sharp like a knife, his eyes were dark like moonless night, and fearless. His skin was smooth and beardless like a girl but there was no confusing the virility of his face. His neck was thick like a bull's and his shoulders were massive and solid like a rock. She could not resist the urge to kiss him. She lifted her head, making a stomach crunch, and kissed him greedily, with the same hunger that the other warrior had been kissing her and she could also feel in his mouth the intense taste of his Lust. She could taste his desire when his tongue reached inside her mouth, feeling the softness under her tongue and deep into her throat. She leaned back and let the other warrior resume the kiss that was interrupted. The warrior inside her was licking her nipple just at the same pace that the one in her mouth was licking the inside of her mouth

With her eyes still closed, she looked around and looked at the faces of the other warriors, they all were each one more handsome than the other. She wanted to lick their faces as if they were ice cream. Their bodies were perfectly formed, with sculpted muscle exactly the perfect size and the perfect shape. She reached out her hand and touched a thigh that was kneeling on the sand next to her. It was thick like a tree trunk, and just as solid. She moved her hand around trying to feel its circumference. It was delicious. She reached out her other hand with similar results. They were all so muscular, and so strong, she wanted them all. The member of the warrior inside her no longer burned. It produced the most delicious sensation pressing against the frontal part of her pussy. It was some sort of appealing tickles that she could not have enough of. She wanted more, she wanted it faster. Soon the warrior was done and she felt an explosion inside herself when he reached deeper and faster inside her. She felt her limbs spasm and a flooding of peace and beauty traveled all over her body.

Before the next warrior could place himself between her legs she sat up to meet him. She grabbed his thick long hair and pulled it back laying him on his back and straddled him. In one movement she took his member that was warm and hard, just right for her hungry self. She dug her nails on the warrior's muscular chest and felt his rough hands caressing her breast. She reached down to lick his face smooth like a woman's and fell the desire in the smell of his breath. Countless epiphytes and mosses were reaching for her body and every bit of hers was being caressed and fondled by the powerful hand of a warrior. There were mouths sucking her breasts. There were tongues licking her back. Her long black torso stretched up to the starts giving more room for the hands of Her warriors to feel her. A thick hard cock found its way into her mouth and started thrusting inside her like the warrior on the ground was doing in her pussy. She had become the altar of The Lust, that the warriors were revering Her with their desire. She was the beach, she was the river she was the impenetrable jungle that the warriors protected. The warriors were the forest, the warriors were Hers.

4.   A PROBLEM OF STRENGTH

Physically José Ignacio was fairly well endowed. Ethnically he was a good example of a Latino; with a complex mix of lineages in his blood. His mother was white, direct descendent from the original Spaniards that colonized Quito, mixed with some Inca and Quichua blood which is common of the people from La Sierra (the Andes). All that he knew about his father is what he had in his genes. He was a heck of a lot darker than his mother, so he need to assume that he got the dark genes from his dad; but he was likely not fully African descendent, his hair was wavy but not curly enough for half African, perhaps his father was mixed with some native Indians. So he had a least two different indigenous lineages in his blood, some African descendent, as well as white Hispanic.

Even when he was young he could see a clear conflict between his grandparents on his mother's side and who his father might have been. Quito society, certainly the people from La Sierra are a close community that has remained mostly white despite of being surrounded by other ethnicities. Externally they talk about being close and homey but once you know them from inside, it is clear that it is simply a racist community that rejects other ethnicities. It was obvious that the union of his parents could not have counted with the blessing of his mother's parents. There was only one picture of his father in his house when he was a little boy, but none as an adult. This united with the lack of pictures of their relationship, wedding pictures and such led to a unique conclusion: she had been knocked up out of wedlock. This, of course, was taboo in the Quito society. It did not matter how much he inquired about his father or details about him, his mother only gave me evasive answers.

The Spaniard part in him could be seen in his factions but nowhere else. At 6 feet 3 inches, probably from his African genes, he towered a foot clear over most inhabitants of Quito. His physical strength could easily be described as herculean. He had always liked sports and had cultivated his strength through several physical activities: swimming, running, biking but most of all climbing. There was something of spidery in his long legs and arms, great flexibility and powerful hands when he was climbing a vertical rock side. But it is not only for his dedication to sports that he had become so strong. He always had been. He suffered, for the lack of a better word, of a mutation in the gene responsible for the production of myostatin; which is a protein responsible to limit muscle growth. Not having a factor controlling muscle growth, his muscles developed much more than it is normal making him abnormally strong even if he did not tried. Although, he had never taken any steroids, nobody believed him because of his protruding muscular development. The Drs. believed that this could lead him to very bad arthritis later in life when his aging tendons and cartilages will not be able to keep up with the muscular strength but in the mean time he had enjoyed of extreme physical strength that have been convenient for his work and a very muscular body that have granted him rather high popularity with the ladies.

Because of his genetic condition, he started walking when he was only 6 months old. His pediatrician indicated that he should not be allowed to walk fearing that his bones would not keep up with his muscle. His mother was extremely worried because he had a physical development that did not match his sense of danger so he often got into more trouble that other kids. Since climbing had been a natural tendency of his, and he had the arm and leg strength to do it, from young age, there was no shortage of opportunities in which his mom found him on top of a closet or bookshelf and there were not few the occasions in which he fell. In one of them he was hospitalized for quite some time but he recovered well without any consequences, to speak of.

When he was a boy in school he realized soon that he was stronger than the other kids. He could make any child cry, even the older ones, just by squeezing their hand with his vice-grip like hands. Some kids would take bets and taunt each other to see who could knock the air of him with a punch in the stomach. Without exception, kids ended up crying with strained wrist when their fist crashed against his rock solid abs. It was not long until the news of his uncommon strength spread through the school and it often became a dare for older kids to try to taunt or bully him. So, for no fault of his own he was often involved in fights in school, and almost invariably with older kids that had come to him looking for trouble. That was what happened with Carlitos when tried his luck with him.

Carlitos was the son of the psychologist that worked at the school but he had some learning disability and had repeated two grades. So when he was in 6th grade he was 14 years old and was much bigger than most other kids in the school (that got only to 6th grade). At 8, José Ignacio was much smaller than him so when other kids dared Carlitos to bully him, Carlitos felt that it was an easy task. After a rash word or two he shoved little José Ignacio by the shoulders making him step back an almost fall. José Ignacio felt his warrior blood boiling in him and reacted accordingly. He never forgot what followed: he took aim and him and jumped straight up in the air to reach his face. His left fist described a vertical arch right above his head catching Carlitos square on the jaw. When José Ignacio landed back on the ground, he saw Carlitos on his way to the ground as well. He landed on his face, out cold. José Ignacio got suspension, as many other times, but the school principal soon realized that most of the times he got into fights, it was with larger kids, so he was unusually lenient when it came to punishing him for fighting.

5.   THE ZAMBO

When the nurse saw the Zambo being brought in a stretcher with a gash on his chest to the small rural hospital of Esmeralda, there was little wondering as to what had happened. Local inhabitants of the town consist of a large working class sector, working at the port unloading the ships, or machete workers in the local sugar cane or banana plantation. Adding the regular influx of sailors that stopped in the town after long days in the sea, you have a lot of men, looking for fun, drinking way too much, and getting into fights. Just about every one carried by their side a wickedly sharp machete, or a knife that used to be a machete but after so much use and so much sharpening the blade had been worn to the size of a very large knife. Late at night, when the drinks steered up the tempers, it was not unusual for scary knife fights to break out, often over a woman, over gambling, or both. This was not the first time that he had this kind of problem judging by other scars she could see on his stomach and trunk.

Working in Esmeralda for more than a year the nurse had seen her share of these kinds of problems. It seemed like every weekend there were no less than two or three of these. However, with the Zambo she noticed something different. For starters he was not black like the majority of the people in Esmeralda, he as a Zambo, a mix of black and Native Indian, which was not rare but not very common in this town. There are local Quichua that on occasions mix with the black people but he did not seem very Quichua. This one in particular looked different from others. His cheek bones were very high, the angle of his jaw very sharp, like chiseled in rock, and he wore his curly hair long down to the shoulders. His brow was defiant, even fierce. He was not the kind of Manabita Indian that was common in the area. There was an air of belligerent on his brow something voluptuous on his lips that made him look really different from other Indian descendants. The Indian and the African had merged perfectly, he has very, very handsome and his built was that of an ox. His arms were clad with bulging muscles and his chest and trunk were ripped and tight. She remembered her classes of anatomy, as she could recognize every single muscle highlighted and swelled. "*Workers at the port, carried boxes all day long loading and unloading ships and developed a formidable musculature.*" She thought.

As a middle class, well-educated Quito woman she had learned proper behavior and to conform to the costumes of the society and never had done anything crazy, or too spontaneous. On occasions she longed for being able to do something crazy. To do something out of control, on an impulse that came out of her guts. Sometimes she wished she could just do something slutty, find a man she liked and sleep with him, just for sex, without any hesitation, or abiding by good manners and cultural rules of how a woman must behave. The Port Zone in Esmeralda was just a place to find them. Every weekend or when any large shipped arrived there was no shortage of horny men looking for a good lay. There had been many nights in which she fantasized with going out to the port and slut herself out the whole night. The Zambo was just the kind of man that she would have wanted to be another woman for. His face was very handsome and his body had a statuesque musculature. She would gladly have him fuck her brains out in out of those nights she felt like it. But these were just day dreams, escapist fantasies that she knew she will never put into practice. She just was not that kind of woman. When he saw her he cracked a delightful smile full of white teeth that made her knees weakened.

She was used to men smile at her, she always had been very popular with men, since she was an adolescent. Boys wanted to talk to her, carry her books, tried to date her. She was the queen of her grade in every year and when her prom day came there was no question who the prom queen would be. Studying nursing there were not many men in her class but there was always a small crowd of men waiting for the nurses to come out of class and there was no shortage of them seeking her favors. Her long curly hair, jet black and shinny, came down to her waist. She was short but her proportions were perfect and she regularly had too many men trying to conquer her heart. In Esmeralda, white women were the minority and she stood out like a sore thumb. Wherever she went there was no shortage of cat calls and men trying to get her attention. So she was always fending off courting men of all sorts.

When she got to the stretcher where the Zambo was he greeted her. "Have I died and gone to heaven that I am seen angels?" He said with a scoundrel's smile on his face. It was a line if she ever heard one. *"If I only had a penny for every time she had heard a line attending men from the port!"* She Thought.

Yet, coming from the Zambo she could not stop but smiling at it. *"Stop flirting you slut! This is a patience. Keep the decor!"* She scolded herself mentally.

She opened his shirt to have full access to his wound before proceeding to cleaning it. She felt a strong whiff of his scent musky and manly and felt butterflies in her stomach.

Her parents were disheartened when she came to Esmeralda instead of looking for a job in Quito. During the time she was studying nursing her mother hoped she would work in a high end hospital where she could meet a young, well-off Dr., and get married. What other reason would a woman have to go to school for? Nursing was a difficult career but it granted the opportunity to work with Doctors, so her mother supported her decision to study nursing. When she decided to go to a small rural hospital her mother could not understand what she was doing. Why? There were good places in Quito to work where she could meet the right Doctor.

The society in Quito comes is a particular ethnicity which skin is fairly white. Their eyes are mostly brown or hazel and their hair varies from chestnut of the Spaniards to the jet black color of the Quichua, and it can be from straight to fairly curly. In contrast people from the coast, where Esmeralda was, were descendant from freed slaves from the plantations and a variety of Manabita ethnic groups so their skin color was predominantly dark. The people from the Sierra derogatorily called the people from the coast, Monos (Monkeys) in allusion to their dark skin. The parents of the nurse could not understand why she would go to work to small town surrounded by Monos! The only comfort her mother had was that at least working in the Esmeralda Hospital she could still meet a Dr. to marry. Obviously the Dr. was white and from Quito, since education was mostly a privilege of the people with means in Ecuador; and people with means were always white.

When the nurse thought of escapist fantasies of finding a man that turned her on and engaging in a crazy relationship of sex for sex, in Esmeralda, she thought how upset her mother would be if she ever so much as dated a brown man, much less a worker without an education or money. She was incapable of straying out of what she was told and how she had been brought up but it amused her to think of that. With the injured Zambo in front of her, her mind was flying. For a second she amused herself imagining to straddle the Zambo on the stretcher and fucking him right then and there. Then she looked as his deep dark eyes exploring inside of hers and was afraid that he could have read her mind at that time and could see exactly how she felt. She felt herself aroused to see his eyes lustily scrutinizing her body. She felt naked and exposed in front of the extremely virile man laying injured in front of her. She put her mind on her job and for a moment could focus on cleaning the wound and getting it ready for stitches. The local Dr. was not in, and he seldom was that late at night, so small issues were for the nurses to attend. A few stitches were well within her skills to dispense, even if she was not supposed to do it. One thing was the law, of course, something different was the reality. Someone had to stitch him up and she readied herself for it.

The Zambo seemed to have noticed that she liked him, or else he was always prodigious in compliments and lines for the ladies. His voice was deep like a foghorn and she could feel the vibration in her stomach when he spoke. When she put her hands on his chest with iodine solution to clean his wound she felt the warmth and firm texture of the pectoral muscles and could not help feeling her pussy do small twist. She smiled uncomfortable thinking anybody could have notice what she was feeling and the Zambo, as if cognizant of her feelings continued with the lines.

"I have never seen a mermaid walking on land." He said. "*That is it, he is probably a sailor.*" She thought.

The nurse had to make an effort to hold her ground and not smile at him. She was ready to let herself go and fuck him in the very stretcher but that was her alter ego, who did that kind of things. She simply tightened her face to restrain smiles and got busy with the stitching.

The wound was some two and a half inches long, not very deep. She expected the Zambo to flinch when she started stitching but he did not seem to have noticed. He was immune to pain or else he was too intent in trying to get her to give him her number or concede to a date when she got out of her shift. She paused to feel his chest with her hand because it occurred to her that it was unnaturally warm. For a second she thought he could be running a fever but he had been drinking, that she could smell, and fighting in a bar so his heat could be for the muscular activity of the fight. However, the Zambo noticed her feeling his chest and wasted no time.,

"That's nice," he said and added "Now I get to feel you too."

This time she could not help but to smile at the daring comment of the Zambo and then had to scold herself mentally "*You are such a slut. He is going to notice if you do not hold yourself*".

She finally was done stitching him up and as she was cleaning up and picking up her materials the Zambo decided to try his luck as he was going to be dismissed soon. He slid his hand by the side of the stretcher and reached for the nurse's upper thigh, moving his hand smoothly to her buttocks. The nurse reached with one hand to stop the progress of the Zambo towards her buttocks and with the other one she poked his recently stitched wound in one side as retribution for his trespassing.

The Zambo released her behind and rolling his head back said with a deep heartfelt chuckle, deep and self-confident, "Ha, ha, ha, you are a feisty one!"

The nurse picked up her things and left to fill out the report. "You need to come in 6 days for me to remove the stitches," she said as professionally as she could.

"It is a date then. I will come to take you out." He replied closing his shirt and getting ready to leave with a vivacious smile on his face.

Sashawarmas,   by Jorge Bandido

"No, it is an appointment," she said trying to be stern but betraying her own words ending the sentences with a smile, despite or her better attempts.

She followed him discretely with her eyes lusting after his body and when he left the threshold of the door her eyes got caught on the eyes of an older lady that often visited the rural hospital. She was an old indigenous woman who often came and sat on the waiting room, not asking for treatment or talking to anyone. She came just about every day in the evening and left at different times at night. The other nurses had considered her someone mentally disabled, perhaps senile. When the nurse's eyes met the eyes of the woman, she motioned to the departed Zambo with her head opening her eyes widely and said: *Sashawarma!*

6.   PLAYFUL TEMPTRESS

On occasions, Maggy played with José Ignacio showing him more of her body.   She always went to the beach in her home town of Esmeralda.   So she had a large collection of scandalous bikinis that she always tried on at home. Every new bikini she bought she would put it on and come out of her room with her breathtaking body to see how they fit on the large mirror of his mother's room.   She would show them to him, model them for him, and ask him how they fit her.

It is not difficult to imagine that with his adolescent hormones and her modeling bikinis that should be illegal, it was too much.   She would entertain herself looking at her body in the mirror, taking different possess, modeling the different bathing suits and asking him if she was too fat.   Like he did not pay enough attention to her body already!   José Ignacio would go to touch her and feel her body and to get drunk with the feeling of her flesh, arguing that she was not fat but just right.   He would fondle her legs and thighs up to her very buttocks.   He would touch and kiss her bare back, her inviting flat belly that called him with the seductive song of the sirens.   She ignored everything as if he was not devouring hungrily all of her body bursting with desire.   After a while she would go back to her room to change.   Some times to come out with another nearly immoral bikini to make his blood boil again.   Between her teasing and his hormones both were making him completely crazy.

One day she was out when José Ignacio came back from school.   She arrived shortly afterward having dropped her daughter at the school.   He followed her to her room but this time he walked in with her when she was going to change from her outdoor outfit to her comfortable clothing to wear at home.

"I am going to change." She told him implying that he should leave.

"Go ahead I don't mind." He told her. She laughed, she told him to get out of her room but since he did not leave she went into her bathroom to change.

José Ignacio followed her there too.   Seen that he was not going to relinquished she started stripping, amused and accepting his new game.   After all, her bikinis were smaller than her underwear; so there was nothing he had not seen already.   First, she took of her t-shirt.   Her breasts were so large, poorly caged by her bra that could barely contain them.   Her belly was flat, covered by a thin hair tracing the sinner's path to her pubis. José Ignacio approached quickly dropping to his knees to be in good position to kiss her below her navel.   He kissed and licked her belly, under her belly bottom, and playing with his tongue in it. She ignored him, or at least tried, and dropped her pants. He helped her pulling them down from their tight fit. Her smooth thighs became available to his hands and mouth. He lowered himself to kiss her delicious skin, that tight and tanned covered her goddess's body. He worked his way kissing and licking her thigh from her hip down to her knee and back up again by the side of her thigh. All the mean time his hands felt her other leg, and her round and tight behind barely framed by a tiny underwear that did not cover much. He went around her back kissing her skin tracing the border of her underwear. Maggy was acting different now. She was not laughing, or impeding his actions. She was panting. She was not stopping his very sensual touch. She hardly moved, and allowed him full contact with her buttock. She was breathing deeply and leaned against the wall as in seeking support. She had felt his Lust and was disarmed and at his mercy.

It was not different that all the occasions that he touched her. She was not showing more skin than in other moments when she was wearing bikinis, but she was allowing him far more license than usual. He was still a boy but he was tall and muscular so he looked like a real man. The act of stripping in front of a man had produced an effect on her, she did not expect. Taking her close off had turned her on beyond what she anticipated and his caresses had pushed her over the edge. She was feeling his warm hands all over her body and she was at his mercy at that moment. Had he known what to do he would have satiated his heart's most intense desire there and then. But at his tender age and without any experience he did not know how to take advantage of the situation. It must have been that he did not take the opportunity that reminded her that he was just a boy. It could have been that he tried to open her bra but not knowing how to unfasten it, he fumbled it. It could have been that his heart was pounding so fast seeing her defenses down that he did not have any control over his hands. When he finally manage to unfastened the bra she snapped out of it and held it in place with her hands and partially recovering, she wrapped herself up in a towel and ordered him out of the room. José Ignacio spent the rest of the afternoon masturbating furiously over and over. She did not come out of her room in the rest of the day. He later learned that she was also recovering from their encounter in the privacy of her room.

Even though he was far from a kid and no longer needed a babysitter Maggy still lived in their house. She did more than take care of him, she took care of the house, cooked and cleaned so even after he was older, and no longer needed someone at home, his mother kept Maggy working for her. It was simpler for his mother, on the one hand, on the other hand, being a good Christian, his mother could not let Maggy go having a baby, and no other job.

Sashawarmas,   by Jorge Bandido

His natural tendency to grow muscle was added by his enjoyments of sport as a teenager. He never lifted much weight, Drs. also discouraged it given his genetic condition. They feared it would be too much but no one could prevent him from doing other exercises like pull ups, running, and climbing. By the time he was 15 he was already very tall and completely muscle bound. As his contacts with Maggy increased in intensity he was able to do more in the way of holding her, and over powering her when he reached under her skirts or reached for other parts of her body. Also when he was fondling Maggy, it was painfully obvious to her that she was not dealing with a young pimple face kiddo but with a rather imposing young man that any woman would be sexually attracted to.

As they continued their games where he touched her and tried to get under her garments, every time more these games turned into tickles and physical games; and every time his strength made it obvious that he was a real man. Later he learned that she was getting as hot as he was during their games but she had the presence of mind to interrupt them before they got out of hand. In one occasion because he knew when she was going to take off and stop the game, he anticipated her departure and straddled her on the bed. He had brought her down onto bed in his room and continued trying to reach under her shirt to get to her wonderful bosom. Maggy stopped laughing seen that he was pinning her down, and the game turned a lot more serious. She tried to held her shirt close against his powerful hands; but the buttons of the shirt flew in all directions exposing her bra that poorly caged her palpitating breast.

He reached for the bra to move it out of the way but she pinned it with her forearm covering her breasts. Her strength was no match for his at this point, so he forced her arm open with one hand and with the other one he reached for her bra and pulled it down releasing the breast that was so badly trying to escape its cage. It came out bouncing and inviting showing it fully erected nipple with the defiant crown of its mountain top. Instinctively, he grabbed it with his mouth and started sucking at it. Maggy was defeated. She had been overpowered by the lust and the strength of the young man. She was breathing deeply, contorting on the bed, clearly disarmed, giving in to her sexual desire. Her body shook with spasm that seemed to flow like current flowing through her body. José Ignacio finally had gotten her breast in his mouth and he was sucking it at his leisure. He was astonished to feel the texture of her breast with her skin so soft and firm underneath. Her nipple hard and peaky felt especially good in his tongue. The smell of her skin of her breast was just overwhelmingly good. He was strong but he was still a boy and did not know where to take her from there. He was overwhelmed by his success. It must have been his lack of resolve at that point that let her get

27

herself together. She turned to one side denying him access to her breast and closed up her shirt. He stood back embarrassed and concerned he had gone too far and let her go.

7.   AN IMPORTANT DISCOVERY

Maggy spent a few days a bit skittish after that day because she realized that he could have taken her all the way, had him had the resolve. However, soon they came back to their typical friendly games. She was more careful now, not to let the game escalate too much that he would be driven again to use force to strip her. This meant that she would leave sooner so their games scaled back down in intensity but continued in a similar way. It was not until he stumbled into a big discovery in which by accident José Ignacio could learn something important that changed the balance of their games forever.

Maggy was talking on the phone, with some of the many men who wanted her. It was not unusual that she would spend long hours on the phone taking with various men. On those occasions José Ignacio would park himself next to her to adore her body and to touch of her what he could. When she was anchored to the phone she would not move and it granted him more time for touching her. He was 15 and his blood was running toxic with hormones. The constant exposition to her body, their games and her flirting was driving him crazy. While she was distracted talking to her friend, José Ignacio got bolder, he stuck out his member to lean it on her bare thigh and be able to feel her. It aroused him the idea of seeing his member touching her coppery skin. However, when she felt his hot member in her thigh, in a reflex movement, she reached with her hand and grabbed it. To his surprise, her fingers wrapped firmly around the middle of his shaft and slid down to the base. She did not move more, neither did he. He was surprised that she was grabbing his member and also of how firmly she was holding it. She was not quite squeezing it, but holding it so tight, as in appreciating its caliper. He knew something was up but did not know what. He chose not to move so nothing would change. He felt a volcano boiling in his groins and getting ready to erupt. Her conversation with her boyfriend became short, and she hardly said anything reducing her talking to monosyllables, but she would not let go of his member which she continue to hold ever so tightly.

Shortly after, she hung up and scolded him for messing up her conversation with her friend who had realized that something was wrong and was inquiring about her change in behavior. However, as she scolded him for putting his cock on her thigh, she still continued to hold his shaft with the same firmness she was holding it all along, as in not wanting to let it go. She had been speaking from the phone in his mother's room and he was seating on the bed. She started moving her hand up and down slowly still keeping his member tight in her grip and without saying a word she knelt in front of him. He watched equally fascinated as terrorized when she put his cock inside her mouth and gobbled it up with her generous African lips. He stood frozen in the spot, not daring to move, not to break the spell. She pushed her hand down as her mouth went up to the very tip. Then took it in deeper in her mouth as her hand went up until it reached her lips. She repeated this maneuver a few times to José Ignacio's delight. He was so excited and being a teenager he was always quick to come. He tried to hold it back not knowing if he should come inside her mouth or if he should tell her he was coming. He did not get the chance to speak, it was not long before he gave her his eager semen deep inside her throat. She moaned as it went inside her; and she swallowed all his essence. Then she licked it carefully clean, pausing to look at it from time to time and tucked it back into his pants. As it was their style, they did not talk about it or made any comments of any sorts. She got up and went to her room and did not come out in the rest of the day. He spent the rest of the afternoon in his room in a dream state remembering what happened.

Their relationship was completely foreign to their personal communication. So he could only guess what was going on her mind. He suspected that his caresses always turned her on even though she did her best to avoid or soften their intensity. She refused to accept his advances thinking that he was just a boy. However feeling the firmness of his erection and the size and girth of his shaft convinced her without a doubt that he was no longer a little boy. His life changed forever. It took him a couple days to recover from what had happened before he went back to seek out her body again. She continued to react the same way allowing him to touch her while keeping a superficial conversation but preventing anything too intense. However, he had discovered her weakness. She was as interested in his member as he was interested in all of her. He would touch her, play with her as usual and when the physical contact was at its peak, just before she had a chance to get up and hide in her room, he would stick his member out and make her feel it with her hand or put it anywhere on her body so she could feel its heat and hardness. Then her resistance would immediately melt and turn into interest. She would end up masturbating him or giving him her delicious oral sex. On other occasions, he would put his cock between her legs from behind and started rubbing in her pussy. As soon as she felt it she surrendered and started rubbing against it herself, back and forth. Things had become substantially better but he still boiled for consummation.

Obviously they had to move to the next level. José Ignacio asked her to let him undress her and to allow him to penetrate her. She was reluctant. However, they had been having a very sexual relationship for a couple weeks, with her giving him oral sex rather often. The point where she would feel bad about corrupting a boy into sex was well passed. Plus he was quite an imposing young man and she herself was very attracted to him. Every time she gave him oral sex she went back to her room to masturbate and she herself had wished to have sex with him for a long time. Yet, still feeling bad about consummation of the act with the boy she asked him.

"Have you ever being with a woman?" It was a rhetorical question but he answered it the right way.

"Yes, I have had sex with a girl in my school". There is no way she believed it since she had seen him growing up and he clearly did not spent any time away from her. However, it gave her the excuse she needed to go the extra step.

Maggy took him to her room by the wrist, she took off all of her clothes and stood completely naked in front of him with her Goddess's body that he so adored. She laid down on her back and he climbed over her to finally satiate his fervent desire. Well, if she had believed him that he was not a virgin, then she figured there that he still was, or had been. He was so turned on, and with so much anxiety of finally being able to make love to her. He was terrified that she could change her mind, and as soon as he penetrated her he ejaculated. It was not a very shinny performance to say the least.

Of course, the body of Maggy, had enough features to keep him busy as long as he wanted and having her undressed, with her huge breast at the reach of his eager mouth, things were different. He sucked her beautiful breasts, she reacted like a she-cat in heat and it was not long before his penis came back up, hard, and hungry. Then, she took charge. She straddled herself over him. Her waist slid easily up and down taking him inside her with a single, secure, deep thrust. She gave him a greedy kiss with her large broad lips. Then it was obvious that she had been holding back all along. José Ignacio never forgot the vivid sensation or her lips on his face. He had the image that his mouth and all his face was a delicious ice cream that she was sucking hungrily before it melted. She was trying to gobble up his face with the same passion and lust that she sucked his member. He had the same image many years later when it was his turn to reciprocate to the world what he was receiving then.

José Ignacio learned that she had had the same lust for him than he had for her. He was no man of her caliper, of course. However, with the constant caresses, rubbings and fondling she always ended up desiring him as much as he desired her. His hands caressed her back her butt and her thighs. The more she tried to consume his face, the more he felt her large breast pressed hard against his chest. She panted, and slobbered him with her hungry tongue as she fucked him and sucked his virginity bobbling out of his face and erupting out of his cock. He ended up sweating, with all his face smelling like sex and sweat of delicious woman. While they recovered on her bed panting, and touching her sweaty body, he was the happiest man in the word. He was almost 16 years old.

The following days were not a lot worse. Their relationship had entered a new level. They had opened the flood gates and now the water ran freely in torrents of sex. All his attempts to have her, all his frustration for not being able to have her for the last 5 years were paying off greatly. His scholar performance came tumbling down because he could not concentrate in his classes. He could hardly wait until they were over, so he could come back to make love to Maggy. While his friends in high school tried to find the way to go out with a girl, or convince a girl to kiss them in the mouth, José Ignacio was tangled up in a relationship of sex with sex with the goddess of flesh that satisfied all his heart's desires. She taught him all the sex that no kid his age knew, and perhaps should not know. Since he came back from school at 1:00 pm they got tangled up in non-stop sex again and again and again all afternoon until she had to go get her daughter from school. At his age with his hormones he always wanted more sex and she herself, never seem to satiate either. At nights when his mother was at the hospital, she would crawl out of bed after her daughter was sleeping and fucked him all night long. She had gone from nurturing protecting mother figure, to tigress of sex that could not have enough of him. He was a very happy man.

8. *ALONE IN THE RIVER*

The black woman woke up in a river boat drifting in the Napo River near midday. Her mind was confused as if coming from a deep dream. Last time she had seen the daylight she was working in the mission in the forest in Waorani territory. She was convinced everything was just a dream except for how vivid it was and the fact that she was naked in a boat floating down the Napo river. The sand? The stars? The warriors and her on the beach? She knew the raid of the warriors on the mission had been real enough her hair still had the acrid smell of smoke in it. How about the other part? Had she dreamt the rest? Had they injected her with some hallucination poison with their darts? She reached between her legs and felt the moisture of her sex. She brought her hand to her nose and her fell butterflies in her stomach when she recognized the scent of the warriors. It all had happened. But why was she in the river now?

Raiding groups of indigenous people normally attacked and kill rival men from other groups. The policy with the women was different though. They raped the women to spread their seeds and took the girls with them. If the woman was young and fertile they would kidnap her too and take her as a wife to bare their children. Why did they not take her. She had felt a deep connection between them. She had nowhere to go now that the protector priest had been killed. She belonged to the warriors, she belonged to the forest. She had felt it very intimately. Why not take her with them?

Alone in the river, not knowing what to do, she felt rejected and abandoned in the immensity of the forest. It was all the more confusing because the legend of the Sashawarma was so well imbibed in the mind of the locals. The Sashawarmas first and foremost guarded the forest from harmful intruders. The mission was clearly a dangerous intrusion on the virginity of the forest. It was perfectly reasonable that the Sashawarmas must have stopped them. But the more traditional view was a gorgeous woman who leads the intruders into the forest and to their perdition. Not a murderous raid of ghost that floated in the night delivering death with spears and poisoned darts. Yet, since the priests are sworn to celibacy, perhaps the Sashawarmas took a different shape. If the target was no interested in sex, as the woman thought the priests were, Do the Sashawarmas takes another appearance? It was too confusing. She had heard that when the intruder was a woman, the Shashawarmas would present themselves in the form of a handsome and beautiful man that would seduce her to the jungle. She never knew if the story of the Sashawarmas was true, what could not be doubted was that the warriors had protected the forest from external invasion. Does it mean they were the real Sashawarmas? Since she was a woman, had they taken the form of beautiful sexy warriors to seduce her? Well, then why not take her with them?

Yet, there was something that did not fit. The Sashawarmas always uses sex to attract their victims. Once in the forest most of them can never come out. Some men have been known to be released by the Sashawarmas after being abducted for them to go back to civilization after they have known The True Lust to spread the seed of the forest. But women never got released. They were kept to contribute with their fertility to the fertility of the forest. Why had she being released? Was she not worth it? She was supposed to become part of the forest, being assimilated in a tribe of Waoranis to bare their children. All the warriors had taken her twice, some three times. They clearly wanted her, why let her go? She had felt their connection. What went wrong? She did not realize that the warriors had had quite a discussion about her after she lost consciousness exhausted of love a pleasure. After they took her in the beach, possessed by the forest's Lust, they had second thoughts. She was human in many aspects but she was so tall and so different that they feared they had done something wrong. Even if she was a woman will she be able to bear their children if they took her? She could be a passing deity visiting the forest. She could be some sort of demon ambushing them. A superstitious fear about who, or what, she was lead them to not take her with them. They have discussed it but decided to leave her in the river providing food and shelter for her survival, in case she needed them.

The boat moved lazily with the current. The sun was merciless beating down on the boat. She sought some shelter in the boat and found some sort of a tarp towards the prow and when she picked up to cover herself with it she found stash of cans of sardines. Good finding, she had not eaten since the previous day and was starving. She realized that the warriors knew that the trip down the river would take several days and they had taken the provision of putting some food and shelter in the boat for her to survive. She felt a warm feeling in her stomach to the realization that they had cared about her survival. They did not just take her in the mist of their lust and abandoned her to her luck. Not completely anyway. Something inside her told her that the warriors were the forest and were watching her to keep her safe her from danger.

As it was inevitable, nightfall came in the river. The pitch darkness of the river scared her. The calm waters seemed to hide terrifying creatures that could come out to get her any minute 15-foot long Black Caiman and 30-foot giant anacondas were common in those murky waters. The very thought of sharing the river with these monsters gave her chills. She thought of approaching the shore and sleep in the shore somewhere but quickly she realized how vulnerable she would be to terrestrial predators. Jaguars were common in the river too. So she opted for tucking herself with the tarp in the bottom of the boat and prayed hoping for the best. However, every time she fell asleep laying down in the mysterious mist of the jungle, she dreamed of the night before, of the terror of the fire, the raid, the exploring hands all over her body, her discovery of the spirits, seeing perfectly clear in pitch black darkness through her closed eyelids, her initiation in the Lust, how she discovered it and how she became part of the forest. She woke up with a jolt, extremely aroused and masturbated. One time, and again, and again, until she ran out of energy and fell asleep exhausted.

This time she did not dream and woke up in the morning well rested and with some sense of achievement that she could not quite understand. She had succeeded in escaping the raid which had killed everybody else in the mission. Was it her merit or the warriors simply spared her for curiosity? Or was it for sex? She had fucked her way out of certain death! Should she be embarrassed that she had been dishonored? Had she sinned having sex with the warriors? She had no choice, alone in the forest and at their mercy. She could have fought. Or could she? She did not even think of it after seeing everybody killed by spears and arrows that materialized in the darkness only to pierce the bodies of those trying to escape the raid. She was so scared that took what seemed the safest way at the time. When her feelings of shame subsided she came back to a feeling of accomplishment that she could not quite figure out. She had succeeded in using her body to save her life. She had managed to turn the tables during the rape and take control of her body and of the warriors. Her feeling of being a giant Kapok tree in the forest, with the warriors revering her body and rendering their seeds for her was strong and felt right. She had been part of the forest when she channeled The Lust. She felt strong, and empowered by that thought.

Three days later the river delivered her to the town of Coca. The local people had been trying to communicate with the mission, and were surprised that all radio contact had been lost a few days back. They were preparing to organize a rescue expedition when the black woman arrived with the news of the raid and her miraculous escape. She did not give details of how she escaped, she said she had escaped into the forest and her dark skin had helped her hide in the night. She was covering herself with the tarp and someone asked about her nakedness. She answered that she had stripped all her cloth in other to escape and not been seeing at night. This explained both her unlikely escape and her naked body. Nobody questioned her anymore and all the interest seemed to had been on the faith of the priest and other white people in the mission. She had nowhere to go, her mother had entrusted her at 14 to the care of the mission. She was almost 17 now and she was alone in the world. Father Carlos, a Spaniard, and a friend and disciple from the murdered father from the same Jesuit church, felt that he had to extend his protection over her. He took her to a new church he was starting in Esmeralda with a similar agreement that the diseased father had taken her. They gave her a place to live and she worked for them in the maintenance and housekeeping of the church; non-unlike the arrangement she had with Father Antonio. For a black woman, without friends of family that shows up naked in a river, it was more that she could hope for.

The black woman took her accommodation by the church and worked in the chores and tasks she was given. She had housing and food and sometimes some money to buy some things she needed. It was not much but it worked. However, her nights were plagued by memories of the night with the warriors. She no longer dreamed about the raid or the fire but she continued to relive the night of endless sex she had with them. She often woke up climaxing in an orgasm, feeling the need to masturbate over, and over, and over. But she was conflicted, she was living by the side of the church, masturbation was a sin and she felt terribly doing it there. Father Carlos made her confess every Sunday after mass but she will never disclose this. Nobody knew about her having sex with the warrior and nobody could know about the rest. Not even the Father. He would most definitely condemn it.

However, her secret could not last long as a secret. A few weeks after the night of the raid she woke up in the morning feeling dizzy and queasy. She realizes that it had been 6 weeks since her last period. She was never late. There can be no other option. She was pregnant. In strictly Catholic culture, living under the care of Catholic Father, there is no wondering what to do about an unwanted pregnancy. She had to have the baby from a father she did not know, even if she had been raped. There was no way from her to know who the father had been of all the warriors that she made love with that night; and even if she knew, what did it matter? They were ghosts lost in the depth of the forest.

She tried to hide it wearing loose clothing but on time there was no way to hide it anymore. Her belly showed no matter how hard she tried to hide it or wear large dresses. Father Carlos was no body's fool. He had kept an eye on her well enough that he knew she did not have a boyfriend or was sleeping around, plus he could do math. It had been the lingering question on everybody's mind really. The story that her black skin let her hide in the forest convinced some people, only those that view her skin color as an oddity but not whoever was paying attention. Raids were known to have a double purpose of protective the territory as well as spreading their seeds. It was well known that women caught in raids were more often raped not necessarily killed. So there was no mystery in Father Carlos mind how she got pregnant.

However, her sex drive continued unabated or even stronger the more her pregnancy progressed. Especially when she walked into the church proper, she would feel so aroused that she had to leave almost right away. She found herself often fantasizing with the statues of the saints in the church, or having ideas about the image of the very Jesus on the cross. She felt embarrassed of having those thoughts, sinful and more importantly she felt there was something unholy about her, about her pregnancy, about her baby. One day she could no longer stand the feeling that there was something wrong with her baby and asked Father Carlos for a confession. She asked if there was something unholy about her baby.

"Your baby is a son of the Lord. You are a sinner, and you sinned when you conceived him out of wedlock but there is nothing unholy about an innocent baby". He told her in a convincing tone. However the woman was feeling such pernicious lust as if her body, or her baby, was reacting against being in the church.

"But I have heard that the Shashawarmas protects the forest and take the women away for their fertility" she argued. "My baby may . . ." She could not finish her sentences. The good priest was understanding, even benevolent about her fear, her confession of pregnancy but his mind could only be pushed so far.

"There is only one God! Idolatry IS a mortal sin. You cannot adore false gods or believe in phony deities. That is what is unholy. Not your baby. Now get out and pray until your faith has been renewed in your heart." He chastised her.

This scolding did not in any way help the problems the woman was having. She had given up in the idea of controlling her desire and simply masturbated nearly all the time to drain her urges. There was no way she was going to bring that to the Father's attention after what he had told her. However, in the small town, in Esmeralda, there was no shortage of alternative consultants on matters of the unknown. She ended up paying a visit to a healer in town who was famous for her knowledge and healing arts. The indigenous woman was of a difficult age to figure out. Her eyes spoke of years gone by; her hair was mostly black with a few gray hair. The lines of her face were mysterious and spoke of old wisdom. Upon arrival her baby in her tummy started to kick as if feeling some imperceptible magic. The healer did not talk to her as if knowing without asking what the problem was and started a prayer shaking a feather brush casting spirits. She spoke mostly Quichua with very poor command of Spanish but the black woman could see in her expression that she was surprised at times and concerned at others. The black woman tried in vain to read her facial expressions and figure out what it was she was doing. The old woman stopped and she took in deep inhalations of air as if using her smell to read what was happening with the woman.

"I don't understand," she said finally. "You have a child of The Lust. It is not possible." She claimed confused and backed away from the woman with unmasked fear. "I cannot help you my child. God Bless you my dear", she said waving her out afraid.

Clearly the consultation with the healer did not do much to put the black woman at ease. Having lost her last hope for an answer she clinged to the words of Father Carlos "*there is only one God*". She turned her last hopes to praying at the church. Her insides were burning with desire the minute she put a foot in the church as it whatever was growing inside her felt challenged by the holiness of the church and tried to fight back; but the black woman only prayed harder trying to ignore her desire. Often as not she succeeded in warding off the lust with the help of her faith, other times she gave up and just climaxed in the middle of her prayer kneeling in the church shutting her eyes tightly and clutching a rosary with a crucifix in her hands with her baby twisting and turning furiously inside her womb. Father Carlos was pleased to see the new devotion that the young woman had found as her birth date drew near.

9.   *ABOUT LOVE AND STRENGTH*

A couple years went by with José Ignacio having the most unusual relationship with Maggy. Because José Ignacio was so deeply entangled with Maggy, in his first years in college he did not have any friends or girlfriend. He was not interested on anybody. He only went to school to take classes but nothing else and he did not have much of a network of friends his age in college. Of course nothing lasts all life. Maggy ended up leaving their house. In a trip back to her home town, she met a fellow of the area that owned a local business. He felt in love with her, nothing unusual, and asked her to marry him. She left, and he was left alone, horny and without any experience of how to get a regular girlfriend. Obviously since Maggy was the one who took care of him since his infancy, there was a strong maternal element, Oedipal, in his relationship with her. Perhaps that is the reason he got a minor in psychology. His maternal figure was split between his real mother who was there but never present, like an unreachable love. The one who he saw far more often was Maggy, with whom he had all the physical contact, far more than any boy should have with a woman. But because she was not his real mother he had the best of both worlds. He could have sex with his maternal figure, at least while it lasted. This particularity of his upbringing was bound to produce consequences in his adult emotional live. Another problem was that he did not learn the regular way to obtain a girlfriend, he never thought of having a relationship that that involved anything other than satisfying primeval physical urges. After Maggy and José Ignacio started having sex there were few words or communication of any sort beyond where she wanted him to kiss her or what she wanted him to do to her. So talking was kept to the minimal. That was the concept of pair bonding he had developed. It was one that only involved sex, and nothing else.

In view of this is not surprising when José Ignacio became an adult all that he wanted from the women was sex. As the child matures, the love for the mother is supposed to be transfer towards a partner that eventually becomes the beneficiary of the feeling of love and sexual desire. Later in his studies of biology he learned that human brains have three parallel systems when it comes to couples. One mediated by testosterone that controls the sexual desire. The sexual encounter and orgasm releases the second neurotransmitter, dopamine, that controls the sensation of seeking out and longing. Last, there is Oxytocin that controls the feelings of satisfaction when a person has the beloved one nearby. So testosterone drives the person to sex. The sexual encounter releases dopamine that makes the person feel good. The presence of the lover when the injection of dopamine occurs tells the brain who to recognize and to seek out that person. Finally, after sex embraces and frolicking releases ocytocin that tells the brain who to cuddle with. This was all simple with Maggy but as José Ignacio transitioned from his relationship with Maggy, he had to learn how to get conquest and love a woman his age, or that wanted something other than sex.

He studied biology at Universidad San Católica de Quito. The alternative was Universidad Central that was free but the level of education was much lower. Universidad Católica was private and costs a lot of money that he, or his mother didn't have but his grandfather had left an endowment for his education so he could afford to attend to a school of much higher means he would have otherwise.

He specialized in botany in particular on ethnobotany and with a strong hobby of epiphytes, plants that live up on branches of other plants or high on rocks, and orchids. He managed to coordinate his love and skills for climbing with his work with epiphytes as epiphytes are difficult to reach from the ground. In Latin America, biology is not considered a real profession. It is not something that will get you a job or reliable employment so few men go into it. Mostly biology is considered almost like a hobby for people who do not need to work, tree huggers and the like (those that wanted to study medicine started directly in a separate school of medicine). Or it is considered a career for women to get some occupation on the side, give them chance to meet a husband while they are in college that will supports them after the marry. José Ignacio loved biology so much that he did not care about the prospect of not finding a job but as a result, he ended up surrounded by women during his college years. Giving the details of his upbringing, this was not necessarily something easy to handle.

After Maggy left, José Ignacio saw himself alone he started paying attention to other women that went to school with him, until then, he had ignored them, being so obsessed with Maggy's body. It was difficult for him to start looking for a partner because he never had the need. He had no experience how to make the transition from acquaintance, to friends, to girlfriend, to lover. In what moment it was acceptable to kiss her? How do you know she likes you? What are the signals that she wants to be taken out to dinner? Or taken to bed? When is she ready for him to touch her breast? When to take off her skirt? These were questions that most men his age would have already figured out during their adolescence but he had spent all his adolescence having wild sex with the Goddess of desire. Once he had a woman in bed, he knew exactly how to proceed but he had no idea of how to bring her from the benches of the university or a dining table to the bed. His only experience had been with Maggy and the procedure was to touch here, touch there, and feel her body assessing her reaction for acceptance but even he knew that the proper path was not to start feeling the body of his female acquaintances. Or was it?

Among his classmates there was a woman called Francia that he really liked. She was short, with dark skin, like him, she had some African ancestor; just like him, she was mixed. This was uncommon in Universidad Católica because economic class and ethnicity ware tightly linked and most brown people could not afford private universities but Francia had a scholarship from sports, since she was quite the athlete. She ran triathlons and her body was very hard and well defined. She wore very short hair like a little boy but with a very appealing body. Her calves were bulky and well-shaped. All her body was all wrapped up by iron cast muscles. Her behind was, African, exquisite, and prominent. Her lips were thick and generous as corresponded to her heritage. It may have been her dark skin what attracted him to her since most students at the university were white Hispanic, Francia and José Ignacio shared that peculiarity of their ethnicity, they were not the typical Quito upper class students, she was obviously from the coast. She dressed modestly and did not show up her forms but there is no way to hide a good derriere from a knowing eye. She did not have the phenomenal set of breasts that Maggy had. Her breasts were rather small, the perky kind, runner's breast.

The problem was that Francia had a boyfriend. José Ignacio knew it because they boyfriend's sister was one of the few friends he had developed in a climbing club he had joined. He knew that Francia's boyfriend was hemophiliac. He also knew that during a bleeding emergency he was taken to the hospital where he received a transfusion, but because the Quito's hospital lacked of a good method for screening for HIV at the time, he was infected with the virus. Francia had been his girlfriend for about a year when he was giving HIV and she saw herself in a very difficult situation. Her boyfriend had acquired HIV for no fault of his own, so she did not want to leave him. On the other hand, to make love with someone with HIV was considered risky, especially back then in Ecuador when we did not know a lot about HIV and how it was transmitted. So their relationship was mostly platonic. What could José Ignacio do with this "intelligence" from his friend that Francia did not have a very active, or satisfactory sex life?

Francia studied biology like him, but her interest was in fishes. José Ignacio knew she spent late night hours in the laboratory by herself examining specimens under a dissecting scope. One evening, he came to her laboratory to talk to her and try his luck. He greeted her *warmly* with a kiss and a long hug, a bit longer and tighter than it was proper. It is fashionable among Latin American to hug and kiss when they meet or say good bye. He just held her a bit tighter for a bit longer to test the waters. She just let him hold her. She went back to her dissecting scope and he started talking to her seeking conversation with any pretext. He sat next to her but his hands were wrestles, touching her forearms, feeling her smooth tight skin of her shoulders. He passed his arm over her, touching her back gently.

"Wow, you have nicely defined shoulders." He commented as he felt up her neck and shoulders. Clearly someone who works so hard for her body would have an appreciation that people paid attention to it.

"You also have very strong arms." she reciprocated with a furtive glance at his massive forearms and bulging biceps; more for a sense of duty than because she felt comfortable talking about that.

Francia allowed him to touch her shoulders and to hold her waist without saying anything. As she did not complain or opposed his exploratory hands he became bolder and starting going farther, staying longer in more intimate zones, like feeling the soft skin in the inner part of her forearm.

"Your skin is so soft. It feels like silk." He commented to justify his caressing her and touching the back of her neck and back of her ears, in what was clearly a purposeful caress, no longer innocently holding her. He continued increasing pressure and she let him. She resisted his siege, silently, without complaining pretending to look into the dissecting scope or doing idle conversation. As she allowed him room for progress he went the next step. When he put his hand on her breast, some small, very firm a perky boobs sitting on her firm pectorals, she covered herself but did not say anything. José Ignacio was entering into a very familiar terrain. It was not very different from his years learning about the woman's body with Maggy, with the difference that he was no longer a teenager, and he had learned a lot how to turn on a woman. Her reaction, or rather, lack of direct refusal, led him to take the next step. He hugged her from behind and started giving her tender kisses on her neck, licking her ears, and sucking the lobes of her ears alternatively.

"You smell so good!" He commented taking a deep breath. His hands closed over her chest, he pressed his chest to her back and himself on her behind. Francia gasped quietly surprised to be held so intimately and covered her breast from his exploring hands that were going directly to them. Yet, continued trying to ignore his advances and pretended to focus in the dissecting scope. This was her last opportunity to speak out to stop him and preventing him from moving any forward but she missed her chance.

She continued to protect her breast and most erogenous parts but it left him way too many opportunities for his exploring hands and lips. José Ignacio could smell her woman's scent behind her ear when he kissed her neck. He took the lobe of her ear and sucked in tenderly, intensely. They continued

42

that situation where she tried to resist the effect of his caresses but allowing him to touch her without telling him to stop what he was doing. He had the image, that he will have many times in the future, that she was a bar of butter sitting on a hot skillet trying not to melt despite the heat from the stove. He noticed that she was ambivalent about his touching her and he knew she was ready. José Ignacio started unbuttoning her shirt, peeling her upper body. She continued her voiceless resistance. She stopped any pretensions with the dissecting scope and started buttoning up back the buttons that he undid but while she buttoned up some he had plenty of time to unbutton more. After two cycles her shirt was completely open and he could caress her breast over her bra. Francia shivered to feel his warm hands on her breast and protected them with her forearms. His hands would slide down her lower belly, and her solid abs and trunk at his will. She had a long brown skirt that covered all the way to her ankles. He lifted her skirt and caressed her legs, her knees, her thighs. Her thighs were incredible firm, even firmer for the tension produced by his trespassing hands and relentless fondling. Her hands were busy protecting her breast. When she tried to hold his wrist to stop him from foundling her the hand would find the breast she left unguarded and holding it firmly.

She was very aware that he was pressing himself against her and trying to avoid it, she backed herself into the corner of the laboratory bench and the wall where she had no choice but endure his trespassing hands all over her body and him rubbing himself on her. He pressed her against his chest and lifted her clear of the lab stool taking her to the ground to get better control of her. He laid on top of her using his weight to dominate her while kissing her in her neck, introducing his legs between hers. This was the same maneuver that he had done so many times trying to make love to Maggy but then he did it between tickles and giggles pretending that it was only a game. Now there was no disguise or pretending. He was trying to take off her clothes to make love to her, they were both perfectly aware of it, and he was not necessarily asking for permission.

With the help of gravity her long heavy skirt played in his favor. José Ignacio moved his hand by her strong thighs all the way to her hip and pulled down her underwear. She tried to hang on to it but the underwear reaped not resisting their tug-of-war. As he pulled down his piece of her underwear, he took another stroll by her fabulously muscular legs. He lifted himself up a bit to pull out his member, and she took advantage of it to turn around and try to escape but while she was in all four, trying to get up, he subdued her again hugging her from behind and flattening her down against the floor. Francia panted of tiredness for the effort trying to resist and José Ignacio panted for the arousal for feeling her delicious body and anticipation of the banquet which he felt it was imminent.

He lifted her skirt completely leaving her in the floor facing down with her delicious and bare behind facing him. Penetrating her was a done deal; at least that is what he thought. He put his hot member on her behind and Francia's whole body shivered to the feeling of the male's hardness. José Ignacio climbed on top of her and started kissing her neck, ears, while his hands caressed her breasts under her bra arousing her inviting her to surrender. He put his member behind her trying to start finding his way inside her. He did not count with her extremely strong legs that closed shot denying him access to her sex. Her powerful legs were straight down with her body stiff that did not allow him to get between her legs. He tried to bend her over to penetrate her but she was like a solid rod of steel and would not give.

Francia painted with her thick lips semi open as if asking to be kissed. José Ignacio longed to suck them but that could wait until he had skewered her. He reached for her pussy with his hand in front of her which led her to make the mistake he was hoping for. She pulled back her pussy away from his fingers pushing her derriere backwards, bending over at the hip, just the movement he needed. He shoved his member between her legs just at the edge of her pussy. She tried to straighten her body again but it only trapped his cock between her legs, right at her entrance. Every new step got him a bit closer and as their two bodies strained physically, his superior strength was paving the way for him. He continued to finger her clitoris in front with his hands to arouse her. Any attempt to lower the contact of his finger in her clit resulted in her bending over and getting her pussy closer to his member. But letting him finger her clitoris was a clear path of defeat for her. She tried pulling his arm away from her crotch but she could barely grab his thick forearm, and feeling it solid like a log, she gave up on that idea. Again, she had to resist arousal or give up. The contact of his finger on her clit, soft and tender was way too intense and she had to lower it, or else she would give out to her own arousal. She felt herself too aroused and she had to stop it at any cost. She pulled back from his finger pushing her behind out. As soon as she pulled back a little to lower the intensity of his fingers on her clit his member found his way inside her. Francia made a last vigorous attempt to avert being penetrated, but he had her completely under his control and she was growing exhausted after the long asymmetrical struggle. He slid his cock inside her in one thrust. Francia let go a deep breath of resignation.

To his surprise she was moist and well lubricated. He could only imagine that it was due to all that fondling. It was at this moment when she finally stopped struggling and resigned herself to let him have her. He turned her head to the side and kissed her lips with gluttony but she did not return his kisses. With her resigned, closed eyes, she allowed his tongue search and explore the softness insider her mouth but did not reciprocate. He had to find her tongue in the back of her mouth where she pulled her away from his. Her eyes were closed, not afraid, not angry, just closed. Her body was inert, not struggling, not cooperating, just immobile. He thrusted in and out of her slowly at first and progressively deeper and faster. She let him do with her as he wished without collaboration or resistance. José Ignacio enjoyed the delicious banquet of her body and came inside her painting with his body over hers. When he finished he kissed her tenderly on her eyes, nose and mouth. She was panting and sweating. It was obvious that she panted for tiredness due to physical exertion but it occurred to him that she might have experienced some pleasure. Her lips were dry for the intense panting. So were her eyes!

10. A SOCIAL ASSAULT

The day was a troubled one. The president was murdered in a freak accident, likely because of his support for the working classes. The people of Ecuador never had a president that looked after them before and the news that this one, who cared about the people, had died in suspicious circumstances had outraged the working class. It started with discontent in the streets but as the mass grew, and they realized how many they were, the situation escalated. Esmeralda was a place of strong racial and socioeconomic disparities, with the very wealthy very close to the very poor. The port and plantations produced a few people that were very wealthy right next to the workers that live in very extreme poverty. Ethnic tensions were also very high, few white people held all the money and power while the black majority was much disenfranchised. It was a keg of powdered ready to go. When the news got out about the president's assassination it provided the spark that was needed.

From big streets demonstration, someone angry chose to throw a rock through a window of a store. The people got in and looted the store. From there it was all down the hill. From one store being looted followed the next and the next and the next until the whole town was in a terrifying state of lawlessness. The wealthy people locked themselves in their mansions or hit the road with their family leaving the town to the poor and needy. At first there was an understandable need for goods, and food, that lead people to the stores. The police could not do anything and they themselves joined the looting in occasions since they were poor and brown as well. Around midday the state of lawlessness was absolute and it was clear that the law of the stronger had taken hold in town. The port was empty, Captains took their ships out to save them from them mayhem, the port workers were in the streets as well as all other businesses. There was a feeling of anger for having had the dear president taken, on the one hand, and a sense of retribution, they wanted to take back from the rich people what the mass felt they deserved. From a problem of economic inequality the situation degenerated to a problem of strength and racial tensions. The poor and brown realized that there was strength in their numbers and their union could mean a difference. Soon the state of lawlessness turned into euphoria celebrating their power and it did not take long before it all started feeling like a party, like a free holiday to do as you please. There was no boss, no police no law at all. After enough booze was running through the streets all restrain went out the window. A white woman walking by the plaza received a few cat calls from drunken men. She disregarded them, as she would any other day, but that day they gave her chase and caught her. She tried to fight back but her attempts only trigger their predatory instincts. They raped her in broad day light without anyone doing anything about it, but quite the opposite. The next white woman that was seeing around was chased and raped without second thoughts. The second floodgates had been opened. The economic tension ran too close to the ethnic one and once the first barrier was shattered they felt to overcome the next. The stores were a free for all and so where any women found alone in the streets. At first they were mostly white women but soon any woman was fair game.

It must have been close to 3 PM the nurse was in the rural hospital, aware of the looting in the city but not worried about it, since the hospital was there to serve the people. There was no wealth, or anything that anyone would seek in there. Everyone in the hospital worked for the poor and brown, they were on their side, so to speak. She was anticipating that it was going to be a busy night when the party mood turned into fight, as it often happened in the weekends and holidays. She decided to take a shower to be ready for the evening. Her sleeping quarters were connected to the hospital main room as where the rooms of all the other nurses. It was a nice perk of the job, providing free housing but in exchange she worked way more hours than her shift mandated since she was there all the time.

Coming out of the shower she heard the commotion taking place in the small hospital. She got herself ready and went in the main room thinking there were lots of patients. What she saw shocked her. There was a small horde of men that were taking over the main hall. Because the highly educated nurses were all white and the men from town where all black or brown, the situation was a Dantesque scene of brown men assaulting white women. Estella, her nurse friend, was up on the hall paralyzed of fear, crying and pleading for mercy while three men took away her clothes fondling and touching her. Rebecca was across the hall from Estella, face down on a stretcher, screaming from the top of her lungs, held down by the arms by black a man while another one was raping her from behind. Mónica, closest to her, on her left, had grabbed a scalpel and was keeping 4 men at bay wielding it wildly towards anyone that drew near her. It was too late for the nurse to hide back in her room, she had been spotted by two other men. She rushed to the shelf where the scalpels were, on her left, aiming to close ranks with Mónica against the attackers. But she could not make it. She was grabbed by one of the men who was coming for her.

She spun on her heels and kneed him in the crotch making him release her. She continued her path towards the scalpels but she was caught again. Two strong arms held her from behind dragging her to a surgery table and pinning her arms against it, facing up. Two other men held her legs and a

fourth placed himself between her legs spreading them apart. She flexed one
of her legs and extended it vigorously sending one of her captors to the floor.
She twisted at the hip, spinning her free leg with all her might and kicked the
one holding the other leg on the face sending him back. She was glad all those
days working out and being part of the Volleyball team had given her strong
legs. Turning quickly she bit the one holding her arms and the attacker let go
of her. As she tried to get up to arm herself, the one that was in front of her
drew his fist back. All she saw a set of dark knuckles growing and growing as it
inevitably approached her eye but there was nothing she can do. Everything
went dark.

****

When the nurse came back, she was back to the position before her brave
struggle. They had pulled out her pants and was naked from the waist down.
All buttons of her shirt had been torn and her breasts where exposed. She was
pinned on the table with her legs spread apart by two strong men, a third held
her arms and a fourth between her legs was pulling out his member to rape
her. She tried to free herself using the same maneuver, but this time they were
expecting it and did not let her go. Much as she tried to shake and free
herself, he was being held firmly by men much stronger than her. She decided
to save her strength to bite half of the face off of the rapist when he came
within range. She just had to time it right.

In that moment, she saw a massive dark fist smash on the temple of the
man that was between her legs. His eyes went unnaturally white and he
dropped vertically to the floor, like dead weight. Since her anatomy classes she
was surprised how thin a plate the temporal bone is and how easy it can break
if hit sidewise. She was pretty sure that that guy was done for.

What followed was a dark tornado of knuckles, and elbows flying over her.
Every gust of wind ended with the muffled sound of fist against a jaw, a
cheekbone or a nose. In the last one her savior reached over the stretcher to
hit the last one of her captors and the ceiling was covered by a dark and
massive pectoral muscle with a small stitched up wound in front of her face.
"*The Zambo*" she thought, and a big relief flooded her soul.

11. THE HANGOVER OF FRANCIA

After José Ignacio made love to Francia, he kissed her for some more time before he let her go from underneath him. She got up and quietly gathered up her cloths that he had pulled out of her in the struggle. He zipped up his pants and left without a word. Once passed the paroxysm of the sexual frenzy and his feverish enjoyment of her body, he had time to think and be tormented by questions: "*Did I just rape my friend? I did not hurt her. Or Did I?*" He told himself. "*She never said the famous 'no' a woman is supposed to say.*" He thought. He did take her clothes off forcibly and he did force her into a position that allowed him to penetrate her but the penetration was easy, smooth and without any pain. She resisted him taking off her clothes but never told him not to do it. Francia tried to prevent penetration, but she never said "stop". Of course, as he thought of that he also realized that it was obvious that she did not want him to do it, not having said it was a rhetorical detail. Or was it?

José Ignacio knew she had not said "no", but he wondered: "*If she had told me not to take her clothes off, would I have listened to her? If she had told me not to penetrate her, would I have obeyed her?*" He was not sure about the answer. He remembered clearly paying attention to what she said with her mouth, as much as he was ignoring what she said with her actions. He knew she did not tell him to stop. She did not tell him to go away. She never said anything close to the required "no" that men need to listen to. He wanted to think that he would have listened to her orders, had she given any but he could not deny that after he was aroused fondling her delicious body and about to feast on her it would have been difficult to stop. It is possible that he would have listened to her at first but after they got into the struggle that he was enjoying so much, he was afraid he would have not stopped then. He did not noticed then that he was "*enjoying the struggle*". The physical struggle of taking her clothes off and subduing her resistance, the conquering of every inch of her skin by physical means had been most enticing. He had enjoyed her resistance tremendously, nearly as much as he had enjoyed of making love to her. The physical strength, the adrenaline rush of the exercise, the feeling of power and over powering the woman he desired was just as enticing as the sexual pleasure but at the time he did not realize it.

It also occurred to him that she was ambivalent about the whole thing. Perhaps she wanted him to make love to her but did not want to be unfaithful to her boyfriend. If he forced her to make love, she could have her clean conscience that she had not agreed to make love with another man while also being able to enjoy some hard sex with a very amorous man who desire her so

49

much that he was ready to take her, at any cost. José Ignacio was learning how much women enjoy being desired and lusted after but he was still knew o the concept. He spent the night thinking what he had done. He went from feeling terribly about it to masturbating remembering the excitement of subduing her and making love to his friend, and then gone back to feel bad for abusing his strength an imposing himself on a woman, a friend, nonetheless. He would have felt a lot worse were it not for the events that occurred three days later.

It was evening, he was wondering about the whole things and not knowing what he was doing he dropped by Francia's lab again. He wanted to talk to her, he wanted to apologize if there was room for that, but most of all, he wanted to talk to her and see how she was doing. After having forced her to have sex, it was stupid to think in going to "*say hello*" but something told him that he should go see her. He felt a longing for her presence that he did not understand quite well. As soon as José Ignacio entered her lab and greeted her she did not show any difference from the first time. As soon as he walked in, she greeted him with a kiss casually.

"Roberto" a graduate student that worked in the same lab "is in his office." She told him.

José Ignacio acknowledged it and followed her to her lab bench where she was, as usual, observing a small fish with the dissecting scope. She was short with him, without the broad beautiful smile of large very white teeth, that often decorated her mouth but she did not say anything. She did not give him any angry or disapproving look and most important of all, she did not get up and took off running, or asked for any help when she saw him come inside the lab. She continued working with him around as if nothing had happened the last time.

José Ignacio had the opportunity to appreciate her body a bit better. She had short tight jean shorts showing her delicious thighs and legs. Her skin was dark and shinny and he could see every single of her muscles drawn in relief. She wore a tan blouse with no sleeves showing her well form upper arms. Her hair was short and practical like a tomboy but he had tasted her body and longed for its feeling.

They talked of trivial things for some 15 minutes. Shortly after, Roberto came out of his office, said goodbye and left. She did not do anything or made any attempt to leave seeing that they were going to be alone in her lab again. José Ignacio had a flash back of the penetration how moist and warm her pussy was and felt an urge to have her again. He cannot say what he was thinking, likely he wasn't thinking. He came closer to her and I kissed her on her neck while she was seemingly busy with the dissecting scope. He continued kissing her ears and soft skin of her neck and shoulders; just as he had started it all three days before. Francia responded exactly in the same way. She did not try to get up and leave, did not tell him to stop or not to do what he was doing. She simply ignored it intently as if it was not happening. He put his hand between her legs and felt her tense skin of her naked thighs and accentuated the tone in her legs and made her look irresistible for his hungry eyes. As the short was tight, José Ignacio realized that it would have a lot more work in front of him to take them off. Yes, he realized that he was planning in taking them off!.

After the first touching and fondling, she moved to a fully defensive behavior not pretending to look at the fish anymore. It was obvious that he was not going to stop there if she did not stop him. He moved into a more direct and active mode trying to take her cloth off. Inexplicably, he went there to apologize for what he had done, and there he was doing it all over again. He put his hands under her blouse and felt her rock hard trunk where he could feel the contour of every, and each of her abdominal muscles and all the muscles of her torso. He started unbuttoning her blouse. Some buttons he undid and other jumped out when his eager hands where working their way towards them. Francia tried to hold José Ignacio's arms to prevent them from undressing her but her hands could barely close around his wrist. She was overwhelmed by the girth of his arms and the power of the man that was lusting for her. She recalled the tidal wave of his lust that had overpowered her the first time and braced for what was coming.

He took Francia to the floor again to use gravity in his favor and started kissing her neck while his hands caressed her breast trying to arouse her and make her surrender to her desires, which he was sure she was feeling. He wanted her to surrender to him before penetrating her this time, that way he would know he did not rape her. She had been very moist the first time, so reluctant as she seemed, he knew she was feeling his touch. It was a battle of wills. He had overpowered her the first time and she only relinquished when he penetrated her by force. This time he wanted her to surrender before he had her.

José Ignacio undid her bra to release her breast so he could have access to them and invite her to surrender by sucking them. As soon as he undid her bra, Francia covered her breast with her strong swimmer's arms. She was strong but not as strong as he was. He opened her arms by force and took her beautiful and perky breast fully in his mouth. It was the same maneuver that he did years before to expose Maggy's breast for the first time, but now he knew what to do. Francia tried to resist. She tried to push him with her arms

51

to remove him from her erogenous zone but he had her elbow grabbed extended to the sides and she was not strong enough to free herself despite her strong and energetic battling.

As Francia struggled to resist him, she panted heavily taking lungful after lungful of the scent of his skin. She could smell the lust on him and was feeling dizzy. She liked him she was attracted to his virility and feeling how he was imposing it on her she had to close her eyes to focus in resisting him. His greedy mouth sucked her breast, feeling the texture of her nipples and firmness of her breasts. He took big breath of the scent of her skin and his brain was intoxicated of femme beyond what he could control. They both were poisoning each other with their scent without knowing it. Francia panted intensely but, again, there was no way of telling if she panted for sexual arousal or for physical struggle. He was convinced that he only had to continue a little longer before she surrendered to her pleasure. He switched from one breast to the other and he was certain that she was melted. He let go of her arms to fondle her behind and thighs.

José Ignacio's hand found her crotch and she squeezed it with her thighs holding it tight to herself. Francia grabbed his head with her left arm holding it tight to her breast while the other hand grabbed a fistful of his hair and tried to pull him away from her. Her ambivalence fully expressed in her actions. Her spine was arched back with pleasure, biting her lips to bleed, breathing heavily, her eyes closed, her brow tight with concentration. His hand was trapped in her crotch, his mouth locked to her breast sucking it ever more intensely.

His free hand unbuttoned her short and started pulling it down. She let go of the hand holding his hair and grabbed his forearm, digging her nails in it for a better grip. His hand continued pulling down her shorts and she let go of his hand to hang up to her short with both hands bending at the hip sidewise freeing the hand that was in her crotch. José Ignacio used both hands to pull her short down overpowering her. He put his efforts to peeling her by force, there will be time later to melt her once she was naked. He saw her skin tense, her ebony thigh muscle, bulging, firm and shiny with a thin layer of sweat that covered her skin. She was wearing a tiny pink underwear that contrasted with her brown skin and highlighted every corner of her charms. There was no need to remove it, he thought, it was so small that he only had to push it aside. José Ignacio took another hungry trip by her goddess legs and placed himself on top of her with one of his knees between hers. She closed her thighs with her iron muscle blocking access to her sex, decided to prevent him from opening them. He forced his way to her breast again forcing her to open her arms again and resumed sucking relentlessly her breasts as he tried to put his other leg between hers against her strong legs. Once both knees were between her thighs, it was a matter of pushing himself inside her.

He had all time in the world. Francia resisted quietly his siege but never said a word asking him to stop or asked for help from the corridors. This time he was sure she did not. Not that anyone would have come since at night the institute was empty but she did not even try. Francia breathed heavily almost without air, between his weight on her chest and the physical struggle to protect her virtue. She was defenseless with her breast in his mouth, his leg between hers and almost without breath. He had the image of a jaguar that hunts a Paca but does not bite down to kill it but barely holds it while it tries to escape. The jaguar enjoys the fruitless struggle of his prey, certain that he will end up satiating himself with her flesh.

It was not clear why she bit her lips from the inside. It could have been to turn into grunts of resistance what were really moans of pleasure, or it could have been to punish herself for feeling desire. With another big effort he managed to introduce his other leg between hers. It was a struggle between his lusty desire for her body or her will to protect it. It was a war of attrition between him turning her on and her resisting her own desires. She was an amazing athlete, far too strong for her size but José Ignacio was inordinately strong and much larger than her. Francia bucked furiously trying to free herself but her strengths were running out. He opened her legs with his and felt her pussy with his cock, just with a thin layer of her underwear in the way. He had wanted to wait there until she surrendered but his desire was burning him and he could wait no longer. He moved the lower part of her underwear to one side. Francia bucked desperately in a last attempt to avoid penetration, to no avail. He slid smoothly inside her warm depths. She was broad and moist to his entrance.

Only then Francia relinquished. Her body went from tense and embattled to relax and limber. He hanged on to her hips to reach deeper inside her. Her pussy was wide and deep. Her lips were swollen part for arousal, part for trauma of her biting them. He could see a redish line in the inner border of her lips where her teeth had pierce their soft skin. José Ignacio ate her lips, licking her eyes, and her ears while his cock enjoyed the banquette of her sex. He felt her buttocks with his hands, and travelled down and up enjoying her firm thighs and legs. She just breathed heavily recovering and letting him have her at his leisure. He made love to her motionless body and came declaring in her ear how much he loved her. After the tempest passed he stayed over her kissing her and loving her with all his heart, thanking her for another journey of delicious sex.

Sashawarmas,   by Jorge Bandido

When they were rested, he got off from her, helped her find her shorts that have been flung away from them. He helped her button up her shirt and found the loss buttons that had flown away during his sexual frenzy. Many buttons were missing so she could not button up her shirt, so he offered his jacket on top so she could be covered; which she accepted. He offered to walk her home.

"No, thanks, I will stay here a little longer picking things up." She replied. "I will give your jacket back next time we meet." But she did not make any eye contact that would let him understand what she meant with it. They kissed good bye and left. It was a regular kiss on the cheek like Latin American friends, not like lovers, and certainly not like sexual assaulter and his victim. Just like the friends they were.

That was not the last time he made love to Francia by force. But this time, he did not feel bad in the least. Her neutral reception after the first time convinced him that she did not feel raped the first time, or whatever happened, had been acceptable course of actions. Furthermore, why would she warn him quietly that Roberto was in his office? It occurred to him that it was a way of telling him: "*don't do anything . . . for now*". He had not raped her but rather he was giving her some love despite her incapacity of accepting it openly. He was giving her the right of enjoying of sex without cheating on her boyfriend.

During that semester José Ignacio made love to Francia at least a couple times every week and she never presented less resistance whenever he started to undress her. If there was any difference was that she learned his moves to undress her and subdue her and tried to find ways to prevent them or blocking him ahead of the move. Every night she was a new challenge and every time he had to do his absolute best to have her. However, she never asked for help, neither did she ask him not to do it. In some occasions he would strip her and get her ready for penetration with his member on her entrance of her pussy but did not shove it in. He would hold her immobilized and just continue sucking her breast of touching her erotically without penetrating her. "*Ask for it*" he would demand, but Francia only would bite her lips with her eyes closed without requesting it. He tried to arouse her more, make her want more to get her to ask for it but he always lost that stalemate. He always ended up giving up to his lust and penetrating her before she requested it actively, surrendered as she might had been. On occasions he would go down on her and eat her pussy. Francia would squeeze his head with her thighs and grabbed fistfuls of his hair. She would dig her nails on his shoulders or any part of his body she got and resisted without moving. He only knew she was coming for waves of current that traveled through her body

54

when he pushed her over the border and the tension of her legs relaxed. Then he would kiss his way up to her mouth. He would feel the smell of rust and taste the blood from her lips, swollen and sensual as it is possible to imagine. Then he would penetrate her without any resistance of her part and he would make tender love to her to his heart content.

"I love you, I love you, I love you soo much." He whispered in her ear when he was coming inside her.

The situation with Francia was not very different from that with Maggy in the sense that he sought out their bodies and they resisted some but were very ambivalent. Maggy was ambivalent for the feeling that he was a boy, Francia was ambivalent because of her complicated romantic situation. José Ignacio was truly in love with her and was hoping that at some point she will leave her boyfriend, or something will happen that she will end up with him. He did not wish ill to anyone but in those days HIV was very little know and there were no drugs to contain it. So deep inside he had the hope that at some point she will be single again and she could be his for real. However, Francia graduated at the end of that year and left town, back to the coast where she was from originally. That is how he lost second love of his life.

12. UNLIKELY RESCUE

The nurse saw the ferocious brow of the Zambo scanning area for more rivals. Then his eyes fixated on eyes of the nurse. She could see the transformation from the belligerent expression to the most charming smile full is very white teeth that illuminated his face when their eyes met. She felt butterflies in her stomach to see the same delicious rascal smile he would use just before delivering one of his lines the day they met.

However the relief the nurse felt when she recognize the Zambo was short lived. After their eyes met, his eyes continued down to her mouth, neck, and collar bone. Soon the look of his face gave her chills in her bones. As his eyes scanned her breast, waist and naked body, his face acquire the most vulgar expression of uncontrolled lust she had ever seen. Her heart froze for a few seconds feeling naked at the mercy of the powerful man. Instinctively she cover her breast with her arms and put her hands over her crotch to protect it from his sight.

He grabbed her by her wrist and looking to the sides of the main room for a good place, found her bedroom door still ajar. He dragged her by the wrist to her bedroom which did not feel very safe at that very moment. She did not dare to resist and took a second look at the four men he had dispatched. They were all motionless on the floor as if they had been hit by a bolt of lightning. The Zambo dragged the nurse in and closed the door behind him. With a movement he ripped apart what was left of her nurse uniform. The other men had taken off her underwear, now she was completely naked. She shyly covered herself with her arms and hands. The Zambo held up her chin and look at her directly into her eyes.

"No," he said with a stern expression that accepted no dissent.

His eyes were way too black with no visible pupil, or else they were all pupil, in the penumbra of her room. The nurse had fought bravely against the other attackers but she had seen how much good it did to her. All that it got her was a swollen eye and bruised cheekbone. Plus she also had seen the ease with which the Zambo dispatched them. There had been no fight; there had been no struggle. His punches had knocked the lights out of each one of them one after the other. Each one of them was far stronger than her and yet, they were no match for the Zambo. Clearly there was nothing she could do to resists him, without risking serious harm to herself. Even the always helpful knee in the crotch could only gain her time for an escape but to where? There was nowhere to hide or nowhere she could escape to. It was silly anyway, she could never reach his crotch with her knees. He towered more than two feet over her. He had no shirt on and she also noticed that she did not reach to the line of his nipples. She could see his iron cast muscles chiseled on his trunk and mighty arms. Clearly any attempt to resist would have been foolhardy. She consoled herself that being raped by one was better than the alternative. If the Zambo had not arrived she would have been gang raped, so in a manner, as she heard the noise coming from outside from the other nurses facing many attackers, she felt that she was the lucky one.

She was nearly decided to accept her faith until she saw him drop his pant and a cock of truly terrifying proportions stood out. She gasped in fear. *"There is no way that monstrosity would fit inside me without tearing my insides."* She thought. She looked at him with pleading eyes hoping he would have mercy but her eyes were met with the same obscene lust as before. She knew there was no way she could get out of it, however she tried. He held her under her armpits and lifted her like a feather bringing her small perky breast to his mouth. The nurse felt the warm mouth sucking her breath so intensely to the point of ache in her nipple. She endured the treatment, glad there was no penetration, yet, and secured each elbow on his shoulders, on either side of his head, to prevent being lowered to his member. She would happy let him have her breasts if that spared her from the imminent impaling.

However, that was a fool's hope. He held her there for short while, to better savor her breast. Slowly but surely he started to lower her down licking and sucking her tender white skin of her neck with his full large sensual lips. She tried to resist digging her elbows on his shoulders to no avail. Not being strong enough to prevent him to lower her with her arms alone, she tried to hold herself up using her legs around his trunk. This was her last hope to resist but it was not such a good idea. All her limbs were not strong enough to resist the strength of the Zambo and now her legs were wide open around his torso. He was facing up sucking her chin when she felt his member at her pussy and tried to resist, a last effort to prevent penetration. His lips met hers and his hungry tongue invaded her licking the inside of her mouth, raping her mouth as he was about to rape her pussy. She smelled his breath, a mix of rum and lust and she knew she had no hope.

She felt his impossibly thick member reaping her insides as it worked its way inside her. She let go of any hope of resisting penetration and tried to relax herself to make it less painful. The nurse bit the inside of her lips not to scream out in pain. She had seen all the jeering and cheering of Rebecca's tormentors to her screaming. Plus there was no help coming, no matter how loud she called for. In fact, screaming will only lure more rapists to the room. She felt her insides burn, his cock went in inch, after inch, after inch, after inch. It was getting hard to breath and she felt queasy as the cock of the

Zambo was reaching so deep inside her. Tears jumped out of her eyes as she endured the excruciating pain. His chest was so broad that she could not reach around with her arms. The Zambo sat down on her bed by the time his cock stopped drilling his way inside her all she could see was a dark wall of pectoral muscles with a small stitched up wound above the line of her eyes. She could feel the sticky sweat on his chest on his unnatural warmth coming out it; glad for a short time that his member was not going any deeper inside her.

She felt short lived relieve when he started lifting her back up but she knew what was coming. After a few inches relief, he sank her back down impaling back on his member. The nurse was helpless with her insides searing with pain as the Zambo's cock worked his way in and out. Blind with pain the nurse commended herself to the Lord. She prayed to God. She asked Him to take her then and there and end her suffering. But she was praying to the wrong side of the isle. That God did not seem to be calling the shots at the time. The Lust was poisoning the air and everything answered to Her will.

After an eternity the nurse felt his rhythm accelerate, she struggled to draw air in her lungs, feeling the Zambo's arms crushing her against his massive chest. His cock drilled even deeper inside her soul as he came inside her. When all was over, he lifted her and put her aside kissing her face as he put her down as a sobbing heap. Her leg felt like they were made from jelly and gave from underneath her when she tried to stand. She had no feeling in her legs, her entrails were throbbing with pain. She breathed deeply in the ground trying to recover. She felt dirty and polluted. She felt humiliated and used, like she was worth nothing anymore. It all was over for her. Suddenly she had another realization: The Zambo was done and in all likelihood he was going to leave. Despite the excruciating pain when he was raping her she found consolation to the idea that she was going to be raped by only one man, not like the other nurses that had a line of rapist taking turns. But as soon as the Zambo left, there was nothing stopping the gang bangers from outside her door from coming and have their way with her.

Even if she managed to lock the flimsy door, it will be no defense for her, not for long anyway. She looked out the window into the thick forest that bordered the town. She could make a run for it. The locked door would get her a couple minutes to jump out the window and run into the forest. When she was a girl, she was very good a climbing trees. If she could just get to one of the tall ones she could quickly get out of reach from any man. She could go up to branches so thin that any large man would not dare to climb. If she got to the forest, that is. There was a 40 yards stretch between the window and the forest where someone could intercept her or chase her down. It was a silly idea anyway. She could not move her legs, or stand up, leave alone race into the forest and climb up tall trees. More than likely she was going to be gang raped like all the other nurses and there was nothing she could do about it. During all her life, she was always the most beautiful woman around. She always turned the heads and got all the attention of the men. She always felt so lucky at having always gallant men competing for her attention. That very charm of hers was going to weigh very much against her right about now.

The Zambo put his pants on but before he left the room he stopped to listen what was happening outside. He paused for a few seconds, looked at her, looked around the room and grabbed her by the wrist lifting her up to her feet with one powerful tug.

"Come," he said.

Numb legs or not, she was dragged to follow him. He opened the door pulling her behind him. She was terrified for what was coming next. What did he want with her for now? He was bringing her naked to the eyes of all the men that were busy raping the other nurses. *This cannot end well.*" She thought.

She saw the four men that had been attacking her still on the floor, immobile, in the very place where the Zambo had dropped them. They were way too still, like inanimate objects. On the left Mónica had lost her heroic battle against the rapists. She was on all four being raped by one man from behind while two other held her by the shoulders and prevented her from moving or resisting. She sported a very swollen eye and a bloody nose to show for her resistance. Estella was laying down on the floor whimpering and begging while a man between her legs had his way with her. Another one flicked her nipple with a sadistic middle finger making her howl in pain. Two other men that were waiting their turn laughed at the "game". They were different men that were having her at first, so the nurse calculated at least 6 by now. As she was leaving Rebecca was still face down on a stretcher screaming with her now hoarse voice when her rapists banged her from behind. She had 4 men waiting that seems especially amused to her screaming. Everybody saw them as they walked by but nobody dared to make a movement towards her, likely due to the terrifying corpulence of the Zambo. It occurred to her that they all knew each other and the new that the Zambo was nobody to mess with.

As she was leaving the hospital she spotted the old Indian woman, the mentally disable one that sat there regularly, the one she had seen the first day she met the Zambo. She was sitting as usual, staring into emptiness, as if nothing was happening. Men were not disturbing her. The nurse was not sure if it was because she was older of because she was not white, or because they knew her and decided to leave her alone. She had bigger concerns at the time though.

The Zambo walked her by town, at a brisk pace as if trying to get to place in a hurry. She had reminiscence of being walked in a hurry by her father towing her by the hand when she was a little girl; such is how the strides of the Zambo compared to hers. In their way she saw the general chaos of the town. Stores being ransacked, people carrying looted merchandise in the streets. She saw 6 more women being raped in the street, most of them by several men, while on lookers ignored them or stood in line to take part of the atrocity. As they walked near some houses she heard through the windows at least 5 other women screaming and asking for help, clearly being assaulted as well. It was a city wide rape fest! Most women she saw being raped were white but it did not seem an exclusive privilege of the white ones. For a second she felt lucky again to be with the Zambo since nobody dared to come near her. Large as his cock was, he was only one, but then she wondered where he was taking her. Her heart chilled when she envisioned a den full of rapists waiting for her. She was nauseated.

13. Back to the Forest

The day the black woman was due the midwife came to her room by the side of the church. The woman prepared her for delivery warning her that first time mothers took long time to give birth and advised her to make herself comfortable. However, in very short time she went into labor and in a matter of few minutes her baby was out, eager to see the world and very much alert. The little boy a mix of the Waorani that had taken her in the forest, and her African blood, and had the making of a warrior. His little arms were strong and he was able to lift his head scanning curiously the world around him. She was overwhelmed with happiness to see the health of her boy and thanked God for giving her such a beautiful boy, and helping her in all the process, hard as it had been.

The joy of the new mother lasted short time. A few weeks within her motherhood she fell asleep nursing her baby on her bed and as she was dozing off when she felt a strong feeling on her nipple; a familiar tension with the warmth of her baby's mouth covering it. She felt something wrong. Her baby was sucking too greedily, too intensely, too intimate. She got aroused by the intensity of the sucking. She felt it radiate into her pussy and felt it turn and twist. She had images of the night in the forest when the warriors were taking her and woke up startled, drenched in sweat and horribly aroused. She could not stop nursing him, he needed food, but also she did not want to stop it because it felt good to have her baby in her nipple. It was not motherly good, but *something else* good. She was getting more and more aroused. She tried to pull her baby away from her nipple but he resisted grabbing it strongly with his gums. She pulled him out forcibly and saw his lips hungrily seek her erect nipple, eager for it. She crossed herself and said silently the Lords prayer trying to ward off her feelings and her thoughts.

It did not work. Her baby started crying from the top of his lungs and her nipple ached with pressure. There was something she could do to stop both. She put her baby back in her nipple, and felt big relief. Her baby stopped crying sucking it eagerly. It felt good to have her baby in her nipple again. So good. Too good! She felt the pleasure spreading from her nipple. She tried to say the Lord prayers again to find strength but the words got choked in her throat, instead a guttural moan of pleasure poured out of her mouth while her body spasms with a long, delicious and intense orgasm as her baby sucked her nipple. She knew there was something super natural about his baby even if she did not fully understand it. The healer had said that much but she did not really understand his connection to The Lust.

Sashawarmas,   by Jorge Bandido

She laid on the bed panting, recovering while her baby finished his meal. She had hoped that all the horniness was a byproduct of the pregnancy and that it would go away after her baby was born. She had never heard her mother or any adult woman talk about this. But of course none wanted to talk about this. It was embarrassing. Certainly no body would share it with the young girl that she was before she moved to live with the priest. And then, of course, there was no way to hear anything about pregnancy horniness at the church. She had a sinking feeling in the bottom of her stomach but she knew it was unfounded. The horniness was her problem, her lack of faith, as Father Carlos had said, her sins. It had nothing to do with her baby. He was innocent. A "*God's creature*" as Father Carlos had explained. But the whole in her stomach would not relinquish despite all the assurance she gave herself that it was all in her mind. With a feeling of trepidation she unwrapped his diaper to find his little penis with a massive erection. The black woman gasped with surprised and covered it up. She knelt by her bed and started praying fervently asking God to spare her child.

The following days passed in a similar way. She was fine feeding her baby during the day but when night time came, the same pattern began. It was worst if the night was moist and rainy and the smell of ripe fruit from the forest permeated into the town from the wind from the forest. She could not afford baby formula and the baby needed to be fed at least twice through the night. The same thought that so many times came to her mind while she was having the horny attacks during her pregnancy came to assault her nights. There was a port a walking distance from the church. There were countless sailors just arrived from long time at the ocean. All of them were horny looking for women to satiate their needs. That is all that she needed. She could just walk to the port and take the first sailor that wanted her. They were ready to pay for sex to the diverse population of hookers that lived out of these costumers. They will be more than happy to do her for free. All that she needed was an hour or so and then she could come back to feed her baby after she had relieved herself. It just felt wrong to have an orgasm while her baby was feeding innocently. But she was not so sure how innocent her baby was. Did all the babies got erections when they fed? She did not know, there was nobody to ask. Go back to the healer? Not likely. The healer had been visibly afraid when she worked with her. "*You have a baby of The Lust*", she had said. What did she mean? How will she react to see her baby. She would never let anyone say anything bad about her baby. It was all her horniness it was all her problem to deal with.

She got her courage to go to the Port Zone. She had never solicited sex from a man. Heck, she had never had sex before the warriors took her in the forest, and she had not had any man since. Her uncle groupings did not really count. Now she was a woman and she was going to look for a man to have sex with. Not like the warriors that took the scare teenager in the forest. She was seeking a one on one sexual encounter with a stranger. She looked at herself in the mirror and she was not bad. She hardly put on any weight during pregnancy, and her breasts were much larger now because of all the milk. But as she was dawning a short dress to head out, her baby started crying uncontrollably. She tried to ignore him telling herself that she would be back soon to feed him but he was crying with such anger that he was choking and screaming every time louder. She could not take it anymore. The black woman lower the strap of her shoulder that held her dress up exposing one of her round full breasts putting it to the baby's mouth. The baby took it and immediately fell asleep, as if all that she wanted was to prevent her from going out.

****

As soon as the baby could eat solid food, she stopped breast feeding him. This helped a lot and she continued as best as she could the upbringing of the baby. One day when the baby was a about two year old she was changing her cloth in her bedroom and felt her skin prickle and her hairs in the back of her neck stood in attention as if someone was watching her. She turned around to see her baby sitting on a chair looking intently at her crotch with eyes eager of excitement. She covered herself feeling modest. Was her baby lusting after her body? Surely it was all in her mind. She thought better of it and she could not believe her baby was actually interested in her crotch. It must have been her ideas. She was the one with the constant horniness and she must be putting that on her baby. Praying was her only remedy and she embraced it fervently. At age 3 she could not help the feeling that he was looking through her dress. She felt naked looking at her son. He would put his hand on her buttocks or breast and caress her in something that very much looked like an erotic touch and worse of all, she *felt* it like an erotic touch. She would scold him and yell at him but she felt beheld by the warriors. It was like they were looking at her and lusting after her through his eyes. She tried to ignore it but she knew it was not her imagination. She turned to praying again and drove her son through the same path.

When he was six, he was in training to be an altar boy. The boy had no interest in playing with other kids; none whatsoever. He acted as if they did not exist. However, any girl older than 11 aroused his interest profoundly. All young women that somehow visited the church were kind with him and greeted him lovingly. But the black woman could see her son beady little eyes look at their breast and behinds. His eager little hands would creep up their thighs and towards their intimates; often startling the girls that attributed the touch to innocence and never thought anything about it. Marielle was 20 and short years old, a teacher of the local school that started working actively bringing her kids to the church to work in the church garden. It was a way of teaching the kids to grow a food garden and help the church produce funding. She had curly brown her, cinnamon skin, thin built, startling hazel eyes, and often wore shorts for the suffocating heat of forest. The black woman's baby was instantly fascinated with her. She took him under her arm and incorporated him to the activities of her students, although her students were far older. The black woman felt sick to see the way her son looked at the Marielle's crotch and how he boldly reached for it when she was standing looking away. For some reason Marielle always acted as if he was reaching for her hand and instead of scolding him, she simply held his hand maternally. As if not noticing what he was doing. *How was it possible? Anyone who looked as his dark little yes could see horniness spelled out all over them.* She thought. His mother scolded him every time he touched her breast and her behind and she expected other women to do the same. It was that new way of teaching in which you are not supposed to scold the kids for any reason!

That morning the black woman was invaded by a feeling of trepidation the minute she came out of her room and felt the moist air of the forest and the smell of overripe fruit and musky scent in the air. She knew what it was associated with and did not like it. That morning Marielle came with other kids for the church garden she did not want her baby to join them as usual. There was something on the air that just felt wrong. However, Marielle had taken a liking to her little boy. The black woman did not want to let him go but upon Marielle insistence she acquiesced. It was in the middle of the explanation for weeding. Marielle went in all four and was demonstrating how to clean the weeds from the tomatoes when her baby grabbed Marielle from behind and started humping her. Her short shorts, her full thighs had finally aroused the thing that lived in the little boy and had led him to grab his teacher. There was no denying that this was sexual humping. Marielle tried to get up but his strong little arms were fixed in her hip bones while he humped his teacher uncontrollably. The black woman ran and grabbed her son from behind finally prying him out of Marielle's rear end. She got up surprised, embarrassed, everybody had seen the little kid humping her. All kids were laughing, all adults that saw it were in horror. Quickly the kids laughter was silenced. The black woman removed her son scolding him embarrassed back to her house and Marielle continued the lecture with the rest of the students. After the class Marielle came to see how the little boy was doing and explaining to his mother that it was ok.

"It is all normal, he was just playing." She assured her.

Sashawarmas,   by Jorge Bandido

"How can anyone fail to see what he was doing? That was not game." She thought but she said nothing. The black woman had seen enough. This was simply another drop in the bucket and she knew what she had to do.

That afternoon she went for confession. During the confession she thanked Father Carlos for having adopted her when she was younger, from having survived the raid on the mission. She then took courage.

"Father, will you take care for my boy if something were to happen to me. If I for some reason were unable to be with him?" She asked him. Father Carlos was taken aback but answered without hesitation.

"Of course I would look after your baby." He replied and explained. "He is also a son of God." The young woman felt her heart sink. She was not so sure her baby was a son of God, not the same God that Father Carlos was talking about anyway. She felt there was a Lust living in him that she could not understand or bear. The words of the old Indian healer came to her: *"You have a son of the Lust"*. She did not want to think of it but she could not stop.

"But why anything would anything happen to you? Father Carlos continued. "You are young, healthy, and strong".

"Nothing father, I just had a bad dream in which my baby was alone." She lied.

"Well so long as I am alive your baby will want for nothing. We do not have a lot of resources in the church but we have enough to support those in need, as you have seen many times". He comforted her.

The black woman did her penitence, said her prayers and left the church with a resolve in her mind. She knew how to set right what was wrong in her life. That night she kissed her boy goodnight. Tucked in his bed, he returned her kiss. No thinking what she was doing she kissed him full in his mouth and gave him a long wet kiss with her tongue feeling deeply the inside of his mouth.

"You will be fine my dear son." She assured him. I will fix what should have been fixed before. She dressed in a white short dress and left the house and walked toward the forest.

****

The following day they tried to find the black woman but there was no sign of her. Somebody found her clothing, including her shoes, neatly folded and put together at the entrance of a path that lead into the forest. Some people said there was a medium size kapok tree that was not there the week before. The black woman had gone back to the Sashawarma where her fertility would render the profit to the forest as it was meant to be. She had gone back to The Lust.

14. MATCHING SOULS

José Ignacio was some 19 years old when Maggy left his life and he was having this relationship with Francia (whatever it should be called) and had started to notice other women. It was not long before he noticed someone who was meant to be a main character in his life. Her name was Mercedes, Mercedes del Carmen. She was also a biology student like himself at Universidad Católica de Quito. They had started together but because he was imbued in Maggy's sex, she was farther ahead in the course work than José Ignacio was. Mercedes was a firm and well planted woman, very much into sports, with strong calves, thick muscular thighs that had no hesitation on showing them off all the way up. She often wore tiny shorts or miniskirts. Her body resembled that of Francia but while Francia was modest and even humble about her body, Mercedes was all the opposite.

Mercedes was one of those ethnic mixes you only find in Latin America. She had white skin but the shape of her body, her behind, her legs and her face was fundamentally that of a black woman, which her mother was, but Mercedes had the white skin of her father, a blue-eyed Chilean immigrant. Her derriere was prominent, well-formed, her belly was flat and tempting with an extremely sexy belly bottom that it was impossible to ignore for the way she showed it off. She did not have the iron cast body that Francia had but it was muscular and firm and she knew very well how to show it and how to tease the eyes of the onlookers with her every movements. Her nipples were belligerent and always on the ready. It was always possible to notice them through her shirt or blouse because they were always on guard and she never wore a bra. Her broad nose, thick lips were sensual, covering her large white teeth that she knew how to flash in wonderful flirtatious smiles showing off her African heritage, all ornamented with curly brown hair to her shoulders.

Her face was comely without being gorgeous. She had suffered a bit of acne when she was younger and it had left its marks. However from the neck down she was a bombshell of sensuality and she knew it; and she also knew well how to use it. Her wide hips moved broadly from side to side when she walked making one dizzy. Her walking was suggestive but it was nothing but the pale reflection of how sensual she moved when she danced. She made love to the music she was dancing to. She made love to everyone looking at her with the spellbinding movement of her hips and turns of her legs and torso. Her palms were broad and she used them eloquently when she talked. Her chest was covered by thin freckles and even though she did not wear any perfume there was no shortage of sexually arousing fragrances around her body. It was only because of the obsession that José Ignacio had with Maggy that he did not notice early this mare in heat sitting next to him in the classes. It is not surprising that when he was alone José Ignacio's eyes drifted towards Mercedes.

José Ignacio had been a student for several years but nobody knew him well. Everybody knew that he had no interest in anybody at the university and after classes he would leave in a hurry. When he started spending more time with his classmates he learned that he was some sort of a mystery for the women that never understood why he was never seen with anybody. Mercedes liked men's attention. This was obvious for the way she dressed, and there was always a small army of men around her. When José Ignacio started showing some interest for her she was especially flattered because he had not shown any interest for anybody (the relationship with Francia was very secret, obviously) and his interest in her made her feel that more special.

One day they were in a small plaza on campus with several people sitting around and chatting between classes. José Ignacio was standing next to Mercedes and she placed discretely one of her hands in the back of his thigh right above the knee, as if acknowledging his presence. She felt the tone of his hamstring and she increased the pressure feeling up his thigh. He tensed the muscle discretely acknowledging her touch and she moved her hand slowly, foundling his thigh, all the way up right below his buttock. José Ignacio did not move but continue varying tension in his hamstring to communicate with her and for her to appreciate. Mercedes continued feeling up his thigh and grouping him with poorly disguised lust and eventually made some sort of comment regarding his strong leg muscles. José Ignacio could not stop thinking that she had felt him and grabbed him just the same way he would have wanted to do to her, were it not because men are not supposed to grope women in public. Yet she had done it to him. José Ignacio learned then and there that there was bound to be something between them but did not imagine what it was going to be or how to make it happen.

One day in a party in the house of one of their friends from school they were dancing a fast merengue. On top of being under the spell of her dancing movements José Ignacio could press her body against his. He felt her firm back, her woman's fragrance, her arms around him holding him just as tight as he held her with her broad palm pressed against the back of his neck holding him close to her with her face nested in his chest, breathing his scent. José Ignacio could not wait any more and had to make his next move but not having experience in dating he had to disguise it somehow.

"I need to go the field tomorrow morning to catch some frogs. Would you want to come with me? It is a pretty creek in the Parque Metropolitano". He offered.

Sashawarmas,   by Jorge Bandido

The school of pharmacy was doing a study with the medical properties of the substance on the skin of frogs that grew nearby. They have hired him to provide with a few of them for the study since he was always in the field climbing and mountaineering. Mercedes accepted gladly to come to the excursion/date adventure.

Although it was true that José Ignacio needed to catch frogs, the hunting of the frogs was only a distraction for what he really wanted. He only wanted to have an excuse to be with her alone and away from her long list of admirers; so he could try to make a move, whatever that move was. He knew she desired him and he was going crazy of lust for her body but he was not a suave lady's man expert in starting something from scratch. He wanted to be alone with her to allow their instincts to act. He felt the forest a place of comfort where the best of his came out although he did not know why.

The next day, when José Ignacio saw her with her tiny shorts and a thin white t-shirt that ended right by her ribs he knew it was going to be a good day. When they met, it also was obvious to anyone paying attention that the story of catching frogs was nothing but a cover. For starters, he was so obsessed with going out with her and thinking what move he could make that he forgot to bring any nets or flasks or anyway to catch or collect the frogs! Yet, she ignored this blatant problem with his story and came up with him to the mountain to "*look for frogs*" all the same. They had the only equipment they really needed: her body and his.

As they went up climbing the creek by little ponds of a few inches deep, they would hold hands to help her, chivalrously and would pass close to each other. He could smell her scent, hold her waist, touch her belly where he would leave his hand a bit too long feeling her skin. He was doing the same thing he had learned with Maggy at first. He did not want to take the path he took with Francia, yet, because he felt there was another way. However, he did not know when was the proper moment to put a definite sexual tone in their superficial flirting other than fondling her body.

José Ignacio would let her go ahead, as a true gentleman on the narrow passages which only granted him a maddening look at her behind as her legs muscle contracted bulging when she climbed with steep steps over the rocks. He did no dare to start a sexual move or break the ice with a kiss and did not know how to move forward. Then José Ignacio thought of breaking the tension when they walked by a deeper pond, about a 3 or 4 feet deep. With a firm push, he shoved her inside the pond, she felled backwards surprised and sunk completely. When she came up, recovering from the surprise she swore revenge between laughter and giggles. Her shirt became completely transparent sticking to her wet body showing her feisty nipples, erect for the cold water. Irresistible! José Ignacio went in the pond with her to tickle her taking advantage of the broken ice and then starting caressing her body without any pretensions. She responded like a she-cat in heat.

She planted a luscious kiss in his mouth and then and there he made love to Mercedes for the first time soaking on the fresh water from the mountain. It was a beautiful lusty beginning that forecasted a lot more of sex, and passion. When they came out of the pond they have been lovers for 500 hundred years.

15. A MATER OF FATE: MERCEDES'S UPBRINGING

As much as José Ignacio wanted to have the relationship with Mercedes that he had with Maggy, they were two different women with two different lives and hearts. Maggy saw him as a pet to spent time with. She clearly enjoyed his body for good sex but she never thought of him as a long term partner. The situation with Mercedes was very different. Their sex was great and it was mostly the only thing they had but that was not all she wanted. She wanted something more long term and more stable. This was a problem, not only because José Ignacio never thought of anything with any woman beyond the sack, but also Mercedes had a particular character that was hard to reconcile with his personality.

Part of the problem goes back to Mercedes's upbringing. She was the second of 7 siblings and the first of 6 daughters. Her older sibling was a boy, Orlando, a year older than her and the pride and joy of her father. After her came Amanda, barely 11 months younger who was almost identical to Mercedes. Mercedes was a very competitive person and she always wanted to compete with her brother and Amanda for her father's attention. Yet, because Orlando was the only boy, her father preferred him over all the others no matter what. Orlando could do no wrong, and she could never be good enough to match him, on the eyes of her father. Because of this Mercedes was always an over achiever but nothing was ever good enough. This was particularly true with physical prowess where she really wanted to excel and be equal or better than Orlando. Nothing she ever did got her father to give her equal attention or the deference that Orlando received for less. On top of this her father was very stern and a friend of giving physical punishment. Whenever any small violation ensued, or what he thought might have been one, he quickly pulled out his belt and gave everyone on sight a good strapping with it. If any time his kids got into any argument or fought those involved would be beaten very severely and the other ones also got "*some belt*" for watching, or for just being there. Needless to say, Orlando, although he also got the belt, his father was far more lenient with him than he was with Mercedes, the one more likely to talk back to her father, or get into any conflict with Orlando.

As Mercedes started developing into a young lady, her body started to turn. Her legs and forms started to shape as those of very sexy woman. At this time her father's attention started to shift to her more. She was no longer the second kid that was not as good as Orlando. She started to catch her father's eye on her own merit. Punishment became less common and he was more understanding. Her father started spending more time in her company, taking

71

her out to places she liked, which he used to only do for Orlando. He was far more physical and loving with her with hugs, kisses and holding her close to him. This was the only thing that she had ever wanted in her life and she finally had it, feeling her father's love and attention like her brother always did. This must have been the beginning of Mercedes appreciation for her body and what she could conquer with it. She would go a very long way in this direction as she became an adult woman.

Mercedes' father had a cabin in the woods, just outside of town where he would go to spend some time alone. It was the worse kept secret, that he had a mistress who he met there away from his family. His wife knew it but she had given up on being jealous. He was a good provider that was always available when needed in the house so his wife, had just given up on that part of their relationship. In the tight Quito society women do not get divorce, if they can help it. They lived together and acted married for everybody but they were not married in practice. That their father had mistress did bother his daughters, all 6 of them as they were coming of age. As it may be expected Mercedes was the one who was the most bothered for the absences of her father as soon as she was old enough to understand what they meant. But when she was turning into a young adolescence, suddenly her father changed. He started taking her to his cabin where he would only go alone. She was the happiest girl in the world they spent the weekend together in the cabin with her dad all for herself. Sitting on his lap by the fire enjoying his hugs and kisses was what made her as happy as she ever thought it possible. They went out hiking, and spent a lot more time together enjoying of her father's physical affection like she only had dreamed of before.

However, her brother did not take kindly to sharing his father's predilection. He resented Mercedes for what she was becoming. As a young teenager he could not help but noticing Mercedes's body, and realizing that it helped her get attention and favors, he started a war against her dressing style. He would call her out for having short skirts, or tight outfits. He would tell their father that Mercedes was flirting with boys, that she had bad reputation as slut, and making up accusations that landed in fertile ground with his father. Since Orlando was the favorite, her words did not carry a lot of weight. It also appealed to her father's sense of jealousy since he himself was feeling the effect of Mercedes' body, it was easy for him to believe what Orlando was saying. Orlando had planted the right seed in the right place. Soon his father was very suspicious and strict about Mercedes dressing style and pretty much appointed Orlando as her supervisor. The positive attention her body granted her from her father quickly dissipated with the new policy of surveillance and control that her brother mustered. She often got permission denied to go out with her friend, if Orlando did not approve. She had to get Orlando to come with her as chaperone so she had to constantly cater and please the very person she least wanted to please. For years Mercedes struggled with this problem. She rebelled against Orlando's oppression. She always tried to push back only to receive more severe scolding and control from her father and brother.

One day, with her being 15 years old, Orlando accused Mercedes of having a boyfriend in school. This was no acceptable in the tight conservative style set by Mercedes' father. Her father was livid with anger to hear that so he pulled out his belt for the standard strapping. It was all the more unfair because all that Mercedes wanted was to be her Daddy's girl and she had no eyes for boys her age since her father had started to take her with him to his cabin. So the boyfriend accusation was most unfounded. However, Mercedes' body had made a turn since the last time her father had given her a strapping. When he bent her over the table and pulled up her skirt to belt her, he exposed himself to the magic effects that Mercedes' derriere was called to produce in every man's mind. After he let the belt fall the first time on Mercedes' behind he felt his heart pounding. He continued nevertheless feeling his blood rush by his ears with every strapping. After the belt smacked her behind the seventh time, her father felt lightheaded and dropped to the ground with stroke. He recovered fully after a couple months. Mercedes could not sit for the next two days but that was the last time that her or any of her siblings got the belt.

A couple years later, during a summer job, she got some money of her own. She used it to buy a bookshelf for the living room that badly needed one. So she came home with the nice purchase where she had selflessly invested her first pay check to make some improvement on the house. Clearly this would grant her some praise from her father. Yet, upon arrival the father inquired where she had gotten the money and ignoring her very logical answer he went with his preconceived idea about his daughter's ways.

"Whore! How did you come by that money? You are sleeping with men for money! You are a whore." He condemned her.

Mercedes was so surprised by the accusation that she could not even rebut it. She stammered trying to find words to answer but no words came out.

"I do not want a whore in my house or the money you made selling yourself." Her father continued.

In another time this anger on her father would have resulted in a serious beating but he was past the time of given her the belt. However, his words hurt far more on Mercedes' heart than any beating would have. Her father had never been able to see her for who she was. The only notice he had taken

73

of her was her sexy body. He never paid any attention to her before she got it, and he could not conceive that she could do anything worthy of being paid some money, that did not involve using her body. Needless to say what Mercedes felt to this new unfair accusation and the obvious implication how her father saw her. The first feeling was of surprise, trying to explain to her dad that the money was well acquired. The accusation of prostitution was well beyond her most bizarre thoughts or possibilities.

Then she went into despair to see her father's absolute conviction that she had sold her body for money. She was a virgin for God's sake! Quickly it turned into uncontrollable anger. All her life she had tried to please her father only to see that he was decided not to see her for who she was. Then all came clear in her eyes like a flash, her father caressing her thighs, and the smooth skin of her belly. His finger playing inside her belly bottom. The strange feeling of him kissing her neck while she sat on his lap in the solitude of his cabin, the tight hugs, the pressure of his body against hers, the "accidental" contact with her breast when he hugged her from behind walking in the woods, him pressing himself on her behind. It all connected. She saw how her father saw her. Mercedes had a sudden realization, as if something that she had known all along but refused to see on its own light. The only thing she was in his eyes was a hot body and the only way she could have made any money was by selling it.

In a burst of murderous rage she got up to go after her father to show him all her wrath, but the minute she got up, her legs gave way from under her. She felt in the ground unable to move her legs. Changing from anger to panic, Mercedes' asked for help, not being able to understand why she could not move her legs. She was taken to the hospital where they could find no reason why she had lost the use of her legs. Once back home she was laid on her bed where she stayed for three days needing help for her basic needs until the feeling and movement of her legs slowly returned as her anger subsided. Later Mercedes understood that she was so angry to the unfair accusation, and to her new discovery of what the relationship with her father had been, that she had a veritable wish to kill him. Not being that kind of person her unconscious had shot down that possibility by preventing her from moving.

Considering all the oppressive upbringing that Mercedes suffer, it is a testament to her strong will that she insisted in dressing in a revealing manner, and succeeded in having an active, and rather fabulous sex life. Like a river always flows into the ocean, the flowers always open in spring, the frogs always call after rainfalls, the lava of the erupting volcano always raises up with its own heat, there are wonders of nature that simply cannot be stopped and Mercedes' desire was one of them.

Sashawarmas,   by Jorge Bandido

Mercedes viewed as part of her identity as a woman to wear scandalous out fits and to show her lusty body in the most appealing way. It is a controversial form of feminism that some people had problems understanding. On the one hand some feminist argued that the woman should not be sex symbol but a person on equal footing than men so wearing attires that draws attention to her body hinders the feminist agenda. However, Mercedes viewed it differently. For her being sensual and provocative was a matter of empowerment. She could use her body to attract attention any time she wanted. She could stop any conversation and turn all heads just by shifting her weight with a sensual swing of her hips. She would smile knowingly as people looked at every corner of her body and being consume by the inevitable lust her presence triggered. She could control any men, and some women, as if invisible hands extended from her body and reached out to hold the observers by their groins with just arching her back lazily letting her shirt raise a little showing her belly bottom and making her small perky breast protrude through her shirt. She could change any discussion or turn any argument in her favor making anyone lose their concentration by finding any excuse to strike a provocative pose. She seemed to hypnotize men with the deliberate movement of her hands when she talked or the sensual way she pronounced some word like "man" or "more" making a long "m" when her lips puckered provocatively. It was like she enjoyed pronouncing the word, as she enjoyed men themselves.

Being sexy for Mercedes was a matter of principle, liberation, and feminism: If a man can use physical strength that his maleness granted him the capacity to yell and impose himself by force unto others, it was perfectly acceptable for her to use her "womaness" to accomplish her goals. The first time she was called a slut she was devastated and offended but eventually she learned to realize that those that called her that were simply sore losers that could not contain their lust for her and not being able to do anything else resorted to name calling. They were her subjects, she was their queen. She ruled their every thought feeling and there was nothing they could do about it.

At the core of this is that she was a very lusty woman. She loved sex, and loved making love to the extreme of her being and it showed. Her constant desire for men overflowed from her out of her skin and spilled all over her surroundings in a fabulous scent that no men could resist. Men were attracted to her like dogs to a bitch in heat, and just like the animal counter parts men were obsessed about her with no regards for themselves or basic decorum. When she looked at a man's body he could tell she wanted to feel it, when her eyes reached his crotch they stood there long enough for him to notice she was imagining his cock. She was the embodiment of lust and desire. Actually, it was thanks to her severe and stern upbringing that Mercedes had learned not

75

to act upon her immense sexual drive. She had learned to restrain herself and act only to the extent that it was acceptable. Her unreasonable father had actually been a blessing; since her desire was far too wild to run lose. She had learned to contain it and to show just enough of it to make men lose their senses while she still could keep a cool head. This was the basis of her strength.

José Ignacio was just as vulnerable to her charm as everybody else, if anything he was especially more so. That was clear to him since the first time he saw her and when they went to the creek "frog hunting". But that time in the pond of the creek where he first took her with so much hunger, something else happened. He had Mercedes from behind with his arms crossed over her chest. In that moment, when he squeezed as he started coming, he bit her savagely in the back of her neck and crushed her against his chest with his strong arm. Mercedes felt the raw hunger of his full desire as she struggled to draw a breath of air, she understood that José Ignacio was driven by the true Lust. The abandonment to his desire for her was such that she was instantly hooked and from them on she wanted nothing but to be the object of his desire, and only his desire. In that moment, then and there they forged a special union that neither of them understood at that time.

16. THE ZAMBO'S SHACK

The Zambo placed the naked nurse face down on the rackety table of his shack and spread her legs apart. The Zambo stopped for a few seconds to take in the sight: her perfectly round buttocks, her tight and shiny skin smooth all the way down to her thighs. Her long mane, cascading in jet black curls all over her back ending right at her tiny waist. She was short in height but had all the curves in the right places. It was surely a beautiful sight to contemplate from where he was watching.

The Zambo placed his cock in her entrance and pushed it softly inside her. The nurse's legs did not reach the floor enough to give her support for a struggle, not that it would have meant any chance for her to resist anyway. She squirmed with her trunk, and uselessly stroked in the air trying to swim her way up the table to avoid being impaled by the Zambo's massive member. He held her by her hips, with her hipbones fitting perfectly in the small of his hands, his thumbs touching each other in her lower back and his middle finger meeting below her navel. He sank inch, after inch, after inch of his erection inside her as she squirmed twisted and clawed to the table to climb away from him; moaning and whining in pain.

The Zambo was fascinated by the view, the contrast between his dark skin on her white silky one. He was also marbled by how tight her pussy was. He was amazed of elasticity of a woman's pussy. Even the smallest ones could stretch and give enough to accommodate in his monstrous member. He never had a pussy that was that tight on his cock and he really liked it. He was going to keep this one for as long as possible. Obviously, she was not the first woman the Zambo had raped but she was the first white one. In fact, she was the first white woman he ever had. What was the meaning of rape anyway? In his mind it was all a gradient of things. Some women kissed and caressed, others moaned and groaned, others begged and pleaded, others bit and scratched, most of the screamed, either for pain or for pleasure. He did not care much for the foreplay anyway. That is what he had heard people call it. All he cared for was to feel the pussy tight around his cock and feel the difference in warmth inside and outside as his barge moved in and out. This gave him added pleasure, making his mouth fill up with water.

The nurse clawed at the table, in pain, biting the inside of her lips, trying to move forward every time he drilled her entrails with his member. As he went in and out all the length of his member, she felt that the Zambo was never going to come and her torment was going to last forever. When he "rescued" her from her four attackers she felt lucky, but soon she realized that he was not a knight in shinnying armor, he had "saved" her just to take her for himself. After the first time he raped her she found comfort on the thought that it was better being raped by one rather than by four. If you could use the words "better" and "being raped" in the same sentence, that is. She was happy to see that he brought her to an empty house since gang raping seemed to be the order of the day in the small town. However, she was alone with him, with no chance of escaping, if he was going to rape her serially, over and over, was that any better than being raped by many? His cock as huge, there was a good chance that other rapist would have smaller members. Why was she was in a position to even consider what would be better between serial, or gang raping?

So much for all those years being worry about not sleeping around, selecting well her partners, making sure she practiced safe sex. Her ex-boyfriend was always annoyed because she was such a stickler for the condoms and never let him do anything to her without the proper protection. She was a nurse for gosh sake. She knew all too well how important it was. Yet, there she was being impaled by a stranger, his dark cock deep inside her, about to flood her insides with his semen, again! Her time working at the rural hospital gave her a good understanding on his kinds of people. There was no shortage of sexually transmitted diseases in the area, sailors getting to land, getting drunk, slipping with whores, or whoever they found. It was a prime arena for venereal diseases to thrive. The Zambo was part of that world and now he was having her at his leisure. Worse of all, she was in such pain that there was nothing she wanted more in the world than for him to hurry up and come. That would end her suffering, for the time.

She finally felt the respiration of the Zambo speed up, his rhythm became faster drilling her insides mercilessly and his hands crushing her hips. The pain was so intense that she thought she was going to faint; but she did not have such luck. Finally in a last ruthless diving inside her the Zambo collapse on top of her and she knew it was over. She could not feel it but she could picture an unstoppable tide of semen flooding her insides. She felt his kisses in her back and neck as he thankfully kissed her after coming. It would have been a tender action, from a lover, if he had not just raped her! The Zambo pull out from inside her to her great relief and she melted to the floor sobbing and crying. The Zambo closed his zipper and looked pensively through the window of his shack to the direction of the port. After a few minutes of consideration he came to her and holding her by her chin talked to her.

"Wait here. It is not safe outside." He told her and left with long strides down the road of the port.

Her throbbing had ended, for now but she was still his captive. When he left she tried to get up but her legs did not moved. The lingering pain and the burning inside her had barely relented; any moving of her legs would only produce more chafing. After a lot of effort she managed to climb on a chair, and help herself with the table to stand up. She felt a tide of semen dripping out of her soaking her inner thigh all its length all the way to her ankle. He had dumped a bucket of it inside her! There was hardly any point in trying to get it out. It was the second time he had raped her, if he had any diseases it was also hers now.

"It is not safe outside" he had said!! Was that a joke? What non-sense was that? He had raped her twice and it was sure to rape her again, if she stayed there. It was her opportunity to escape from him. The door was unlocked she could just leave. *"But go where?"* There was no safe place where she could go at the time. In the current status of lawlessness of the town, with everybody running crazy letting their worst instinct go, there was not a chance in the world she would be able to make it to safety without being jumped by somebody else, perhaps many! When the Zambo walked her from the rural hospital to his shack, she saw 6 women being gang rapped in the streets, on top of the other nurses that were being raped in the hospital. She could try to make a beeline for the church hoping that there she could be protected but it was in the main plaza. She was a regular visitor and she knew if there was a place where she could find help was at the church under the protection of old priest. No one knew how old he was but he had seen the town grow and everybody, even the worst rapists would take pause before getting into the church and profane both the house of God and the domain of venerable holly man. But it was a moot point, she would never make it there safely. It was a long way and she was sure to be caught by someone before she got there.

To make matters worse she was completely naked. In a normal day she could never walked anywhere in Esmeralda without eliciting countless cat calls, and comments from men in the neighborhood. She regularly heard from beautiful well delivered complements to her beauty that nearly made her stop and thank them, to the most fouls and vulgar expressions of what they wanted to do to her. It was obvious that in that current state of chaos, the latter was going to prevail. She saw the lusty stares as she was being walked naked through town, the only reason she did not get jumped earlier was because the Zambo was so scary that nobody dared to dispute him his prey. Yes, that is what she was, a prey.

She had to reconsider the "protection" of the Zambo. There was no doubt in her mind that he was going to rape her again when he returned. He did not seem to have any remorse for what he had done and she knew she was not the first woman the Zambo had raped. Staying there was sure to get her raped again but trying to escape could get her in more trouble. Large as his cock was, she got to rest between one and other rape, if she was taken by the

79

crowd, there would be no rest and to mercy, even if some of the other men were smaller. In the end, the fear of diseases made her stay. If she was raped by many she got a higher chance of getting more diseases. She found a shirt from the Zambo in his closet and put it on, as not to be completely naked when he returned. His shirt covered all the way to her knees and she was swimming inside it, like a dress, but it was better than complete nakedness. She went on her knees and prayed for the best.

The Zambo returned about 40 minutes later carrying two large sacks of food that he had obviously looted from some of the nearby stores. She was relief to see him alone. Something inside here still feared that he was going to share her with his buddies. He looked at her wearing his shirt and smiled. A broad charming smile full of white pearly large teeth that she had liked so much the first time he came wounded to the hospital. She could not imagine how she had being so wrong as to be attracted to someone like him. He came near pointing to the bags.

"Cook." He told her. "*He wants me to make him dinner! That's it!! I am his bitch!*" She thought. Her feminist vein felt offended by the command. She never thought of herself as a traditional woman that cooks for a man and serves him. She was about to protest when she realized that asking her to cook for him was the least of the impositions that he had required of her! She swallowed her pride and got busy. She explored the bags of goodies, pulled out a chicken some veggies and made a casserole with white rice. While she cooked she kept an eye on the Zambo. He took a shower and came back with just a towel wrapped around his waist. She could notice the bulge of his member on the loose towel and felt chill in her blood when she thought he was going to have her again, but instead he started tuning up the a small radio he had busily trying to get the news of what was happening in the convulsed country after the assassination of the president. Once he got a station he liked, the Zambo spent the time pacing through the house and looking long at the road that lead to the port, as if trying to read the future of the small town at the end of the road.

When the food was done she brought it to the table where the Zambo sat to eat with good appetite. Seeing that she stood on the side he continued with his habits of monosyllabic commands.

"Eat." He ordered.

She sat at the table and served herself a couple spoonful of rice but she could only nibble her food. Her stomach was tight up in a knot. She knew that it was her, what was for dessert.

17. A RELATIONSHIP WITH MERCEDES

José Ignacio romance with Mercedes was extremely intense. She was delicious and incredibly lusty. He loved having sex with her and she would never say no. He had recovered his Maggy and felt very happy. They did not have anything more than sex but then he did not know there was anything else to be had with a woman. Mercedes and José Ignacio continued to see each other during the following couple weeks, but as they started to become more familiar with each other jealousy struck him. The problem was that after he started seeing her more regularly, he felt what all men would feel in the presence of Mercedes body, a strong call of desire, so he was prey of the most extreme bouts of jealousy. He felt a blinding rage, to see her showing too much of her body or moving it in a way that appealed the attention of other men. He started taking issue with the people she hung out with and made it clear to anyone who would listen that Mercedes was taken, and people better listened. He also made sure to inform Mercedes that there was a new dress code she needed to abide to. He banned all the revealing outfits, nearly immoral miniskirts and thin blouses that she often tied up above her belly bottom or that simply were see-thru enough that she did not have to do anything to show her torso. Her breasts were small but her nipples were shameless and always poke the blouse as if trying to pierce it.

José Ignacio did not remember how many times he sent her back to her house to put real clothing on. She would complain and resist his command.

"You are not my father." She would spit back at him.

But when she refused to put a thicker blouse on or a longer skirt, he would take action. Once, she was chatting with some friends while she was waiting for him in the lobby of her apartment building. She was wearing a plaid mini skirt that ended miles above her knees and was intended to steer men's passion. Her loose fitting t-shirt was so short that ended just below her breast exposing her whole abdomen. If she were to lift her arms the lower part of her breast would be seen underneath; which was just the same because the fabric was so thin that one could make out any bit of relief of her small tempting breast.

He felt so angry to see her doing what he thought was, flirting with them showing off her fabulous body that his mind went blank and some part of his brain took over. He held her softly by the back of her neck and lifted her chin to him, as in placing her to kiss her but once there, he squeezed the back of her neck so hard that brought tears to her eyes. When she realized she was in trouble, he let go the pressure somewhat and told her gently in her ear.

Sashawarmas,   by Jorge Bandido

"Is this my girlfriend or is this a filthy whore? You better get back and put some honest woman's cloth on before I rip it all from you and leave you naked." He purred softly in her hear.

Mercedes knew that he was not bluffing and not wanting to be embarrassed in front of her friends she kissed him with a peck on his lips and pretended that he was just being sweet. She swallowed her anger and went to her house to change. At first this kind of situation was a common occurrence and pretty much the way they started all their dates. She would try to exercise her freedom against José Ignacio's commands, he would oppress her and make her abide. She would complain, mutter under her breath but she always ended up complying. So they were working out somewhat of a relationship, also out of the bed. This was no very different than the same kind of relationship she had with her father, except that her father no longer exercised physical domination or punishment on her, José Ignacio had taken that role. She loved his strength but was afraid of it because she feared he would use it against her if he felt compelled to it.

Mercedes's body was not only delicious but there was something special to her when she made love that truly captivated his heart. Her face was reasonably attractive, not particularly beautiful. However, when she was making love she would close her eyes experiencing so much pleasure that her face irradiated an inexplicable beauty. Her mouth parted, half way open while she panted, and her expression of supreme pleasure made her become the most beautiful woman in the entire world. As her orgasms built up she released a soft scent of ripe pineapple that only became stronger and stronger as she came close to her climax. On occasions, a soft amber glow shone all over her body when she was coming. The first time he saw it, they were making love by a lagoon near the sunset and he believed it was the reflection of the sun trickling through the leaves of the rainforest reflected on her sweat-covered skin. But as it became more intense he realized that it was her own glow coming through her skin as she came into pleasure. That was the first realization that he had that there was something supernatural about Mercedes' desire.

His relationship with Mercedes continued with ups and downs. In bed they were phenomenal together but he was worried that he had not seen the depth of their passion and feared of what might lurk in there. His passion for Mercedes was so strong that when it was good and they were in the same page it was great, she would glow with love when they had sex and he was truly happy. However, when they fought, it was equally strong. He felt such strong urges to own her body, to possess every inch of her flesh that he got in very dark vortex of anger, and jealousy that scared him to what he could do. The intensity of their love was so strong that he feared it could be their demise. It was nothing he could explain rationally, it was just a fear of something he knew existed in the depth of their love that he was not sure what it was, but knew enough to feared it.

Superficially, he thought that it was that they did not share a lot of things intellectually because all that he sought in Mercedes was sex. Being brown and poor after suffering discrimination all his life he had a natural tendency to seek changes in the status quo. Mercedes on the other hand was a very conservative person politically speaking. Her white skin spared her of the prevalent discrimination in the country although her African genes were very prevalent in her. If they ever started talking about anything that was not biology or sex, they would immediately start fighting very adamantly; which in a manner was the closest to the intensity with which they had sex. Often it was the constant search of this intensity what scared him. He felt there were depths in their relationship that he should not tempt.

However, as they were working out a relationship Mercedes had to go to the field to do her field work to the Yasuni National Park, in the Amazon forest where she was doing a research project with radio telemetry on medium size carnivores (ocelots, margays and such). She left but because José Ignacio was also a biology student he managed to find a way to go to the field and spend a week every month with her. It was a perfect week. They made love from the first moment he arrived and did not stop until the time he left. There was no moment in which they were not either working in the field or having sex and often both. Between sex and sex they would go to the field to track her animals, it was unusual when they did not make love in the forest both naked in the jungle in intimate contact with nature. He could always find an orchid at hand and surprised her with a romantic present of an exotic flower. At the end of the day they had a light dinner in a common cafeteria and back to bed to make love all night long. In the heat moisture of the forest, his desires seem to be even more intense than usual and he would never stop. Mercedes often had images of being part of the forest, the branches of a huge tree, some animal making love in the darkness, or she saw all the pollen of the a tree being funnel towards her vagina as if the pollen knew how to fertilize her. Tiredness was afraid of José Ignacio and did not touch his body. There was no pause during the whole week he was there. After José Ignacio left Mercedes could not walk for the intense chaffing, and needed to sleep for two days straight to recover from the lack of sleep.

Unfortunately, after his Mercedes week, he had to come back to Quito to take classes and to work. It is not difficult to understand that having a woman like Maggy all the time for his leisure since he became of age, and having such a delicious lover at the other side of the country, it was unbearable to be doomed to celibacy for three weeks. Not only was it difficult to restrain himself from jumping the first woman he ran into every morning but it had physical repercussion in his body too. He would masturbate several times a day but it did not help a lot. Most of his classmates were women and his lust positively poisoned his mind. After a few days without having sex, he would feel increasing pain in his testes as if they were to exploit. It was as if he had a vice grip in each one of them that prevented him for doing anything. He did not know it then but it was part of another physical condition that had developed as a consequence of a childhood accident.

In the one hand there was his physical need for sex but on the other one was that his relationship with Mercedes scared him. His relationship with both Maggy and Francia had been intense an sexual but he did not feel the feverish need to possess them. Maggy had boyfriends at school and eventually got married. Francia had an official boyfriend too. None of this bothered him in the least. This was very different with Mercedes. He desired her so intensely that he did not want anyone around her. He felt so possessive of her that he did not want any other men to get a glance of her body, or a whiff of her scent. He felt trapped for how badly he craved her and it made him angry. When they were together he would possess her but he could not avoid wondering what happened around her body when he was not around. Who looked at her? Who did she talk to? Did she smile to other men? He knew she liked men's attention and it made him rabid not to be able to watch her when he was not around her. His feelings were so intense, that he feared them. He feared not being able to control himself if he got too angry He feared what he may do driven by his jealousy, to her, to others. On occasions he felt he should find someone different. Someone who gave him the same good sex, with a hot lusty body but that did not trigger in him such strong possessiveness. Someone like Francia, for instance.

He started for the first time in his life having female acquaintances that he did not try to make love to. In particular, he became friends with Amelia, another biology student. Amelia would often chastise him for being with Mercedes and dared him to say one reason not sexual for which they were together. Racked his brain as much as he could, he never succeeded. In reality it was not so much that they did not share other things, the problem was that sex with her was so overpowering that his mind could not stray from it. Amelia would try to set him up with other women, part for thinking that they were better for him and perhaps part to get even with Mercedes who was madly in love with him, and with whom Amelia had some history with. Amelia coached him in manners and ways with women. Dos and don'ts.

Sashawarmas,   by Jorge Bandido

Since he only knew the sexual part, she was instructing him in the ways of being gallant and getting to seduce a woman.

Amelia had a very beautiful cousin, Marlene, who studied pharmacy and sometimes came to their part of campus to hang out with Amelia. One day she challenged José Ignacio to pay a compliment to her that was not just a line. He never had any illusions with Marlene because she knew him from Amelia and she had made sure to tell her cousin to stay the heck away from him so, they had somewhat of a friendship as well. When Amelia challenged him to pay a compliment to Marlene, he did not know what to say but quickly it came to his mind.

"You must be quite dumb because it would be unfair that God had made you this beautiful and also smart." He told her.

Marlene had moment of hesitation while trying to figure out if it was a compliment or an insult and after a second broke out laughing at the witty remark. She held his face with her hands and putting her sensual lips on his give him the sweetest of kisses.

"That was a very special compliment." She told him.

It was just a short, only lips, kiss but it felt so good! He felt his heart racing and tried to continue it, but she pushed him back laughing.

"No, I am wise to you," she said; and she pushed him away.

18. HER CAPTIVITY

Daniela bit the pillow tightening her fist on the linen in pain when the Zambo impaled here from behind. Biting the pillow was the only way she could withstand the pain without screaming. Her gums had become sore and often bled for biting the pillow so hard. She had bite sores inside her lips for biting them when a pillow was no available. Her palms were bruised of digging her nails in them making a fist to focus her efforts. The Zambo massive chest loomed like a roof over her while he shoved himself inside her. He was so large and she was so small that she fitted in a small cave between his chest and the bed. That is where she lived and what her life had become. It was the third day she had been his sex slave and it did not become any easier. The first day he raped her 6 times, during the day and all through the night. She did not count the second day because it all merged together on her mind as a continuous state of being raped without pause. Often she woke up with a nightmare of being raped, half of the time to realize that it had she was not dreaming.

She had resigned herself to it, and she had tried to gain herself for the idea that it was her new reality that she needed to accept. God send us challenges all the time to test our faith. Hers was just tougher than others. When she saw that he was going to take her she prepared herself. She breathed deeply, trying to relax her pussy. She even fingered herself a little trying to get some moisture to lubricate herself but there never was enough time for it to fully work, the minute he felt like it, he shoved his manhood inside her without much warning or consideration, leave alone foreplay. It did not help that she was raw from the first times and he never left enough time for her pussy to recover before raping her again. It was only fitting, men with so much muscle also have a lot of testosterone which produces the sex drive. She had always been attracted to muscular men but now she was experiencing what it really meant.

Even between one rape and the other he always wanted her next to him. His member seemed to get somewhat softer after coming but never flaccid and would become somewhat smaller but it always had a terrifying girth. He was most of the time pensive, listening to the news but required her to sit on his lap or on the bed next to him. His mind was seemingly somewhere else but his hands were on her: holding her buttocks, playing with her nipples or absentmindedly caressing her crotch and putting his fingers inside her. There was nothing of her off limits; she was simply a body for his amusement. At one time he heard the news about a military Junta trying to get formed to take the government back. It might have upset him quite a bit. He was fondling her buttocks and when the news came in the radio he shoved one of his fingers up her butthole. Daniela panicked because up to then she thought she had it as bad as it was possible, being raped vaginally over and over, but then she realized that it could be a lot worse. She prayed God to divert his mind from that path. She could not imagine the pain if he shoved his gigantic cock up her ass. She closed her eyes and prayed, and prayed, and prayed.

****

She had always been very beautiful. She was used to always have men's attention and always felt blessed for her beauty. At some point she convinced herself that the Zambo's attention was a compliment for her beauty. He could be out there raping as many women as he wanted with his herculean strength, yet he had chosen to have her only. It was a stupid consolation and she knew it. Yet, she needed something to hang on to in her life. She needed to see some good side to her predicament; and this worked ok.

After the Zambo came that morning he collapse over her letting his large humanity lay on top of her as deadweight. She unclenched her fist and let go of the pillow. His cock was still inside her but at last he had stopped shoving inside her. Soon it would slip out, she thought. She felt her teeth loosening and her gums throwing, but it was over . . . for now. Her concern now was to draw breath under her large captor. She heard him breading restfully with deep inhalations and long exhalations. Great! He had fallen asleep! He woke her up, fucked her for what felt like an hour, and now he wanted a nap! She was tired too. She was tired of him, tired of being raped, tire of not having any hope. She wanted her suffering to end, she wanted everything to be over. But at that time, drawing a breath of air was more important, she had to crawl from under the Zambo so she could free her lungs to expand. It was a small bed even for a single person. Certainly it was small to share with someone the size of the Zambo. He was hot like a furnace. Sleeping next to him meant to be in a constant state of sweating, both for his heat and the moist heat of the surrounding rainforest.

She managed to slither from underneath him and went to the bathroom to wash. She put on one of his shirts that fit her like a long dressed and went to the kitchen. She was getting used to the routine of being his woman. He had already had her that morning; the next demand was breakfast, why not do it ahead of time and save the humiliation of being bossed around. She contemplated by the thousandths time the possibility to escape to the town. "But to go where?" The country was still on chaos and the town was in a scary state of lawlessness. Things could have calmed some but there was no

87

guaranteed that she was not going to be assaulted if she went to town. She did not know if being serially raped by the Zambo was better than being gang raped by many. What happened to the women that got gang raped? She had seen the hostility of the men raping Rebecca and the bruises in Mónica's face. The racial tension of the town was being expressed in violent ways against the white men, their wealth and their women. Likely all other women that were raped had been kidnapped to be someone sex slave like she was. At least with the Zambo she was safe. All that he wanted from her was sex, if she gave it to him she could be fine. He was not going to hurt her, beyond the damage his cock had done inside her, that is. She wished his member was not so large, or that his libido was lower, or that she was not so raw from the constant rapes. She remembered the tale that people in the Andes said about the spectacled bear, El Salvaje (the savage), as the local called it. They claimed that a bear would kidnap a maiden and take her to his den. There he would lick the sole of her feet so much that it would leave them tender, so the maiden was not able to walk and that way prevented her from escaping. That was pretty much how she felt, kidnapped by a large beast that kept her to his pleasure.

While she was in the kitchen with a big cleaving knife she considered like so many other times to take it to the Zambo. She could sneak up to him while he was sleeping and slid his throat. It could be a swift movement that he would not be able to stop. If she did it right he would not be able to retaliate and would die of a quick death. Nicking the carotid artery will also do the job. It will produce so much bleeding that he would die in very few seconds rendering her free. A deep cut in the stomach could also do. She recalled her anatomy classes. The abdominal aorta, goes deep by the stomach; the mesenteric arteries were also all over the area. With a deep cut, he would bleed to death in a few minutes. Then she could remain hidden in the shack until the town calmed the same way she was, but without being raped. The only thing was what to do with his body. She could not carry it and in the sweltering heat of the forest it will decompose quickly.

She was absorbed in these thoughts and did not realize that her legs had brought her up right to the side of the sleeping man. She was surprised to see herself by the bed holding the knife just inches to execute her thoughts. She did not recall moving out of the kitchen! Something in her was taking over and she did not know what it was. All she needed to do was a quick movement with her arm and it all would be over. There is no way she could go through with it. On the one hand was: What if she missed? What if he woke up just before she could do it? He could hurt her very seriously. It was all day dreaming amyway. She was not able do such thing. She walked back to the kitchen. She was a nurse for crying out loud. Her deal was to heal and help people, not to kill and stab them. Plus she was a good Christian. God presents us with challenges and it is up to us to show our devotion to His teaching. This was just a test to her faith for her to pass. Resisting was the proof of her true faith. She did a quick mental calculation. The time to remove the stitches from the Zambo's wound was overdue. She put some water in the fire with a small sharp knife to remove the stitches when he got up.

****

Breakfast was almost ready when the Zambo came out of the shower. He was not wearing a shirt as usual and his skin was covered by tinny drops. It was not possible to tell if it was water or sweat, likely both. There was something unnatural about the warmth of his skin, his skin was always moist with fine sweat, even after a cold shower. In the sweltering heat of Esmeralda even her skin was often moist. Before she set up the table she brought her supplies to the table.

"Let me see your wound." She told him using the commanding voice that medical practitioners use when treating a patient.

He presented it to her and she carefully reached in with the sharp knife next to his chest to cut the stitches one by one. While she was at work he had an appreciative look in his eyes, admiring her work. Or was he admiring her? When she was done he pulled her face toward his and kissed her mouth with a soft, deliberate kiss feeling with intense contact between their lips. She did not quite return the kiss but she let him do as he pleased with her mouth. She felt overwhelmed by the intense sensation. The nurse realized that after all the sex he had demanded from her there has been little kissing. He liked sucking and kissing her breast but never her mouth. When he came he would covered her with shallow tender kisses in her back or all over her face but wet, mouth-to-mouth kisses, the kind that lovers give each other, had been missing. This one was perhaps the longest and the tenderest and without knowing why she felt her eyes welling up.

When she was done she set at the table and sat next to him. She knew that it would not be long before she was asked to "give her services" to him and saw with anxiety how he finished his breakfast. When he was done he pulled her over his lap. He pulled up her shirt/dress leaving her completely naked. He looked at her long jet back mane cascading down her body, in large curls, half masking the small perky breast and produced one of his charming smiles full of large white teeth. He started kissing and sucking her breast intensely. She felt his strong manly smell and the deep sensation in her nipple traveling down her body. He sank his mouth in her neck and kissed her licking her ear lobes. She would have felt disrespected for the touching and aroused by the caresses, but in that situation, she knew it was just the path to being impaled mercilessly one more time. He lifted her and straddled her over his lap to lower her as it has been happening so often. She reached down and felt his large member about to make contact with her pussy as he lowered her. This time she had the nerve to say something.

"Wait", she said, holding his chin and kissing his large thick lips apologetically for interrupting.

She reached over the butter on the table and scooped three fingers full of butter to lubricate the Zambo's member. She smeared the butter all over it and dutifully impaled herself with it. She took a deep breath of air and let it go slowly as she lowered herself on his cock. She held herself on his hips to control the penetration. It was a long way to the bottom but since she was controlling it she could pull up sooner before getting all the way to the end. She started working on it with the help of the butter and managed to get most of the way down. The Zambo let her do and used his rough and callous hands to caress her breast. One of his large hands covered most of her chest when he was foundling her. Her reached behind her and squeezed her buttocks hard, appreciative of her tone. Her eyes were closed, the brow somewhat screwed up, her beautiful mouth half open as she let air in and out slowly concentrating in the task of relaxing herself to allow his member in. Her raw insides still hurt but she could tell that this was a way to make her life a lot easier given her new situation. Feeling in control the element of fear went away and she managed to relax herself more to better accommodate him insider her.

Because now she was doing all the work, his hands were free to caress her body. She felt his warm hands squeezing the back or her thighs to the point of ache. His other hand came to the front scraping her nipple when he squeezed her breast so hard that made her gasp. He took a look at her goddess body with her back arched backwards, and facing to the heavens, screw up her brow, and biting the inside of her lips, and two small tears streamed down her perfect cheeks. The pain of his hands squeezing her breast, her thigh and the rawness inside her collided in her mind making her let out a little whine. She took a deep breath opening her eyes to see the perfectly muscular chest of the Zambo, with all his muscle protruding and well defined. To her surprise her pussy was all the way down in contact with his pubis. It was the first time she took it all in without feeling her insides tear. She breathed deeply in relieve. She moved up and down with a slow rhythm not as deep, or as hard, as he would do it but something she could tolerate and that would also give him the orgasm he wanted. He must have enjoyed the sight of her diligently fucking herself with his cock because it was not long before he squeezed her tight against his chest when he was coming but now she was fully relaxed and wrapped her arms around his chest. Her hands did not meet behind the back of the huge Zambo but she could feel his chest, his magnificent muscles. She breathed closely inside his skin and felt the musky scent that was now familiar to her. She let her tongue timidly out, enough to taste his skin and figure out for once and for all if it was sweat or water.

19. THE TEMPTATION OF THE BODY

It was a rainy day in the Yasuni rainforest; one of those in which there is no wind, no storm or lighting. It was just a continued down pour as if the station had moved under a gigantic waterfall where it rained with no end for days and nights. Even the mosquitoes were afraid of coming out of their hide outs for fear of being knocked over by a bombing drop of water. The frogs walked around in broad day light because the whole place felt like a swamp. José Ignacio had come to Yasuni for his share of Mercedes and to help with her field work but the rain prevented the use of radio telemetry equipment. Mercedes was dedicated to work in the computer with her advisor and José Ignacio spent all day alone, bored to tears, only having Mercedes at nights.

In that opportunity there was a new person in the station. A tall woman daughter of an Italian family, Claudia, was 5 feet 9 inches tall, had a fine Greco-Roman nose reminiscent of a bird of prey, a fresh personality, an athletic body, a delicious behind, very short shorts, and legs that went on for miles and miles. She was a med student but she was interested in biology of primates. Someone had given her a howler monkey that had been raised in captivity as a pet but now they wanted to put her back into the wild. Since they have an important social structure it was not possible to just turn her loose, she had to be introduced into a group where it could have the social life they need. Claudia brought her monkey and she was working with some American primatologists in the field station (most scientists in the station were Americans) that were studying a population of wild howlers and also had a group in captivity where they were studying diet.

José Ignacio liked Claudia since the first moment he saw her, he kidded around with her, flirted with her a lot. She knew he liked her and seemed flattered by his attention. He could notice how Claudia looked appreciatively to his muscular body and glanced at his bulging biceps whenever he moved his arms. Because it was so hot despite of the rain, he wore no shirt showing his hard body covered with a film of sweat that never evaporated in the heat of the jungle making the tight skin over his muscles shine. It was obvious that she was physically attracted to him. This day he was in the lab of the station where she was preparing food for the monkeys. He approached her and started kidding around and flirting with her and practicing some of the advice Amelia had given him to properly court a woman.

José Ignacio had noticed how she responded to his flirting and took a bolder step. They were both sitting at a table next to each other. He had started the touching game, putting his hands on her knee as they talked and feeling the internal part of her thighs tenderly. She ignored this obvious touching. He felt the moisture of the forest air and got the certainty of what to do. He got his member out of his pants and moved her hand under the table for her to grab it. If it had worked so well with Maggy why not try it again? She was surprised to feel his thick hard cock on her palm but she grabbed it and held it firmly, looking at his eyes in surprise. Without skipping a bit he approached her and caressed her thighs. She felt the coarse skin of his hands touching the inner side of her thigh and took at big breath of air inhaling his scent holding it in suspense feeling how his hand progressed towards her. Claudia felt current traveling through her body and let go a deep calming breath when his hand went down her leg and away from her pussy. He stopped his hand ever so close to her pussy but without touching it, and traveled his way down her thigh to the knee caressing the soft skin of the posterior part of the knee. But shortly she took another deep breath feeling his hand coming back up around her thigh stopping just before making contact with her pussy again; teasing her and seeding longing for his touch. At the same time he stuck his mouth into her neck and kissed her neck seeking her ears. She continued holding him with one hand while breathing irregularly following the touch of his hand. She was completely disarmed. Feeling the girth of his erection, his hands traveling her forms, he climbed towards her breast and felt her nipples feisty and perky. He gulped her mouth hungrily and kissed her sealing her mouth with his. She responded in kind, like a woman answers to her lover. Instinctively she started to stroke him slowly up and down.

There was nothing obvious in their communication, even mutual flirting, that would tell him that she was going to give to such move but there was something in the smell of the forest that told him she was his. In that moment he could have taken her all the way to the end because he had her suspended by the string of his desire. However, someone came to the laboratory where they were and they had to interrupt themselves. He put his member away, in a hurry and both pretended that there was nothing happening. The person pick up a jar from a shelf and left almost immediately so they were soon back alone. The problem was that it gave Claudia the break that she needed to recover her defenses. When they were alone again, he tried to pick up where they left off but she stopped him.

"No wait! Mercedes is my friend. I can't have anything with you." She told him moving his hand away from her thigh.

Clearly, it was not easy to explain why he would be interested in Claudia having Mercedes with him, in nearly the same place. The closer he felt to Mercedes the more he could peek into the depth of their passion and the more he wanted to run away and find somebody else that gave him the same good sex but without the raging intensity that scared him so much. The love she produced in him was great but he feared what he could do with the jealousy and anger she also had a way to produce in him. So he was always in the lookout for a woman that was as hot as Mercedes but that somehow did not steer his dark side so much. In fact, Claudia was perhaps, someone with whom he could find what he really wanted. Since his mother was a nurse, there was an attraction to her since she was a student of medicine. She was hot as hell, and she could perhaps be a good substitute for Mercedes in bed that did not torture his sense of jealousy and possessiveness.

On the other hand the same argument that she could not have something with him because Mercedes was her friend said without saying that the problem was not that she did not like him. The only objection for them having a relationship was Mercedes. This would turn him on even more and made him angrier. However, it was the only argument he could not fight. He was not a suave man with women but even he knew that telling a woman: "*Oh, no. I am with Mercedes just because I am enslaved by her sex, but I am actually looking for another girlfriend.*" Was about the worst thing he could do to get her favors. This sounded very bad on the one hand, on the other hand, it was not credible. Explaining how afraid he was of the deepest feelings Mercedes triggered in him was long and complicated; unless someone knew him very well. His fear to the intensity of his passion was something that he felt at some level but he himself did not understand it well. She will never understand it. So, he did not bother saying anything.

"Oh, she is busy, and I am sure she would not mind." Was the only thing he could come up with but even he knew it was lame.

"I don't think so. I am sorry for what I gave in there but it is best if we just stay as friends." Replied Claudia getting up and going away.

José Ignacio tried to corner her again several times during the day to resume where they were interrupted but she rejected him every time. When he insisted in touching her disregarding her objections, she simply left the place where they were and went to a place where there were other people, mostly American biologist. As he had tasted her lips and felt her curves he was poisoned. His member had felt the soft stroke of her caresses and wanted her. He needed to have her. If Mercedes had been around he would have relieved himself on her, if nothing else but she was busy in the computer room with her advisor.

In the evening, though he saw an opportunity when she was going to take a shower. She was staying in a house on the station with concrete walls and a very high ceiling (about 20 feet tall) where the walls did not get all the way to the ceiling; they stopped 4 or 5 feet short of meeting the ceiling. This is a kind of construction common in very hot places to allow the hot air to go out. But it is possible to get into any rooms if one can climb over the walls, and climbing was his thing. He waited outside her room and gave her enough time to undress. He climbed up the wall using some furniture that was next to it with his member out and ready. He was hoping to get her alone, locked up and peeled which would have made very easy to take her back to where he had her before and finish the job. But he jumped the gun. He got there just as she was pulling down her shorts before getting into the towel, a bit too soon. As soon as she saw him she pulled up her shorts immediately.

"What are you doing here." She asked surprised.

It was a rhetorical question as he was going at her with his erection out and ready to take her. He jumped on her and clobbered her on her back on her bed sticking one leg between hers. She had felt him, and he had felt her desire. There was a deeper connection he knew existed and he wanted to bring it to the surface. He knew all that he had to do was to overcome the initial resistance, the superficial concern about Mercedes, and he could gallop this mare for many miles. He grabbed both her wrists with one of his hands and used the other one to caress her breasts and fondle her. He kissed her neck and mouth but she would denied him her lips and would turn her face preventing him from resuming that hot kiss that got interrupted. Claudia was surprised and did not react to escape but once he had her under his control she objected vehemently his actions.

"Let go of me! Don't! Let go! What are you doing? I am Mercedes's friend! I am going to tell her! Now! I mean it!" Protested Claudia vehemently.

José Ignacio tried to shot her mouth with a kiss but she continued to avoid it and asking him to free her. It was dinner time in the cafeteria and there was no body in the area of the rooms. On top of this the deafening sound of the rain on the tin roof of the station made it nearly impossible for anybody to hear anything just a few feet away; so he was not too worried about her protestation. With his warm cock on her terse thigh, his thigh on her pussy feeling its heat, he was where he wanted. His hands felt her forms arousing her. His wrestles lips sucking her ears and neck, arousing her. He knew she had no chance of resisting. She was as good as his.

This was no unfamiliar terrain for him. This was exactly how he forced strip Francia so many times but with the advantage that Claudia was not nearly as strong as Francia. He knew that leaving her on the fire a bit longer she would end up melting. However, Claudia was not as ambivalent as Francia was about being taken. For starters she told him from the get go to go away. Despite the first acceptance of his touches early in the afternoon, she told him with no ambiguity, and repeatedly to leave her alone. However, her rejection was because of Mercedes, but he also knew that she desired him. He knew that if he could touch and caress her some more, he could turn the tide in his favor. The problem was that Claudia knew it as well. She could feel the effect of his hand and his touch. She knew where it would lead her and she had no intentions of letting it happen. She knew she was not strong enough to resist him. She knew that she was lost and there was only one possible outcome from the path they were in. Decided to change it, she started calling out for help.

"HELP! HELP! I AM BEING RAPPED!" She screamed from the top of her lungs.

He put her breast in his mouth and started to suck it intensely. She was overpowered by his strength and by the musky smell of his skin. The more she struggled the more she inhaled his scent. Her nipple quickly turned sides and started playing for him. She felt his warm mouth, sucking her nipple so greedily. She felt a wave of lust traveling from her nipple down her body and making her pussy twist. Claudia tried to free herself but slowly she noticed how her desire was winning the battle inside herself. He was so unbelievable strong and so masculine. How can a girl resist him? Her unfaithfully nipple was working for José Ignacio inside, and the rest of her body was following its lead. Even the other nipple that he was not sucking was aching with anticipation and longing for the man's virile touch. The heat of his body was radiating over all of hers, and her struggle for resisting was tiring her over and forcing her to inhale more of his musky smell, that she realized too late, had some magical aphrodisiac properties that had already taken hold of her. She was panting both with pleasure and tiredness and ready to give up to the lust he had seeded in her.   Her vocal cords, the only part of hers that had not yet surrendered to his desire, made a last call for help.

"HELP! HELP, I AUMMM" Claudia called but could not finished as he possessed his mouth before she could finish. His tongue went inside her licking lovingly her inside, the inner part of her teeth and the softness under her tongue. She had no way of resisting and gave him to his kiss. His lips caressed hers with an overwhelming sensuality. Her pussy made another twist and, to her chagrin, she felt how her hips, with a mind of their own, raised forward to press her clit in his solid thigh. She had surrendered to his lust.

However, Mercedes was done working in the computer lab and was looking for José Ignacio. Other people told her that they had seen him hanging out with Claudia during the day and her antennas got in alert. She had seen the sexy Italian hotty around and knew José Ignacio's raw lust and charm. That was a bad combination without her surveillance. She went to Claudia's room suspecting they could be having an affair, but when she approached the door she heard the last of Claudia's call for help and called her.

"Claudia, are you OK? What's wrong" She called from the hall. Mercedes' voice gave Claudia a last hope for resistance and called out one last time back asking for help.

"OOUUMM" Grunted Claudia with José Ignacio still blocking her mouth with his.

He was exploiting for penetrating her for once and for all but he needed still some time to get there. She still had too much cloth on. If he had waited 3 more seconds before making his move, she would have moved away from her shorts and he would have gotten her naked and defenseless. By now he would have impaled her. But to pull down her shorts was a major step that was going to take time. With Mercedes outside the door he did not have a lot of time left.

Mercedes heard enough to know that there was a man trying to force Claudia and being a biological station where most scientist were respectful foreigners, she could imaging easily who the perpetrator was. Mercedes climbed up the wall as José Ignacio had done. Once on top of the wall she could see him pinning Claudia on her back trying to make love to her, not precisely with her approval. Mercedes was afraid of heights and she took some time seeking a way to climb down without having to jump from the height where he had jumped. This gave him enough time for José Ignacio to pull Claudia's shorts down, but doing so he lost his position between her legs. He only needed to open her legs again and penetrate her but Mercedes seeing the situation got courage and jumped.

José Ignacio managed to get between Claudia's legs again and he could feel her pubic hair in the tip of his member. It was just a matter of a thrust to impale her. However, just at that very time Mercedes threw herself over him clobbering him off Claudia, freeing her from his grip. The strong man grabbed Mercedes, hot and horny as he was, shoved her in all four on the bed; pulling down her shorts in one single move. José Ignacio shoved his member inside Mercedes deep and hard pressing his chest on her back and his pubis on her behind.

"AAAUUGGMMM" Mercedes, who was dry, let at a long grunt of pain when he impaled her but made no attempt to resist.

97

Claudia, who was ready to escape, turned around to help Mercedes who was paying the price for saving her. Claudia tried to push him away hearing Mercedes grunt and seeing her fists cramp on the linen of the bed and her brow screwed up in pain. José Ignacio came out and went in a second time hard and deep drilling her deeply. Mercedes let go a lout groan of pain again while Claudia rained punches on José Ignacio's back trying to fee her friend. When it did not work she dug her nails on his back. José Ignacio, impervious to Claudia's attempts, rained kisses equally on Mercedes' neck, back, and shoulders. Claudia was overcome feeling the hard muscles of José Ignacio's back and its perfect definition.

At the third rocking of the boat Mercedes started lubricating herself and her groan of pain turned into moan of pleasure. She could see waves of lust shoving Mercedes' body forward and backwards every time he thrusted inside her. Seeing how Mercedes did not struggle or complained Claudia stopped punching him, part for how useless it was proving to be, part for how overwhelmed she was to feel José Ignacio's body and scent, and part because Mercedes did not seem to want help.

Everything indicated to Claudia, it was her time to leave both lovers at it, but she stood bolted to the ground unable to leave the scene. Something close to envy invaded her to see Mercedes mouth half open, panting with her eyes closed taken with such raw lust. It was like something of her was there. If nothing else, it was José Ignacio constantly calling Claudia's name as he kissed tenderly Mercedes' ears and neck. It was as if all that lust was intended for her. Against her better judgment, she placed her hands on his back and torso feeling the sweat permanently that covered his slick skin and clearly marked muscles. She took a deep breast and felt again his musky smell. The first time she smelled it was a bit offensive to the nose. The second time she felts some sweet aftertaste that made it somewhat appealing. The more she smelled it the more it grew on her, by now it has an addictive feeling to it; that she could not have enough of. Then she noticed how it started to acquire a mixture or the smell of ripe pineapple.

Claudia never knew why she did it. At that time it felt like a good idea. Claudia straddled José Ignacio from behind and encircle his bull's neck with her forearm trying to strangle him, still somehow trying to pry him apart from Mercedes but she was not sure if it was to protect Mercedes or to take José Ignacio for herself. She was breathing very heavily with arousal. Her naked torso came in intimate contact with the strong man's unnaturally warm back. She took a deep breath by his neck and felt a spam of Lust traveling through her body and condensing in her pussy that gave another powerful twist. Holding his thick neck from behinds without thinking what she was doing she licked the back of his neck sucking his skin all the way to his hear. She felt that salty flavor of his skin, and the potent smell that it radiated and she could not help by rubbing herself with his behind. *"What are you doing? He is raping your friend! You need to hurt him, not lick him!"* Claudia scolded herself but she could not stop doing what she was doing. She flattened herself more on is back. She reached with her hands for his nipples and dug her nails on his massive pectorals. She licked the lobe of his ear, taken by his flavor, tears of emotion exploding out of her eyes as her pussy did wild summersaults out of her control.

Claudia managed to control herself enough to slide down to the floor shivering again and stood frozen watching the scene. Claudia was reaching the level of addiction. She felt her pussy turning and churning with the scene of the woman so powerfully taken. In the darkness between the two bodies she could not see his member going in and out of her friend but she could picture it in her mind. She had held its impossibly thick caliper that morning filling up her whole hand. She knew she had to leave but she could not muster the strength for it. Her mouth filled up with water as she found herself panting in arousal when his rhythm fastened. Claudia saw his hands squeezing feverishly Mercedes breast as he called Claudia's name declaring his love for her. She reminded spellbound to the scene until Mercedes' amber glow became brighter and then went extinct slowly. This last change and the collapse of both bodies on the mattress was what finally made her recover the control of her legs and leave the room.

It is not normal that a woman accepts that a man makes love to her calling her by the name of her rival but Mercedes knew him well and she knew that while she had him between her legs she was the one calling the shots no matter what he said or whose name he called out when he was coming. After they came, they got dressed and went to Mercedes' room without having dinner. She was embarrassed of what the people might have heard and did not want to be in public.

"You are such a pig! You were going to rape her! A friend of mine! You are despicable" She chastised him.

But all response she got was him sealing her mouth with a long invasive kiss, driving his finger inside her until she started panting again. Then took her one more time. He might have done her 3 or 4 times that night, with lust fueled for the recollection of the encounter with Claudia and enjoying Mercedes gorgeous body. While he was doing her, Mercedes let him be but as soon as they we were done she resumed her scolding and name calling.

Claudia had to had nowhere to go after leaving her room. She was too aroused to be in the presence of people and she had no cloths on at all. She headed towards one of the trails that lead into the forest where she could avoid running into anybody as night was falling. She felt in the jungle she will be able to find some relief. It was raining so hard that she felt the warm water of the tropical rain flooding towards her nipples and cascading down the peak of her breast. The rain was so sick that she could only see 5 feet in front of her but she knew the way well. She stepped into the trail where the forest canopy took the brunt of the rain but there was still a lot of water dripping on her from the branches. Then she stopped and crossed her arms over her breast to stop the gentle rubbing of the water falling from her nipples. She felt her own hands and took a deep breath. She smelled like the man. She smelled like his body. "*Gosh, he smelled so good. Why did I resist?*" She had been horny all day since he first kissed her and put his member in her hand but her better sense of good behavior had prevented her from acting on her desires. Now she repented her resistance. "*It could have been me taking him in.*" She felt with longing.

His sweat had stuck to her when she climbed over hm and now she smelled like his skin. She smelled her arms and shoulders. She rubbed her hands on her abdomen and brought her palms to her nose only to feel her pussy do a summersault to feel his strong scent impregnated in her skin. Claudia rubbed her skin with her hands using the abundant rain water falling on her to wash down his scent from her body. His scent refused to leave her skin. Her hands caressing over her body steered up his musky smell and made her have shivers on her spine. Instinctively she reached for her pussy and the very contact of her hand made her climax alone and naked in the jungle. After coming she calmed herself down, wiping the water from her body not realizing the part of her that had gone down with the water into the intimacy of the jungle.

****

Both Mercedes and José Ignacio consumed in their lovemaking the day before had not noticed Claudia's actions, and attempts to stop José Ignacio at first to protect Mercedes but later to take him for herself. Next day Mercedes was embarrassed with Claudia for what he had done and made the mistake of asking him to apologize to her. They went both to where Claudia was, in the lab, same place where the prior day he almost had her. However, instead of a regular apology for something wrong he had done José Ignacio offered different apology.

"I am sorry your body is so delicious that I could not contain myself. I am sorry your smile is so sweet and your laughter so sensual that I did not have the strength to stop." He told her turning on the charm and continued. "In fact, it is mostly your fault for being so beautiful that you made me lose my control!" He continued.

His "*apology*" was so shirtless, that Claudia had no choice but to break up in a nervous laughter at the shameless way of expressing his desire for her body in front of his girlfriend.

Laughing at his lack of restrain it was obvious that she liked feeling desired in that way. José Ignacio had Mercedes, who had an excellent hot body. His lack of restrain over Claudia could do nothing less than rise her self-esteem. Obviously, if having Mercedes, he still wanted Claudia so badly, was a testimony of how desirable Claudia was. One thing he was learning about women, was that low self-esteem was a very common threat among all of them; even among those that did not have any reason for having self-esteem problems. In other words, instead of apologizing for assaulting her sexually, he managed to wash his actions into a joke, a game of more flirting and seduction that could only open his opportunities farther in the future. Claudia felt completely naked to José Ignacio's desires and all she could do was to laugh nervously and seek help on Mercedes whose stare she could not hold much as she tried.

Neither José Ignacio nor Mercedes were aware of the effect that their love making had made on Claudia the night before but from the first interaction in the lab the day before he knew that there was connection between them and so he was following his instinct. With her acceptance of his game it was obvious that, were it not for the obstacle of Mercedes, Claudia was well within his reach. This was also obvious for both women. So, from that day forward, Mercedes kept him under extremely close surveillance. Claudia avoided being with him alone, as if he had the plague. She would always try to be on the presence of other people. He would touch her breast when they encounter each other or grabbed her behind when she passed but she knew better than making a big deal out of it. He inspired in her an intense lust very unfamiliar to her and she knew it was best to avoid it. Before going to bed she would find Mercedes and make sure she was guarding him before she undressed but in the shower she always fantasized with him breaking in a taking her in the shower as she had imagined him taking her under the rain in the forest trail.

Sashawarmas,   by Jorge Bandido

That week ended and between Mercedes guardianship and Claudia
avoiding José Ignacio, he did not manage to have his way with her as he was
hoping. Mercedes and Claudia became best friends partially, because they
have similar characters and liking but mostly because Mercedes wanted to
make sure that Claudia was on her side and not as a rival. Mercedes hated to
be depending on Claudia's restrain to keep her boyfriend from misbehaving.
She trusted Claudia's friendship, and she never did anything that gave her
reason to believe that Claudia liked José Ignacio but she feared that no woman
could resist his desire once she had felt it.

20. A SLIPPERY SLOPE

A lot of the relationship between José Ignacio and Mercedes out of the bed involved a battle of wills between him imposing his ways to her and she resisting it. It was the closet to making love when they were out of the sack. At first he thought it was because he had to possess her to control because her she was so flirty but later he realized that it was a way of seeking the intensity of the encounter that he was so addicted to with their sex. Clearly, there were no few occasions in which the confrontation led straight to bed as well. Her risqué dressing was probably her own version of the same thing. She had found her father's attention by showing her body and even though it resulted in a lot of strict guarding and oppression, it also meant that her father was paying a lot more attention to her than before. The same was true about every other single man in her life. Controlling as José Ignacio was, it simply made her feel the more special. In a manner he took the role of her father in guarding, her and taking the antagonism with her regarding the exposure of her body. This is the reason of both, her acceptance of his imposition of a dress code and her constantly challenging of it. He was the strong figure that would angry easily and take action physically if provoked. Nobody in her life, other than her father had ever done that. So she found a comfortable, or at least known, area to communicate with him. Also because she viewed him as a parental figure, she would readily accept demands from him, and be more than eager to please him. When he showed attention to another woman she did not see it as a fault of his for liking another woman she saw it as she needing to try harder to get his attention and earn his favor, just like she once tried with her father over his preference for her brother.

One day he found her in a mall, when she did not know he was going to be there. José Ignacio was livid to see her dressed provocatively, head turning actually. He did not say anything then, but took her to a hotel room to have sex but as soon as he closed the door of the hotel room, he gave her a small amount of money.

"Why is that? She asked confused.

"Well, you are dressing like a cheap whore, I am paying your fee." He responded biting each word with anger.

"I can dress however I want. You don't own me." She spat back angrily. "Do you want to make sure I dress like you want? Then be with me. Stop courting other women. If you are not watching me you will never know how I am dressed," she said defiantly. That was the wrong approach with José Ignacio when he was jealous.

"I do own you. You are not going to blackmail me." He replied purring dangerously at the time that he pull her hair down forcing her to look up at him. "You do as I say because you are my woman."

It was a fine line for Mercedes. If she seemed not to accept his possession of her as a property, she risked physical punishment. But she hated to be dominated. She knew the safest way was to divert his anger towards sex, then he would take her and be sweet and loving again. She remembered her dad beating her and José Ignacio was far stronger than her dad, even if he did not use a belt. While having sex they were definitely in a plane field and that was where she needed to go.

"Of course I am your woman, I am all yours. I only want you to give me all your love, all your attention. I don't want you to seek any other woman." Replied conciliatorily Mercedes.

"So why were you dressed like a whore if you were not with me." José Ignacio continued without letting her off.

"I wasn't dress like a . . . I am sorry. I am sorry. I won't do it again." Replied Mercedes knowing that arguing about her dress would only get him angrier.

"How sorry?" He said not relinquishing and still holding her hair down to force her eyes up towards him.

Mercedes replied kissing his lips and trying to smile to divert him from his path of mind.

"Get the soap and froth is well with water." He ordered her. Mercedes heart sank.

"No, no, please." She pleaded.

She hated when he used sex as punishment. She hated to be taken in the ass, and she knew he would do it to make a point. Their sex was so special that she hated for him to use it against her. She liked so much a proper penetration and he seemed to enjoy just as much doing her in the rear.

"Let me suck you. I will suck you really good." She offered reaching for his member and stroking gently. "I will swallow it all, like you like it." She begged upping the deal.

She was a lot more inclined to give oral sex. Preferably as part of foreplay in regular intercourse, but she was not a fun of having him come in her mouth. He would shove it too deep and made her gag when he was coming. Plus and then he wanted her to swallow it which revolted her. It was another level of the domination game he liked and she rather had vaginal sex where she could do him as she wanted.

She dropped to her knees and took it in her mouth stroking it with her hand all its length. José Ignacio took a deep breath and accepted her penitence. He liked seeing Mercedes on her knees, in the same position she would use to prey to the Lord, sucking his cock with her generous African lips. It was a position of submission that strengthened the point he wanted to make. By the time he came in her mouth his anger had dissipated and she was glad it all was behind.

Another point working in José Ignacio's jealousy and rough treatment of Mercedes was that he felt enslaved by his desire for her. He felt that he could not measure up to her desire and her lust and he made up the difference by physical strength and oppression. On the other hand, she felt quite the same way about him. She was captivated by the way he lusted for her, for the intensity of his desire. She felt the most special woman in the world when he was squeezing her with his arms at the moment of his climax. His extreme jealousy, although she often complained, it told her how much he cared. Even if he slept with another woman on occasions she knew she was the one he felt the need to be possessive with. Somehow she knew, perhaps better than him, how deep his sexual desire ran in his souls. It was very clear to her that so long as he had access to her to satiate his lust, she could count with his attention, and his protection. Since sex was about the only thing he seemed to want, it did not matter if the strayed with other women. She knew the other ones could not rival her in the sack even if they were prettier. She was deep inside a girl that had found a way to use her body to please her father and unconsciously she saw him as her father. That is why she would tolerate all the physical abuse and impositions from him while she had always been very vocal for women liberation and feminism.

In his side, he was stepping on a slippery slope. Mixing sex with power was a completely strange for him and that he never knew in his relationship with Maggy, it was present in a manner in his relationship with Francia, the conquering of her body as he stripped her, was very much a matter of power although he did not see it except later in life, as an afterthought. However domination and sex mixed very natural with Mercedes. He was finding it a delicious and inebriating cocktail, that added to the fear he already had of the intensity of their love.

One day there was a party at the university at the end of the year. Mercedes was back from the field for the Christmas celebrations. Tropical countries do not have cold season so Christmas parties are very much parties, like any other: music, dancing, drinking etc. Amelia's a cousin, Marlene, came to the party. She was a mulata, (mix of black with white) with thick eyebrows that framed her caramel eyes. She might have some Quichua blood as well as most of the Quito people do. Her eyes were some darker tone of hazel, downright captivating. Her ethnic mix was delicious and all men were attracted to her. She also was smart and funny. The problem was that being a cousin of Amelia who knew him all too well, Marlene had been warned very clearly about José Ignacio being hook with Mercedes. But in this party in the school, she had been drinking and he noticed her defenses were lowered.

He invited Marlene to dance, kidded around a little and seeing her vulnerable, took her with him away from the crowd hoping to seduce her. They went to a hall in school, hardly hidden and started making out. Because José Ignacio used to work in the herbarium, he had access to the prep room, where after the staff had left he had all privacy he wanted. This worked as a charm; it provided a private place to have sex to any woman he seduced without having to spend money in a hotel room. He was working on Marlene in order to take her to the prep room and he knew that it was only a matter of arousing her a little more since she had a one too many drinks, and she was kissing him passionately. However, Amelia had seen them leave the scene and came to her cousin's rescue, finding him fondling Marlene all over. Amelia gave José Ignacio a shove an a piece of her mind; and took Marlene away from him.

"Hey, I really like her. I have good intentions." He protested but Amelia did not believe him for one second.

"If you are serious with Marlene you would stop all other flings, break up with Mercedes, and try again when she is sober." She chastised him.

José Ignacio came back to the dancing arena to see Mercedes dancing with another man. He had not forbidden her to dance with other men but she knew all too well that he did not like it. But the problem was not that she was dancing but how she was dancing. She was far too close to him and he was holding her way too tight. José Ignacio could see their bodies rub and touch as their dance and he saw his hands traveling up and down her back and even feeling her derriere. That was definitely over the line. She knew better than to let somebody else touch her. Mercedes was never shy to express herself. She would tell a man that he is out of line, without any hesitation. But in this case she let her dancing partner go way too far without doing anything. *Did she see me kissing Marlene and wanted to get even?*" He thought. He did not know if she did it because she liked the other guy or to make him jealous, but jealous he became.

106

Sashawarmas,   by Jorge Bandido

José Ignacio felt his rage growing in him and taking over his body. He did not remember getting to Mercedes from the dancing arena. This was not uncommon during his rages; which later he discovered had a good neurological explanation. It had not been a pretty sight. After decking her dancing partner and making sure that he would not get up, José Ignacio grabbed Mercedes by her hair and dragged her out of the dancing floor by her hair troglodyte style. As they walked away, he could not erase from his mind the image of her being fondled by another man and her letting him touch her without complaining. He felt his blood boiling with blind rage. When there was no one on sight, he confronted her with what she had done. At first she tried to deny that she was doing anything but eventually she snapped.

"I saw you kissing that woman". She retorted. That was the wrong kind of answer. José Ignacio pulled her hair back forcing her to look up at him.

"I can sleep with anyone I want and that does not give you the right to do anything in exchange. You are my woman and I will not let my woman be a slut for the pleasure of other men." He and told her, spitting the words with anger.

He continued his march to the prep room dragging her by the hair; calling her whore and every other dirty name he could think of a. She knew how to handle his jealousy. After the first misstep of confronting him she went quiet and did not argue. She simply let him do as he pleased, which regularly it was making love to her. After making love to her, she knew, his anger would subside and his love would come back up again.

José Ignacio pushed her face down on his desk at the prep room and without wasting any time he pulled up her skirt and pull down her underwear. Rage was burning inside him, he wanted her to feel pain, and without giving her any preparation, shoved his hard member full of anger inside her. It slid all the way in, easily inside her well lubricated pussy. This was not abnormal because Mercedes got wet extremely easy and she had known, since he dragged her from the dancing arena, that he was going to fuck her. However, it occurred to him that she was lubricated because she liked the other man touching and feeling her body. He felt anger burst through his temples. He wanted to hurt her and he knew how to do it.

José Ignacio got both her wrist behind her with one hand restraining her from moving. He got his member out of her, placed in the entrance of her asshole, and shoved his shaft in with fury. Then Mercedes tried to squirm when she realized that he was going to fuck her in the ass but he had her well immobilized. Mercedes screamed and he felt all the muscle of her body and her torso contract in pain. He pressed her nape against the desk to subdue her and shoved the rest of his member in, until he felt her hard muscular butt in his pubis. Mercedes cried and screamed begging forgiveness. He had taken her in the ass before but he always used some lubrication, vaseline or soap, at the very least. But this time he penetrated her dry, with anger and without any preparation. She was in pain, and he knew it. But not only that, *he liked it.* He liked it very, very much. Mercedes begged for forgiveness and promise not to do it anymore but it was not enough. José Ignacio continued merciless going in and out with unmitigated anger. He was delighted to see her in pain. He loved her screams and moaning of pain and he was enticed by her pleading of mercy. He wanted to teach her a lesson for trying to escape his control and domination. He was inebriated of pleasure drinking up her pain.

He gave it to her with full thrust. Every time enjoying more her cries of pain, her abundant tears covering her face and how her body twisted and contorted every time his cock went in. She had hurt his pride and he was making her pay for that. When he came, as usual, the rage gave way to his true love and he showered her with loving kisses, sweet and tender on her neck, her teary eyes, licking and kissing her salty face. Her body inspired him trust, tenderness and love.

"You will always be the true love of my heart." He declared between kisses and caresses.

She swore never to make him angry again and they both kissed with love. There will come a time when José Ignacio was not proud of what he did. Not only it was horrible to have abused of his physical strength to force her and hurt her. It was unforgivable to have enjoyed her pain. Besides, what moral authority did he have to be jealous. If Amelia had not stopped him from seducing drunk-Marlene, he would have been having sex with another woman at the time when she was only dancing with another man. What reason did he have to be so jealous? Much less to hurt her? But at this time he did not realize that he was enjoying a little too much the venom of mixing sex with violence. While he exerted his physical dominance over her body, she was also exerting her own. She had him firmly by the cock and he knew he could get from her all the sex he wanted, even if it hurt her, so he never failed to come back to her, even if he had flings with others. Her unconditional acceptance of him was the hook that had him. The sexual connection between their souls ran far deeper than any of them imagined.

21. BACK FROM ESMERALDA

The bus arrived to Quito at the crack of down. It had been a long ride through winding roads from the forest to the mountains. It has been 18 months since she left Quito for her new job in Esmeralda away from her family. She had never been out of her house. She lived with her parents in Quito while she was going to nursing school, moving out was prohibitively expensive. On the other hand her parents would never let her move out by herself. "*A decent woman moves from the house of her parents to her husband's.*" They would tell her with finality. Perhaps that was part of the reason that she wanted so badly to move out. The job in Esmeralda was OK. It paid a bit better than those in the city because everyone wants to live and work in the city and few nurses are willing to move to rural facilities, and for a good reason as she learned the hard way. But more important than the money was the fact that there *was* a job there for a new graduate, while any hope to work in Quito had to be as a sub, for hours, no benefits, until she acquired some experience that made her competitive. Going to the rural facility was a way for her to get some chevrons and be able to come back to be competitive in the job market.

Her parents were not thrilled that she was moving out to a small town because they had never relinquished control of their only daughter. But her mother had worked on her father to agree with the hopes that a small town could change her ideas about marriage. Rural facilities also had a lot of young doctors that are required to work for two years in rural community. Her mother was certain that in a small town, there would be a young doctor that would fall for her overwhelming beauty. The sacrifice of letting her go on her own to a town could pay off in terms of giving her the chance to find a good eligible doctor to marry. She got plenty of requests, to be sure. Most of them just wanted to get in her pants, which was something she was used to since she was teenager; men seem to have only that on their mind. There were some that were more serious and considered something beyond bed, but she had not been crazy about them. For starters she never thought of going to school, or working on a hospital for that matter, as a way to find a husband. It was all her mom's machinations. When her mother was using those arguments to convince her father to let her go, she just played along. Going to Esmeralda was a good move for her future. In that score she and her mom were in agreement. Only that her mom was thinking on her catching a doctor for husband, while she was thinking on getting professional experience and becoming better qualified for her job. So, she never intended to live in Esmeralda all her life anyway. She just hoped she would come back on her own terms.

Sashawarmas,   by Jorge Bandido

But, despite it all, she was back. She was wiser. She was stronger. She had grown up more than she would have ever imagined. She could not say she came back triumphant, as she once hoped, but she came back alive. And that was more than she thought was going to happen in the last few days since the social explosion in town.

She had spent all night thinking what to tell her parents. Obviously they had to be worried with the news about the turmoil in town and all the lawlessness that engulfed the whole country after the assassination of the president. They would be happy to see her safe and sound but she worried on what would happen when the happiness of seeing her alive wore off and they wondered what had happened to her. How has she managed in the middle of the craziness that went on?

She could not possibly tell the truth. For starters she was embarrassed of what had happened. Being rape was a big stigma to bare in Quito society. Plus telling it would be reliving it and it was much too painful for her to talk, or even think, about it. She could not accept the idea and she felt that if she made up a different story and believed it well enough her whole trauma was going to go away. If she denied that it ever happened, she could move on as if it had not happened. At least that is how her mind was coping with the situation.

Her story she came up with was reasonably believable. It touched on all the things that her parents cared about. There had to be a man who protected her, as it kind of happened, but this man had to be not interested on her. Otherwise she would have to explain how she kept her virtue. It was the fiancé of Mónica, her friend nurse at the same hospital. As the story went, Mónica's partner came to the hospital and rescued all 4 nurses from the facility. He owned a local supermarket franchised and took them to one of his warehouses that was well guarded by his security guards. This story had a male hero, as they parents expected. It had also a believable story that the benefactor was completely altruistic, and did not ask anything from her. Also, it explained how she survived for 3 week in hiding. There was plenty of food and supplies in the warehouse of the supermarket. When the order was restored Mónica's boyfriend had simply had given her a ride to the bus station because she wished to come back. When she eventually told it, the story sailed smoothly. Her father insisted in thanking the man that had protected his daughter. He wanted to invite him for dinner or somehow show is gratitude and insisted in knowing who he was. Daniela had to come up with some excuse, delayed, procrastinated hoping he would forget but at least she had dodged the main part of the problem

Sashawarmas,   by Jorge Bandido

Of course the reality had been quite different. She replayed on her mind a million times the last day of her captivity. She had woken up early and was making breakfast as she knew was her duty, when the Zambo came out and turned up the volume of the little radio. The narrator was loud and even ceremonious: "*The constitutional order has been restored. The military junta conceded the government to the vice-president. The rule of law has been restored*". It took the Zambo a few seconds of reckoning after which he rushed into the bedroom to put on a shirt and pick up his machete. He came out in a hurry, held her face between his hands and looking straight into her eyes, with his eyes so dark that seem to lack a pupil.

"You need to go home to Quito. It is not safe here anymore." He told her with his deep foghorn voice: She was surprised at his tone but nodded consent like a school girl.

He kissed her tenderly on her forehead and left the house with a gust of wind. She looked out the window and saw him running with long powerful strides towards the plantation that bordered the forest. His machete folded by his forearm, his arms swinging at the rhythm of his runner's strides. He clearly was going to hide in the forest but she had no idea why he was doing that. If the order had been restored, who was he hiding from?

Not a moment too soon. As soon as the image of the Zambo disappeared from the small window a powerful kick made the door shake on its hinges. "This is the National Guard. Open the door" There was no time to answer, a second kick made the door fly open and a contingent of heavily armed guards poured in the house baring their arms and checking, rooms and closets. She was petrified next to the kitchen sink when she saw 8 men getting in the house. She was glad she was wearing one of Zambo's shirts that cover her up to her knees. It was far more than she had been wearing during all the time she was the Zambo's captive. He wanted her to be naked most of the time.

"He is not here sir." Came the report from the guards that were searching the house.

"Where is Jose Ignacio Guzman?" The head of the operation asked her with a commanding voice.

It occurred to her that she never knew the name of the Zambo. Words seemed trapped on her throat while she hesitated uncertain that they were actually looking for the Zambo. But there was no confusion.

"Tall, Zambo, very strong, very dangerous." Described the head guard seeing her hesitation. She took a deep breath and she will never know why she said it.

111

"He went running on the way of the Port," she said pointing out the other window, in the opposite direction that the Zambo had actually departed.

"Thank you ma'am," said the head guard formally and ordered the rest of the crew out on the chase of the Zambo.

She saw them running at fast pace towards the Port and wondered why they were looking for him. "*Very dangerous.*" He had said. That was true enough. The people that were trying to rape her in the hospital had been knocked unconscious with just one punch. But dangerous to whom? There must have been a reason. The Zambo certainly knew they were coming after him. He did not even have breakfast and had departed in a clear farewell, without intending to come back. She also wondered why she sent the guards off his track. She should have turned him in for having kidnapped her and raped her serially for days on end.

"*Go home. It is not safe here anymore.*" Were his last words to her. She was so conflicted with herself and about him. May be he had protected her from far worse violations. It was hard to believe considering how he had had raped her repeatedly. And then the other questions: Who was he? Was he involved in some politics? The guards did not seem to be too worry about law enforcement, rather it seemed like they were looking for political agitators and those that might threatened the newly established order. That must be why he ran into the forest. Regardless he was gone from her life forever.

The nurse fixed up her shirt/dress to fit her better. She did not trust that the order was that well restored or even what that meant. Yet, she went down the street that connected to the town, on the way to the port. All she was wearing was the Zambo's shirt that best fitted her, no shoes and nothing underneath. She felt rather vulnerable. However, the town seems to be going back to normal. The last time she had walked this path there were women being raped at what seems like every street corner. She was positively terrified. But now things looked different. There was trash in the streets, general disorder as the day after a big party when people start waking up with the hangover; picking up the wreckage of the night before. That was the feeling the whole town had. Instinctively she went to the church where the old father Carlos likely had the only operation with common sense to help people in need. She was not wrong. There was a small crowd of people, mostly women that had realized it was finally safe to be out on the open and they all were asking for some help. Some needed food, others sporting reaped off rags, evidence of the sexual assault they had suffered, needed clothing. All of them needed healing of their soul.

Sashawarmas,   by Jorge Bandido

She joined them, part of her nurse vocation lead her to participate on the providing of help and giving out food. After all she had been relatively safe during all that time and she had not lacked water, food or shelter. Father Carlos recognizing her as a regular attendant to Mass, called her over. Explaining that she was a nurse got her to operate a basic first aid kiosk that was unmanned and with several people in need. Then she had people, protection from the church, and a mission that matched her soul. Towards the evening when the needy were winding down the father called her.

"Thank you very much my daughter. You have been very helpful. You may go home now." Told her appreciatively the old priest.

But of course, she had nowhere to go. Despite the seeming calm of the town around the church, she did not dare go to the rural medical hospital where she had been living. The whole thing was ransacked anyway. She did not dare to even go back to the place and just did not want to see it again, not wanting to relive the experience.

"Actually father, I do not have a place to go. I am from Quito and lost all my belongings. I thought of getting money from the bank to buy a bus ticket to go back but I loss all my documents of identification. I have nowhere to go. If I could spend the night here, on a bench, tomorrow I will try to find my way back." The Nurse asked, hoping the priest would let her stay around in any capacity.

Fortunately, the old priest new everybody on town and was well respected by the whole community. He talked to a boy that helped him in errands after which the boy took off running at the speed of light, as if the future of the planet depended on the speed of his feet. Ten minutes later the boy came back solicit with an answer to the father's query.

"Go to the bus station and ask for Anibal. Tell him I sent you. I thank you for all your help here my daughter. May God bless you," the old priest said.

She did as instructed. Anibal, a heavy set bus driver on his 50s gave her a warm smile to hear she came recommended by the religious man.

"I am sorry I lost everything. I do not have a ticket" The nurse excused herself embarrassed. Anibal's benevolent smile open wide and friendly.

"I am always honored to help a friend of father Carlos, my dear. Have a sit right here behind my sit". He told her

That is how she found her way back to Quito without owning anything, not even the shirt/dress she was wearing.

113

Of course her parents were happy to see her. After a few minutes of disbelief and happiness.

"Could you not have at least called? The news from all over the country was unsettling but the news from Esmeralda were the most disturbing. We were worried sick about you!" her father asked reproachfully.

Luckily her mother scolded him for not being nice to her. The nurse explained that she did not have phone access anywhere and told them her precooked story.

Soon she got rested, obtained new copies of the documents she lost and started looking for another job. The job market was still difficult but at least she was safe now. She had a place to sleep, three meals a day and she could save all the money she made, which was not much. She was getting settled. She was a hard worker that soon was noticed as someone to keep around and, although permanent jobs were scarce she started getting lots of sub gigs that helped her get back on her feet. She was feeling better and happier and the nightmare from the kidnapping in Esmeralda was slowing fading away. She no longer woke up in terror reliving the fear of being raped and the memories of those days started feeling like a book that she read or a movie that was very vivid.

The memories of the last days in Esmeralda would have gone away altogether were it not for the fact that she was feeling a bit weird in her balance, her scent of smell was very intense and her appetite was very random. She went from ravenous to not wanting to eat, to puke. She never had any appetite issues when all her friends were starving themselves to look skinny. She was just the perfect weight without ever trying at all.   Then the final confirmation of her fears finally came. She was late!

22. THE ANGEL AND THE NURSE

Exxon had received a permit to start exploration in the rainforest, in particular inside the Yasuni National Park. The mood in the country was torn; some people liked the income that oil exploitation would bring for the cashed strapped country. Others were unhappy due to the environmental consequences. Clearly exploiting oil in the National Park could not be good for nature, the wildlife, or the indigenous people living there. However, the National Park was managed by the government and the new government was on board with it. They evacuated temporarily all the people from Yasuni station with the excuse that it would be uncomfortable for them to be there with the crew of engineers and geologist. However, everybody suspected that the exploration activities were very destructive and they did not want the scientist to witness them. So Mercedes was in town for a whole weekend, after which they could return to the field station. José Ignacio had not been feeling well in those days. He was very bothered by the exploration because he feared the worse and he felt very close to the forest. Also stress for school was getting the better of him, a few drinks with dinner and a full stomach did not help his condition. He was with Mercedes in a hotel room enjoying their love when he had an episode of his disease. He had not had one in years and as usually when it happened, he had forgotten all about them and hoped they were gone for good. However, that night shortly after making love to Mercedes, it struck him.

It progressed the way they normally did. His stomach seized up and stopped moving. Everything between his ribs and his groins were perfectly still and fell hard and stiff. It was like his guts had turned into a 1000 pounds rock that was sitting on him and did not let him move. His trunk was under intense pain and the only movement that happened was reverse peristalsis. His guts rejected everything in it all that he could do was vomit. Every 10 or 15 minutes he was attacked by a convulsive bout of vomits that lasted one minute or two. Then brief relieve came to his body while his guts settled and then the stillness came in with more excruciating pain. He had suffered of these episodes for all eternity and they could come once a year, or every other day for no apparent reason. However, he had noticed that stress and lack of rest made a difference. He had not had any episode for at least three years and this one got to him with vengeance.

After the first hour in this situation Mercedes got worry, since she had never seen them, or even knew about them. She took him to the hospital, against his protestation.

Sashawarmas,   by Jorge Bandido

"There is nothing they can do for me. It will just go away later." He protested.

There was no medicine, anti-emetic or any other treatment that could help him, save for time. After 12 hours or so, the episode would end itself and he was going to drift into a state of sleepiness. The next day his whole body would ache as if he had been ran over by a truck and the following day he would feel just fine. This was the course that these episodes always took and he was resigned to just wait them out, instead of subjecting himself to more testing and medicines that he knew would not produce any results. However, he was in no condition to resist and he let Mercedes take him to the university hospital.

He barely recalled anything, hospital lights, stretchers, a bucket for him to puke when the bout came and holding it, the most beautiful woman's face he had seen in his whole life. "*An Angel!*" He had the sudden realization that he had died and gone to heaven.

His mother, a very religious woman, brought him up under a deep catholic upbringing. When he was a boy she insisted in having him be an altar boy to help the priest in the Mass.

"Your father used to be one when he was a boy." She would tell him encouragingly.

That was about the one thing he ever heard about his father. He had seen a photo of a young dark kid dressed as an altar boy and a priest. When he asked any more question about his father that was the end of it. Yet, despite how religious his father had been or how religious his upbringing was with his mother catechism really did not take on him that deeply. As soon as he had any level of independence he stop going to Mass, against his mother's protestation, and for most part he called himself some sort of an agnostic. However, experiencing excruciating pain, feeling at the edge of life and death, it was comforting to think in a superior being that was there to take care of him. He was seeing the angel with his own eyes, so he let himself believe.

It did not make sense that being dead and in heaven he was still puking and is so much pain but he was in no condition to subject his situation to rigorous deductive reasoning. The angel holding his head while he vomited had the most fine beautiful face, huge brown eyes, small delicate lips, sharp pointy nose, nacreous impeccable skin dressed up on nurse scrubs. In the haze of his illness he could see the white skin of her bosom with scattered moles contrasting with nacreous background. Her cleavage was discrete and modest but it was clear that her breasts were round and full. On occasions a wave of lucidness flashed over him and he reached over to feel her breast. The gentle but firm hand of the angel grabbed his wrist and moved his hand away putting it by his side. On occasions he heard Mercedes' voice, on occasions he met the caramel brown of the angel's eyes, every time more he wanted to put his face between her breast but the cramps of his stomach and his confused stated made him wondered in what stage of the afterlife he was in.

The night turned in to morning and as the sun rays were coming in he felt the familiar sensation of relief that came and the end of the episode. Slowly he felt into slumber state that would end up with very deep sleep. When he woke up it was evening again. Mercedes had left in the morning when his situation got stable. He looked around and saw the angel, likely in her next day shift, checking up on him. She looked at him and gave him the most charming smile when she saw that he was awake.

"How are you feeling champ?" She asked him with bright smile and warm tone.

He mumbled whatever answer he could to the effect of feeling better. She was not an angel, just an extremely beautiful nurse that was taking care of him. Being the son of a nurse himself, he was often inclined to think highly of them. He had seen her face all through his agony, her devoted attention to his disease, and her charming smile. He had the vague recollection of feeling her but he was not sure he had done it and if he did, she did not seem to hold any grudges.

As José Ignacio recovered his mental clarity he tried to sit up to start a conversation with her, he most certainly wanted her number. She told him briefly what he knew what had happened, puking, non-responsive to drug, moaning in pain, until he felt a sleep.

"Had you had that before? Do you know what triggered it?" She asked.

He explained to her what he knew about it, which was not much. She explained in technical terms what exams they were doing to him and what the process was to find out what had happened. Then he learned that she was not a nurse, she was a medical student in training. He tried to continue a conversation away from his disease trying to engage her personally hoping to get her number and asked her out later. However, she was decided to keep it professional and talk about his disease. She wanted him to come the next day for some medical examinations and to see the Dr.

He was always mindful of Drs asking for spurious test just to charge for them but the university hospital provided free care for all students and taking the test would grant him an opportunity to see Gabriela again, the medical

students he was so smitten with. When she was leaving to fill out some forms
he let it out.

"I do not recall well but last night I seem to remember that I. . . . ahem . .
." and he trailed of not wanting to finish the sentences but his eyes when
down to her breast in explanation. "I was not myself at the time but I seem to
recall . . ."

Understanding, Gabriela laughed a soft sensual chuckle. "Oh, yes! You
did. Repeatedly!" And turning around left the room.

An actual nurse made an appointment with him to have a CAT scan of
his head. This was most odd because his problem was a digestive one, what
would a CAT scan of his head tell her? Honestly, he would not have cared
about keeping the appointment but going back there could get him another
chance to see Gabriela again and hopefully score a date with her. He had the
test but could not see Gabriela, that day. His hope was that she would be
there when he met with the Dr. to talk about his case.

His suspicions were right. Gabriela worked regularly with that Dr., in a
apprenticeship style. He met the Dr., a neurologist, and Gabriela was there
learning and contributing.

"Here we can see small L-shaped scar in his brain between the Nucleus
Accumbens and the Amygdala and with a branch from the Amygdala to the
Ventral Tegmental Area, just under the Hippocampus. The Amygdala is the
center of the primitive brain. It regulates primeval urges like the control of the
digestive system, fear, anger, and sex among others. There is no surprise the
scar triggered these episodes." Explained the Dr. "It seems like when the scar is
irritated in may swell producing pressure in this area stimulating the function
that these centers regulate."

Clearly the digestive system is part of the primeval support system of the
body. When the scar acts up it puts pressure on these centers which sends
them wrong and confusing messages. That, the Dr believed, was what
produces the episodes. It had the benefit of explaining why they went away by
themselves (exhaustion of the neural pathway involved) and why the
gastroenterologists had all been so stumped with the problem. It was not
about the guts, even if the guts were how the problem manifested itself.
However, the position of the scar also affects other centers. The Ventral
Tegmental Area and the Nucleus Accumbens is also known as the reward
pathway of the brain. It is where the dopamine receptors are and that part
that tells the brain when something pleasurable has happened. The
Hippocampus, along with the Amygadala, are involved with memory of
pleasurable events and has to do with the subject seeking them out. These

118

centers are known to be critical in drug addicts since the drugs stimulate the reward centers and the memory of them is what drives the addicts to seek out the drug so intensely.

"These kind of injuries are also involved in compulsive drug addiction. Do you consume any drugs?" Asked the Dr. very professionally.

José Ignacio never had any inclination for any drugs except for some drink now and then. He knew no addiction except for addiction to sex. So he shook his head. The next part of what the Dr. said was more troublesome for him. As if she had read his thought.

"This injury may produce inappropriate sexual behaviors because the person may seek the reward so intensely that it would overlook social rules of normal social behaviors. It may produce risky and extreme sexual conduct. It is in fact, similar problem with drug addiction except that it is sex itself that becomes the drug." She explained. "Have you have any issues in your sexual behavior?"

José Ignacio hesitated to answer and kind of shook his head but with far less conviction than he had denied taking drugs. It was a bit awkward because the Dr. was a woman, in her 40s, very well kept. She was slender yet toned, her breast were well formed if not too big. She was a very attractive woman in general. Also the gorgeous Gabriela was there, he felt weird talking technically about sex with them. Certainly, because extreme and inappropriate sexual conduct was something that other people, like Mercedes, kept saying about him. There were no shortage of times when he took her constantly for days on end during his visits to Yasuni that she would declare that he was the worst *sex addict* in the world. But she was just been hyperbolic, right?

"This injury may continue acting up or it may stop all together." The Dr. continued, "It may also produce problems in irritability, anger or aberrant sexual behaviors. Have you experience any problems in controlling your temper?" She inquired giving a brief pause before she continued. "It can also produce hypersexual activity as well as the opposite: depression, lack of interest in anything and impotence. The hippocampus is involved in depression as well as the opposite, maniac over stimulation of the mind".

Again, Mercedes would agree that he suffered of hypersexual activity and surges of anger but he was not sure he wanted to talk about it with them. He was painfully aware of the presence of Gabriela in the room. He certainly did not want to talk about his girlfriend in the presence of Gabriela. He did noticed Gabriela's eyes looking into a notebook but not writing anything as in trying to pay attention while pretending otherwise. After all he had reached for her breast during his episode. He was not convinced that his behavior was

119

wrong or extreme, and he certainly did not want to let Gabriela know of anything that may scare her so he denied all accounts of unusual sexual behavior. Plus, was his sexual behavior really extreme? What does inappropriate really mean? Mercedes would have said he was guilty of both. The thought that he may develop impotence was also very scary. If anything identified him was his erect penis. The thought that it may not get hard was downright scary. So he pushed away that thought from his mind and denied it all.

"The pressure on the hippocampus can produce episodes of bipolar activity. Either make you very active and unstoppable or sink you in deep depressions. Because it affects declarative memory, people with this lesson may have an extremely good memory or the opposite. Have you experience any of this?" The continued the interrogatory.

Now he had an explanation of his near photographic memory that helped him so much in his classes despite the fact that he was always thinking of sex and studied very little. He recalled having moments of extreme excitement and going on doing things for days on end without getting tired and needing minimum to any sleep. These were often linked with being with Mercedes working in the field all day and having sex all night, not leaving her chance to sleep, or doing her while she slept. He did not suffer from depressions, unless she meant those moments where he was angry all the time and nothing in the world seemed to be right for him. He attributed those to the unfairness of society, and how brown people were discriminated against at so many levels. Mercedes used to call his dark moods. Yet, he had no intention of confessing any of that in the presence of Gabriela.

"Well, I am glad to hear that. I will put you in some antiflamatory drugs to prevent the stomach episodes for now. If you were to develop any of these other symptoms come back to me we can help you and treat you for those too." Offered the Dr. amiably.

As he was leaving, he worked out the courage to ask Gabriela for a date. After all, he was a biology student their field were not that far apart. Also they were very much of a similar age, because in Ecuador students get into medical school straight from high school. So, he asked her if he could take her for a cup of coffee after her shift. It was a bit of a gratitude offer for her taking care of him. Or at least that is how he played it out.

"My shift is tonight but I get of work at 5 pm. Then I have a couple hours". She replied lukewarm.

He was not sure she was that much interested in a date with him as she was curious about his condition. The brain lesion was uncommon and the

Dr. was interested in his as a case study. So, perhaps Gabriela wanted to get some more data on him. Either way it granted him the date he wanted.

They went for coffee and he discovered how much he really liked her. Not only was she beautiful, she was smart, sweet, extremely warm, and caring. She started to look like a person he would consider seriously as a partner. They made plans for a future meeting, a real date. He played his cards right and at the third date he managed to kiss her and they kind of became boy and girlfriend. She asked about Mercedes since she brought him to the hospital, spent all night with him, and she was clearly worried about his condition.

"She is just a classmate, we work together sometimes." He evaded this question.

He was not schedule to see Mercedes in another three weeks. However there was a glitch. As José Ignacio started dating Gabriela she would not put out. She was very catholic and a virgin. She would not have sex out of wedlock because it was sinful. Being attracted to a very catholic nurse, or med student, was very much what Dr. Freud would predict of him, since that was a very good description of his mother. His mother was also short, petite, and very white. He was so interested in Gabriela that he accepted her conditions of no sex, but of course he hoped, and constantly tried, to change her mind. He boiled of desire to make love to her but she would not hear anything about sex before marriage. They would go out, make out, he would caress her and touch her forms but she would not allow anything she thought of as sinful. He was going crazy!

After having all his relationships being so intensely sexual since he was a teenager, he had to have a teenager relationship after being and adult! Even copping a feel earned him a scolding. Obviously it could not work out, making out with her got him so horny, so he had to go to Yasuni to meet Mercedes where he would get even and exhaust all his lust and frustration for not being able to make love to Gabriela. The first time he saw Mercedes after starting seeing Gabriela he fucked her for 36 hours straight not letting her go to the field. It was far more than usual but Mercedes was used to his extreme lust. Plus, she loved being desired so intensely so she dealt with it even if she was sore after the first few times. This became the routine. He would gather up desire and lust with Gabriela and drain all of it with Mercedes for one week of the month. His emotional life had gone from being very simple with one woman that gave him everything, Maggy, to have two women and still not feeling satisfied.

Gabriela's mother was very strict and guarded her very carefully. José Ignacio was not allowed to visit her if there was not a chaperone at all times.

121

Gabriela had to come back home in a very strict, and early, curfew when he was with her. One day, José Ignacio went to visit her and Margarita, her younger sister, was supposed to be the chaperone. When he arrived she told him that Gabriela was not home yet. She was held up in traffic coming back from school, so he saw himself in her house along with Gabriela's sister. Margarita was strong minded opinionated who, although she was still a teenager, rebelled against the iron hand of her mother. Margarita did not have the supreme beauty of Gabriela, but you could not share genes with Gabriela and not being at least fairly attractive. She taller than Gabriela, with smaller breast but very perky ones and long well tone legs. She was also very curious about men and about her body. In no time José Ignacio realized that he could exploit her rebelliousness and curiosity. Being alone in the house could only result in one thing.

José Ignacio ended up making love to Margarita in the coach as he waited for Gabriela's arrival. She was the first virgin he ever tasted. Her skin was so soft and so white, her breast were so tender! He could barely imagine what it would be like to have the very Gabriela. When they were done, he did not want to wait for Gabriela anymore. It would have been awkward to see Gabriela after making love to her sister and he did not know what was going to happen later. They agreed to keep it very secret, Margarita told Gabriela, that he had called to cancel and she never told her that he had even been there. It all worked out well. He tried to coordinate other times to meet with Margarita again to relief himself but her mother's surveillance was way too tight. Short time later Margarita got knocked up by a neighbor and was force to get married. José Ignacio continued to date Gabriela who was the only woman who had inspired him anything beyond just sex, but sex itself was out of the question with her.

When finally Gabriela agreed to let José Ignacio make love to her, he was the happiest man in the world. He took her to a beautiful hotel, spent the night together (pretending she was in the hospital during her shift to dodge her mom's surveillance). He made love to her slowly, tenderly with all his love. Next day he felt that he did not need anything else in the world. He did not have to continue going to the field to relief his needs with Mercedes. He was bewitched with Gabriela's beauty for months. The only reason he remained with Mercedes was to relief his needs with her. So, once she agreed in having sex, he had no reason to continue with Mercedes. Plus, it allowed him to avoid that intensity that scared him about his feelings for Mercedes. He felt there was a darkness that she steered that no other woman did. Not understanding what it was, he wanted to move away from it.

Sashawarmas,   by Jorge Bandido

He went to Yasuni to finish up his dual relationship. However, when he saw Mercedes in person he felt his knees weakened. The moist air of the jungle got in to his lungs and the familiar smell of over ripen fruit that you can feel in some part of the forest got the better of him. Her body was so luscious, the shape of her thighs was so perfect and her skin so tight. Her nipples became hard to see him and he could see that through her t-shirt. His body had a conditioned response to her presence and it demanded he abided by it. He could picture how much fun it would be to take her. How easy it would be to get all that pleasure; and he could even feel the warmth of her pussy on his cock in anticipation of taking her. So he preferred to take a last taste of her before giving her gave it up. José Ignacio made love to her long and hard. He tried to work up the courage to tell her then but it seemed rude to break up with her just after having had sex. He waited a bit, out of courtesy, but by then he was horny again, and since it was the last time, he went for seconds before ending their relationship. He fucked her for 4 straight days trying to exhaust all his lust for her body, before he could break up their relationship.

José Ignacio eventually managed to tell her that he was in love with someone else and he was not going to continue with seen Mercedes. He told her about Gabriela, since she had seen her when she brought him to the hospital. As faith would have it, it was Mercedes who insisted in taking him to the hospital where he met Gabriela!

"Asshole." She yelled punching him on the chest.

Understandably, because she realized that he had that plan all along but instead of telling her from the beginning he had fucked her brains out first and then told her about his determination. Being used for her body was a feeling that was very familiar to Mercedes. Although she often accepted it, she never liked it.

After she protested, complained punched him and called him all kinds of names she came up with, she started crying. He hugged her comforting her but feeling her hard body next to his, his member got hard again. He touched her here, touched her there. He placed her down on her bed and took her from behind one more time. Loyal to her motto of life, she let him make love to her as he pleased. José Ignacio ended up staying all week with her. During the last days he made love to her just as regularly as he had in the past. She would become from angry to sad alternatively which only meant that he made love to a woman who was angry punching him or to a woman who was crying and needed comfort. It did work as comfort because after making love they always ended up with mutual kisses and tender caresses that united them so strongly. It was just like usual except that this time it was good bye.

123

23. TAKEN

Heartbroken, Mercedes took a break from her work at Yasuni and sought comfort in an unlikely person: Claudia. They had become good friends since Claudia refused to sleep with Jose Ignacio despite some obvious attractions. At first there was a bit of tension because Mercedes was worry of Claudia's charms taking José Ignacio away from her. José Ignacio would declare shamelessly how much he lusted for her and Mercedes saw Claudia as a real threat. Lust was the main drive of José Ignacio towards Mercedes and Claudia was a real rival in that very field. It did not help that Mercedes knew that at first she had given to José Ignacio's advances and had made out with him, even stroking his member! Mercedes was worried that once a woman had felt his caliper in her hand, she could not help it but wondering what it would feel like to have it inside. She would have been far more worried if she knew what seeing José Ignacio taking her with such lust had done to Claudia's feelings the night she disrupted his attempts to force Claudia. Regardless, Claudia had been firm regarding not wanting him both vocally and in her actions. He continued to make advanced at her and she continued to turn them away. When Jose Ignacio dumped Mercedes, she was crushed. She had a bit of hesitation in telling Claudia that they were no longer together because she feared that Claudia may see the path clear now. Of course, Claudia would have to contend with José Ignacio's new girlfriend. But if she could not have him, what did she care who did?

Their friendship was a fluid one, nevertheless. They saw each other often, they both liked hiking, contact with nature, and exercising. They have taking to running together, hiking and going out. Claudia's family came from old money and her family had taken a liking to Mercedes. Since Claudia was the only daughter, they had adopted Mercedes to come along in parties, and family vacations to the ranches and various properties they had all over the country. It was because of this that Mercedes had sought refuge in Claudia after José Ignacio.

"You really need to forget about him and find someone who really cares about you." recommended Claudia.

This was a very sound advice and Mercedes knew it. However, she had not lost hope that José Ignacio would get back with her. In fact, she knew it was only a matter of time. There was a Lust connection between them. She felt it deep inside her, regardless what her mind told her. That is why she had not sought any boyfriend. She knew that José Ignacio would be back and if she slept with another man, he would not like it. Both her and her boyfriend could be at peril.

In fact, far from listening to her friend, Mercedes took exception to this kind of comments. *"Why does Claudia want me to find someone else?"* If Mercedes was no interested on José Ignacio or if she found somebody else, that would *really* clear that path for Claudia to get on with her man. Was Claudia truly telling her that for her benefit? Or did she had some hopes to one day take José Ignacio inside her as Mercedes so badly longed for. The Lust that possessed Mercedes for Jose Ignacio was such that she could not be objective, or imagine how a woman would not desire anything other than having him. José Ignacio had such a charm to attract girls. All girls at the university wanted to bed him. For Mercedes it was his passion what made all the difference. He was so horny! Her nipples ached to his touch. Her pussy was constantly wrestles when he was around and she could not think of anything but having him back with her. No woman could resist being desired so intensely. Once a woman had felt it, she could not resist it. If Claudia had grabbed him and he had fondled her, she was done for. Mercedes was convinced, it was too late and Claudia could not be trusted. Had Mercedes known that Claudia had licked and kissed José Ignacio's neck, and that she had masturbated rubbing herself on José Ignacio's back the day Mercedes "rescued" her, she would not have gotten any were close to her. Deep inside that is partially why she went to Claudia being in her company was a better way to keep an eye on her. She knew the little med student he had dumped her for would not last and then José Ignacio would be available again.

This time Claudia had invited Mercedes to the property her family had in the Oriente, in the Amazon jungle where Claudia's father owned a cattle operation including large extensions of pristine forest, not far from Yasuni. For Mercedes coming to the forest, along for vacations, not for work, was a rather unusual thing. However, Claudia had taken upon herself to be Mercedes companion while she grieved for the break up with José Ignacio and had dragged her to the forest in a vacation trip. The cattle ranch section was of little interest for both of them but the other part contained a gorgeous pristine primary forest that they both appreciated very much. The call of the howler monkeys at the crack of dawn, the mysterious sounds of the night with countless of frogs calls, the myriad of calling birds in all direction bringing the forest alive at sunrise, was something special that had its own healing power for the soul.

During this time the forest did not sound as mysterious or mystical as she always felt it when she was in it. More mysterious was a black water Igapó in the property. Black water Igapós are bodies of still water in the Amazon that on occasions can be quite deep. Because they always have water, many animals live nearby or come regularly to drink or to stalk other animals that do. Black Caimans, monstrous anacondas, and huge carnivorous fishes were known to inhabit these kinds of places. Nutrients in the rain forest are limited because the greedy plant absorbs it very quickly so waters and soils are normally very poor in nutrients and few algae grows in these waters making the water very clear. The only thing that prevents the water from being perfectly clear is the presence of tannins. Leaves that fall from the surrounding trees decompose very slowly making the whole Igapó like a giant tea solution. The flat slope of the area and thick radical system of the surrounded vegetation prevent water from carrying many sediments even in the most heavy down pours. So it is possible to see into the water for a few feet except in the deepest parts in which the water takes a mysterious dark color, fertile for fears of unknown forest creatures from the deep to germinate.

Mercedes was a bit intimidated by the Igapó when she saw it first. She had seen others before but somehow she felt that this one had something else in it; something darker and mysterious. However, after a couple days she grew used to it. They bathed in its shallows, sunbathed on its white sands and went bird watching and canoeing around it towards the early and late hours of the day looking for rare birds. That day they had come to the shore to sunbathe and to swim in the Igapó as many other days. It was 3 in the afternoon and the sun was blistering hot on the sky. The fresh water of the Igapó was inviting. The first few inches were warm like an old soup but as soon as her feet got in the deeper part she felt the relieve of the coolness from the deeper water. She walked a bit more up to her waist line and sat on the clean sandy bottom to cover her body with the refreshing water.

Mercedes had moved faster and Claudia was still on the shore when she turned around and saw Claudia pulling off her t-shirt exposing her athletic upper body with well-toned arms, perky breast. She could see the sun shining on her abs in her flat abdomen and hourglass body as she continued stripping down to her bikini. When Claudia bent over to pull off her shorts, Mercedes could see her well defined calves, her long legs went on for miles, perfectly shaped thighs, and prominent and round buttocks. Boy was she hot! No wonder José Ignacio had tried so hard to have her. Claudia had a prominent Roman nose, green eyes, she was taller than Mercedes for almost a foot. Claudia's breasts were about twice as large as hers, firm and round. Her arms and shoulders were well defined, muscular and yet, feminine. Claudia's upper body was clearly superior to hers. Although Mercedes' hips were wider, Claudia's tiny waist made her hips look quite wide. Mercedes felt better about the comparison with her lower bodies. Mercedes buttocks were more prominent and rounder. Her thighs were thick and muscular. She knew that José Ignacio really liked that. He was not into chicken legs. But looking at Claudia with her small bikini she was not so sure anymore. Claudia's legs were endlessly long, all the muscle could be noticed as she walked and her derriere, although more discrete than Mercedes', Claudia's behind was so round and looked so tight that Mercedes was not certain that José Ignacio would prefer hers. *"Yes, I definitely had to keep Claudia in my team!"* She thought.

Claudia joined her and they were swimming happily pushing away the choking heat of the jungle. Suddenly Mercedes had a bad feeling. Her original sensation of there being a presence in the deep came back in full force. She stopped and listened. The jungle had gone suddenly very quiet and very still. Not a bird sang in the whole forest. Not the slightest breeze blew and all the air felt heavy with moisture. The air became thick with smell of over ripe fruit and musk that she felt somewhat familiar but did not know what it was. Mercedes felt the hair in the back of her neck standing on, and felt goose bumps all over her body. It was there!

"Claudia, we need to get out of the water. Now!" Mercedes urged as she started to walk out towards the shore.

Mercedes felt how the water was pressing against her skin with unnatural intensity. She felt the pressure on her behind, her thighs and her crotch far stronger than it had any right to be. As if the water was intend on having her. She felt the water moving over her skin, she felt its touch obscene and purposeful. Claudia was walking out next to her when she gasped in surprise and looked around herself trying to identify what it was.

"Did you feel it?" Asked Mercedes.

Claudia nodded looking at her with fearful eyes. Mercedes' nipples stood in attention to the intense feeling of the water in her skin. She felt fresh water zipping very directionally between her bikini and her skin between her legs. She felt its greedy touch and she knew they had to get out.

"Hurry up let's get out" She urged Claudia extending her hand to help her out.

Claudia grabbed her extended hand and followed with terrified eyes. In a few more steps the water was only a foot deep but the film of water that still covered her body seemed to have its own ideas. Mercedes herd Claudia, who was a foot behind her, gasp and stopped. Mercedes turned around and saw Claudia collapse to her knees clutching her crotch with one hand and her breasts with the other as if trying to hang on to her bikini. A film of water ran thick over her skin groping her intensely. Claudia fell in all four with a guttural sound in her throat, looking at Mercedes with terrified eyes as a pleading hand tried to reach in her direction. She tried to talk to Mercedes but her words froze in her throat and only a groan game out. "Ouuunngggh".

Sashawarmas,   by Jorge Bandido

Claudia had a quick flashback to the night in the forest under the torrential rain when she had gone out of her sleeping quarters where José Ignacio had tried to take her. She was naked under rain with rivers of water running done her skin, cascading down from her nipples to her waist, soaking her pussy, and trickling down to the jungle's soil. She was feeling the forest Lust.

Mercedes saw Claudia's eyes loose contact with hers and became empty, as if looking nowhere, as if she had departed elsewhere. Claudia's knees spread apart; her elbows were down to the sand. Her lips brushed on the surface of the water kissing the Igapó and she bent back her spine raising her behind, presenting herself. Mercedes felt again that strong scent of musk and overripe fruit and felt strangely aroused by the scent itself.

"It's the water!" Mercedes cried and tried to reach Claudia to drag her out of the water.

Claudia let out another deep moan. Her knees spread out farther and her pussy came down to the floor of the Igapó bringing her hip and her crotch under the water. She inhaled deeply, her spine arched back and Claudia presented her face to the sun. Her eyes were closed to the sky. Her face received the amber light of the afternoon and showed her beautiful expression of unrestrained pleasure. Her fist grabbed handfuls of sand and she let out another deep groan from deep inside.

Claudia crawled in all four towards the edge of the water and collapsed face down on the sand, her bikini gone. Claudia was completely naked, breathing heavily clutching her breast and reaching between her legs. Claudia convulsive body was trashing on the sand picking up a film of sand on her skin as she rolled on the wet sand out of control, her eyes closed and her faced tight in a deep expression of ultimate pleasure, as if the water in her skin, or the sand of the Igapó were making love to her.

Claudia's green eyes open and look into Mercedes's eyes but Mercedes and for an instant she seemed to have made eye contact but quickly her eyes became estrange and lost focus. Her eyes were wide in amazement, her pupil was huge taken most of the iris. Mercedes could tell that she was in a different place moaning and groaning with pleasure. Mercedes remembered the many times that José Ignacio had pointed out that she became the most beautiful woman in the world when she was having sex. She always felt that is was him just flattering her; but this time she could see what intense pleasure did to a woman's face. Claudia was in the category of extremely beautiful in a regular day. At that time, in the throes of such intense pleasure she was downright captivating. There was a presence taking Claudia. At first Mercedes was

128

scared but soon fear was replaced by something else. She started feeling hornier and hornier. Even jealous, Claudia obviously was having a good time. The smell of ripe tropical fruit and musky tangy scent became stronger. Then she knew what it was so familiar. That was the scent of his sweat. It always made her horny to smell his sweat and that smell was all over the Claudia whiffing around them. He was having her!

Claudia got in all four with her knees wide apart. Her eyes closed, her face tight, tears of emotion welling up her eyes. She was panting so heavy that every exhalation was a long deep moan. Mercedes looked at Claudia's perfect body. Her elbows on the sand, her spine turned back, her buttocks sticking out as if allowing for an easy penetration. Mercedes was torn. She no longer worried about her but instead she wanted to be her and experience what she was feeling. She wanted to be part of what she was experience in any way or form. She realized the somehow he had managed to send his essence and was finally having his way with Claudia. She was jealous and she wanted him inside her. She was so horny to smell José Ignacio and see Claudia's pleasure. Mercedes felt this irresistible attraction to her convulsing friend. She was gorgeous, she was hot, her face had breathtaking beautiful with her expression of infinite pleasure. She felt a strong urge to have a cock and fuck Claudia's beautiful body. Soon Claudia started screaming climaxing on the river sand. Mercedes could not hold it any longer and rolled Claudia on her back, straddled her and kissed her in her full in the mouth deep and long. Her tongue went inside Claudia's mouth licking the internal softness of her gums and under her tongue. Claudia's mouth was full of sand that she had picked up trashing on the beach. Claudia reciprocated her kiss, her eyes closed, recuperating from the deep intense orgasm moaning softly with satiated desire. Mercedes tried to find him in Claudia's mouth, to no avail.

Mercedes was frustrated to have missed him, jealous that Claudia did, and extremely horny for the whole scene. She came down in a full contact with the Claudia's relaxed body. She felt the touch of her nipples in her own and felt shudders down her spine. She pressed her pussy on Claudia's toned thigh and felt a wave of pleasure traveling through her body. She continued kissing Claudia's lips, and rubbing her nipples on Claudia's breast. The whole scene had made her so horny that she came rubbing herself on her sleeping friend.

Claudia transitioned to relaxed deep sleep naked on the sand of the Igapó. The wind picked it up and the smell of overripe fruit and musk left. José Ignacio had consummated his goal, he had taken Claudia in front of her just as he intended the first time, without Mercedes being able to do anything. Mercedes understood there was a deeper connection between José Ignacio and the mysterious jungle of the Oriente. She felt strange at her reaction to

Claudia's pleasure. She had never been attracted to women and had never had any intentions or wishes to have sex with a woman. She knew that the Forest and José Ignacio were connected. There has been something of José Ignacio in Claudia's body and blamed on that the whole situation.

When Claudia woke up she looked sheepish and embarrassed. Possibly for finding herself naked on the beach of the Igapó, but Mercedes could not help the feeling that Claudia was embarrassed for something she had done. Mercedes knew that José Ignacio had had something to do with it. Did Claudia know it too? Had Claudia seen José Ignacio making love to her? Mercedes was pretty sure that she never noticed that she was kissing her, so her whole behavior had to do with something she had experienced in her strange sexual trance. Mercedes never talked with Claudia about what happened, but whenever there was any mention about the Igapó Claudia always looked guilty and changed the topic.

24. HER BELOVED BABY

The nurse took the pregnancy test just as a protocol but she knew all too well what the results would be. She was pregnant. She remembered the boyfriends that she had had and how careful she was in always practicing safe sex to prevent pregnancy first and foremost. Because her partners had been good decent men, and the risk of venereal diseases was minimal. Then the Zambo took her and had his way with her over, and over, and over, for days on end. Her main concern had been a sexually transmitted disease. That she ruled out as soon as she came back having done all the tests available. What she did not expect was that he might had knocked her up.

Then it was clear for her why the Zambo, who could have had any woman or women in town, chose to stay with her. Clearly his primeval instincts were finely attuned to her hormones and had identified her as a fertile partner. She remembered him taking deep breath smelling her breast, her neck and her lower belly, just below her belly button as if inhaling a delicious nectar from her body. The blood of the warriors ran thick on his veins and his contact with nature was far closer than most of us that live in cities and have left our original roots many years ago. The Zambo knew she was fertile. That is why he would not stop doing her during all of her captivity.

All of a sudden she realized that the time she spent as a sexual hostage of the Zambo will be with her forever. She had always been a good Catholic. The idea of having an abortion was well out of the question even if it meant baring the baby of a rapist. "*Would he have his genes too? Would his baby become, on time a rapist as well?*" She wondered. "*No. There were no such things as 'raping genes'.*" She answered herself. She was going to bring him up in a good manner, loving others, loving God, and respecting women. All the Zambo would give him would be his strong genes; he was certainly a good stud, if nothing else. She actually felt blessed to have a baby growing in her tummy. She always wanted to have babies and the idea excited her regardless. It was a very inconvenient time, she had no money to support him, and it would have been nice to have a father that could help her with the kid. Nevertheless, she was pregnant and she was going to love her baby as any baby deserved to be loved. Her parents would help her with the money needed, obviously. That was a comforting thought.

Wait! Her parents had a very different idea of what had happened. They were all very conscious of women who sleep around and got pregnant. Countless times she had heard derogatory and snide comments about some neighbor or distant relative who got knock up out of wedlock. They would be ashamed to have her daughter be pregnant without a husband. Likely they

131

would not turn their back on her, or her baby, but she was going to catch some flak for that. They could not know she was knocked up in Esmeralda. They have all accepted her manicured story about Mónica's boyfriend saving them. It would be best for them to think that she got pregnant here in Quito sleeping around as many of those women they chastised. She wanted to hide the shame of her rapes. Sleeping with a boyfriend and being knocked up was something that has always been on her radar and at least she knew how to deal with it. This was true even if the boyfriend disappeared and wanted no responsibility with it. The idea of confessing been having raped serially was entirely different story that she was not ready to deal with.

Of course, there is issue of the math. Anyone can count 9 month and when the baby is born, it would be easy to know when she was impregnated. She could always argue something about having an early baby. She was the one with medical background after all, she could think of something half believable. She hid her pregnancy as much as possible. She was small and skinny, which gave her a lot of room to hide her pregnancy using larger clothing and such but her baby was growing large, clearly taking after his father, and when she was six month pregnant there was no way to hide it anymore.

She was living at her parent's house. She could not afford her own place so when she could no longer hide it, animosity started developing with her father.

"I had a boyfriend at work and it did not work out." She would replied defensively the day her father finally asked her about the father of the baby.

"It did not work out? I think it worked out just fine! Look how pregnant you are!" Her father retorted bitterly.

Her mother was not any happier but seeing how angry her husband was, she often took her side trying to diffuse all the tensions. She had accepted that her daughter was also one of those sluts that let herself get knocked up by a boyfriend that disappeared. Oh well!

When the day came she was scared to death of the process but she did not want an epidural. She wanted to feel her baby, she wanted to be fully aware of it and her heart was so full of love that it helped her fight the fear. Her baby turned out to be just as determined has his father. As soon as she was barely dilated the contractions came strong and back to back and the baby nearly crawled his way out. Strong powerful lungs were evident as soon as he came out. When the nurse showed him to her indicating that he was a boy, she was absolutely happy.

Sashawarmas,   by Jorge Bandido

"What is his name?" the attending nurse asked.

The new mother had not thought about it but when asked, she answered
without hesitation:

"José Ignacio Guzm . . . Carrera. Jose Ignacio Carrera." She could not
give him the last name of his father, so she gave him hers.

The magic and happiness of her new baby healthy and strong came with a
couple problems. One is that he was a very large boy, it was difficult to say
that he was a premature baby. Of course, the other problem, is that her baby
was substantially darker than she was. It was obvious that her father was black,
or at least very dark skinned. It was more difficult to make up lies for both
issues than just come clean. She decided to come clean and explain what
happened. However, before she could say anything her father asked her point
blank.

"Where you raped?"

Daniela could not tell why this question offended her so much. Surely,
she had been raped. She had been raped repeatedly. She had been a sexual
hostage of a man who did not seem to know satiation. His sex drive was
fueled by the magic essence of the rainforest. She had endured more rapes
than anyone could imagine. But what bothered her was not the question or
even to talk about it. What offended her deeply was the context. Her father
had been happy to swallow the tall tale of the miraculous escape and hide out
in the warehouse. He was bothered, but also had bought the story about the
Quito boyfriend that had left her. She was deeply offended that he had
believed all those, unlikely stories as they were at first, but now he had decided
against them seeing than her baby was brown. Clearly, in his mind this
boyfriend was a white one, or else this new enquire would not make any sense.
Obviously, if she had a boyfriend that knocked her up, if she had consented in
sleeping with a man, he had to have been white. Right?

Why could she not have had a black boyfriend, that left her? This is what
her more recent story suggested. Why did her father directly assume that she
had been raped, just because her baby had dark skin? This was so offensive for
her. In fact, the first time she saw the Zambo in the hospital with a gash on
his chest she had the hots for him. She was downright horny to have him.
She had erotic dreams with him the following few nights after she treated his
wound in the hospital. Had she not been so predisposed against his kind of
people, she would had been interested on him; may be even consented to date
him! The reason she never considered seriously to go in a date with the
Zambo, or any other person from Esmeralda, was because deep inside she
"knew" she could not, should not date a dark person. It was her father who

133

taught her all that prejudices and racist biases that she still had despite how much she despised them. She was quiet and did not answer.

"Where you rape?" Her father demanded.

Why was it so important for her father to know? She had a brown baby and he, liked it or not, had a brown grandson. Those were the cold facts. She knew her father was a good Christian that would never dream of doing harm to a new born or to deny him the love that he deserved by being a son of God. Would it make any difference if she had been raped or just consensually knocked up? If she had been rape, she was a victim and not a horny careless slut that just got herself knocked up. If she was knocked up by having consensual sex with a brown man, she would meet the typical stereotype of horny young white woman eager for a black cock. That was the scorn that her father wanted to avoid. But she felt offended for how worried he was about society and what people would think at the time she was so happy for having a healthy strong baby. She thought for a few seconds and answered.

"No, I was not raped."

She could not swallow the concept of associating her baby to an act of violence and abuse such as a rape. She wanted to love this baby for the rest of her life and she did not want the stigma of a rape associated with him. She wanted her baby, and everything around him to be pure and beautiful. Certainly, the first time the Zambo took her it was rape, no discussion. There is no doubt she was serially raped the next few days. But on the fourth day something happened. She accepted that he was going to penetrate her regardless and tried to find ways for it to be less painful. She would try to get herself lubricated, by touching herself, when she knew it was happening, or she would use soap or butter to help penetration. She was so raw from the first few days that lubrication did not help as much but it was still lot better than what had been happening.

The fifth day in the afternoon she was coming out of the shower wrapped on a towel and the Zambo got her in the bathroom with intentions of taking her.

"No, wait, a lady needs her own time alone," she said and pushed him out of the bathroom playfully.

The Zambo acquiesced rolled his head back with a deep hearty laugher.

"I knew you were a feisty one." And let himself be pushed out of the bathroom.

Not for long though. Five minutes later the Zambo walked into the
bathroom again. Without saying a word he lifted her off the ground as if she
weighted nothing and inverted her upside down. She hanged on to her towel
as well as she could as he dove with his face in her pussy. His lips were
unnaturally warm kissing and licking her sex. She hanged upside-down with
his erect cock dangling by her face. Or rather, her faced dangled by his cock.
Like everything else, she had no saying on what happened. There was nothing
she could do but let him kiss her pussy and lick her clitoris at his leisure. It
has been established that she was his for his pleasure anyway.

At least, this was not painful as the penetration, even if it was undignifying
to hang upside down when he ate her. Dignity was the last thing she had, and
she felt the Zambo licking away the little of it she had left. She grabbed his
member with one hand noticing that her fingers could not round the full
thickness. "*No wonder it hurts so much to take it in.*" She thought. Once she was
there she put it on her mouth. If she could give him a blow job she may spare
herself another impaling. She had to part her jaws almost completely to take it
in and all she got in was just the tip. It was silly, she thought. She could never
suck it. He continued working on her while she admired his hard rock abs,
the ripped muscles of his legs and thighs that resembled tree trunks. He was a
wonderful specimen, downright statuesque. Pleasured surrendered her in that
position and soon she was panting and feeling great desire, kissing and licking
his cock for the lack of something better to do. When he righted her up, still
suspended on his arms she enveloped his trunk with her legs, while he kissed
her breast taking long inspirations taking in all her scent. He lowered her like
he had done the first time in the hospital but this time she wanted him in.
She knew taking in whole thing would hurt but getting some of it in would
feel good. It felt really good! Her arms spread out from one to other of his
massive shoulders she felt his warm skin that was perpetually covered by a film
of musky sweat that smelled like the jungle in a hot day. When he lowered
her and their mouths were at a level, she kissed him. It was her who initiated
the kiss on his large sensual lips that she had desired the first time they met.
She sealed his lips in a long deep kiss that brought her so much closer to him.

By the time she was lowered to his cock, she was dilated and well
lubricated. It was still a bit sore but that time she could say she actually liked
it. As the time passed she realized that if she took control of the penetration
she could manage to do it without full depth all the time and lower
substantially the amount of pain. She had learned the rhythm of the Zambo
and had joined him. She learned that caressing his testicles while she was on
top straddling him made him come quicker. She did not have to fully impale
herself on his shaft, she could do it maneuvering until the last minute. When
he was coming all bets where off, he would shoved it deep inside her but it was

far shorter time than taking it all in through the whole intercourse. When they were done, she felt quite proud of having taking him all.

The sixth day her blood was running positively toxic with hormones. She could not have enough of his cock. She had been bitten by the true Lust and was experiencing Her effects. His cock was permanently hard and she was getting good use of it. She straddled him, while he was sleeping and impaled herself on its full length. She pressed her small hands om his iron chest and reached over to lick his sweat with her tongue. That was the precise dream she had the day after she met him in the hospital when he was wounded. She wondered how the same cock that hurt so much the first time was feeling so good now. He woke up and started kissing her. His lips were so large, so meaty, so warm. His callous hand covered her buttocks and moved up and down her thighs as she worked her rhythm. She felt her climax coming and dug her nails on his muscular shoulders. She bit his face with hunger, she bit his chest hard digging her teeth on his pectoral as she collapsed over him. She was his, her heart and soul belonged to him. She wanted nothing else in the world that to be his woman and make love to him for the rest of eternity.

The following days were the same. She was all over him, always wanting more and more sex. It made a lot of sense now. She was ovulating in those days. That is why she was so horny. *Then* is when she got pregnant. She was not impregnated during a rape or an act of power and abuse. She was knocked up during a deep act of sensual, passionate love making. All the time she had interpreted her giving up to him sexually as the results of her prolonged captivity. She knew about Stockholm syndrome. A hostage may end up establishing a rapport with her captor where all the options of escape are not viable. That is how she had explained to herself her torrid affair with the Zambo after a few days being his captive. Regardless, whether it was result of the captivity, she ovulating that day, or the Lust from the forest that had found Her way inside her. The conception of her baby had been the result of beautiful passionate love making. She repeated with conviction.

"No, I was not raped."

Her father's face fell apart by the implication: she had had a brown lover. Her father looked to the ground, took a deep breath, got up and left. Her mom broke up crying, sobbing uncontrollably. The odds of snatching a good husband were a lot lower with a brown baby, even for her daughter with her incomparable beauty. It took them a while, they tried to hide the baby from their friends but eventually the little brat with his charm and chubby cheeks got to them. Likely they did not stop being racist, but they made an exception for their grandson, even getting really protective if any of their friends made any snide comment about his skin color, or lack of father. This is the reason they all were so worried when the baby had the accident

The little one was exceptionally strong. He started walking at 8 months of ages and had no sense of what danger was. A good primate, he was always climbing up everything he could get his hands on. Because his little arms were so strong he could pull himself up in situations where most kids could not. The mother always thought that the Zambo was a creature of the forest. The natural strength of her baby could easily be explained by the strength of his father. Whatever it was that made him so strong, clearly had been passed on to her baby. Most native Indians live in the forest and climbing on trees is part of their daily routine. The Zambo clearly was part native Indian. She recalled his high cheekbones and ferocious brow. This conclusion came on stronger later when her baby revealed his temper and started getting in all kinds of fights in school, his baby's disposition for violence, which was not lacking on the Zambo, as well as his resolution to never give up in a fight regardless of who he fought with, was definitely linked to his warrior genes.

Little José Ignacio must have been 4 years old or so, when he was climbing on the bookshelf, that was not fully loaded with books. When he reached the top, his weight made the shelf top heavy and the whole thing came down landing the kid on his head. He was out cold when he was found and the Daniela rushed him to the hospital. He had a skull fracture and luckily was large enough that the skull was not presenting such containment to the brain. Since brain injuries tends to swell. It is this swelling that is the problem when the swelling of the brain is contained by a complete skull, there is a lot of pressure on the brain tissue which results in necrosis: death of the brain tissue. The nurse was sick to the thought she may lose him. However, the fracture on the baby's skull was so massive, and the skull so young, that it allowed for swelling without producing so much damage.

25. STAKING HIS CLAIM

José Ignacio's relationship with Gabriela worked well, except for the excruciating lack of sex. Shortly after Gabriela consented to have sex, and José Ignacio had broken up with Mercedes, Gabriela had remorse for what she had done. She repented for her sin, and decided to go back to celibacy, imposing celibacy on José Ignacio at the same time. One day, being unable to endure the pain of his testicles that abstinence gave him, he hopped into a bus and went to Yasuni seeking out Mercedes. They had broken up but he knew she was always a save solution for his desire and decided to seek her out.

José Ignacio arrived in the evening when he knew dinner was taking place. Arriving to the cafeteria he greeted Mercedes from behind surprising her. She stood up turning around and saw her man. His scoundrel's eyes, his sharp jaw line, long jet-black curly hair to his shoulders, and his charming smile with huge pearly teeth that always made her knees weaken. She felt her heart skip a bit. He was there and he was there for her, she knew that. She could picture in her mind his statuesque hard naked body, with all his muscle ripped and chiseled and his massive cock hard and ready for her. She knew that was in her very near future. When her eyes went down to his crotch she could see it bulging with desire for her and felt happy to be back to normal.

However, his surprise arrival to the station showed him more than he wanted to see. Walking in the Cafeteria in the evening, he saw Mercedes sitting very close to another man, David, an American researcher studying in the same station. There was no mystery looking at them that they were a couple by his hungry beady eyes spilling lust when he looked at her body. It was a very common sight among men that talked with Mercedes. But those that had actually tasted her showed an especial feverish look of being lost in lust when they looked at her crotch. This one had a serious case of the disease and José Ignacio knew that she had let the hogs gorge themselves in what belonged to him.

Mercedes saw the instant transformation of José Ignacio's face from beautiful and charming to threatening and scary. The ferocious brow of the warrior came out in full force giving his face the most terrifying expression. She followed his gaze and found David as the target of José Ignacio' displeasure. She was painfully aware of his Herculean strength and short temper when he was jealous, and feared what could happened.

José Ignacio felt a rush of blood in his brain, his eyes sight got blurry with jealousy and walked up to him with big strides. He grabbed David by the arm and shoved him aside making him fall awkwardly from his chair.

Sashawarmas,   by Jorge Bandido

"Who the fuck is he." He demanded.

"No one he is just a friend." Mercedes replied trying to appease him

"Your friend? He told her in a menacing tone grabbing a handful of her hair and pulling it down forced her face upwards towards him, drawing her very close to him. "Did he fuck you? Friend don't fuck."

Mercedes grabbed his thick forearms and uselessly dug her nails in it. It never worked, he did not seem to have a pain threshold but it made her feel better.

"That's not your problem. She spitted back at him, tears of anger and impotence coming out of her eyes. "You left me for another woman."

This was the wrong way to go about with José Ignacio when he was angry and Mercedes knew it but she herself was very affronted. He stuck his hand down her pants and grabbed her pussy

"You are my woman, and I don't want my woman giving her body to other men and you know it." He purred back in her ear with his deep threatening voice.

"You don't own me. I am a free woman." Mercedes retorted with tears coming out of her eyes in anger. "Plus it was you who left me for another woman".

José Ignacio planted a long kiss in her mouth sealing it with his lips and making her shut up. All this happened on a cafeteria with no less than 10 or 12 people in attendance. He was making the point of humiliating her in front of her friends to stake his claim on her body. He was hurt to the thought that Mercedes was with another man and he wanted to make her pay. Pulling her hair backwards he was arching her trunk back everyone could see him grabbing her crotch. He found the entrance of her pussy and stuck his middle finger inside her. Mercedes could not protest to the public humiliation because his tongue was deep inside her throat and pulling her hair backwards he had her almost out of balance of falling. Her hands were hanging on to his forearms as much for balance as to dig her nails on him. With his finger inside her he could play her as a well-tuned instrument for his enjoyment.

Mercedes felt angry for having been left, humiliated for his entrance in the room claiming her as his property, impotent for not being able to fight him off. She was also scared of what he might do if he knew about her new boyfriend. She could also feel his lust, his power, his unbelievable strong arms. She could feel his jealousy and his desire for her body that always melted her. She also was feeling his thick finger inside her and she was feeling

139

the effect. His musky smell was overwhelming. She was torn between the feeling of humiliation and her lust for his sex. He was in control. He always was. There was nothing she could do. A voice came from behind José Ignacio

"Dude what are you doing. Let go of her." It was David that was bravely standing up behind José Ignacio demanding he stopped what he was doing.

Mercedes fell José Ignacio's muscles go very still, very tense. Not a fiber in his body was moving. She was terrified of what this meant. She knew him and how bad his anger could become. He was going to tear David to pieces! It was bad enough he suspected that David had had sex with her; David was now challenging him of what to do to his woman. Mercedes broke the kiss, now that José Ignacio's mind was somewhere else, and yelled.

"I am fine. He is not hurting me". She said hoping that David would stand down and not provoke the rage of her Herculean lover towards him. If his anger was towards her, she could steer it towards sex, but there was no telling of what he would do to another man. José Ignacio let go of her and, drawing himself to his full height, he slowly turned to face the man who had dared to order him what to do about his woman.

"Who the fuck are you and what is your problem?" José Ignacio asked in a low pitch murmur almost like threatening a purr. "Did you fuck her".

David had a strong urge to leave the place when stared down by the large man and almost repented to have said anything but his held his ground. Mercedes came around between both of them, shoving José Ignacio back said

"Of course not, my love. We are just friends. He is nobody. I am yours, nobody else's". She tried to appease him.

David felt the sting of the statements: "*He is no body. I am yours*" but realized that she was trying to save him from harm.

"You are damn right you are mine," said José Ignacio grabbing Mercedes and turning her around. He grabbed her by the crotch as before and got his other hand under her shirt squeezing her breast. Mercedes collapsed grabbing both forearms with each hand. She closed her eyes half in pain for the squeezing of her female parts, half feeling his intense masculinity, and half to avoid eye contact with the onlookers that were witnessing her humiliation as a woman. Yet, she had the presence of mind to save David from another foolish action.

"I am fine. He is not hurting me. I like it. I want it". Mercedes said out loud as soon as she could draw another breath.

140

Sashawarmas,   by Jorge Bandido

It was clear that she was just discouraging David, or anyone, from further crossing José Ignacio. But the words echoed on David's head "*I like it. I want it*". He knew deep inside that she was telling the truth.

26. HER PENANCE

José Ignacio dragged Mercedes from the cafeteria to her bedroom at the astonished sight of all researchers. Mercedes was relieved for the time; it was important to bring him away from other men or people he could hurt. Also, in the privacy of her room she would not be humiliated for whatever she had to do to appease him. She will have to answer a lot of questions. She knew she was not out of the woods yet, but things were moving. After he had an orgasm things will improve a lot. She still might face some punishment, but at least it was now between her and José Ignacio; nobody else would be hurt. She knew he would never hit her, beyond, say some spanking that often lead to sex. He would never do any real harm to her, beyond some savage sex but again, it was part of their relationship. He was driven to her buttocks so intensely, he always ended up spanking her in that kind of situation. In the worst case scenario he would fuck her in the ass, which she really disliked but taming him was what matter the most at the time and she understood it was a price to pay. She may go for a few days sore when she walked if he fucked here in the ass too hard, and would not be able to sit if he spanked her but if José Ignacio went after David there was no telling what he could do to him. Together, alone, she could steer anything towards sex and dodge must of the violence.

"Who was that guy?" He demanded getting in the room.

She knew she had to walk a fine line. Lying to him would guarantee him getting angrier and more violent if he found out, but all the truth would also get her in trouble.

"He and I have been seeing each other." She answered.

"Seeing each other? I don't care who you *see*. Did he fuck you?" He demanded.

"No. We just started being together a couple days ago" Mercedes lied. She had to!

José Ignacio kissed her mouth tenderly. His hands caressed her breast, not with anger as earlier but tenderly with care and love. His mouth slipped down her neck and took her other breast in his mouth. His unnaturally warm mouth was sucking her breast lovingly. She had a hard time believing that she was going to get off so easily and she was getting very turned on. His mouth went down to her belly bottom; he always loved playing with it. Even when they were not having sex, he would put his finger in her belly bottom to just feel it. Mercedes was relaxing under his touch. His smell of musk was arousing her as it always did. He went down her belly bottom on his way to her crotch and took a deep breath feeling up his lungs with her scent. Suddenly José Ignacio pulled out and faced her.

"I thought you said that you did not have sex with him." He asked.

Mercedes' heart sank. It was as a rhetorical statement. How could he know she had slept with another man by smelling her lower belly? There was something mysterious about him and sex so she knew lying again was not a good idea. He knew the answer and she had better come clean.

"I was afraid you were going to get angry. I am sorry." She answered pleading to him.

"You are sorry? Sorry for what? For sleeping around or for lying?" He demanded.

"For both. I am sorry. I did not know you were coming back. I swear. If I had known, I would have waited for you. I thought you did not want me anymore." She begged.

"So you let him fuck you." He answered accusingly. "How many times did he fuck you?"

Mercedes broke up in deep sobs. "I am sorry, I am sorry. I will never do it again. I swear." She said pleadingly.

"Answer my question." He demanded in a soft voice that was no less threatening.

The best answer was "*only once*" but if he caught her, she would be in really deep trouble. She wondered if he would also be able to smell in her how many times they had had sex. She had to say something credible.

"Five times" She lied presenting all the finger in her hand. "We just began a few days back."

"Only five times? We normally fuck that many times in a single night." He answered skeptical.

"He is not you, he does not have your appetite, you are different." She said finally able to answer honestly without sinking deeper.

"Ok, and how many spanking should I give you as punishment for every time he fucked you?" He asked holding her hand up for her to tell him.

Again, she had to walk a fine line not to anger him more. Zero was out of the question. If she said a low number, it would not help her case that she was truly sorry. If it seemed she was trying to get away with something it would

143

backfire in the mind of her irascible lover. Of course since he was holding up her hand the ceiling was 5. Dutifully she put out 3 fingers, the best compromise balancing the two extremes.

"Ok, place yourself." He accepted.

Mercedes took a resigned breath and kneeling on the floor she laid down on her bead presenting her rear end for spanking. She was not sure it was better than being fuck in the ass but she did not get to chose on that matter. He had decided spankings. She was glad he had accepted some terms for calming down but still dreaded the 15 spanking she was going to receive. This was the one time when she regretted having such a herculean lover. José Ignacio lifted his powerful arm and whacked her hard on her left buttock. Mercedes broke up crying in protestation.

"I did not know you were coming back! You told me you had a girlfriend and that you were leaving me". She protested.

A second spanking just as hard as the other landed on her other butt cheek. Mercedes yelped in pain. She was crying in pain, in anger impotent to fight against the unfairness of the situation.

"You left me. What was I supposed to do? Become a nun?" She complained.

"Who fucked who?" He ask angrily

"What do you mean." She asked confused.

"Did he fucked you or did you fucked him?" He demanded.

"What is the difference?" She asked confused.

"Don't be coy. You know the difference." He answered threateningly "Did you let him enjoy your flesh, and suck on your tenderness. Did you suck his cock? Did he use you to relief himself? Or did you fuck him? Was it you who went out of your way stick his dick in you looking for sex?"

Mercedes was again had to walk a fine line that will determine if what directions the events took. What was less likely to anger him? If he had taken her, she was not as much a participant. If she said she had done it, it was mostly her fault. She knew that he was protective about his property and he felt her body was part of his property. If she had let a stranger take her for his pleasure that would anger him too. She was tired of trying to balance what would be the less of two choices and answered him honestly:

"I was horny. You had left me and I wanted to have sex. If he had been a hornier man, I would have fucked him a hundred times. I also have my needs.

144

I wanted to fuck. I wanted to fuck and you were not around." She answered with a bit of spite in her tone.

"I knew it!" He answered turning her on her side with ill contained anger in his low accusing voice and continued: "You are such a slut that you could not keep your legs closed." He said spreading her legs out.

"I am not a slut. I am a woman who owns her own body. I wanted to be horizontal and you had left me. I am free to sleep with whoever I want. It was you who left MUUUUGGGHHH." her voice trailed feeling his cock inside her.

He was taking her in a sidewise position with was the only position that Mercedes felt some pain when penetrated, if she was dry. Mercedes groaned.

"If you don't want me to sleep with other men, be with me." She responded gambling it all. Her voice still breaking with sobs. "I will fuck any and every man I want to if you are not with me."

"You are a dirty whore that all you want is to feel a cock inside you; isn't that right." He replied thrusting inside her deeply. She hated being called a whore but she thought for herself that he had stopped spanking her and was fucking her now.

"Yes, I am a slut. I will love a dick inside me. I rather have your cock because it is delicious but if you leave me I will take any other cock." Replied Mercedes defiantly. "Do you understand me?"

"If you ever fuck another man, I will beat the crap of the two of you and then I will fuck you so bad that you will not walk again. You filthy whore."

"I am not a whore. I am woman. I am your woman." Mercedes said her voice interrupted with his thrusting.

"You are not my woman if you are fucking other men, now, are you? No, you are a whore, a skanky. filthy whore." He said, his hands crawling over her breast; his mouth kissing hers, his tongue licking her face aggressively.

Despite his aggressive tone and all the insults he had stopped spanking her and he was in fact, making love to her. She knew that once he came, his mood will mellow considerably. Somehow she had given him the right answer. Clearly, what he liked so much about her was her desire, her passion in bed, her lust. If that same lust that he loved on her was what led her to sleep with another man, then it was part of the woman he loved. If it was her enjoying sex, if it was her desire running loose and guiding her actions, it was part of the woman he loved and he was far more willing to forgive it. On the other hand if she had let another man take what he felt was his, then that would infringe on his property, as he saw her. .

"I am not a whore. I am your whore. I love your cock, your love." She said returning his kisses.

"How did you like it fucking him." He asked her spiteful.

"I didn't." Mercedes answered with full honesty. "He is not you. He does not have your cock. He does not have your arms, and muscle. He does not have your passion. I only like when you fuck me." Mercedes replied from the bottom of her heart.

"Say you are a whore. Confess it." He urged her. Feeling his rhythm fasten, she knew he was close to coming so she played along.

"Yes, I am whore. I am a whore. I am a filthy whore". She said panting. "I am yours, yours, your whore. I'm your whore." She added holding her breath in anticipation of his climax.

Right on time, he started coming, with deep thrust inside her and his powerful arms hugged her crushing her against his chest. His teeth sank in the back of her neck with a brutal bite that often marked the peak of his orgasm. José Ignacio came inside her with all his love and Mercedes felt full of life. Mercedes was happy. She had him back. She had managed to diffuse the bomb. She did not know about the other woman that he had left her for, but it did not matter. His member was inside her, his arms were wrapping her, squeezing her against his massive chest and that was all that mattered. It had cost her two spanking but it had been far less than she feared. There would be time to explain to David.

It came to prove what she already knew: Being his woman meant pain. When he was about to come there was this ambiguity. On the one had she was happy to feel his passion and how strong his desire was, on the other hand she knew it always involved a crushing hug and a brutal bite in whatever was closest to his mouth at the time of his climax. His abandonment to the passion of sex was such that he turned completely predatory at that time and she liked nothing more than to be that prey. Once he had been sucking her boob when his orgasm came. It was so painful that she actually fainted. She sported a big bruise covering her whole breast for the following two weeks. Yet, she would not have it any other way. She was his woman. She loved his passion, his desire, even if it came with some pain associated with it. Plus, after his orgasm, there came the sweetest shower of kisses and tenderness. It always made it all worth it.

146

27. JUGGLING TWO TORCHES

José Ignacio was still seeing Gabriela whom he hoped would recovered from her apprehension to pre-marital sex and continued to relief himself with Mercedes regularly in the field station. A couple months later Mercedes finished the field work and came back to the university while writing her thesis. It was a good thing because he could continue having sex with her more regularly with Gabriela still withholding sex.

"You are still seeing her?" Mercedes asked indignant when she found out. "What was all that jealousy with me for having sought somebody else? You spanked me and were going to beat up David!" She pressed him.

"Look, we are a polygynous species. Monogamy is a social construct that does not adapt to reality." He explained using biological arguments to support his position. "It is that way in the animal kingdom. When the males are larger it is because it helps him have several females. The larger the male the more females it monopolizes, look at Elephant seals, or mountain gorillas. They are much larger than the females so they can have many of them. Look how much larger than you I am. It is natural that a man has several partners, not the other way around".

"Well I don't want to date a gorilla or a walrus; I want to date a human being that lives in society. We are not animals, we are people and we live in society. This society is monogamous, there are even laws against bigamy." She retorted trying to hold her temper.

"That is the problem with this society. We need to change it and go back to our roots. We need to obey to the call of our nature. Native Indians in the forest are polygynous. That is what we are." He replied.

It was an old argument that they always rehashed without any solution. However, his position was set. He was going to keep Gabriela as his girlfriend and have Mercedes as his mistress. Mercedes hated to be the backup yet, she accepted her position of *"the other woman"*.

There was not really a choice for Mercedes to make. Leaving him was out of the question. Both because she loved him so much that she rather had him shared than not at all. She was addicted to his sex and his lust. She could not conceive not having him in some way or form. Besides, leaving him would have meant force celibacy for her. He would never let her have another partner. He knew where she lived; she was going to be still hanging out with the same people. If she dated somebody else he was going to find out and repeat the scene from the field station. It was not safe for her or her boyfriend. But then again, she really did not want anybody else. She only wanted him and she knew she could keep him if she played her cards right. On time, she knew he would come around. Knowing that Gabriela did not give him sex, and knowing how sex-driven he was, made her optimistic that she could prevail. Mercedes accepted that he had Gabriela for diners, and movies, while Mercedes was his woman for wild sex. Gabriela was the princess of the dinner table and Mercedes the slut of his bed. Doubtlessly Mercedes knew, and better than José Ignacio did, what really mattered to him and she knew that even though they saw each other behind the curtains, she was the one that gave him what he really wanted. So long as his member was inside her and it was her who his arms squeezed when he was coming, she knew her position was safe.

The situation with Mercedes was difficult to understand. What did she want with José Ignacio? She wanted what most girlfriends do, she wanted him to stay with her, to get married, and for him to be her husband. The difference is that Mercedes was used to be mistreated and to endure a second place. Her father always preferred her older brother no matter how hard she tried to be liked and loved by him. So, it was natural for her to try harder the worse she was treated. One thing that José Ignacio gave her, even as she was his second woman, was a very passionate love and desire. Even in in this, there was similarity with her relationship with her father. It was the lure of her body what ultimately got her some of her father attentions. So, the relationship with him was mirroring very much the relationship she was familiar with.

On occasions he would call her "body" or "behind" reducing her whole being to a body part he was thinking of. He said that to annoy her but it brought the point that it was her body what held him to her. He desired her the way she wanted, with more strength and intensity that she has ever experienced. His inability to leave her despite him being in love with another woman, as he said, was a testament of how intensely he desired her. If Mercedes knew something about her body was that her body would secure her more attention than anything else she did. While she was unable to control the love that a man could feel for her, she could manipulate very well the level of desire and lust she produced in him. So giving him the sex he wanted gave her control over something that she did not have in other relationships. He, like any addicted person, always thought that he could quit when the right woman came along but Mercedes knew that he was addicted to her sex and her particular way of loving him. That is why she tolerated all his infidelities because she knew that he was coming back to her one way or the other. They both gave each other what they needed the most. That is why when he got married many years later she reacted in a disastrous manner. Part of their

148

relationship unwritten contract included that he could sleep around, even try to sleep with her friends, as with Claudia, but with the condition that she was was going to keep him in the end; that was what she really cared about.

José Ignacio continued dating Gabriela going out with her in romantic dates. When their date ended, Mercedes was waiting for him to make love all night long. Mercedes knew the bus station where Gabriela took the bus to her house and waited for him there. Because of her curfew, Gabriela had to go home rather early. Mercedes was often on the station when he walked Gabriela to it. Mercedes ignored their arrival to the bus station, pretending she was just another person waiting there. Gabriela did not remember Mercedes from the time she took him from the hospital and as Mercedes pretended not to know either one of them, on occasions they spent 20 minutes in the bus station all three together. During this time Mercedes took the time to take the measure of Gabriela, make a note on her clothing demeanor and everything else about her that she could criticize later. When Gabriela got in her bus she would then turn to him, make some disparaging remarks about Gabriela's dress, or height and go with him to a nearby hotel where they made love which was the main reason for their lives.

Mercedes had accepted her role of second place so well that she helped him in whatever he wanted. After spending the evening with Gabriela, touching her, and trying to convince Gabriela to go to bed with him, José Ignacio was so aroused that making love with Mercedes, he would come very quickly. Mercedes ended up also accepting that. When they met she would masturbate him knowingly that he would come very quickly and then she started to make love to him heating up new semen that was truly hers. As her body was so sensual, it was easy for her to get him hot after having come. In fact, it was not unusual for her to make him to come two times back to back. What of that was a consequence of his brain injury, or his natural tendency to sex he could not tell, but it did not matter.

On few occasions José Ignacio succeed taking Gabriela to bed. Of course, those days Mercedes waited in vain for him to show up so it was not easy to conceal from her when he had slept with her rival.

"You fucked her didn't you?" Mercedes would ask in anger.

There was no point in trying to deny it, so he did not try. Rather he used it to provoke her.

"She is so tender and her pussy is so tight. I need to be careful not to hurt her". He would reply shamelessly, hugging Mercedes and pinning her both arms to her side to prevent her from hitting him. This usually took a little more work in his side since the bed was something Mercedes felt was hers but even these events were forgiven as soon as he started making love to her. He would lick her hears and fondle her body knowingly that exciting her would help her temper. She loved when he ate her, and he would resort to this strategy to easily calm her down when he had slept with her rival. He could not complain. He would have rather have everything in one woman. He rather loved one person who did not scare him but this was a close second. With Gabriela he had the most beautiful and pure romance and with Mercedes he had the hottest passion in bed. He just could not give up any of them. This also kept the scary part of being with Mercedes at bay, since he could step out when things got very intense and he feared being seduced by darkness.

There was a fatidic day in which Gabriela decided to drop by his school to give José Ignacio a surprise visit in his office at the herbarium. With the bad luck that when she did not find him in his office she peeked in the collection room only to find him climbed over Mercedes, who was naked, in all four, while he was banging her from behind. Gabriela did not even imagine that he could be unfaithful and was completely flabbergasted when she found them having sex. Mercedes who never liked her position as second woman, decided to take her revenge. Gabriela was the woman that had taken her boyfriend away from her. Gabriela was the reason she was degraded to the position of "*the other woman*". Her father had another woman, and she always hated women who take other women's man. Yet, Gabriela had made her one of them. She was the reason she had to wait in the shadow for him to get free before they could be together. Gabriela was a lesser woman than her. She would not even give him sex! Why did he even like her? She knew why. Gabriela had a prissy little face. She had a very beautiful face in all honesty. But she was skinny, she did not have the luscious body that Mercedes had. There was no sensuality to her forms. She was modest and did not show off her body but her body did not compare with Mercedes'. Gabriela was just a pretty girl. Gabriela was the kind of woman that Mercedes always felt jealous of. All her life she had seen boys being attracted to pretty-faced girls. Well, Mercedes did not have a cute face but she has all the curves to make up for it.

Seeing Gabriela out of balance, Mercedes took advantage and decided to take her down.

"Don't be so surprised we are having sex. We have been lovers for more than a year and I am the reason he always goes to '*do research*' to Yasuni," she said as she made air quotation marks and continued. "He kisses your pretty little face during dinner but I am the one he fucks. Do you know what it feels like to take his cock inside you? Do you know what he is like when he comes? Have you felt crushed by his passion with his mighty arms when he is coming?"

Sashawarmas,   by Jorge Bandido

Mercedes continued merciless and moved her hair to one side to show a bite
mark on her neck: "This is what he made me when he was coming two days
ago after you both had pizza. You had pizza but he had me".

Gabriela's face of astonishment continued to grow as her eyes filled up
with tears. To make sure there was no doubts, Mercedes told her all the places
they regularly visited, where Mercedes used to meet him afterwards, and the
place where Gabriela got the bus for her house, even the tree where they have
carved their names with a heart.

Mercedes did not even bother in putting any clothes on and continued
telling her all these things showing her delicious body that Gabriela was in
competition with. José Ignacio had nothing to say and Mercedes would not let
him contain her. She hated Gabriela and unleashed all her frustration for
being "unseated" and did all she could to hurt her. José Ignacio saw no way to
fix the disaster. He could not deny what Gabriela had seen very clearly and
there was no point in denying all the other things that Mercedes was saying.
He did not want to be with Mercedes anymore because he resented the way
she had gone out of the way to hurt Gabriela, who he loved dearly. As for
Gabriela, there was no way of fixing the relationship after that.

28. HEARTBROKEN AND EMBARRASSED

Heartbroken as José Ignacio was for the loss of both his girlfriends, he started anew. Amelia was probably one of the few females friendships he did not eroticized. They shared a good friendship and being alone, she kind of took him under her wing. Amelia never liked Mercedes for some of their previous history. Before José Ignacio came into the picture Amelia was starting a new relationship with a new boyfriend and Amelia was really excited about it. There was a long weekend in which Alvaro invited Amelia for an escapade to a house in the beach he had reserved but Amelia had plans to go with her family elsewhere. Apparently Mercedes got wind that Alvaro's failed plans and invited herself to go with Alvaro. They spent the weekend together in a house in the beach. Alvaro swore that he loved Amelia and nothing happened during that weekend with Mercedes, but this was hard to believe by looking as his glassy eyes when he looked at Mercedes crotch. It was obvious that he had been trapped in Mercedes' gravitational lust field. Men never recovered from that. Amelia always told José Ignacio to break up with Mercedes because she was no good for him, and she was glad to see that he finally did it.

In those days there was a party at Amelia's house. It was a family gathering but since José Ignacio was heartbroken, and he was her good friend, Amelia invited him to attend. Obviously, Marlene was one of the persons attending the party and he saw as a chance for him to start out with a good foot a new relationship. However, Marlene knew about his recent emotional collapse losing two girlfriends and did not want to be the one on the rebound. The party went on, José Ignacio had fun, a few drinks. Adding them to the heartbreak and his attraction towards Marlene, it was a bad combo.

They were dancing a fast merengue where he held her very tight to himself and feeling her bosom press against his chest. José Ignacio was horny, heartbroken, and drunk, so he continued dancing with her very tight ignoring her request to lower the pressure. In middle of the dance he got more excited and put his mouth to her neck and started sucking her neck working his way to her ear. She bent her neck covering it with her chin but this simply put her lips at his reach for easy access. José Ignacio kissed her full on her mouth holding her tight against his chest. Marlene pushed him away and broke free leaving him dancing alone in the floor. He was excited and followed her trying to hug her and kiss her.

"Jose Ignacio you are too drunk. Keep your hands off me." She would tell him while keeping his hands of her body as if he was an annoying fly getting to the food.

He continued to follow Marlene fondling her. Marlene liked him, she knew he was Amelia's good friend but she was not happy about his approach to courtship at that time. So she kept a delicate balance of not rejecting him too forcibly but tolerating far more than she would tolerate from anyone. Eventually she decided to go in the bathroom and lock herself in it to avoid his constant harassment and to let him cool down. It was a bathroom by the kitchen that one day would be the scenario of important events that turned José Ignacio's life around. Unfortunately for Marlene she did not get to close the door before José Ignacio had his foot in. He shoved the door in and shot the door behind him.

"Jose Ignacio, calm down. You are too drunk and you are being a jerk." She protested facing him, and trying to reason with him but he had his member out already and pinned her against the sink.

He hugged her, kissed her mouth. He got his hands on her behind and rubbed his cock on her thigh. It was not his proudest moment to say the least. He was very drunk, emotionally destroyed, horny and he really liked Marlene. He lifted her skirt well enough to pull down her underwear but she was wearing panty hose. It made it a lot more difficult for him to get to penetrate her. Fortunately, Amelia had noticed what happened and got in the bathroom with them to help pull her friend off Marlene.

It was a situation that a sober José Ignacio would have condemned very much. He was trying to force his friend during a family party. Emotional stress and alcohol was a bad combo for his brain injury and his primeval instinct were running out of control. Luckily now Amelia was teaming up with Marlene and between the two of them they prevented him from striping Marlene enough to force her. Amelia held his arms from behind pulling him away from Marlene. Marlene did what she could to hang on to her clothes. José Ignacio member was out he was rubbing it on Marlene's thigh. It was not possible to keep it quite from the rest of the party because now Amelia had the door open and was trying to drag José Ignacio out of the bathroom to give Marlene a way to escape. Marlene's father was in the party and, of course, did not take kindly that someone was trying to force his daughter in the bathroom. Marlene's father was a big guy with short temper. He was not bigger than José Ignacio but he was a Cornell on the army and always had his gun nearby.

When Amelia realized that he was trying to come in the bathroom to get José Ignacio, she switched positions and tried to block the door barring his entrance. Marlene also panicked to the thought of her father shooting her friend because she knew of his temper. Both of them came to the door trying to block the door and prevent Marlene's father from getting to him. Seeing

153

them distracted, José Ignacio pulled down Marlene's panty hose half way and put his member between her legs. Marlene struggled to prevent José Ignacio from raping her while at the same time protecting him from her father. José Ignacio continued humping her until he came and smeared his semen all over her thighs and crotch. Amelia's mother and her sister, Marlene's mother, noticed what was happening and between them all managed to get Marlene's father from the door. Once having come, José Ignacio became a lot more docile more obedient. As soon as there was an opening Marlene and Amelia rushed José Ignacio out to the back door and out of the house while his wife and her sister prevented the Cornell from getting at José Ignacio.

Marlene, Amelia, and Amelia's sister helped them drag him, out of the back door and out of the house. The party was divided between those containing Marlene's father from getting to José Ignacio those trying to get him safely out of the house. José Ignacio had borrowed his grandmother's car to come to the party because the buses did not run that late in the fancy neighborhood. Marlene, Amelia, and her sister dragged him to the car then they realized the other problem.

"We can't let me drive in this condition." Amelia pointed out.

"But if Dad gets to him, he will shoot him. Letting him back in the house is not an option," Marlene said.

José Ignacio had stopped to try to force Marlene but his member was still out.

"Put that thing away." scolded Amelia.

"I want to you put it away," he said presenting it to Marlene.

Amelia was getting very tired of him and shoved him against the car, grabbed his cock and put it away as she let out a long list of insults.

"We have to make sure he sleeps on his car tonight, he cannot drive that way," said Amelia's sister.

"José Ignacio give me the car keys." Demanded Amelia.

"What for?" He asked seemingly unaware of what happened.

"You have to sleep in the back of your car, you cannot drive." Explained Amelia.

"I will go in with Marlene, she can come in the car with me." He put as a condition.

"She is not going to go in there with you. You need to go to sleep," said Amelia trying to take the keys from his hand.

"No, I will only go in there with Marlene to make love to her."

Amelia's patience was running very thin by now. "Ok, she will go in with you. Open the back door for her to be able to go with you." Prompted Amelia's sister.

All the alcohol that José Ignacio had drunk was finally taking their toll on his awareness. He opened the door and sat down on the back seat.

"Now go in there and sleep but give me the key before you go." Ordered Amelia.

"No, I will keep the keys. Marlene come in." He called stubbornly.

Then Marlene showed what a good soul she really was.

"If I give you a kiss you will give me the keys?" She offered with a charming smile as she who talks to a baby with a tantrum.

"No, I want to kiss your breasts." He demanded.

Marlene gave a nod to Amelia and her sister and consented. She came to the door of the car and opened her shirt presenting her breast in front of his face. José Ignacio took them greedily over her bra and reached his hands to her behind. Marlene let him fondle her one last time. However, in order to touch her derriere he put his keys down. Amelia quickly snatched the keys from his lap. Between Amelia and Marlene shoved him in the seat and shot the door of the car. He was so drunk that he felt instantly asleep as he laid down.

29. ALL IN ONE

Of course José Ignacio had the biggest moral hang over the next day. When Amelia told him about what he had done, he was so ashamed of himself that he did not know what to do. Part of him told him that he had to apologize but the other part of him told me that he had gone too far for apologies. The only decent thing he could do was not to see Marlene ever again and spare her of his presence. It was all the same. He had to go to the field to do his field work so he had to move to Yasuni for several months. He did not have to see Marlene or anybody else for a long while. However, before he left, Amelia told him that he had to talk to Marlene and apologize. Dutifully he called her and asked her to meet with him. They agreed to meet at Amelia's house. He did not have a face to show to her parents but Amelia assured him that her parents were not going to be around.

Marlene came and they talked. He told her his very best apology for how badly he had behaved, blamed it all in the alcohol and his weak emotional state and begged for forgiveness. Marlene was very nice. She realized how truly sorry he was. She smiled at him with such a beautiful eyes, she talked to him so sweetly, and kindly that she made him feel a lot better. Soon they were just chatting. They were telling him what he had done, recalling the mess he had made laughing and reminiscing of it with such a good mood that really made a big difference. He got more and more embarrassed to hear all the details he had forgotten seeing how lightly they took it made him feel better. but He probably would not show his face to that house to face Amelia's mother or anybody else but the two people he cared about where there laughing it off.

José Ignacio was going to the field the next day. As he was leaving Amelia's house he kissed Amelia good bye. He was not sure about Marlene. A kiss in the cheek is standard way to say good bye among friends but he did not know if he was in that category on Marlene's book anymore. However, as he said good bye from a distance she smiled at him.

"Come here, give me a kiss." She invited him.

He went near her to give her the expected kiss on the cheek but she held his face with both her hands and gave him a sweet kiss on his mouth. She smiled at him tenderly.

"Call me when you come back". She told him melting his soul with the depth of her caramel eyes

Sashawarmas,   by Jorge Bandido

José Ignacio went to the field dreaming of Marlene. He had always liked her. In that party at the university he got to kiss her when it was her the one that had some extra drinks but Amelia prevented him from taking advantage of her. He was glad of that, because there was a real prospect now that he was single. He had assured Amelia that if Marlene accepted to go out with him, he would stop seeing all the others. He really liked Marlene but he was not sure he would have been able to stop seeing Mercedes or that he would not see Gabriela. Now it had happened the other way around. He had stopped seeing them and now Marlene was giving him the green light. As she told him later, the spectacled that he made of himself from the depth of his drunkenness was, at some level, touching for her. José Ignacio went to the field but got the first excuse he could come up with to come and see Marlene. It was a short visit and the only thing in his agenda was to see her. Marlene was gorgeous, dark curly hair, long and feisty all the way to her waist, with a better than average set of breasts. She was smart, interesting and loved his sense of humor. She accepted dating him, sober and single as he was now. She had no objections to premarital sex, had wide lusty hips, great in bed. She studied pharmacy so she had somewhat related interest in biology. Since he was into the ethnobotany, there was a direct connection to pharmacy. Finally he had found the person he had been looking for. She did not inspire in him the maddening intensity that Mercedes did. His career required that he went to the field, with the plan that Marlene would come to visit monthly while his field work lasted.

It was a good plan, as he conceived it but it did not turn out quite as easy. The place where he was doing his field work was the same where Mercedes had done her work. It was full of memories of his relationship with Mercedes. To make matter worse, her advisor, an American researcher that managed substantial funding, offered Mercedes a job doing some more work in the field with him. They went now to live in the same place where they had had so much wild sex during the field work of her thesis. She lived a couple door down his room in the same building and it was not possible not to run into each other all the time. Not having any woman in that place, José Ignacio was in really deep water. To make matters worse, because Mercedes was not dating José Ignacio's dress code did not apply.

To further taunt him, she put on completely immoral shorts that would stop the traffic in any street and tiny white t-shirt, that did nothing to conceal her always feisty nipples. Mercedes entertained the idea of dating someone to make him angry but figure that it was not wise to tempt her luck so much. José Ignacio was torn between the lust for her and his need to stay straight and not cheating on his girl. He felt that even after all the problems Mercedes would still take him if he asked. She was not dating anybody at the time and

157

he knew that it had to toe the line acting as he wanted his girlfriend to behave. However, he was worried to slip off the wagon and the consequences it could produce. It sure would feel good to have her but then what? He had something good with Marlene and did not want to risk it.

It did not help that he started being bugged by the suspicion that Mercedes was sleeping with her boss because they spent so much time together. He had always being a jealous man and he never stopped seeing Mercedes as a property of his. The idea another man was enjoying the delicious forms that she constantly modeled in from of his room was unbearable. It made him crazy to look at the movement of her hips when she walked and the constant insinuation of her forms that he had loved so much. He knew how much pleasure was in that flesh and it killed him not to enjoy it. There was no way her boss did not see it, and he was convinced that he was, at least courting her. He knew also how much Mercedes liked sex, and he felt there was no way she was not getting laid. He despised her for having gone out of her way to hurt Gabriela. He also despised her for inspiring such uncontrollable lust in him. Her body inspired him gratitude for all the pleasure that it had given him. But at the same time it made him angry that her body had him prisoner of his desire. He hated her because all that he could think of was on galloping her sweaty body all night long. His desire for her was so intense that it was precisely that intensity that scared him. Plus, he was aware that so long as he had the obsession with her there was no way to have a real relationship with somebody else, not even with Marlene. If only Marlene was with him all the time I could have endured it better but having sex only a few days a month was beyond him.

José Ignacio did well despite how hard he wanted Mercedes. To his credit, he managed to not break into her room in the middle of the night. Many times he saw himself looking at the top of the wall of the room where Mercedes slept and mentally figuring out how easy it would be for him to climb up the wall and satisfy his unquenchable lust for her. In fact, likely he could just as easily walk through the door, since he felt certain she did not luck her door at night, to allow him easy access to her. However, it would have meant the end of something really beautiful he had with Marlene, and there was no way of making sure that Mercedes would not repeat the same number with Marlene that she did with Gabriela. There was no way he was going to risk his relationship with her.

One day there was a celebration in the station. A friend of Mercedes' was having a birthday and they were celebrating in the cafeteria where everyone could attend. José Ignacio chose not to go not to increase his temptations. It was hard enough to contain himself from jumping her when she walked by his room door but if he had a drink or had the relax environment of a celebration, it would have been way too easy to slip and fall off the wagon. He went to bed early hearing from his room still the noise typical of people having fun.

****

José Ignacio woke up with a sharp pain in his chest in the middle of the night. As his awareness came back he realize that Mercedes, who had taken a drink too many, was in his bed, biting his chest with anger. In pain, he acted by reflex and pressed her face against his chest. This maneuver works well to prompt release from a bite because the person biting experience pain in her face and lips that often leads to ending the bite. As soon as she let go of him, Mercedes started insulting him.

"You are such an asshole, you fucked me, you used me and then you left me for that prissy little whore." She told him crying and planted another brutal bite in his face, next to his chin.

Enduring the pain as well as he could he pressed her nose to make her release him. She opened her lips and continue breathing through her mouth but did not release him. After a while she let go of him and unleashed another long list of insults and names and gave him another bite in his neck.

Mercedes cried with rage and humiliation remembering the situation with Gabriela.

"She is not half the woman I am. Why do you prefer her prissy little face over me?. She would not even fuck you. I fuck you. I do you all night long, as long as you want. All that time. Why do you prefer her." She continued scorned.

José Ignacio had preferred another woman, a lesser woman than her. She let go of his neck and gave him another excruciating bite in his shoulder. She would not let go. Her teeth clamped down on him like a vice grip and he could not find a way to make her release him. He felt tears flowing from her eyes in his shoulder while his own tears came out of his eyes in pain. He pressed her face against his neck one more time hoping to force her to release the bite. As soon she let go of him, he grabbed her face with his hands to control her and keep her teeth away from him. Obviously, she bit his hand instead.

José Ignacio noticed her skin of her body in contact with his. He felt her hot and moist pussy rubbing against his thigh. "*She stripped before getting on my bed.*" He thought. He felt her greedy pussy gobble up his member, who unbeknown to him had hid her call and was ready for her.

159

Sashawarmas,   by Jorge Bandido

Mercedes' anger was intense but her pussy was lubricated and warm. He slid inside her with no resistance and started doing her, trying to ignore the pain of her bite. He focused in making love to her, in and out, in and out, all in, all out. He knew from their relationship that making love to her was the only way to tame her when she was angry, which he had used many other times when he had missed a date, for another woman. Slowly, he felt how her teeth unclenched from his shoulder as she started to pant softly. Her rage was giving to pleasure. He continued doing his job until she finally let go of him.

In the penumbra of his bedroom José Ignacio could smell of ripe pineapple filling up the whole room. He noticed her expression of ultimate pleasure that she adopted when she was enjoying of sex with her full generous African lips discretely exposed her large white teeth. He loved caressing her lips with his and feeling the higher part of her gums inside her lips with his tongue. That gave him an especially intimate sensation of closeness with her only comparable with the deep sex that they were practicing. In her breath he could feel the smell of alcohol and the unmistakable smell of iron oxide. Blood! She had drawn blood with her bites! Mercedes shone with the amber light that only she emitted, when she was having a very intense orgasm. Connected in their mouths and sexes they came to a long and deep conciliatory orgasm. They fell asleep exhausted and slept tangled up with their arms, bodies and legs.

Next day, José Ignacio woke up and did not know what was going to happen when the vapor of the alcohol had dissipated. Sex with Mercedes was delicious. They had done it the night before as the only way to stop her from biting him but he did not have any intentions of giving up his relationship with Marlene. So he wanted to make love to her one more time before everything went back to normal. He had already cheated on his girlfriend, for no fault of his own. He may as well enjoy it one more time. He parted her legs and reached for her pussy. As soon as he felt her pussy ready he penetrated her while she slept. She woke up impaled from behind and started making love to him without skipping a beat. When they finished it was the time to talk. With the morning light he could see the results of the bites from the night before. He had bruises in his face and neck and two cuts in his chest and shoulders where she had drawn blood with her teeth. Nothing serious but it was going to be difficult to conceal them from Marlene.

"Look Mercedes, I lust after your body to the level of illness but I am in love with Marlene and all that you and I can have is sex in the shadows, nothing else." José Ignacio told her trying to draw the lines where they belonged.

160

Sashawarmas,   by Jorge Bandido

"If you love Marlene, why did you have sex with me?" She asked him
shortly.

He had no response to that question, obviously. He could have argued
that she got him sleeping but he knew when he had been bested and knew
when to shut up. He was strong enough to have repealed her if he really
wanted. Plus the morning sex was all his initiative.

"Because I can't resist your body. It is my illness. My addiction. You can
fuck me anytime you want. I cannot resist you but that is all that will ever be
between us." He told her with all the honesty of his heart.

He did not know then how true it was and what it would cost him
eventually. He also warned her that he was not going to allow her to sabotage
his relationship with Marlene, whatever it took. Mercedes got up, put on her
cloths and left his room without saying a word.

Mercedes continued tempting him with her ridiculously tiny shorts, her
wonderful movement of her hips when she walked but she did not make any
more moves on him. His hormones were betraying him, he wanted woman,
and he wanted her body. He woke up at nights drenched in semen after
dreaming of her. Worse of all, he could not go to Quito to see Marlene until
his bruises healed. When they did, he took impromptu trips to Quito so he
could relief himself with Marlene but he could only do so much of that do to
his field work. Marlene did noticed that his love making was far more
animalistic and salvage but she attributed it to the time without seeing each
other, not noticing that he was in fact draining his lust and frustration at
Mercedes in her body.

One day when Mercedes was in the shower José Ignacio could not stand
hearing the shower and knowing she was naked under it. He resigned himself
and made his decision. He was going to have her. He thought of breaking in
it through the window of her bedroom, but tried his luck with the door first.
It was unlocked for easy access, as he had known all along. He took her in the
shower, enjoying her soapy body, as he had planned once with Claudia.
Mercedes had her eyes closed of having soaped up her face, when he walked
in. She heard the shower curtain be moved and stood still waiting in
anticipation. She felt his hand around her belly bottom, and the warmth of
his chest on her back. His other hand came scratching her nipple and
squeezing her breast to the border of pain. Mercedes curved her back pressing
herself on his groin and taking a deep breath reached out with her arms
around his neck. She smelled the scent of her man and maneuver her behind
to find his member. Loyal to her style, Mercedes let him act at his leisure and
allowed him to make love to her for a short eternity in that very instant. Their

161

silent war had ended. She had won squarely and he was her hopeless prisoner. She did not say anything about Marlene. She put no conditions. Actually, being "the second woman" in theory, she spent more time with him, since he only saw Marlene when he went to Quito or a couple times that Marlene came to visit for a few days only.

Mercedes and José Ignacio went back to make love uncontrollably, all the time as it was their style. To her credit, Mercedes never told Marlene anything. Neither did she make any other scene when Marlene came to visit. She would simply stand aside and pretend José Ignacio did not exist while Marlene was with him. Although Mercedes behaved well, there was no shortage of rumors in the station and when Marlene was around, Mercedes made sure to wear even sexier and more scandalous clothing to make sure that it was not possible that anyone could be in her presence without looking at her body. Knowing José Ignacio's past with Mercedes, Marlene was regularly very upset and bothered for the shameless way that Mercedes dressed, knowing that they slept very close to one another. When Marlene left, Mercedes would get into José Ignacio's room to make love to him she galloping him into their mutual orgasms she held against him in a long litany of complaints.

"Why don't you have enough with me? Why do you put me as second? I am a better woman than her? I am second to none. Why don't you choose me for once and for all? You are a whore, a male whore". She complained.

30. A RACY ISSUE

José Ignacio finished his field work and came back to Quito. His
relationship with Marlene had survived him living next to Mercedes for 6
months. He really wanted for things with Marlene to work so once he moved
back to Quito he stopped seeing Mercedes all together. However, Marlene got
an opportunity to go the US to continue her education. She left with
promises of love with José Ignacio but it was clear that they could not keep the
relationship going long distance. So José Ignacio went back to be alone. The
natural things would have been to resume his relationship with Mercedes, but
his fear of the feelings she aroused on him was too strong. He preferred to
find someone else, with whom the relationship would not have a darkness and
intensity that it had with Mercedes. In the city he could avoid being in the lust
gravitational field that she created and try to have a semi-normal life.

Universidad Católica de Quito was private school, among the best
education that money can buy in Ecuador. José Ignacio's presence in it was
rather unusual because his family were not well to do people. His mother
worked as a nurse in a hospital where despite her education her salary was
rather basic. So she could not pay for his education there and in Ecuador
education was pretty much a privilege of the well to do in those days.
However, his grandfather had let a trust fund on his name to fund his
education. Aware of the need of cultivating the mind, he had made it a
priority when he passed on. José Ignacio's mother did not have a choice in the
use of that money because it was earmarked for José Ignacio's education. It
was not clear to what extend that might have been a slight to his mother, since
she was in big need of money herself, leaving money for his education
bypassing her needs was perhaps a way of his grandfather to settle some score
between them. Perhaps it was the resentment of his grandfather against his
daughter for her being knocked up by a brown man which brought shame to
their family in the tight and gossip ridden Quito society.

Although, he got the benefit of a good education, there was no way of
ignoring that he did not belong at Universidad Católica. There was a clear
parallel between ethnic and social status. Those that can afford and education
in a private university are by enlarge, white people. Even if white means
something different in Latin American than in other places. Many of these
"whites" would be called Hispanic in the US and often they had a strong
indigenous component but their skin was very much white. When José
Ignacio walked around a crowd of students he was always, by far, the darkest
person and about the very few that have an African ancestor. Superficially
there was no discrimination towards brown people because you could not find

the racial violence that you could find in the US. Police are normally brown too, and the violence against the poor, although present, came across as just that: violence against the poor, not racial violence. However, José Ignacio's brownness was always present in his treatment with other people who were surprised to hear that he was from Quito. Most people believed that he was from the coast, a "Mono".

When he at first drifted towards Francia he thought that she simply looked more like Maggy than any other. However, it could as well had been that she looked more like him than the others, she was African descendent. Something similar could be said about Mercedes. Although her skin was white, her morphological features were very much that of a black woman, more on the lines of the etnicity that he was attracted to. However, other women in the university were not indifferent to him. He certainly had appreciation for the looks of other women and since he was so different, so unusual, so dark, and tall they were often interested in him as well. His muscular body and good sense of humor always helped and he never had any problem getting some attention or a date with women, once he learned how to ask them out. In fact, he found it surprisingly easy to get them to bed as if it was all that they had in mind. However, most women, with the exception of Mercedes, were reluctant to start a real long term relationship with him. Often he heard the excuse "*Mercedes is my friend*". This excuse did not hold a lot of water. On the one hand he was no longer seeing Mercedes officially but since they had a history of splitting and coming back their friends still saw him as a couple. Where the excuse really failed was that "friendship" with Mercedes did not stopped them from sleeping with him, it was just an obstacle to date him in a regular basis.

The fact that he was sought out just as a cock to fuck and nothing beyond became painfully obvious when he went out with Elena, a gorgeous woman, 5' 9" with long auburn hair and very shapely body. She did not show off her body at all the way Mercedes did but she was every bit as delicious. She had larger breasts and a scent so provocative that would give him an erection of only inhaling near her. They went out and after minimal dinner talk they went to a hotel room. They both wanted it so badly that as soon as they walked in the door they were tearing each other cloth apart and doing it frantically until they both were exhausted. As they recovered panting next to each other they stroke up a lively conversation about life and what they wanted in the world; where they were finishing each other sentences and laughing at how much in tune they were despite the early of their acquaintance.

It did not take long before they were going at it again, and again through the night. Elena was the loud kind and when they were making love she soon

164

was crying out loud moaning and howling. In the moment of her climax she was downright strident. He loved the abandonment with which she gave herself to sex when they were alone. The next morning they were full of each other and full of life. He in particular was full of illusion since she was someone he really considered for a long term, and she was so good in the sack that he knew he would not miss Mercedes. Their connection was so intense that he knew she was the right choice, he felt all the passion but she did not steer the darker feelings that Mercedes had a way of steering. At least not at that time. Beyond the good connection they had what really told him she was the person was the scent of tamarind she emanated when she was aroused. However, the next day when he saw her at school she was cold and standoffish. He tried to kiss her when he saw her but she stood back. When he sought her mouth for a kiss she presented her cheek, in the normal way of Latin American fashion to greet among "*friends*". This was surprising because they had left that morning feeling very close to each other. Through the day he had a hard time trying to figure out why she was so cold with him.

In the evening he met her outside and followed her to her car. In the parking lot, she was again warm, and even loving. They went out for something quick to eat and had the greatest time together. There were moments in which the wind brought to him her scent and he felt butterflies in his stomach and an irresistible desire to get closer and get drunk with her scent. The next day at school she was again, very cold as if she did not want to be seeing with him. He understood and gave her some space. At the end of the day he asked her out again. She had some hesitation at first but accepted. This time they skipped dinner and just ate each other. Her scent of tamarind flooded the room just upon arriving and he simply wanted to live inside her for the rest of his life. They slept so close with all their bodies in contact, his cock inside her never went soft, and stayed there until the time to continue making love to her. She looked so full of life and so happy when they were in bed, her orgasms where so intense and so easy that he knew that she was the one; and he knew that she felt for him just as strongly he felt for her.

"I feel so good with you, want to be with you all the time. I have never felt so close to anyone this way. I want to give you the best of me, I want to breathe your name all the time. I want to have you and only you. He declared passionately.

"Yeah, I also want to fuck you 24/7. You are so delicious, I can't stop myself", she said kissing him tenderly. But he noticed the obvious lack of the other part.

Of course he was sorely disappointed the next day when Elena became just as cold and distant when other people where around. It was driving him crazy.

Sashawarmas,   by Jorge Bandido

He decided to wait until she was alone to talk to her and ask what the problem was.

"Nothing, I was busy talking to our friends." She answered evasively.

This was disconcerting because she could have greeted him and still talk to their friends. He wanted to see her again that evening, heck he wanted to see her all the time, he was deeply in love with her. But she told him she could not see him that night.

"How about tomorrow?" He asked hopeful. Elena thought for a moment

"Let's talk tomorrow, what did you have in mind?" She asked

"I truly don't care, I was thinking a movie, dinner, hike in the mountains, anything so long as it was with you." He replied cheerfully and continued, "I just wanted to see you because I feel really well with you."

Then without thinking much he felt that there was no point in hiding what he felt anymore and decided to declare his love to her but not having other way to do it, he did it with a song. In the middle of their conversation he broke into song singing "Algo Contigo" ("Something with you"). As the lyric goes

Is it necessary for me to tell you
that I am dying to have something with you?
Have you not realized how difficult it is
for me to be your friend?
I can no longer come near your mouth
without desiring it to insanity
I need to know your life
To know who kissed you and who shelters you
Is it necessary for me to tell you
that I am dying to have something with you?

He was a more than passable baritone and the lyric was perfect for what he felt. As his song progressed he could see her eyes, welling up with emotion, the expression of her face, and he knew he had touched her. He could see how she was hanging to his every word.

"Come with me, let's be you and me." He told her. She hugged him tight and he was a happy man.

They went for a romantic dinner, talk about their life, what they wanted, they even talked about children, how many they wanted. They talked about politics, their need for social justice in the world, their passion for conservation, their love for dogs and other animals. She was his perfect

166

woman and they both knew it. They had a beautiful evening that night and he wanted nothing else in the world but her.

José Ignacio was going crazy the next day to see that Elena avoided him very actively. He did not want to pressure her because he wanted her to feel relaxed about him. He gave her a couple days of break in which he did not seek her out although they kept running into each other in the halls. Eventually he asked her to chat. She was hesitant, still avoiding him. He had to clear things out and brought her with him to the herbarium where they would have some privacy. He wanted to make sure she was not around of other people. By then it was clear to him she was embarrassed of other people knowing they had something, perhaps because everybody still saw him as Mercedes' partner and she did not want to be seen as stealing her boyfriend. But for him it was more important to know what her problem was; and of course, he found out.

Once they were in privacy he held her close to him, kissed her in her cheeks, ears and neck. She accepted them for a short time but then she asked him to stop.

"Yes, José Ignacio, I do want to have sex with you, I always do, it is always great, but a relationship cannot be based just on sex. There needs to be something else," she said to his surprised.

Clearly she did not feel the way he felt. A bit taken aback for the news

"Well but you clearly like me. Let's let it develop, something will grow in you." He replied optimistic.

"I have thought about this, and I know what I feel. I like sex with you but nothing more. In fact, I feel like a slut going out with you just for sex without feeling anything else for you." She explained crushing him.

This stung at so many levels for one that he felt a world of things beyond sex for her but it was clear that she did not feel the same way. It also stung because that reminisced what he felt for Mercedes. He loved the sex with her but that was about the extent of it. Elena just had more clarity in her mind and honesty with him because she knew there was no chance. This was not that different of how he felt about Mercedes except that he could not, or would not, give up on Mercedes' sex. Elena just had stronger will than him.

He could recognize that his request to date for some time so see if something grew on her was the same position that Mercedes was trying with him. The reason Mercedes was willing to continue with him, despite how clear it was that he only wanted sex from her, is because she knew that the sex was a strong hook for him and he would not leave her so long as she gave him the sex he wanted. IN the meantime, Mercedes was hoping for other feelings to develop. Elena just had more control over her sexual desire that she could override it. But he continued trying to get her to give him a chance.

"Even if you were right and the time came when I felt something else, we cannot be a couple. What will people think? And if it gets serious, What am he going to tell my parents? They will never understand. So it is better to stop it now before it gets any further." She explained.

Now some of the truth started to come up. She was embarrassed of dating a brown man. He was OK to sleep with in a slutty moment but not dating material, and certainly not someone to take to your house and introduce to your parents "*they will never understand?*". Understand what? He swallowed hard trying to discern what was Elena and what was the society talking through her. In their few conversations it seemed like she was a progressive, open minded person. However, there is no shortage of the so called "progressive" that like progressive ideas but not applied to them, not with them, certainly not in their family. She was OK with the idea of inter-racial couples but she did not want to be part of one? Now, what really tipped the balance and made him lose everything was her reply to his next comment.

"My love, society will eventually learn and accept interracial couples. It won't take long," he said holding her close and trying to convey his feelings, But to his chagrin she said something that turned the tide completely.

"Also, even if we got together and had babies, what will the kids look like?" She continued her objections.

He froze in the spot understanding the implication of her question. Up until now, he have been thinking that her position was being between a strongly racist society that do not see dark people as equal to the white ones and her attraction to him, only physical as it may be. Up until this point he viewed her as someone confused, trapped between her neutral position, and her family and society. However, this last question flaunted it too clearly in his face: She was the racist! "*What were they? Two different species? What did she mean saying: 'what would the children look like?'*" She was too far into the culture and prejudices. Boy had he misjudged her!

Being heartbroken, confused and getting increasingly angry both at her and at himself for having misjudge her so badly, he felt the need to answer her question.

"I will tell you what our kids will look like". He said firmly with his voice full of poorly contained rage.

Sashawarmas,   by Jorge Bandido

In one movement he pulled open her shirt sending all the buttons of her shirt flying in all directions, tore her bra in the front with his fingers and held one of her breast fully in his hand.

"Look at the color of my hand on your breast! Do you see the difference? Our kids will be in between, browner than you, whiter than me, like coffee with cream. Will they look like Martians? Will they look weird? Abnormal? Wrong?" He asked squeezing her breast to the point of aching, mirroring the pain of his soul.

Elena was petrified at his violent outburst and the feeling of his hand firmly grouping her exposed breast. Her eyes were wide open with surprise and fear, and her lips slightly parted. Absolutely irresistible. He kissed her mouth covering it all with his thick lips and licking the outside of her gums possessing her mouth entirely. His hand went to her trousers and opened it up while she was immobilized against a filing cabinet. He slid his hand from her breast up towards her throat, rounding it easily with his fingers and putting just enough pressure to make her eyes stare with panic, her hands hopelessly clamped in his thick forearm. He pulled down her trousers with underwear and all and spun her around, bending her over on his desk and pulled out her shirt completely. She was in the same position and in the same place where he countless time took Mercedes in their escapades and just like that he impaled Elena from behind holding her firmly by her throat, pinning her with his other hand on the desktop. A soft moan escaped the grip of his hand on her throat while a very paralyzed Elena, with panic drawn all over her eyes, let him do with her body as he wished.

It took three back and forth to get the whole cock in. Elena, groaned interruptedly as the pressure on her throat allowed it. He saw her delicious behind, her auburn mane cascading on her, yes, very white and silky skin. His other hand traveled from her buttocks up her back and her shoulders, coming to the front on occasions to feel her full breast. "*Gosh she is hot! My God I loved her!*" He thought. He wanted her for him so badly but he was so hurt for what she had said that he was choking in his own feelings, just like she was choking with his strangling hand.

He came thrusting deep inside her, pressuring his pubis on her round and magnificent buns and much to his chagrin his lips, very close to her ears, let out the last thing he wanted to say at that time

"I love you, I love you, I love you sooo much".

He collapsed over her back and let go of her pulling out from inside her. Elena turned around instantly clutching her throat gasping and looking at him with terrified wild eyes. He fell on a chair taking in the situation, what he had done and how Elena was reacting. After a couple seconds of hesitation Elena pulled-up her pants, turned around and took off running out of his office and out of his life. He debated for a second to chase after her in order to straighten out what had happened but he knew everything was over between them.

José Ignacio sat on his office digesting what just had happened. Elena was the woman that he wanted the most in the world. In the exchange she had the realization that she was a racist and the only reason she was with him was, in her own word, "*feeling like a slut for sleeping with the brown man*". She clearly enjoyed feeling like a slut long enough but seeing that he wanted more she gave herself away. That had produced his violent outburst, but was it justified? He tore her clothes off and took her without any consultation or permission. He did not rape her, though. She said she wanted it. " *Yes, José Ignacio, I do want to have sex with you, it is always great, ..:*" she had said. Plus she did not object in any moment, yet, she could not have said anything when he was choking her with his hand around her throat. Plus, one thing is a conversation one may have with a woman analyzing a relationship. The situation did not involve a fluid communication you would expect of a regular foreplay. She was certainly terrified when he did it. Could she have objected if she wanted? He attacked her and quickly enough his hand was around her throat preventing her from making any noise. Then he was subduing her pretty forcefully. In fact, this is the first time that Elena did not moan and howled in pleasure when he made love to her. He recalled the interrupted choking groans she let out. Was she trying to tell him to stop? What have he done? He was slipping down a slippery slope and did not know how to stop it. Worst of all he had lost the love of his life, again.

Elena did not realize she was naked from the waist up until she was in her car and even then, she did not much care. She started her car drove home without much regard for traffic signals or traffic safety for that matter. She rushed to her house, escaping from José Ignacio, the university, even herself, and her own feelings about him. Walking into her house with her arms crossed covering her bare breast there was no denying something had happened.

"Who did that to you? Are you ok?" Her father inquired.

"A man at the university" she mumbled full of fear.

"Who was it? Which man?" He pressed her.

Elena could not believe the words that came out of her mouth but once they were out, there was no taking them back

Sashawarmas,   by Jorge Bandido

"A dark man ".

To her credit after all the questioning that followed Elena did not say she
had been raped. Neither did she identify José Ignacio as the attacker. When
she was asked about it, she denied, but most people still assumed a sexual
assault that had not succeeded. The descriptions of a "dark man" lead to the
conclusion that it may have been someone not from the university, certainly
not a student, since there were very few black or brown students. Her father, a
very influential contributor to the university, demanded more security for the
students. Poster went up warning about sexual violence on campus and
guards increased their presence. José Ignacio was often carded by new guards
who did not know him but being a student he was always let go. Despite of
the precautions Elena never came back to school. She did not know how to
handle seeing Jose Ignacio again. She knew there was no future with him but
she desired him too intensely. She had been bitten by The Lust. For years she
had wanted to move to another country and took this possibility to go the
Germany to finish her studies. No, she did not speak German at the time but
it did not matter. Her father had all the resources to oblige and her happiness
was the only thing that mattered to him

31. THE NURSE'S REALIZATION

Her baby was still in the ICU but the news that morning were very comforting. She was not sure she could believe them or not and she feared having false hopes. It had been several weeks since the accident and many things merged together from the last few days. Because she was a nurse, she was far more knowledgeable than most parents about the true problem that her baby faced and the possible complications. Since the skull was still not that hard and it broke in several parts, the problem was somewhat ameliorated. Regardless, the baby was in the ICU, in coma for several weeks. Her friends at the hospital tried to support her but the regular optimistic lines that would work to uplift the hopes of other patients did not work with her, she had used them way too many times not to know what was happening in real life. So these days were especially hard on her. She remember in a moment of despair thinking what she would do if the worse were to happen.

When she first realized she was pregnant, she was very conflicted but now she knew that her baby was the best thing that had happened to her in her whole life. If she lost him her life would be so empty that she would not be able to carry on. Suddenly she had a strong realization. She had never felt so sure about anything in her life: If she lost her baby she would get another one. Not any baby, she would try as much as possible to get this one back. If her worse fear were to come to occur she would go to that very place, to Esmeralda, and look up the Zambo, to ask him to make her another one. It should not be difficult to find him, and once she did, convincing him to take her should be no challenge if the days she spent with him were any guide.

She was not sure if she had dreamed it. She recalled the night before a familiar woman walking in the hall outside the ICU in Quito. Because of her time in Esmeralda, she could tell she was a person from the coast, just for her dressing and demeanor, but there was something oddly familiar about her. She was an old, Indian woman, with very dark skin and wrinkles beyond years. Not a lot of gray hairs, Indian people get few of them. She recall watching the old woman with curiosity as she paused on the hall in front of the ICU and as if knowing in what direction her baby was, she put her chin down and said a silent prayer, that the nurse could not hear, but she was certain it was not in Spanish. When she was done, she made a gesture with her hands, turned around and left. The nurse thought of following her and asking who she was and what she was doing there but stopped herself. There were other patients in the ICU. Nobody could tell who she was there for or what she wanted. What did it matter anyway? She had just stood outside of the unit and did not do anything, just a prayer. She herself had said countless prayer during the

172

last weeks. In fact, her life had turned a bit into a permanent praying, since there was nothing else she could do.

When she finally talked to the Dr. she was relieved, her baby had finally started to turn for the better. He was still far from well, or out of risk, but it was the first time in many days that she got something that resembled good news. In the following days her baby continued to improve, the swelling continue to go away slowly but surely. Eventually all the swelling was gone and the doctors were amazed that the little guy had managed to pull through with no visible damage they could tell. They feared that he was going to have motility problems, or mental retardation, for some damage that the brain might have endured due to the swelling, but there was no way of knowing it at that point.

With her baby back at home and out of danger, she realized the true impact that that Zambo had done in her life. Since she first saw him she was attracted to him. He had after all saved her from a gang of rapists. Barring the first days she was his captive, she had enjoyed very much being his woman. She could have ran from the first day but she felt it safer with him. Last but not least, he had given her, her beloved baby and nothing had made her happier in the world. She had decided to look him up to have him make her another one, if she lost her baby, but once her baby was out of danger, she still thought: *"Does he not have the right to meet his father? Does not the Zambo have the right to know he has a son with me?"* Likely he would not care much. Likely hers was not the only child he had, but it was the one he had with her. She decided to go to Esmeralda to look him up. Talk to him. She had to process what had happened. This is what her friend, a therapist, would tell her. She had already forgiven him for raping her but she wanted to tell him so. She wanted for her baby to meet his father. She would not ask anything from the Zambo. What could he give her? She had enough money to get by with the support of her father and her job. It was far more than she could expect the Zambo to provide, even if he was willing to do so.

She decided to go to Esmeralda to seek him out. This was not an easy decision, though. She had to go back to the place where everything happened, and it would likely relive in her all the fear, all the pain and the trauma, but she felt it was the right thing. After little José Ignacio was out of danger, she took a few days off at work, her parents could take care of her baby while she was gone. Of course her dad would object it, but he was famous for not understanding emotional needs. She was sure her mother will support her and between them they could convince her dad. She was an adult woman anyway even if she was living in his house and depended from her parents economically. It was her call at the end of the day.

173

Sashawarmas,   by Jorge Bandido

As she rode the bus she tried to picture what it would be like to be there. To see the town she last had seen ransacked by the social explosion. It has not been such a long time but it felt like a life time ago. She tried to imagine what the reaction of the Zambo would be to see her. How he would react to the news of their baby? He was quite the flirt and likely would make a pass on her, as he did the first time they met. She was not so sure about the news about the baby. Would he be happy? Angry? Would he even care? She would settle for neutral, but she feared anger. Deep inside she hopped he would be happy to see her. She knew he would want to have her, but beyond that she was hopping for an positive emotional response. She hoped he would be happy to know about their baby and she fantasized with him wanting to meet him. She could imagine his large muscular arms holding the small delicate toddler. Wait! Was she imagining too much? What did she really want from this adventure? In a sudden realization she told herself. "*You slut!*"

For a second she had thought: "*what if he wants to rape me again?*" Then she realized that it would have not been possible. He could not rape her because, she realized, she wanted him. She wondered if he would try to seduce her. What would she do? The whole thing was supposed to be about her baby but when she caught herself imagining the Zambo's muscular arms, she realized she wanted him for herself. She had made no plans for accommodation in Esmeralda. Sure, there were a lot of hotels that should be available in the low season but she had not thought of staying there. Unconsciously, she realized that she was planning with staying with him, as his woman.

What was she thinking? She wasn't. This made her accept what she had not dared to think that she wanted him for herself. Not as the father of her baby, she wanted him as her lover, she wanted him between her legs and inside her as he so often did when she was his captive. She wanted the Zambo to make love to her like they did with hunger and deep passion before the abrupt end to their love affair. While her baby was in danger she realized how horribly sad she would have been if she lost him. Her happiness hinged on that baby being alive and doing well. She wanted another one, that way she would not be as vulnerable. The trauma of being knocked up and dealing with the aftermath for the first baby had been difficult but the second one would be very different. She felt a big relieve like someone who just discovered a big truth and a weight is lifted from her shoulders. She was not looking for the Zambo to tell him about their son. At least that was not the only reason. She was looking for him to make love to her, restart that romance that got interrupted, have him make her another baby, and have him in her life in a permanent manner.

174

32. AN ADDICTIVE COCKTAIL

The oil company had continued their work in exploring for the presence of oil in Yasuni. It was a National Park and these activities would be forbidden but the government was complicit with the actions of the corporation. The exploration of the forest consisted on putting explosive charges all other the area and detonating them at the same time to register with fancy sound sensors how long the wave took to get to the bottom and come back. Because sound travels slowly on liquid the more solid ground they found, the quicker the sound bounced back. When there is a lot of liquid, as in oil deposits, the sound takes a lot longer to come back. In the mind of oil engineering's, this is "little disturbance". However, for a nature loving biologists like José Ignacio, the sole presence of the oil operation in the forest was downright sickening. Having scattered explosions go off all over the forest was completely unacceptable. He knew he had a special connection with the forest, and although he did not fully understand it, he knew he was at his best in the pristine place. His eyes and smell were sharper, he could hear things that others people could not. With his heightened senses he could finds all sort of flower, small insects, hidden fungi. The full diversity of the forest was open for his scrutiny. The sole presence of an oil operation in the area made him positively altered. To make matters worse, the abrupt departure of Elena from José Ignacio's life was a heavy blow. Not only did it produce immediate repercussions on his health triggering one of the episodes of his illness, but also it made him reassess what really were his options regarding female company. It seemed like he was going to have to settle for those women who would accept him, skin color and all. All of a sudden Mercedes was not only a wonderful lay, she was also a person who really wanted him for who he was and was willing to have him all the way. His fear of darkness got pushed to the background.

Dropping by the field station in Yasuni and taking Mercedes was easy enough, yet, there were things beyond the physical attraction that scare him from the relationship with Mercedes. There was an element of force in the relationship with Mercedes that was similar to what he had found so appealing of the relationship with Francia. It was somewhat of a relationship of power and domination, that they always worked out when they disputed every inch of Francia's skin as he tried to undress her. They fought heartedly until he conquered one breast. Then she surrendered that but continue guarding the other, and the rest of her. Francia would defend every bit of it and accept the conqueror inside only after he had prevailed squarely in the last struggle. The only time she did not fight was when he wanted seconds. After making love to her, José Ignacio often stayed a few minutes and then wanted more. In those occasions Francia, naked as she was would let him have her the second time without further resistance. It was like a mutual understanding that he had earned her for the day. Jose Ignacio found something similar with Mercedes but he was adding an emotional domination, on top of the physical one, to the mix. Since Mercedes did not deny him her body, he had found a way to make her resist him and fight with him before sex. He would find a way to make her angry. He would give her some money when they got to the hotel as one would do to pay a prostitute. Or he would tell her how he lusted after her friends or even sisters, and ask her to help him fuck them. This was sure to make Mercedes mad, once she was angry he started to undress her and then she would fight him off. He got the chance to force her, after he subdued her by forced, they would make love and she would forget all about his insults. Including power and domination in his relationship with Mercedes was the ambers of what would become a wild fire.

Being alone, and horny after he recovered from Elena's abrupt break up, he went to Yasuni to see Mercedes and explore what would happen between them. Despite the fact that he never promised anything when he was with her and Marlene, Mercedes had not taken anybody else. She either learned from the last time, or managed to hide it well enough from José Ignacio. At any rate if she had someone, she dropped him the instant she saw José Ignacio come back to her life. However, that week Mercedes was busy processing data in the lab with her boss. Some sections of the study site were out of reach for oil exploration anyway. He went mostly to make love to her but when she was busy all day in the computer lab. It was like the time he ended up meeting Claudia. He was bothered by all the time Mercedes spent with her boss and was always suspicious of her boss wanting to get in her pants.. Everybody wanted it, why would not he? Even well behaved white Americans had to be susceptible to her charm. Of that he was sure.

José Ignacio was bothered for not being able to be with Mercedes but also there was some restlessness in his soul. He did not feel right, like a piece of him was missing, or in the wrong place. He went for walk in the forest. This always brought out the better of him. However, there was something wrong in the forest that day. He could feel it. There was way too much wind, hardly any moisture and the forest was plagued by the smell of burned gun powder from the explosions of the exploration. Every time he tried to connect with the forest, that came so naturally, he felt more and more that the jungle was different; out of balance. The flowers did not have the color that they normally did. The vines in the forest made treacherous ladders that the monkeys were afraid of using. The wind inside the canopy sounded like a howl of pain, as if the jungle was suffering. He picked up a flower he knew well, to regal himself with the sweet scent of its calyx but instead he was stung in the nose by the acrid smell of dog shit. He was feeling dizzy with the hot wind that blew inside the forest, where no wind has any right to blow. His vision became blurry and something took over him as in automatic pilot. He saw himself from the outside, like he was an observer on his own life.

In his way back he walked by "the jacuzzi". The Jacuzzi was a water pump that brought water from the water table to feed a temporary lagoon where animals had more water to withstand the peak of the dry season. The water came out a 6 inches pipe that poured generous torrent of water in a sort of cement pool that was about 15 feet across and about 2 feet deep. From there the water spilled into the lagoon. This was a wonderful opportunity for anybody to refresh themselves from the taxing heat of the tropic. This was just what he thought would help him at that time.

In the Jacuzzi he saw Charo who had the same idea. Charo was a biologist that studied birds and had a beautiful body. Her face was not very attractive, but her body was downright magnificent. She was a close friend of Mercedes and shared with her the lack of modesty when it came to bathing suit. Charo was wearing a tiny bikini, ridiculously small, that barely cover anything of her crotch or her voluptuous buttocks leaving very little for the imagination. Her breasts were small, yet both boobs spilled all over the sides of the extremely small bra that barely covered the nipples. When José Ignacio saw her, dizzy as he was, he felt his cock stand in immediate attention. He nearly gasp in surprised when he saw, from outside his body, the most vulgar expression of lust on his face. He walked in the Jacuzzi to refresh himself and to start a conversation with her. He could not stop looking at her body, and his face evidenced the lust poisoning his mind was suffering. He could not keep even a superficial conversation to mask his intentions. The wind was very strong but it was hot and dry, almost burning, not like a cool breeze that would have felt good in the heat of the jungle. There was no moisture in the air and his skin went very dry. He approached Charo with ill-disguised lust and put his hand on her knee. He moved his hand up her inner side of her thigh seeking her pussy. Charo moved away and removed his hand away from her leg quickly when she saw his intentions.

"Oh, you thighs are so beautiful and so tight." He told her as he continued moving closer to her body. Charo backed away from him reading his intentions.

"Jose Ignacio, stop. I am a friend of Mercedes and you know it." She warned him.

This was the same line of Claudia, and it never deterred him of what he wanted so he continued.:

Sashawarmas,   by Jorge Bandido

"Oh she is busy, and not around now is she? I am sure she won't mind if I took a small bite off you." He continue to approach her as she backed continue to back away from him.

Because the pool was circular he could have followed her while she backed away all day long. She did not want to turn her back on him, judging she could not outrun him. Her anti-predator instinct kicked in. It was too late for an escape, fight was her only choice. But the predator in him was also kicking in high gear. He saw himself from the outside grabbing Charo's leg below the knee and held her to prevent her from evading him and reached with his other hand behind her waist locking her against the side of the pool. Charo tried to push him away in his chest, to no avail. He had his member out already so when he secured her by the waist he was able to press it, hot and hard as it was, on her crotch.

"Stop it. I am going to tell Mercedes." Charo protested ordering him repeatedly to leave her alone, while in vane tried to push against his massive chest.

His arm around her waist locked her and the other one grope her all over her body. He had her secured in a place, unable to leave, and unable to prevent his hands for touching her. It was not very different than the time he assaulted Claudia in her bedroom except that Claudia had given the go ahead at first and then changed her mind. The other difference is that he assaulted Claudia in her bedroom, in the middle of the activity in the station so Claudia's calls for help were bound to be heard by someone. The Jacuzzi was remote from people's activities and the jungle was his accomplice. On top, there was a loud engine of the pump drowning a lot of Charo's screams for help. So there was not going to be anybody coming to her rescue. Charo was surrounded by the forest' Lust and on the grips of one of Her progeny. The Jungle was being raped by the Oil Corporation and She was fighting back.

In the struggle to free herself from his grip one of Charo's small breast broke loose of the small bra and came out hard and erect. This was not very difficult to happen because the bra was indeed very small. This tilted the scale in his favor. He remembered all the times that Maggy came out of her bedroom to flirt with him and to model her tiny bathing suits for him. *"What kind of women wears such small bikini anyway? Her bikini was even smaller than that of Mercedes' if this was possible. Obviously she wanted to provoke men to lust after her".* He thought. He was just rising to the occasion. He took a deep breath next to her boob and felt her smell or a woman merging seamlessly with the smell of the jungle and he knew he was doing the right thing.

178

Sashawarmas,   by Jorge Bandido

He brought her towards him and gulped her small boob completely in his mouth. He sucked it greedily while his hands continue fondling her thighs and her pussy. Charo protested, trying to free herself and punching him as she could. She punched him in his back and shoulders but his superior strength had her subdued. He could see himself from the outside subduing Charo against the Jacuzzi's wall at the same time that he felt the texture of her breast in his mouth. He was witness and perpetrator of the strange scene. The forest was reciprocating through him where it knew how to strike. He had her back against the border of the pool. He grabbed her elbows and forced them behind her preventing her from using her hands except for scratching him, but this was little considering the banquette he was about to have. He had forced her in a position from which she could not move and all that she could do was to resist arousal. He had both her hands held behind her back, his cock was rubbing in her crotch, and his mouth sucking her boobs greedily. She was done for!

José Ignacio had, again, that image from the times when he forced Francia, of a bar of butter sitting on a hot frying pan, trying, to no avail, to not melt with the heat of the stove. Because the bikini was so small, he did not even had to pull it down. He only had to secure the angle of penetration and thrust it in. He only needed to suck her breast a little longer to arouse her more and he could savor her biscuit in the water, just like the first time he took Mercedes in the Parque Metropolitano. It was a done deal. In a regular scenario his aphrodisiacal sweat would have poisoned her mind and she would have surrendered already but the water from the Jacuzzi and the strong wind washed it all away. The forces in the forest were out of balance. The harmonious dance of desire and lust had a taste of resentment and retaliation that was cramping its style.

He let go of her arms to position her waist better for penetration. However, Charo was not, yet tame enough and when he let go of her hand she sank her nails in his face. He was surprised by this sudden and violent attack and let go of her briefly. She stood up to leave but he recovered quickly and grabbed her again pulling her towards him. He was convinced that he was only a matter of arousing her a little more but in that moment Charo unleashed a brutal knee in his crotch that took him to the ground. Charo used this moment to take off running covering her breasts with her hands, as the bra fell in the water. He felt on his knees with cloudy vision feeling that he was going to faint but fearing to drown in the Jacuzzi if he did. José Ignacio held on to the wall of the Jacuzzi and climbed up it using his arms; he had no control of his legs. He felt great relief to see himself in dry ground before he fainted.

He woke up a later without knowing where he was. Everything came back to him shortly after, when he felt the excruciating pain from his groins irradiating through his body. He noticed that the sun was substantially lower than when he was trying to make love to Charo and concluded that it had been some 2 hours since. The pain on his groin irradiated from his ribs to his knees and he felt as if he had a vice-grip pressing in each one of his testes. He tried to get up but he had no strength in his legs. He waited, at least another hour before he could stand up. Slowly he walked to Mercedes' room, where he was staying. Each step he gave was as if someone hit each one of his testicles with a hammer.

He crawled in Mercedes' bed and tried to recover. In the evening Mercedes came back wondering where he was and surprised to find him in bed.

"I am not feeling so well." He explained.

She took a shower and invited him to have dinner in the communal cafeteria but he declined. She left. Coming back after diner, she got in bed with him trying to have sex since they had not done it since that morning. As soon as she touched him he felt unbearable needles digging in his testicles.

"No, not now." He refused her.

Mercedes was flabbergasted since it was the first time ever that José Ignacio refused having sex. Assuming he had an upset stomach because he did not eat, she feared he could be about to have one of his episodes. She left him alone and fell asleep hoping he would get better. Next morning, Mercedes sought to have sex again, and again José Ignacio turned her down. His pain had subsided some but he did not want to chance it. Mercedes got up expressing concern for his health but when out to work again in the lab.

During his convalescence in Mercedes' bed José Ignacio had a chance to reflect on what he was doing. Was he trying to rape Charo? When it was happening he did not think he was doing it. It was as if it was not him but somebody else outside his body. Yet, he was feeling on his flesh her skin, her hard body. It was like he was the jungle's wind that was touching her. He certainly felt her nipple in his mouth when he was sucking it. While he was doing it, it felt just right. It could not be wrong. Could it? Replying the image in his mind what he saw from the outside or what felt in person, it looked wrong, very wrong. But it was only in retrospective. Her body was so luscious and her bikini so tiny she obviously wanted a man to take her. Pretended resistance was a common strategy in many animal species to assure the male is truly interested. He was just showing his interest. Some females reject systematically all males so the one who is strong enough to take her by force gets to sire her offspring. That is how she selects for the best genes for her babies. Taking her despite her protestation was just the way of the jungle. However this was him reasoning things away. Was he trying to rape Charo? The question became more and more incisive in his mind and he knew the answer but he just could not accept it.

He would have never done anything to hurt her. With Francia he always caressed her enough for her to get aroused until she surrendered. By the time he penetrated her she was well lubricated and willing, even if she never asked for it. That was exactly what he wanted to do with Charo. Yet, something inside him told him that it was different.   Charo was vociferous about not wanting him to touch her. What was the difference between that and raping her? He always saw raping a woman as a despicable thing to do. A man should never use his strength on a woman. Tenderness and chivalry were the ways to act around ladies.

His mother always made sure he understood respect for women, even though she had little influence in his upbringing because she was always busy in the hospital. Yet the way he had learned about women with Maggy involved touching feeling and stripping, mostly by force. Then he realizes that among all the teachings a mother may do to her children, the mandate of respect women's was about the only thing she had been very adamant in teaching her child. He did not recall her teaching him respect to adults, not stealing, not lying, or any of the other things a mother wants her children to learn. Just the issue of respect for women's will. This was especially odd because the other parts of his education was pretty much entrusted to Maggy, a teenager girl with no more than second grade.

In all fairness, José Ignacio never had any problems with respect for adults, lying, or stealing. He was always a very well behaved boy. His only behavior issue as a child was getting into fights, but this was largely not his fault, save for his immense pride about himself and his persona. His mother seem to have accepted that this was part of her son's personality she could not change and always tried to keep him from being expelled from school, with very little punishment against him for his feisty tendencies.

Wait! He never had any problems with lying or stealing but he always had issues about women bodies. Was it a natural tendency of his? An innate one? At this age in his life he realized that his upbringing with super sexy Maggy was rather unusual. He knew that it had to do with his tendencies towards the girls. While it is true that he was very young when Maggy moved in with them, it was also true that, young as he was, he started noticing her body.

Now he knew about his brain injury he had since early childhood, but this was not something that his mother would have known early on when she was so adamant teaching him to respect women. Every time there was any news about a rapist in TV she would go off against the perpetrator condemning him very strongly. Often she would address him face to face: "*A man never does anything to a girl, she does not want him to do to her.*" Had she noted something on his behavior that was prone to that issue?

Another issue that bugged José Ignacio was that he never understood the relationship between his parents. There was no picture of their wedding, or honeymoon or any other picture of them for that matter. The only picture he ever saw of his father was when his father was an altar boy. He had his mother's last name, so it was pretty obvious that his parents never married. The lack of pictures and recollection of his father suggested that he had never been present in his life. He knew his grandpa would never agree of her getting together with a brown man, as his father obviously was. Did she have an affair and got knocked up? He recalled isolated arguments between his mother and her father, often dealing with women liberation and women freedom.

A couple times the argument ended abruptly when his grandpa said something to the effect of: "*Wasn't that what happened in Esmeralda?*". When this happened his mother would go immediately very quiet and very angry but she would stop the argument right away, relinquishing her point on women liberation wherever she stood. What had happened in Esmeralda? He never got that answer. He knew that his mother had worked in a rural hospital there and that she had good friends in that small coastal town. Those were the ones who recommended Maggy to come to work for her. But other than that, he had no idea of what might have happened. On occasions he suspected that it had been something shameful that his mother did not want to talk about. He thought that his father was from Esmeralda and "the event" had been her being knocked up by a boyfriend. Was it the link with women liberation? Being knocked up? It worked as an explanation for a while but then he had a new question. "*Had she been raped?*" That would also explain why there was no picture of them as a dating partners. Was he the result of a rape? Was his father a rapist? Was that why his mother was so adamant in him learning to respect girls? But there was actually a picture of his father that she had. It did not make sense that a rapist would give his victim a picture when he was a boy? It must have been a boyfriend.

As his mind raced feverishly over these issues he went back to recalling the events in the Jacuzzi. He was trying to make love to Charo but he noticed how much he had enjoyed her struggle. When a jaguar catches a prey, it sinks its teeth on it to kill it. Does he like doing it? Does it enjoy killing its prey or is it just a natural necessity? Well-fed cats still kills birds and lizard. Is it for pleasure? There is no denying seeing a dog with a squeaky toy. The more it squeaks, the more excited the dog gets and the more intently it bites it down. José Ignacio felt a pit in his stomach to this comparison. It was so true! That was exactly how he felt when the woman struggled against his advances. That is why he often got Mercedes angry, to enjoy that struggle. He felt downright predacious. He could not deny that to peel the woman slowly conquering her body as she resisted was spellbinding. That was the same he experienced with Francia and enjoyed so much of Claudia when he tried to take her. He recalled breathing deeply and getting assurance in his soul that he was doing the right thing. Did he have rapist genes? His mouth felt up with saliva to the recollection of fondling Charo and sucking her breast and the pain in his testicles came back with vengeance. José Ignacio spent all morning in bed and it was not until well pass noon that he felt like he could get up to get something to eat, more than 24 hours after Charo's aggression.

Mercedes came back in the evening and sought out to make love to him one more time. He did not feel the pain any more but when she touched him the pain came back and worse of all, his cock did not get hard

"What is wrong? What happened to you?" Mercedes asked very surprised.

She tried to suck it to get it hard, despite her dislike for giving oral sex, but he stopped her because it brought in unbelievable pain. . José Ignacio panicked because that was one of the issues that the Dr. had said could happen because of his brain injury: not being able to have an erection and he was feeling in total despair. He explained everything to Mercedes hoping she will help him overcome his erectile problem. When he eventually told her the entire story, Mercedes got really angry and celebrated Charo's actions.

"You were trying to rape her and she gave you what you deserve." She chastised him.

This stung very badly because it precisely what he feared.

"I was not going to rape her. I was going to make love to her." He defended himself. "It is not right that she used violence when I was just caressing her. What right did she have?"

He had not applied violence why would she. His way to seducing women did not involve any violence. He was strong enough he could easily force a woman into position and rape her. If they were not immediately willing he would encourage them by touching caressing until they changed their mind. At least that was his idea of it. There was nothing wrong with that. No violence. Nobody got hurt. He would never penetrate a woman that was not lubricated or willing to take him.

"You tried to rape Claudia and now I am glad that Charo put you in your place." Mercedes spat at him.

"I am not a rapist." He retorted stung because deep inside he feared that very issue, but he could not reconcile who he was, or who he was supposed to be, with the image on TV of a rapist that his mother so seriously condemned.

If a woman truly did not want him to make love to them she had to free herself from him or resist his caresses without becoming aroused. That was natural selection. If a man was able to convince a woman to have sex by touching her, he deserved to have her. Those were the terms in which he tried to make love to Charo. Charo had stepped out of the rules and instead of resisting she had taking the path of violence.

Mercedes was angry that José Ignacio was, again lusting after other women, and celebrated that he had being hurt.

"You deserve it for being such a pig." She chastised him.

For José Ignacio this hurt even more to see his girlfriend side with someone who had attacked him and he was truly scared about his member no working anymore. José Ignacio felt that attacking his genitals would have been something that Mercedes had some stakes on.

"It was a disproportionate response. I was trying to give her pleasure. What Charo did was like me hitting you for siding with her. It hurts that you take her side but it is a feeling that I had to respond with words not violence." He argued. "What if I would hit you for siding with Charo? That would be disproportionate. Wouldn't it?".

"Oooh that would be so macho of you to hit a woman. I dare you hit me." Spat back Mercedes defiantly.

Taking the line the hook and the sinker he placed her on the bed as her father used to and dropped a powerful palm on her butt to make her shut up and get her attention.

"Don't hit me!" Mercedes roared angrily and tried to get up but his hand on her back prevented her from getting up.

"This is what Charo did to me. I was kissing her and she hit me." José Ignacio replied.

Of course Mercedes' father used to hit her a lot when she was a girl and after she was not so much of a girl, he still continued to hit her. José Ignacio

184

only spanked her, he never hit her in any other way, and it was mostly because he was so drawn to her butt, and there was always a sexual tone to his spanking. But Mercedes did not take well being hit in any way; even if it was for sex. However, when José Ignacio spanked her she stopped glorifying Charo's aggression.

Then he decided to spank her again to get her to protest even more and to make his point of unbalanced response. He spanked her hard, with all his hand on the other buttock. Mercedes became even angrier with increscent rage and he felt a warm feeling travel his body from the arm pit of the arm that he hit her with, all the way to his groins. He pinned her down on the bed and pulled down her short exposing her delicious derriere and gave her another loud spanking. Mercedes squirmed and roared in anger and again, he felt the warm feeling traveling his body and soothing the pain that he have been having for the last 24 hours. Disregarding her rage he straddled her facing her behind and started spanking her time and time again; using both arms one on each buttock without pause. Mercedes cried in impotence yelling insults with every spanking. But the more he spanked her, the more that Mercedes wallowed in anger and impotence, the stronger a current of euphoria travel all over his body. The Jungle was feeling the white man's violence with the generalized explosions all over the forest and She was striking it right back the way She knew.

Each spanking was a new demonstration of anger, and a new contortion of her body in impotent rage and a new warm familiar feeling in his body as if it was something he had been doing all his life. As if he was hiding the call of his own nature. Each tear that Mercedes shed, each moan of pain, it was a new breath of warmth and relief to his body. He felt a new sensation that he had never experienced. It was one of power. When he forced Francia he enjoyed the feeling of victory in a battle and when he finally penetrated her, she surrendered and he made love to her lovingly. With Mercedes it was different. There has been for a long time a situation of emotional domination, now it aroused him to feel her rage and impotence. He got excited to feel that he could do anything he wanted to her and that he was her absolute master. Her firm and muscular buttocks could support quite a beating so he could hit her as hard as he wanted, with his powerful arms, without being worrid of doing her any real harm. He could vent on her all the frustration for not having been able to have Charo and all the anger for Mercedes taking her side. But there was something else. He could never satiate his newly found pleasure and became instantly addicted to it.

A strong down pour began and the noise of the rain on the tin roof, muffled Mercedes' cries of pain. Thunders overwhelming every sound contributed to mask what was happening in their room from other people from the field station. José Ignacio spanked her mercilessly until his palms ached of how hard he was hitting her. He could see the rosy mark of his hands stamped on her buttocks where he could clearly make out the red print of every finger on her skin. Eventually they all merged in a bright redden surface. He was drunk with a new feeling of euphoria and pleasure he had never experienced. José Ignacio relished in his new found position of absolute power over his lover's body. At every spanking he felt that his member started to thicken and grow. At every spanking it became larger and harder. He was aroused to hit her and to feel her impotence in repressed moans. He finally felt a huge erection, inebriated with power and lust.

He climbed down from top of her and opened her legs placing his hungry member in her pussy and slid it inside, the whole thing in a single movement. Mercedes felt his cock hard and firm impale her and broke up crying out loud in pain. She never liked to cry when he hit her because she felt inferior, weak. She felt that if she could repress the urge to cry she was holding her own against his strength. But this time she was too angry, felt impotent against the abuse of strength. So she let go and screamed in pain as it felt best. He pressed her against his chest, moved it out completely, only to impale her over and over and over. He felt split inside him. One part of him relished incredibly the forceful conquering of her body and her contortion of pain. His mouth felt up with saliva to hear her scream in a predatory reflex. But another part of him was terrified to see how much he was enjoying it. He felt he was raping Mercedes and he was loving it. His soul was torn in two opposite directions. One that was feasting on the pain he was inflicting on his beloved and another one that felt horror of what he was doing. The law of the jungle can deliver atrocious death and beautiful life all at once. Terrifying darkness and beautiful light fit so naturally side by side in the recesses of the forest. That summarized José Ignacio's soul, which was made of jungle.

By the time he came inside her, his dark side had subsided. He came swearing to her his eternal love, her screams were a soft grunt in her sore throat and her face, with swollen eyes, was covered in tears. Soft tears of rain were trickling all over the forest as well. Amber rays of light from the afternoon sun trickled softly through the bedroom's window. He licked lovingly her copious tears. He continued kissing her with love because she would not stop crying. He ignored her protestations and continued covering her skin with his kisses.

"I am sorry to hit you my love. I was feeling very frustrated," he said between kisses; but something on him was torn on how he could have done it and how different it felt just before coming. She forgave him for hitting her but asked him to never hit her again. She had not stopped crying when his cock became hard again. This time he made love to her tenderly. As usual, she acquiesced to his desire and let him satiate his needs on her body.

That was not the first time José Ignacio hit Mercedes but it was the first time that he realized how much he liked it. José Ignacio realized he was on the strong side of testosterone. That is the hormone that produces sex drive as well as muscle development and he had lots of both. But he also knew that the same testosterone is associated with violence and aggressive behaviors in the animal kingdom as well in humans. He did not know the hidden power of the venom that he had consumed and the seed that was germinating in his hyper-testoteronized body. It was a new experience for him. Why did he like it so much? Was he a real rapist? Was it why he enjoyed hitting her so much? Did he inherit raping genes that he could not control?

He knew from psych classes there was a big deal of power and domination in the raping as sociological phenomenon. He really enjoyed the domination and pain Mercedes experienced. He had started his sexual life with Maggy and stripping a reluctant woman is how he learned about sex. It was not his genes, it was his upbringing that lead him to enjoy it so much. Like a very addictive drug. He never had sex with violence and the other women he had sex with never experienced any of this. He recalled the words of the neurologist who had seen him: "*This injury may produce inappropriate sexual behaviors because the person may seek the reward so intensely that it would overlook social rules of normal behaviors. It may produce risky and extreme sexual conduct. It is in fact, similar problem with drug addiction except that it is sex itself that becomes the drug*". Surely his brain injury was acting up again and that is why he felt so overwhelming need to have sex with violence.

He came back to Quito. He remembered spanking Mercedes and got aroused with the only recollection of his misdeed. He went back and forth from feeling bad for having hit her and then feeling so much pleasure recalling what he did to her. He often masturbated remembering it and something in him realized that the passions that Mercedes inspired him were too intense, both the good ones and the bad ones. He could not accept who he was when he felt that pernicious lust when he was with her, and blame it on her. He had to learn to control it if he was going to continue with her or those were passions that could end up consuming both of them. Fearing that this could escalate to more intense situations that he could not control he tried harder than ever to find someone to inspire him something just as intense but peaceful. His attempts to separate lasted little because he always yearned to make love to her again when they were separated. He would make love to other women but those were sexual relationships that did not inspire him the overwhelming lust that Mercedes did. They did not have the intensity of the domination games and violence that he got with Mercedes.

33. INTRUSION IN THE FOREST

The Peruvian president had given consent for the oil exploration in the Amazon Amazon. This was a controversial maneuver because most of the affected area was pristine rainforest that had been to that date part of a Woaorani reservation. Woaoranis were famous for not being friendly to intruders and up to this date they have protected their patch of rainforest from western influence. The decision of the president to allow oil exploration in this area was very much money driven but with little consideration of the impact it would do in the ecology of the system was well as the local inhabitants. Everybody was opposed to it but the Woaorani warriors were the ones that were most decided to do something.

As the operations began the workers met resistance just entering to the area with warriors running the workers away from the area. No one was hurt because the spears and arrows were intentionally shot near the operators. But they sent a clear message that trespassing would not be allowed.

Yet the government had deal with the oil company. The next group of oil workers came escorted by heavily armed national guards. Then the situation became more difficult. Woaorani warriors had expressed their determination of not allowing the oil workers into their land and just as the national guard showed up with displaying their guns, the warriors showed in force. The scene was nothing short of Dantesque. On one side of the narrow river were military soldiers armed with automatic weapons in combat gear. On the other side a battalion of Woaorani warriors lined up with arrows and spears with combat painting in their body. The confrontation was eminent. The Woaoranis s stood in line for an easy execution with the machine guns from the other side but the river was not wide enough to spare the soldiers of the arrows. Nerves were tense. The drop of a needle would have been enough to trigger a disaster.

Locally local inhabitants of nearby town showed up with cell phones recording what was happening. The ease in which this kind of news travel now a days gave pause to the Cornell in charge who was ready to order the butchering of the whole group of indigenous warriors and the situation was diffused. Images of the two groups about to fight were broadcasted around the world and the government changed tack. However, they di not just give up. For the next four to six weeks, dozens upon dozens of dead warriors turned washed up on the beaches of the rivers in the area. The oil companied tried to spin the situation saying that it was conflict among the different Woaorani tribes but it was clear that the wounds were produced by western guns and not arrows or spears. Regardless, the oil company got the Woaoranis to move back into the forest and started operations in the area that had been cleared.

There was local outrage on the communities both the people and scientist of the area. However, the oil company managed to block any media development and the world did not find out about this new offense against the forest and their people. Yet, the Forest was hurt. Her Woaorani protectors had lost a stand, the Forest was in defense mode and activated all of her defenses.

34. BITING BACK

The psychology student came out of the gym late at night after a long day of studying, nearing the finals. As the stress of the exams became stronger, she needed more hard workouts to clear her mind and keep her sanity. There was nothing she relished more like the endorphins rush in her brain after a hard work out that let her exhausted before going to bed. The only catch was that in the day when she arrived to school all parking spot were taken and she always had to park far from the gym. The walk through campus, late at night was a bit scary. It was dark, all alone, with abundant gardens that made the campus pretty during the day but that highlighted its solitude, and made it scary at night.

She was told many times not to be out so late but she could not help it. It was the only time she had to work out and she was not going to give it up. Also, the crowd that worked out at that time was more mature. Not so many young meat heads pumping iron, hitting on girls, and being disrespectful. Rather there was a more thoughtful crowd, more interesting, and all around cuter, in her mind. There were two men on the weights machine working out across the gym that were clearly checking her out. The one with the big muscles was physically attractive but his working partner, the skinny one with the sweet smile and the unruly bangs was more her type. She could see them in the mirror of the wall, checking her out and talking about her, while they thought they were seen and being slick.

She was not the show-off kind of girls but her legs were well formed, her behind was hard and prominent, well deserved for the squads and exercises. In the gym was the only place where she wore tight spandex, that were revealing of her curves. She was just not interested in attracting that kind of men in general, but in the gym, she wanted to feel free and because the men at that time were more mature, she felt safe dressing sexy. She even felt a bit slutty sometimes. The cute one with the sweet smile had her fantasizing and getting aroused. She would have given him a sign were it not because she feared that the other one would get confused and take the sign for himself, instead of his skinny, more timid friend. But it was all day dreaming anyway, she did not have time for that. She was a senior and she needed to finish her degree soon to move on with her career, the last that she needed was a romance with all the distractions that it involves.

As she walked she noticed that the hall was long, dark, and away from most people activity that late. She sensed the hair on the back of her neck stand on end but she did not know why. There was nobody around! She had some sense of security on her speed. If she felt any danger she could run like the wind blows, there was no chance a robber or any attacker could catch up with her, unless he himself was also a national medal winner in 400 and 800 meters, as she was. She no longer ran competitive track but she still had it. She sped up the pace to get quicker to her car. She entertained the idea breaking into a gallop and end up her work out in force and also to get out of that dark hall that gave her the creeps, but she decided that it was all in her mind.

Suddenly two strong arms wrapped around her from behind pinning her arms to her trunk. She was lifted of the ground life a feather and taken into the bamboo garden, to the right of the hall, and away from people that may possibly pass. She screamed in surprise. As soon as she realized that she was being attacked by a man, she screamed from the top of her long.

"HELP! HELP!" She yelled as hard as she could while she also tried to free herself but her captor arms were solid, like made out of steel.

She tried to kick him in the nuts with her heels but that did not work either. She continued screaming from the top of her lungs asking for help before she was taken too far away from the main hall. A powerful set of teeth clamped on the back or her neck biting her. Her attacker brought her deep into the garden and took her down to the ground lying on top of her. She struggled to free her arms but her attacker had his left arm around her body, pinning her left arm tight by her trunk and holding her right forearm with his hand. With his body on top of her she was completely immobilized. She screamed asking for help but she was creaming straight into the dirt, her mouth filling up with grass and dirt. The bite in the neck was just adding pain and restraining her from doing any resistance.

He was biting her on the neck so hard that she was shocked by the sheer pain. The bite was just in the part of her neck where she regularly got tension headaches when she was stressed. She had been battling a headache for a week because of the exams and the bite was just aggravating it all the worst. She felt, it would develop into a full blown migraine if she did not stop it soon. She screamed more with all her lungs but all she got was another mouth full of grass and dirt. There is no way her voice could had gone very far. Being so over powered and in so much pain she tried a different approach. She stopped yelling and went still trying to negotiate with her attacker. The pressure of the teeth in her neck lowered considerably as soon as she stopped screaming, although he did not fully let go. It was a welcome relief on her pain and she felt she could try to talk to him.

192

Sashawarmas,   by Jorge Bandido

"Please sir, let me go. I have some money in my pursue, may be $30 or $40, you can have it. Also, my bracelet is silver. You can get good money for it. You can have it all. Please let me go". She begged.

But to her chagrin, what came back was a command in an extremely deep voice, almost like a purr.

"Strip".

She panicked now seriously and resumed screaming as hard as she could. No longer it was clear that her attacker wanted to rape her but also the voice was so unnaturally deep that it made the her of her neck stand on end. The was something malignant on that voice that she could not understand but she fully felt. She went back to struggle trying to free her arms and trying to free herself with all her strength and the pressure of the bite resumed in full force.

There was no mystery from the beginning on what his intentions were; since he had her immobilized with only one arm, the other hand was fondling her thighs, buttocks, reaching between her legs all the way to her crotch from the very first moment. She tried ignore the sexual undertone of her attacker, but seeing the direct request that she stripped, made it impossible for her to ignore that it was a sexual attack, not a robbery. She knew all the tricks to defend herself: the knee in the crotch, the unexpected elbow, the claws on the face. But they all required that she were facing her attacker, or at least had the capacity to use her hands or legs. Instead, she was pinned on the ground, immobilized; the pain of the bite was blinding her. On top of it, his weight was squashing her and she could hardly breathe. Any efforts to scream, or to release herself, just required her to breathe harder. With her face shoved on the dirt, getting air, involved breathing in some dirt.

A million things rushed through her mind while she tried to think of what to do. She recalled a conversation she heard from her uncles, one of whom was arguing that a true rape was very rare. "*If a woman does not really want to have sex, she can always avoid it. It is like threading a needle that does not want to be threaded*". He had declared.

She felt offended when her uncle said that but now she wished there was some truth to it. If she only resisted she could avoid being raped. She had always been strong and quite able to defend herself, but now she was so overpowered that she saw no possible action. She continued to hope someone will come and stop the assault but in the mean time she only could do was to resist as much as possible. She felt his hand founding and groping her in such an intimate manner. She felt so abused, so disrespected feeling the hand of a stranger press on her crotch. It was such a special part of her, and this stranger was touching her so insolently. She only needed to wait for someone to come.

Sashawarmas,   by Jorge Bandido

Surely someone heard her screaming; at least the first few screams before she was brought behind the bamboo and forced to scream into the dirt.

She took a break from the struggle to save her strength and felt just a rush flowing over her body when the pressure of the bite lessened again. The cessation of pain, felt so good! His smell was overwhelming. It was some sort of musky offensive smell to her sense. She felt it filling up her lungs and taking possession of her body. Suddenly it dawn on her: Negative reinforcement! It consists in providing an aversive stimulus, the bite, until the subject performs the desire behavior. He was putting pain on her until she relinquished the struggle. She knew how effective classical condition is to change behavior and realized that he was, literally, domesticating her to allow the raped. She had to avoid it at all cost. She went back to scream and try to free herself but her screams were as useful as her attempts to freedom from the powerful arm and, as she could have predicted, the bite came down in full force, twice as hard as before. Her vision got blurry and she thought she could faint.

She recalled a documentary that she had seen of lioness taking down a young buffalo. The animals was far bigger than the lioness and fought back at first but having a lioness clamped her jaws around her throat it just stood there resisting the bite of the feline without trying to escape or fight. She did not like where it was going. The lioness ended up eating the young buffalo. She thought of herself as the prey that fought to defend her flesh from the predator intent in feasting on her. IT was all too similar to the documentary! The sweat of her skin gave her attacker a salty flavor that made his mouth water a little. She continued screaming resisting the pain but the pain and despair won turning her screams into sobs. Her voice was growing hoarse anyway.

She felt her nipples twist with the wave of euphoria that travelled through her body when the teeth of her attacked release her neck. It was the closest to a feeling of elation she had had in a long time. Being calm and quiet beat the alternative for a long shot, even if that mean lying under him and letting him fondle her forms. She had to think of something. She started to come to term with her situation: there was no help coming her way. It was all up to her to get out of this one. He was not stripping her though. With his free hand he could have pulled down her pants and being so strong he could have raped her already. Yet, he was just fondling her instead. It dawned on her: he was waiting for her to surrender herself to him! She knew from her studies that there is a big deal of power and domination in the sexual assault; far more than just sexual desire. All she had to do was to outlast him and she could win this stand-off, and remain unrapped.

194

Sashawarmas,   by Jorge Bandido

How long could she resist? How long could she wait? It was hard to
breath and even when she was quite, he was still biting her neck, just not
digging his teeth in her flesh mercilessly. Her migraine came in full force. She
saw numbers traveling in front of her eyes when she closed them. His smell
was intoxicating. She needed to end it. She could not endure it any longer
She considered surrendering. Letting him have her. The penetration would
probably hurt but it was working towards a solution. He was far too strong for
her to resist, if he started to undress her. So, it was not her call ultimately. In
the path she was in, she was up to endure a lot more pain, and still may end
up being raped in the end if he chose to take her. All that pain would have
been in vain. She tried screaming with the rest of her forces to see if she could
get somebody to save her. The bite came back with vengeance. She felt a jolt
in her neck and the pain went up 5 folds. She felt warmth spreading all over
her neck. She realized that it was blood flowing from the cut his teeth had
made. It was too much!

"I give up! I give up! Please don't hurt me anymore! Tell me what you
want me to do." She pleaded.

"Pull down your pants." Came back the same unnatural low pitch voice
came back right in her ear.

The release of the bite felt incredibly good. Like a whole new sensation of
pleasure. She accepted it. No one could have that voice pitch. The sense that
she was dealing with an evil force came back to her and overwhelmed her
senses. She was torn. She knew there was something evil on her attacker, but
it felt so good to feel the relief of pain. Her life of catholic upbringing flashed
in her eyes. Martyrs have to resist evil, endure pain. They need to fight
against temptation. God would help her if she believed. But her pain was so
intense that she had lost faith. She was not giving up to a temptation, she just
wanted the pain to stop. The end of pain felt so good. She accepted that to
give up her body was a reasonable price to pay.

It was the only solution and she resigned herself to it. If she letting him
win spared her the damage he was doing to her, it was better than the path she
was in. She took a deep breath and reach with the little movement she had
with her hands to pull down her sweat pants as she was instructed. She pulled
them down to her knees and spread apart her legs positioning herself for
penetration. She felt the delicious sensation of his teeth finally letting go of
her neck. The warmth spread broader on her neck and upper back and she
knew she had taken the right choice. She could picture her upper shoulders
drenched in blood. She was happy that it was just one rapist. Often one rapist
will leaves after the deed, but when there are several, the odds of battery and
further abuse are much higher. She relaxed her pussy as much as she could

195

preparing herself. If she cooperated, it would hurt a lot less, that she knew.
She had endured enough pain already. She felt an impossible thick cock at
the entrance of her pussy and took in a deep breath and let it go slowly. Her
attacker had let go of her arms and was holding her by her hips bones now. It
allowed her to put her elbows below herself and raise her head to take a clean
breath away from the grass of the garden. The relief for the neck bite felt very
good and she accepted anything that was coming as a just price to pay to end
her suffering.

"Aauugh." She groaned when the first three inches went in. She let go of
all the air left in her lungs slowly and prepared herself for the reminding of his
member. She felt him sniffing her neck, and softly licking and kissing her
neck and ear lobes on the other side of her head that was not bleeding, as if
drinking in her smell with great pleasure. He grazed her ear lobes almost
tenderly. All she had to do was to let him have his way with her and she
would quickly be free.

"Hummmph". She grunted feeling another length of his member getting
inside her. One of his arms was in front of her chest holding his weight while
the other one traveled up and down her body under her clothing, feeling her
skin and her forms. His unnaturally warm lips were kissing and licking the
other side of her neck with the same tenderness than the aggression which
with his teeth a minute ago were digging in her flesh on the other side. She
had managed to lubricate herself a little bit. She definitely made the right
decision, she thought.

When the last length of cock went finally in, he started a slow, rhythm
with long thrusts pulling a long stretch of it out and going back in, full length
until the whole member was all the way in again. She knew the drill. She
knew what to do. She soon will be free. It could not last long. His right hand
came around her hip towards her lower belly and tenderly felt it, placing his
warm hand right on her womb.

Her womb! She recalled the day of the month. It was new moon! She
recalled with terror that was ovulating that day!

"Wait! I am ovulating today! You are going to knock me up. Please sir
stop. Do not get me pregnant!" She pleaded.

However, her attacker did not seem to hear. If anything his rhythm
became faster and more intense. She went back to try to struggle with all her
force to free herself from him, to no avail.

"Please sir let me go. I will jerk you off. I will do anything. I will blow
you but please do not come insidguumgh". Her plead was interrupted when

196

his powerful thrust shoved her face back in the dirt filling up her mouth again with grass and dirt.

His rhythm was growing faster as his cock when in and out full length in every thrust. She was desperate at his impending ejaculation. She felt his powerful arms crushing her making all her vertebrates crack under the pressure. She tried to breath but the pressure on her chest was so hard that no air came in. His orgasm was imminent. She continued to try to plead for him not to come inside her but she had no air in her lungs and nothing came out. just a mute gasp. She tried to breathe again but her lungs could not expand. She tried to breathe again, and again, without success. It did not work. She feared he would break her ribs. His rhythm continued accelerating as the pressure of his arms squeezing her against his chest. She tried another draw air again, and again, to no avail. It all went black around her.

35. LOOKING FOR THE ZAMBO

When Daniela arrived to Esmeralda, she felt a knot in her stomach. Some of the most traumatic moments of her life came back to her and for a second she felt fear that the town was still stuck in that heinous time. However, soon she noticed the normal functioning of a small town where the rule of law was, mostly, in control. She got off the bus and walked the path all the way to the house where she had been sex slave during the social explosion. She relived the street in the days where every corner showed an evidence of the mayhem that had engulfed the city. The stores being ransacked, women being raped in the streets, all the lowest instinct of the populace running lose. She was glad it was a lot calmer now.

She took a deep breath when she got to the Zambo's shack at the edge of the forest and wondered if she really wanted to see him or if deep inside she hoped not to find him. She knocked at the door with her heart pounding in her chest and it opened lazily with its reluctant hinges that barely held it complained for having to open.

"Hello!" She called. "Anybody home?" She called the second time before crossing the threshold.

The house looked empty but somehow still had the flavor and personality of the Zambo in it. The kitchen table where he first had taken her in the house was still there. In the same place in the same complicit attitude it had had that day. The kitchen did not look very different except that there were no pots on the sink or on the stove. She went into his bedroom to see the bed where she was taken so many times, both by force and willingly. It was naked of linen, and showed the sagging in the center where the heavy body of the Zambo had made its dent.

Daniela stood there for a while thinking what to do. There was no evidence that he was still living there or that the shack was occupied at all. She looked at the window that faced the forest and recalled the last time she had seen the Zambo escaping the guards that, he knew, where coming for him. She could still see him with the machete in one hand folded by his forearm balancing his arms back and forth as he sprinted into the forest with his perfect stride. Why were the guards looking for him? Clearly they were not arresting all rapist, they would had had to arrest most men in the village. Plus there was a whole delegation of some 8 guards that had come to arrest him. "*Tall, Zambo, very strong, very dangerous*", had been the words of the lieutenant that lead the commission when he described him to her. There was no doubt the words were accurate. The physical description was obvious. She had seen

198

what happened to the men that were attacking her after the Zambo had given them a punch each. Nothing but one single punch had been enough to knock the lights out of them. Yes, strong and dangerous were true too. But one is only dangerous to those that are their enemies. Why was the Zambo an enemy of the guards? They came after him in force after the uprising was overcome. Was he involved in some political issues? Was he part of activist cell that tried to destabilize the government? No other reason would explain why the guards came after him as the first thing when the order was restored. She did remember that he was very worried about the news in the country, as if having a lot at stake on the outcome of the vacancy of power. This interest in politics stroked her as unusual from the beginning if he were just another port urchin or a worker in the plantations. They often do not get too involved in politics. Sadly the time she had spent with him they never talked about hardly anything. She loved his deep voice and it always turned her on, to hear it. That is after the deep fear for the first days had been overcome.

As Daniela was leaving the house having lost hope to find him there, she was surprised to find a short, white middle age man coming in the house.

"May I help you miss?" Asked the man.

"Oh, I am looking for a man who used to live here. Do you know if anyone lives here now?" She asked.

"Nobody lives here darling. I own the house and it has been vacated for a few years. No one wants to live here." Replied the middle age man.

"Do you know José Ignacio Guzman?" Asked the nurse with a glimmer of hope she may be able to find him.

"Yes I do. He was my tenant for a while but he disappeared right after the revolt. He owed me three months of rent. The few belonging he left did not compensate for hardly any of the bill he left." He replied bitterly.

"Do you know where I can find him?" She asked without much hope, due to his attitude about the man.

"I sure don't. Nobody does. Last he was seen was when the order came back after the revolt. He was seen running on the road to the port. He might have escaped on a boat. Who knows what dirty business he had been involved with?" Replied the man.

That was her lie! That is what she had told the guards when they enquired about him, but she knew he had gone the other way. This led her to conclude that the Zambo never came back to Esmeralda. Did he disappear in the forest? How can someone do that? She felt a pit in her stomach to the thought that she may never find him, and realized how much she loved him and how badly she was hoping to find him.

The nurse put her feet back in the path to town. She did not know where to look for now. She could wait until the night and go to the bars by the port. She knew he was the kind to frequent those places. The night she met him he had been brought in wounded with a cut on his chest after a bar quarrel. She was not especially thrilled to go at night to a bar where there would be zillions of men looking for women that were guaranteed to head on her. Most of them, she was sure, were involved in the rape fest that seized town the day of the revolt, so these would be not only drunken sailors and port workers out to get laid but men that were capable, and had, raped defenseless women. However, that was the only chance that she could get news about the Zambo. She was torn.

36. RE-RAPED

Jouvet woke up disoriented in the university garden dark at night. Her neck was sore, with a suspicious warm spreading over the upper back. She was bleeding! Suddenly the whole thing came back to her. The attacker! She looked wild eyed around fearing he was still there. She could not see much in the dark but something told her that she was alone. Her attacker was gone. She looked for her belonging, and found her purse and wallet. It all was there. He did not rob her, he just raped her and left. She stopped to think of that again. *"He only raped me"*. Yes, it could have been a lot worse. She was alive, even if she had to go to the hospital for stitches.   She got up and put pressure on her wound with her hand over her t-shirt and ran to the closets entrance of the university where a unit of campus security could be found. She told them about her attack and asked for help. The attacker was likely gone by now but she needed medical attention.

****

The day of the deposition Jouvet woke up determined. She had endured all the paperwork, invasive intimate exams and farther humiliations the night of the attack and she wanted to make sure her attacked paid for what he did. It had been very taxing after being raped. She endured the medical treatments from the stitching of the wound on her neck, the pelvic exam and all the other humiliating exams collecting semen samples and studying her insides for evidence of lacerations and injuries. But all that was behind now. She had done her part. All she needed to do now was to render a testament of the attack and let the police do their work. With DNA samples collected her attacker could be identified unequivocally and locked up in jail.

She was a bit disappointed to see the office where she was going to render her testimony. No fancy declaration room like in the movies, rather a middle of the road desk, where an officer sat taking notes while another one ran the questionnaire. It was in the middle of a big room that contained several cubicles, with other desk of the same style nearby and people going back and forth, phones ringing, and people talking to each other from desk to desk. There was not going to be a whole lot of privacy for her declaration. She swallowed and walked in the room. Talking about being raped was not something she was looking forward but the idea of being overheard by other made it all the more uncomfortable. Yet, she had to do what she had to do.

"Good morning Miss Tami, have a seat. We will be taking your testimony" greeted the receiving officer. He was a Hispanic man of 30 something, medium built and professional demeanor. The other officer with an air of supervising the interrogatory was also Hispanic but of African descendant, the typical brown color of generations of mixed heritage likely from the coast. She sat down as instructed trusting that it would be over soon. She would have preferred to be interrogated by a woman but she did not think that was in the cards. She recounted everything that she remembered as it had happened the day of the attack.

"Can you describe for us what your attacker looked like?" Asked the interrogating officer.

"Actually, I did not see him. He got me from behind in the dark and pinned me to the ground. He never let me look at his face or at him for that matter. I passed out from the pain and not being able to breath, and by the time I regained consciousness, he was gone." Replied Jouvet.

"So you don't know what he looks like?" Inquired the officer to be sure.

"He was very strong and big. Not fat, tall and very muscular. His arms were very thick, very strong". She added.

"That does not give us a lot to go by. Did you see his hair? Do you have an idea of how old he was? Clothing?" The officer explained.

She could not answer that. Trying to give them as much information as she could she added

"He was very big", a bit embarrassed looking from one to the other officer sitting on the table.

"Yes, you already told us that he was big, not fat but tall and strong. Do you have something else?" Asked the officer losing a bit his patience.

"No, I mean his member, was very large. Uncommonly so." She said now color rushing to her cheeks. The officer exchanged a glance with the one sitting next to him.

"We need some physical characteristic that we can put out in and order for his capture. Otherwise, we will not be able to identify him." He told her with finality.

"But you have DNA samples of him the Drs collected, . . . in me. Surely you can find a match and find out who it was." Jouvet argued starting to lose hope.

"Miss Tami, we cannot go and get blood samples from every man in the city to match with the samples obtained from your attacker. In fact, we cannot force a person to give a sample unless we have a very good reason to suspect his guilt, probable cause. You have to give us something of his physical description in order for us to start a search." Explained the officer.

"He was black, I think," said Jouvet.

"Do you think?" Asked the officer frowning a little.

"I can't be sure because it was dark and he got me from behind" She added.

"So you did not see him." The officer said trying to get the facts straight.

"I did not see him but I think he is black, I could smell him all around me. His smell was very overpowering, very unique." She continued trying to give them as much information she could.

"Did he *smell* black" The officer asked now frowning heavily.

Jouvet realized how it sounded. She looked nervously from the officer to the other one sitting next to the table.

"I did not see him but I think he was black. That should help to find a suspect in the university. There are not a lot of black men on campus." She answered with pleading eyes asking for understanding looking from one to the other.

"Look darling, if you want us to be able to find this guy you have to give us something more than a smelly black guy with a big cock". He added.

A generalized snort and laughter coming from all over the room told her that other officers were not as busy as she thought and had been eavesdropping in her interrogatory. "We cannot stop anybody with this information". The officer continued losing his patience.

Jouvet felt heat building up in her face as embarrassment and anger colliding in her mind with full force.

"Look, I was raped, brutally assaulted by a man because you have failed to provide security for the citizens. Instead of taking me seriously you are here laughing at me?" Jouvet retorted tears of anger and impotence coming out of her eyes.

The officer lean back a little, exchange another glance with his partner and told her in calmed but stern tone:

"Ok, explain to me how he raped you to get a better idea of what happened".

Jouvet could not believe the question. What was he asking?

"He grabbed me from behind and bit me. He pinned me down, he . . ." She trailed off not sure what the officer was asking since she already had referred the whole story before. How much detail did he want? What did it matter? "He held me from behind, immobilized me pinning me against the ground. I screamed but he had me facing to the dirt. He bit me very hard and held me pinning me down. I could not breath with his weight on me. No one came to help me and he ended up raping me." She concluded.

"Miss Tami, the forensic exam found no evidence of physical struggle typical of a sexual assault. No scratches in your skin, no skin of the attacker in your finger nails, things that unavoidable happen in a sexual attack. Your underwear was not torn, or showed evidence of tugging. How did he strip you?" The officer confronted her.

Jouvet was shocked by the question and realized that a straight answer would not help her case. "I . . . He bit me so hard, and he would not let me go. What was I supposed to do?" She answered her voice trembling.

"You have not answered my question." The officer replied sternly.

"He had me immobilized, I was afraid he was going to kill me or hurt me more than he had already." Jouvet answered between sobs.

"You still have not told me how he stripped you. Your clothing was not torn, or showed evidence of physical struggle." Replied the relentless officer.

"I took it off because I was afraid. No one was coming to help me. I could not fight him off. All that I could do was surrender," said Jouvet sobbing.

An extremely insulting "Ahh!" of understanding traveled over the room at her reply.

"What was I supposed to do? I was alone. He was hurting me so bad. How much pain does a woman have to endure? How much risk? I did not know how much he was going to hurt me if I did not cooperate. There was no police around to help me." Jouvet asked disconcerted.

"So you did cooperate." Added the other officer that has been quite up until then

"Damn you! Who do you think you are?" Spat Jouvet rage spilling out of her.

"Look, Miss Tami, I don't think you bit yourself that way on your neck. That is a nasty bite and the person who did it needs to go to jail. Why don't you tell us the name of your boyfriend and where he lives. We will grab him and match his teeth with your wound. If there is a match we can force him to give us a blood sample. If his DNA matches the sample from the forensic exam, we can put him away for 3- 5 years for domestic violence and battery." Replied the officer with a conviction that made her wonder why she was even there.

"Wait! I was *raped*. He is not my boyfriend. I don't know him or where he lives. Why would I say he raped me if it wasn't true?" Answered Jouvet in disbelief.

"Unfortunately it is not uncommon that some women get mad with their boyfriends for cheating on them or other reasons and accuse them of rape to get even. The bite he gave you deserves jail. You have a much better chance with an accusation of battery than insisting on the rape scenario. Believe me." Recommended the interrogating officer.

The woman could not believe what was happening. "B . . . But . . ., I *was* raped. I am not making it up. Surely the forensic exam shows evidence of it". She stammered.

"Well, the forensic exam is inconclusive. There was no evidence of fighting or physical struggle. They did not find the unequivocal injuries you expect from a forceful penetration. There are some lacerations to be sure but it is within the kind you would find in, . . . well, in a consensual intercourse with someone with a big penis." An eruption of laughter roared all over the room.

Jouvet's heart fell. She knew it was a moot point and said nothing. She had collaborated in the penetration eventually, to avoid being farther injured, after having resisted so much pain from the bite. The officers managed to quiet all eavesdroppers and prompted her.

"Look, the judge is a woman and she hates men who beat up their partners. I assure you that if you give us this guy he will pay. But the case for rape is weak at best. You have no sign of struggle. Your nails have no skin from the attacker. You have no, bruised, scratches from his attack or any other damage beyond the bite. The way it looks to me is that your boyfriend and you got into some rough sex and he overdid it. We can put him away but you have to tell us who it is. If you insist in the accusation of rape by an estranger, this guy will walk, even if we catch him, which I don't think we can. It will be his word against yours. The lack of physical struggle will tilt the scale in his favor."

Jouvet stood up and left the room disheartened. She came to accept her situation and there was no way she could convince them she had been raped.

205

Sashawarmas,   by Jorge Bandido

To the psychological harm of having been raped, she had to endure the second raping by the police officers and society that did not believe her.

37. THE PORT ZONE

Before she realized what she was doing the nurse feet had walked her to the small rural hospital where she once worked. Why had she come here? She had lived here for a year and a half, before the revolt when she was kidnapped. Up until that day it had been a good place for her. She had learned independence from her family, economic independence, a place to live, a group of friends. She had learned quite a bit about being a nurse and even a lot of the Dr's. duties. Her experience in that place had been extremely valuable in her later professional life. Yet, the last time she saw it, it had been invaded by a gang of rapist that were taking all the nurses. Because education was a privilege of the white people all nurses where white; and the native inhabitants of Esmeralda were mostly black, Indian, or brown. The sight of it was a horde of black men raping all the white women. It was an unlikely "thank you" for their effort providing health care for them.

One of the reasons that she wanted to work in Esmeralda, of all places, was that she did not subscribe to the racist stereotypes of her upbringing. She liked the idea of being out in a rural hospital providing health care for poor people with fewer opportunities and she liked the idea that racial barriers were not an issue when it came to health care. Even in Ecuador where the brown people did not have access to education, health care was free. It was basic health care but health care nevertheless. She wanted to be part of that and that is why she went to Esmeralda against the better judgment of her family. She was revolted by the thought that when the rule of laws when out the people from town had gone out of their way to find and rape the white nurses that were there to provide health care for them. The very idea made her sick. These men had proven right all the stereotypes against the black and brown she was trying to fight. It contradicted all her values and principles and she did not want to think about it. She did not want to try to explain it away with some sociological argument about structural violence, but she could not ignore how real and traumatic it had been. So she had kept it at arm's length and decided not to have any thoughts on the matter. That is why when she was coming to Esmeralda, she did not make plans of coming to the hospital but her feet had decided differently and had brought her there. Now what?

She walked up to the reception counter looking around and seeing how little it had changed since she last worked there. The tables were in order and things seem to be working well. To her left she saw a stretcher. The same one where Rebecca had been gang rapped and screamed from the top of her lungs asking for help. To the right was the place where Estella begged to her assaulters and back to the end where she had last seen Mónica in all four being raped by one and held by others that likely were taking turns on her. IN the back was the stretcher where she had fought the attackers until they over powered her. Her stomach tied on a knot and she had to sit in the waiting area to recover. A few minutes later her fears dissipated. The rural hospital was working just the same way that it had been when she was there in its good days and she felt better, almost at home.

She stood up and approached the reception desk not knowing what to say and upon lifting her eyes, they met with those of another woman with an expression of surprise and recognition on her face. She was a bit taller than her, with brown hair to the shoulders, tan skin from the coast, vivacious brown eyes and full lips.

"Daniela! It's you?" It was the exclamation of Mónica when she recognized her old friend from the hospital.

Both nurses came together held each other in a tight embrace reconciling and reconnecting all the time they had not seen each other.

"I did not know where you were. I did not know if you . . . I am so glad to see you doing well," said a Mónica teary eyed. "I saw you leave and I was afraid... I am so glad to see you here." She continued not daring to speak out her fear that Daniela might not have survived that day, even now that she was seeing her safe and sound. Both women cried on each other shoulder remembering silently the ordeal that they both had survived.

Daniela, herself had wondered in her lonely nights what had happened to her friends in the hospital. After the Zambo took her she had no idea of what had happened to them during the weeks of lawlessness that followed the social explosion. With any luck they had been taken by a single man to enslave them for sex like it had happened to her but seeing how things were she feared they might have been victims of far worse abuses than she had. Clearly, like her, Mónica had survived it. Daniela wondered how she had managed. Where had she hidden? Did she run into the forest like Daniela herself planned at some point? Or did she just survived being rapped over and over, by man after man, for days on end? She did not know and she did not want to ask. Whatever she had done, she had survived, like herself, she was standing there with that ordeal behind her.

"What does not kill you makes you stronger," Mónica said out loud as if having read her thoughts.

"Yes it does." Replied Daniela with a sigh.

They both had wished they died on their particular times. All the stronger it had made them. Nobody but themselves knew what they have gone through and nobody knew what it had meant, or how they had made it. They both were survivors and they forever shared that deeper level of sisterhoods.

Mónica moved to hostess mood showing Daniela what was new in the hospital and making small talk. She dropped nonchalantly how hard the work was, being so understaffed, in case that is why Daniela was there but not addressing the point head on.

"How long are you in town for" Mónica asked finally prompting her to speak.

"I don't know. I probably should be heading back soon." Answer Daniela somewhat distracted in her own thoughts. Mónica, being the frontal person she was addressed the issue head on

"Why don't you stick around we need more nurses". She offered.

"No, I have a job waiting for me in Quito," She answered and after a pause she said: "I have a baby." She added looking into Mónica's eyes in a tone of confession. "I need to go back to him".

Mónica was surprised to hear it. It did not escape to Mónica's attention that Daniela said nothing about a husband.

"Oh, congratulation how old is he." She inquired hugging her.

"He is 4 now." Daniela answered with her frank eyes looking straight into Mónica's given time for her to do the math.

Mónica made a small gasp and opened her eyes widely when she understood what Daniela was saying without words. She hugged her.

"Oh Daniela, I . . . oh my God! I . . ." Mónica was undecided if she should show pity, anger, or happiness to the news.

"I love him. He is the light of my life." Daniela came to her rescue. "I would not have it any other way."

Mónica's eyes welled up with tears and she exploded in relief laughter hugging her friend.

"Congratulations! I am so happy for you. Where is he? Why did you not bring him over? ".

"He is with my mom right now. But I could not bring him anyway. He had an accident and was in the ICU for a long time." Daniela explained but tranquilized Mónica's concerned look. "He is fine now but when he was sick I realized I had to come to find his father." Daniela paused briefly but looking at the inquiring look on Mónica's eyes she continued.

Sashawarmas,   by Jorge Bandido

"When he was so sick and I thought I was going to lose him. I did not know what I would do if I lost him. I felt . . . Well, I think he has the right to meet his father. And his father has the right to know he has a son. Now that my baby is safe I came to look for him to talk to him." Daniela explained dutifully justifying her trip to Esmeralda.

It took only a few seconds for Mónica's eyes to recuperate her vivacious spark, letting her mouth drop she told Daniela, wide-eyed, slapping her in the shoulder.

"Awk, you slut, you fell in love with that big Zambo!" Mónica said in mock accusation. Daniela looked down embarrassed and smiled in consent. It took Mónica all of 3 seconds to figure out what had taken Daniela years to understand.

The two nurses hugged each other and laughed like teenagers that just shared a big secret about boys.

"I don't know what I will do but I need to find him and tell him about our baby. He has the right to know." Insisted Daniela recovering the sober rational angle on the situation. But Mónica wouldn't have any of it.

"Yes, and while you are at it you can ask him if he cares about a quick fuck, won't you?"

Now it was time of Daniela to slap Mónica's shoulder.

"It is not like that! He is gone though. It does not really matter, I went to his place and the house is empty. The land lord told me he has not seen him since the day of the revolt." Daniela added.

As Mónica looked expectant of Daniela finishing what she was hesitant to say, Daniela continued.

"My only hope is to look in the port zone to see if I can find him there or if someone knows about him."

"Do you want to go to the port zone at night? Where all the horny sailors are looking for hookers or any place to put their dicks in?" Mónica inquired with some irony.

"I know it is stupid. It will never work." Daniela admitted reluctantly.

"You cannot go alone there, obviously but I have a friend that can come with us. He will be happy to help us." Offered Mónica.

"A friend?" Now it was Daniela's turn to be suspicious

"He is a friend," Mónica said defensively. He delivers supplies to the cafeteria. He is big a muscular and has been very helpful." Added Mónica, as Daniela was holding her side so they would not split of laughter, Mónica continued.

"He is a handy man that has helped me a lot in my house." Seeing that she was sinking deeper and deeper in her own hole, Mónica rushed to come clean.

"He is gay! I tried to get him in the sack one day that he came to help me install an AC unit in my room but he turned me down. Nobody knows he is gay but after turning me down he explained it to me so I would not feel rejected. Ever since, we have become good friends. Sometimes he invites me to places when he needs to pretend he is straight for social occasions and I help him with that. I am his 'beard'," she said doing quotation marks in the air. "He will be happy to escort us to the port zone." Mónica added while Daniela wiped her tears of her face.

"Why don't you come to my place for the afternoon and we can head to the port at night. Where are you staying anyway?" Mónica said trying to change the theme since Daniela looked she was going to pee on herself.

Both nurses composed themselves and by the end of the shift they were heading out when Daniela stop on her tracks just as she was leaving the rural hospital.

It all made sense all of a sudden. That is where she had seen her before. Daniela spotted an old Indian woman sitting in the waiting room of the hospital and she could tell exactly the other times she had seen her before. She was, to be sure, a regular to the waiting room in the hospital. She was not a patient, everybody had grown to accept her as an elderly, perhaps mentally disable, woman that sat there all the time for no apparent reasons. However, Daniela could remember exactly three other times where she had seen her. The first time the Zambo came to the hospital with the gash in his chest she was sitting there and as Daniela followed the Zambo with her eyes leaving the hospital torn between her woman's desire and her professional ethic and Quito upbringing the woman had pointed at him with her head as he walked out and told her "*Shashauarma*".

That is the first time she actually noticed her beyond her passive presence in the hospital. The second time was during the social explosion when the Zambo walked her out naked to his shack. She was sitting in the same place she was now, with the same attitude despite the mayhem. The third time had been a couple weeks ago when she had seen that woman in the hall of the

211

hospital in Quito saying a silent prayer outside the room where her baby was struggling for his life.

Daniela approached her and asked her.

"Ma'am, do I know you?"

The old lady simply looked at her passively neither nodding nor denying knowing her. Her eyes were gentle, almost a smile drawn in her mouth; but even that was hard to read. Daniela could not stand any longer the weird silence talking with a person who would not talk to her, yet did not refuse to.

"Where you in Quito at the ICU of the main hospital?" She asked point blank.

Seen her desperation the old Indian woman gave her a nod. A single moved of her head down and up. Breaking into tears Daniela inquired.

"Did you save my baby?" With the same gentle yet blank stare the woman shrugged her shoulders imperceptibly.

Daniela leaned over to make close eye contact with the indecipherable eyes of the old woman.

"Do you know where Jose Ignacio Guzman is." She asked hoping against hope that she would give her an answer.

She thought that her eyes had pointed to the side of the building where the forest began but she could not be sure. Her eyes were so sank in her sockets so deep that it was difficult to look into them. However, as hard as she tried to establish a connection with the mysterious woman, her eyes glazed over her as if not seeing her.

"Daniela, that woman always comes here and sits there. She is not well on the top. I don't think she can tell you anything." Added Mónica seeing that Daniela was losing it.

As the brief window of communication had passed, Daniela stood up thanked the woman as she left, but she was not sure why.

38. THE DOCTOR'S DATE

The Dr. woke up alone as many other days and readied herself to go to work. It had been very much the same since her husband left her. A dentist, he had taken off with his dental hygienist. He did not even have the merit of originality! That explained all the days "working late" that she used to complain about. It was rather typical. A man on his fifties leaves wife for a woman on her twenties. Her mother had warned her of that: "*Now that you are 40 you need to work extra hard so your husband does not change you for 2 of 20*".

A professional, with a lot more invested on her life than just her looks, she never thought that could happen to her. "*There are men who don't appreciate the true worth of women, but my husband was not one of them.*" She thought. She learned bitterly how wrong she was! As the time passed she blamed herself more and more. All the time she spent at work, teaching classes at the university, seeing patients in her practice. She could have used that time to spend with her husband, and used their money to travel and enjoy each other's company. But she had invested all that time in her career. As a result, she had a great career but no husband. Often she went back and forth to what she should have done. Would he not have left her if she had not been so involved with her career? What if she had given up her career to make her husband happy and he still left her as she got older? There were plenty of stories of that sort.

It did anger her too that nobody thought anything of her husband in his 50s taking off with a girl in her 20s but if she ever took a man younger than her, say mid 30s, there would be all kind of criticism about her dating a younger man. Why was society so unfair when it came to women? She never felt for the typical woman stereotype in Latin America where women stays at home and depends on their husband. Instead she was smart, empowered woman with everything going for her. But it did not matter how liberated she was, dating a younger man was out of the question. It would be so frown upon, and being a professor at the university surrounded by younger men, there was no telling where that could go.

To make matters worse, she was horny as hell. There was nothing she wanted more than to be bent over and banged like a screen door in a hurricane. Even before her husband left, she did not have much of a sex life. Her husband was having plenty of sex on his own, anyway. She would masturbate when she was home alone. Even when they were together their sex was mild at best. She never had a relationship of wild sex, even when she was young, she had always been very thoughtful about her partners. Since he left she had been hornier and hornier and she did not seem to get a hold on her urges. Where was she supposed to find an older man that was available and interested on a woman like her? She was still beautiful, she thought. She was in good shape, very fit and healthy but still, at 42 any bimbo 20 years younger would give her a thought competition. Her only chance was to have a man that valued her brains, her personality, who she was beyond the flesh. The problem was that she was not itching for a thoughtful loving partner. She was actually aching for a good fuck, a horny lover that wanted her flesh feverishly and with urgency. It was a lost case. She would never get it.

Arriving to her practice she felt a pit in her stomach when she saw the first patient waiting for her. It was a man, in his low 20s, strong and muscular, coppery skin, curly dark hair to his shoulders, eagle like nose, and thick, kissable sensual lips. He looked perturbed, wild eyed. Many of her patients were, she was a neurologist and often people that came had quite a range of neurological issues. She remembered him from the first time he came. He ended up dating her student resident at the time. He had a lesion in his brain from a childhood trauma. It did not seem to produce much of the expected symptoms beyond a digestive syndrome that was more of a low intensity seizure rather than a digestive problem. She greeted him and started asking the regular questions finding out about his problem. He seemed to have had some sort of hallucination, perhaps associated with his neurological condition. She was interested in him because he was quite an interesting case study she was hoping to publish for how unique an illustrative his condition was.

During the examination, the Dr. could not help but appreciating his muscular build, thick torso and neck. His face was so beautiful and so masculine. His jaw lined was carved with a chisel in sharp angles. His skin was smooth and dark and unnaturally warm. His scent was masculine and overpowering. It gave her butterflies in her stomach to walk around him and to feel his skin with her hands. She was finding it difficult to concentrate but when he spoke to her with a voice deep like a foghorn, she felt her knees weakening. Although she was a neurologist and never had much of a need of a close physical examination, beyond MRIs and equipment-based tests this time she told him to take of his shirt to do a full physical examination. She was always so formal and so "by the book" but this time she wanted to indulge herself a little bit. She gasped when he pulled out his shirt and she could appreciate his fully develop muscular chest and ripped abs. She asked him to lay down and placed her hands on his abdomen. His skin was so warm, but she knew that he did not have a fever. It was just his organic heat radiating from him. She used her stethoscope on his chest but she could not help but placing both her hands on his skin, and sliding them over his chest and abdomen feeling appreciatively his physique. She felt her pussy make a summersault and she knew she had to stop. She realized she was fondling her patient far more than she needed but she did not care. She wanted to indulge herself a little more

She fantasized what it would be like to have an affair with him. She was so horny, she was ready to fuck the first man she found. This one was about perfect for what she wanted. Her ex-husband was a skinny nerd, with whom she never had much passion anyway. In her insistence to seek value beyond the flesh she had denied herself the possibility to consider a partner that was a jock, one like this, pure muscles and pure meat. But now she was a divorcee, and free. In the presence of such human specimen she entertained the idea of having sex with someone quite the opposite to her husband. A beef cake like her patient was about right. She was longing to feel his body and to look at him naked. She entertained the idea of asking him to take his pants off for a complete physical but she could not find an excuse to make it justify such request. After all she was a neurologist. The torso examination was already a stretch.

After the first part of the interview, his mood calmed down from the hallucination he had and started making more sense. In a normal situation she would have told him to put his shirt back on for the conversation but she was enjoying too much the sight of his naked torso. She even felt her mouth water a little when he moved his arms making his muscle bulge even without doing a forceful contraction.

"I had a strange dream that I was assaulting a woman in a garden in the middle of the night. IT was very, very vivid and this morning I woke up in the very place that my dream was. Is it possible that I was doing tings without my own consciousness? Other times I have seen myself from the outside doing bad things." The patient explained.

The Dr. heard him and could not help fantasize of being that woman and being taken by him. She herself was feeling like assaulting him. Yet, it was all in her deep desire. She was a professional that will not act upon her urges. Not with a patient. She explained to him how visions and feelings during neurological episodes were very vivid and felt very real but they were not more real than any other dream or fantasy. Often neurological patients experience phantom smells of things that are not present. His eyes opened widely when she mentioned it.

"Have you smelled things that were not there?" She asked.

The patience thought of it. "Sometimes I had felt weird smells that do not belong to the situation, but not in my dream last night." He replied.

Sashawarmas,   by Jorge Bandido

Then she noticed that his eyes were looking at her body. She could see his eyes searching for her forms under her medical gown, as if he just had discovered that she was a woman and was exploring her. He switched to something she could have sworn was more of a flirtatious conversation with her. Would it be possible? Was he really flirting with her? Her pussy made another somersault when he flashed his delightful smile at her after saying something that sounded like line about her but line or not, it made her feel good. She succeeded at pretended to ignore his comment and in keeping her mouth straight and not revealing the smile that his flirting had put in her heart.

There was no way she would act upon the attractions she was feeling. For starters he was 20 years younger than her, he was likely a student at the university, it did not matter if he was not her student. Not to mention that it would be most unethical to sleep with her patient, even if she could put the stigma of the society aside about being a cougar. Reading her notes she recalled that his brain lesion was such that stimulated his libido, and the reward center of the brain. Patient with this lesion typically show extreme sexual behavior, and lack of restraint. That was pretty much what her horny self was asking for: *"a strong hunk of a man that would take her without restraint!"* But, how unethical would it be for her to indulge in her sexual attraction with a patient knowingly that the patient very disease made him more vulnerable for any sexual advance. The more she thought of it the more she convinced herself that it was out of the question, but the more her pussy ached to make and advance and take him for herself. It was all the more difficult because he continued to flirt with her flashing his gorgeous smile and making her stomach vibrate with his deep voice. She could not stop looking at his muscles and felt herself hot and aroused as she struggled with her urges.

The Dr. stepped away from the examination table to take a break for herself fearing she was not going to be able to resist her yearnings any longer if she continued under the influence of his scent and his presence. She approached her desk and pretended to read some notes but her mind was taken over by lust and she could not concentrate. It did not work. She tried to write something but she could not get her pussy to stop twisting and turning. Then she took a deep breath feeling something and got a lungful of his scent again. She felt his presence right behind her but she did not dare to turn around to see if it was true. The hairs in the back of her neck stood on end and her knees buckled into weakness just instants before she felt it. His arms wrapped around her chest and his mouth dove at the lobe of her ear deep and warm. One of his hands dove for her crotch while the other one grabbed her breast pressing her hungrily against his chest. His mouth licked her neck with the same lust she was feeling for him.

216

Sashawarmas,   by Jorge Bandido

"Did I give him the 'come on'? Did I hinted him to proceed?" She thought afraid
that she might have provoked his actions. He had read her thoughts to the
letter and was doing precisely what she wanted him to do. Her patient lifted
her like a feather and turned her around facing him. Instinctively her legs
opened wrapping around his waist as he pressed her against the nearest wall.
Her skirt was modest but allowed for easy access to her sex. He opened her
shirt pulling it apart and sending all the bottoms flying in all directions. Her
bra snapped like a twig on his fingers and her breast were out full and eager.
She felt his warm mouth taking her breast in and sucking it intensely. .

She never knew when he took his member out, but she felt it pressing on
her underwear warm and hungry. Likely he took it out before he approached
her. He moved her underwear to one side and cleared the path for
penetration. The Dr. bit her lips in the inside to prevent herself to make any
noise that could attract attention from outside but also to prevent herself from
doing any protestation or objection to the course of action her patient was
taken. The last thing she wanted was to say something that would make her
patient stop. There was nothing she could do about the deep felt grunt that
came out of her throat as he impaled her with his thick member. She bit his
thick lips and groaned with pleasure, her mouth watering and overflowing
with lust as she kissed and licked the virile face of her lover.

*"Wait! What are you doing? You are fucking your patient! His disease gives him
lack of sexual restraint. You are taking advantage of the disease of a sick man."* The
Dr. scolded herself. But she realized that there was nothing she was doing. In
fact, there was not much she could do. He had taken her with his strong
arms, lifted her off the ground and was pinning her against a wall, screwing
her without any consultation. The only thing she could have done was to
voice disagreement, or ask for help. But there was no way she was going to do
any of that. She was longing for a good fuck for months, and she was finally
getting a pretty good one.

In fact, being an empowered woman that always takes control of things,
being taken hard in an animalistic fuck like he was doing was an entirely new
experience for her. She was always in control and she always had very slow,
soft sex. The notion of being taken as roughly as he was taken her was new
and completely arousing. She grabbed his curls with both fist and kissed his
lips and face hungrily. She took a deep breath to feel up her lungs with his
scent and got a subtle smell of blood. Her medical training kicked in and she
panic fearing she might have drawn blood biting his lips. She paused and
lifted his lips trying to assess the source of the blood. There was no evidence
of injury. But the there was a thin red line at the base of his lower teeth, just
by the gums. It seemed old blood, not something new. However, she had to

give up in her examination as he continued to pound her against the wall. She left herself be pounded into a convulsive orgasm. When her lover put her down she reached for her desk and grabbing a pen and said somewhat flustered.

"I need to up your medication!"

39. ROLE REVERSAL

More than a week went by before Mercedes could sit down after the spanking bout José Ignacio gave her. A few weeks later, the oil operation seemed to have done some bad things. A large section of the forest was shot down from researchers visit and rumor that a boat containing many barrels of chemicals sank and the content was spilled in the pristine waters. It was uncertain if it had been some of the activities in the Peruvian side or something that happened directly in Yasuni. The Oil company managed to keep secrecy and all that people could know were rumors. The park management had closed up large sections and it was not sure it is was to protect the scientist from exposure to the chemicals or to prevent them to see the damage the oil company was doing to the last few relics of pristine rainforest left on earth. Because she could not go to the field Mercedes came to Quito for a surprise visit to her lover.

José Ignacio himself, had done a lot of thinking about his relationship with Mercedes and his life in general. Something felt wrong with him and he attributed it to the turns his life has taken. He was getting used to the idea of having Mercedes as a permanent partner, fear of his passion for her or not. He was a bit worried of how much he enjoyed spanking Mercedes and feared that there was something in him intrinsically perverse that got stimulated with that kind of behavior. On top of this, he was feeling strong stress for the courses at the university. TO add to it, the situation in the Amazon, with the oil company intruding in native land really bothered him. He felt it was an offense to the environment that he loved but there something intimate personal on this that affected him. He had not been himself in the last few weeks. With all those things compounded on him, he was wondering even who he was.

When Mercedes came to the university she found José Ignacio on a bench with Valentina and Beatriz at each side of him. Beatriz, a blondish girl, with wide hips and a pretty face was on his right holding his forearm with one hand and the other one on his shoulder. Valentina was looking admiringly at his pectoral muscles and bulging biceps. Mercedes could tell that Beatriz had slept with him already for her demeanor and familiarity she leaned next to him. It was clear that she felt very comfortable with his body. She could also tell that Valentina had not for the way of immense desire and anticipation she looked at him. Mercedes was very familiar with the feeling. José Ignacio seemed to produce that in just about every woman. It was a special talent of his. She would have burst with jealousy in other situation but she knew that none of these were rivals for her; not really, not with her around. He might sleep with them but they will scatter around like roaches when you turn on the light, the minute she showed up. Mercedes stopped some ten feet from them and interrupted the story he was telling to the swooning women.

"Hey, Don Juan! Are you going to say hello to your woman or are you going to flirt with the girls all day long?"

José Ignacio was surprised to find Mercedes in Quito and took him a second to take her in. She was wearing a flowering flowing skirt many inches over her knees showing her magnificent and tanned thighs. She wore roman style sandals that strapped around her ankles all the way to her ripped calves. Her shirt was tight up above her belly button with just one button well below the line of her nipples. There was no hint of a bra and the shirt was cut so low that watching from the right angle one could take a look at their defiant nipples. In a regular day this outfit would have earned her a scolding from José Ignacio but she has caught him with two girls feeling him and not expecting her, he reacted to the pleasure that her sight produced him.

"Oh wow, what log did you fall from?" He asked.

"I just dropped from the jungle to have you dear." Mercedes said walking slowly up to him swinging her hips defiantly side to side.

Ignoring his admirers, she straddled him and kissed him full on the mouth. Instinctively he reached for her thigh under her skirt all the way to her behind. She grabbed his other hand and placed it firmly on her breast, taking a deep breath of pleasure when he squeezed it. She broke the kiss turned her face to the heavens with her eyes closed feeling the pleasure of his hands on her body and drove his mouth to her other breast. She felt a jolt of current to feel his warm mouth taking in her breast above her shirt as it was. She grabbed the hand from her breast and brought it to her mouth. With her eyes still closed, she pulled out his ring finger and stuck it in her mouth driving it in slowly through her generous African lips all the way down and moved it in and out as if it was a dick she was sucking. By the time they came back to the world Valentina and Beatriz were far gone seeing Mercedes display of territory.

It was no more and no less than the Mercedes equivalent of the claim that José Ignacio had done foundling her in the cafeteria when she was talking with David in the Yasuni station. It was just less violent but containing the same message: "this is mine and I can take it at will". If José Ignacio was going to spank her and take possession of her as property, it was only right that she did the same thing. Mercedes got up and stood up in front of him pulling him by his wrist.

Sashawarmas,   by Jorge Bandido

"Come on. Let's not waste time," she said and dragged him out of the plaza.

They went to a hotel where they could regal themselves to their passion. After the first frantic love making that normally was too in a rush and too desperate for their mutual hunger for each other, they had a chance to frolic on bed celebrating their love. Remembering something, Mercedes straddled him and grabbed fistfuls of his hair next to his ears and told him looking him straight in the eyes:

"You slept with the little slut didn't you?" Surprised by the unexpected question he played coy.

"What you mean my love?"

"Ah, don't pretend you don't know. You slept with that whore of Beatriz. They were both drooling over you. Beatriz was leaning by your side. I can tell when I woman had tasted you. They become zombies that can only think of fucking you. You fucked her didn't you?" Mercedes asked him still pulling on his hair with both hands.

Mercedes anger always turned him on and reminiscing on when he had Beatriz he started getting aroused again. He lifted her slightly and slid his cock inside her before he answered.

"I was horny my love, and you were not around. She has a nice tight ass". Mercedes jerked in anger pulling his hair harder and biting his chin.

"Aaarghh. why do you do that? You are such a slut. You are a whore, a whore. The minute I turn around you stick your dick in the first slut that you have nearby. Do you think I like that? You hit me so hard last time. Don't you think I deserve a little loyalty?" She told him impaling herself repeatedly with his member pulling on his curls.

"I don't want to share you with anybody. You are mine. As much as I am yours and you don't let any man come near me, I want the same thing with you. No woman can come near you. Sometimes I wish I were a man to beat the crap out of you for being such a slut. How would you like that?" She asked increasing the strength in which her hips met him and taking his member deeper inside her.

"But you are my love and you know it." He replied somewhat amused.

Mercedes collapsed over his chest anger relinquishing to pleasure. She let go of his hair and ran her palms over his solid chest and shoulders.

"I can't beat you up but I will beat the crap of any woman I see near you." She conceded inhaling his musky scent deep in her lungs and biting his chest.

221

Sashawarmas,   by Jorge Bandido

She panted still driving his member in full in and out of her. She licked his sweaty skin and felt she belonged to him more than ever.

"I just want to be yours and you to be mind. If I had you with me all the time, none of this will happen. Let's move in together. That way I can satisfy your sex all that time." She asked, probably by the hundredth time.

"Yes, my love whatever you want", said José Ignacio, who was panting heavily as she drove him to climax.

It was one of the many times she got a positive answer in those circumstances. She knew that it will not necessarily be honored after he came, but in that time it felt good to have him give in to her. At least, when they were having sex she called all the shots. He squeezed her tight as he was coming and she abandoned herself to being his.

After they recovered from love making Mercedes continued interrogating him. She knew he had slept with other women, and she hated the answers she knew she was going to get but she could not help inflicting herself that level of pain.

"Who else did you sleep with? The other girl was dying to have you. You did not do her did you"? She asked unable to help herself.

"Nope, not Valentina, I would rather had done Beatriz again rather than her". He replied.

"I will put a chastity bell on you before I leave and when my contract is over, I will come back and we will move in together and you will never sleep with anybody else." She ordered pulling on his curls again and talking very close to his face, intoxicating herself with his aphrodisiac scent. Since it turned him on, to see her anger, he told her.

"Well you are not going to be very happy to hear who else I slept with."

"Who?" Mercedes asked preparing to snap.

"Gabriela." He answered wrapping her with both arms and preventing her from punching or being able to hit him.

"NOT HER". Mercedes roared with anger "She is the one woman I will not let you have anything with. Did you really see her? Mercedes asked hoping it was just him trying to get her angry.

"Yes, I ran into her when I was coming out of the hospital. She greeted me smiling and asked me if I wanted to have coffee. Before I knew it we were banging like rabbits. She changed a lot since the last time I saw her. No need of begging, no need of convincing, no deep resistance to sex from the former

222

days. She said nothing about God, Catholicism, or the sin of fornication. We just fucked all night, good and long. She is just as beautiful as she was but now, she really likes sex. I invited her to meet again two days later and we also went at it all night long, not even dinner. She went from not wanting anything to do with sex to just wanting sex." His arousal mounting remembering sex with Gabriela and enjoying Mercedes mounting anger.

"I don't want you with her". Mercedes commanded hammering every word.

"She lets me do anything to her I want. She takes in the rear, no problem." He explained.

"No, pleaded Mercedes, I don't want to have to deal with her again. Please tell me you are just making me angry! Mercedes pleaded at the border of tears, anger surrendering to fear.

Because it turned him on so much to talk to Mercedes about other women, and since Gabriela was such weak point for Mercedes, José Ignacio doubled down

"Also she can really suck a cock. She looked unbelievable gorgeous smoking my cigar with her princess's little mouth. She also had a special talent for it. She doesn't have a gag reflex, she can take it all in her mouth, deep into her throat, only stopping when her nose touches my pubis. I try to deny her my come to make it last longer but she is so good at it that she always made me come so hard.   Also, she swallows it as if it is a delicious cream, and licks it clean thoroughly when I am done. On time I pull out just before coming to splash her princess's face while she tried with her close eyes and open mouth to capture as much as she can. She was so beautiful giggling with her mouth sprinkled with semen all over!"

Mercedes was destroyed. She dropped to his side sobbing defeated. Gabriela personified the type of woman she always was jealous of, with a pretty face, small frame, and perfect Barbie proportions. Since she was little she was jealous of this kind of girls and it was only when she developed her sexual forms that she felt she could compete with them. The first time he dated Gabriela she took comfort in the fact that Gabriela did not give him any sex, so she had the sex side way open for her and she knew that is what José Ignacio cared the most about. If Gabriela was going to give him also the sex, there was nowhere for her to compete.

"How long have you been seen her? It has not been that long since you were with me. You can do me however you want. I will let you do me in my rear, I will suck it whenever you want. I will do everything you want me to do.

223

Just dump her. Break it up with her. I don't mind you sleeping with other women, but not her." Mercedes begged.

José Ignacio got again very aroused to see Mercedes total surrender and wanted to test it.

"Turn around" He ordered her.

Mercedes knew she had to make good on her promise and acquiesced laying down on her belly and presenting her behind for him to take. Since his member was already lubricated from the former love making he put it on her rear. Mercedes let out a long breath to relax herself at the time that he shoved it up her rear end.

"Uugggh" grunted Mercedes, biting the pillow her fist crisped on the linen paying the price for her submission.

José Ignacio showered her with love and kisses in her neck and upper back. Nothing turned him on more than her absolute surrender to his pleasure. Accepting him in her rear without protestation was a new event in her relationship and aroused him to the extreme. It did not take long before he was coming inside her impaling her rear. In the frenzy of the love making he promised her that she was the only one and promised to abide by her request that he dumped Gabriela but Mercedes knew it was during sex promise, which he often reneged of. He came crushing her hips, as he often did and they both fell asleep depleted of love making

****

When they woke up in the morning Mercedes tried to get a straight answer about the future of his relationship with Gabriela. He was evasive and assured her that she was the one he preferred.

"I will take her when you are not here but you are now my official girlfriend. She is the mistress now, and you are my girl on the eyes of everybody" He assured her.

Mercedes was angry at this prospect but it did occur to her that this was an improvement over the former deal. If she had José Ignacio for dinners and movies, "the prissy little girl" did not stand a chance against her in bed, even if that meant that she had to work harder in pleasing him in the things she did not like. She knew that José Ignacio was a "butt person". In that she had a big advantage over Gabriela. When it came to derriere, José Ignacio would clearly prefer hers, even if she was not crazy about anal sex. With the blow job part, she had to do some work. She did not know about that talent that

Gabriela had to take it all in. She could also see how he liked so much her beautiful face sucking his member. She herself felt that Gabriela's face was astonishingly beautiful. She was not sure how she could compete with that but she felt her sexual creativity was good enough that she could at least draw a tie, if she dedicated herself to give him oral sex as he wanted.

Mercedes was so upset about the news of Gabriela coming back to the scene that she missed a big flag with the story; but once she got to terms with the new challenge and how she was going to face it, it came to her mind.

"Wait, you met Gabriela because you went to the hospital? Why were you at the hospital?" She asked knowing that her lover was the portrait of health and he never went to Drs. If he could help it.

"Well, I had another episode, I think. So I went to see that Dr. that saw me before" José Ignacio explained.

But Mercedes new him well. He had had other episodes since. To have gone to the Dr. this time, there had to be something else.

"Do you "think" you had an episode?" She inquired now in full inquisition mode.

"I don't know for sure. I woke up one day with all the symptoms of having had an episode, the pain in the trunk, some dizziness, generalized stiffness in my stomach. I had a dream, I think, about being in a garden in the university assaulting a woman from behind. This was an stranger that I have never seen before. But when I woke up I found myself in the very garden where I had the dream in the university. I don't recall going there at all. It was a very vivid dream, more like a hallucination. Because my symptoms where the same than the episode I went to the Dr. to seek her advice" José Ignacio replied.

"You assaulted a . . . What? So, . . . so was it a dream or not? Mercedes asked perturbed.

"The Dr. said it must have been a dream. She thinks that I might gone in a semiconscious state that is why I got to the university. Not fully awake, not fully conscious. So, I might have incorporated the places I saw before falling asleep into my dream and built it into my dream. It was really unusual. Normally I have conscience through my episodes, and remember everything but this time it must have been different. The Dr. had told me that my condition could continue the same or change for no particular reason. She placed me in a stronger treatment and she says it should be ok now." José Ignacio explained.

Sashawarmas,   by Jorge Bandido

Concern over the health of her lover overrode the jealousy with Gabriela and Mercedes cuddled inside his chest.

"I don't want anything to happen to you," she said, kissing his chest and feeling his warm arms around her.

They spend more than a week together before Mercedes had to return to the field. There were plenty of times to rehash the discussion about Gabriela. Mercedes was unhappy about Gabriela's return to the scene but she could see that she was now the official girlfriend. Gabriela was "the other" woman. Gabriela called several times trying to schedule a date but he turned her down because Mercedes was in town. She could see there had been an improvement from the former situation and was decided to take advantage of it as much as possible.

Suddenly the roles had switched. Now Mercedes was his official girlfriend while Gabriela was his mistress of the shadows with the advantage that Mercedes knew about Gabriela so he was not risking surprises. Gabriela drew comfort from the fact that she was getting even with Mercedes and Mercedes was happy that she was the one who he took out for dinner. Both devoted themselves to please him in bed as much as he wanted because there is where the competition was. Because he was so hooked with Mercedes body, they still spent a lot of time having sex. Even though Mercedes was the official, they spent about the same time with José Ignacio. He would take a week a month to be with Mercedes and she would come to Quito for another week, to be with him. The other two were Gabriela's. Her new devotion to sex was moving for José Ignacio and all the more he appreciated her company. She was still a devoted catholic but now she had sacrificed her soul so he could have her body.

It was different because now Gabriela was not the hope of a beautiful fulfilling relationship. She had switched from not wanting anything to do with sex, to having enough with just sex. She no longer inspired him the illusion of love and bliss that she once gave him. Although both relationships were very sexual there were very different in their essence. With Gabriela he had an extremely beautiful woman to make love to. He loved to taste her and adore her delicate forms. After love making her face was often all slobbered by his licking her greedily. But he had to make love to her tenderly not to hurt her because she was so fragile.

On the other hand Mercedes gave him a different kind of sex. She was a strong muscular woman with whom he could have hard rough-and-tumble sex. Her pussy was deep and broad. He could plunge in with all his gusto and she was always wet, wide and hot to receive him. Of course he loved the

226

nymphomaniac expression of ultimate pleasure when she had his member inside her. He adored her smell of pineapple and the amber glow of her skin in the moment of orgasms so he always worked with her to get her there. Their relationship was somewhat bipolar going from perfect bliss in bed to moments of where power and domination ruled the day. It was very different, no better or worse. Gabriela showed a 100% submissive to his desires of her body. With Mercedes, he enjoyed a good fight.

With these two women he had little time to dedicate to school. He was between the beautiful princess of an enchanted castle and the intense passion of a Brazilian whore. He was obsesses with the sex of both of them. His life was turn into a constant search to find more ways to make love to them, long forgotten where the dreams with Marlene or Elena.

40. INSIDE HER SKIN

She got the call shortly after noon. Deep inside her she had been waiting for that call since their the last time she saw him. When her secretary told her about the call, she felt butterflies in her stomach and picked up the phone feeling like a little school girl whose boyfriends finally called. She felt her heart fill up with joy when she heard his deep voice and she was even happier to hear his request.

"I want to see you now." He told her.

There was sense of eagerness in his voice and her loins ached reminiscing of him. She knew she wanted to *have her*, not just see her. She immediately cancelled all patients of the afternoon and the classes she was scheduled for; and told her secretary to tell anyone who called that she was not feeling well and had gone home.

She walked up to her car with her heart pounding. Her lover had told her to meet him up there. As she approached her car his big arms hugged her from behind. One of her hands sought out her breast while the other dove down straight for her pussy. She covered herself protectively.

"Not here, not here. We are on campus." He scolded him breaking free. "Get in the car, we are going to my place." She ordered him.

Driving to her house she tried to make some small talk but she was so horny that it was hard to concentrate even on driving. She had relived countless times the time he took her in her practice and had not stopped waiting for the moment to have him again. She was fantasizing about taking him to the point that she was close to get into an accident three times in the way to her house. After a lifelong of being responsible, professional and thoughtful, she was now doing something completely crazy and out of character. Having an affair, with a younger man, a hunk of meat as anyone would put it, was as far from her character as she could imagine. Yet, here she was doing just that.

He did not help her driving. At first, he keep insisting in putting his hand in her crotch which got in her way of concentrating in her driving. "Keep your hands to yourself". She scolded after a near collision for her being distracted. IT did not work so well because he followed her order to the word. He sat sidewise in the shotgun sit and open his trousers. His impressive cock stood out as he stroked it gently up and down looking at her.

The Dr. could hardly concentrate in driving taking sidewise glances at her lover masturbating looking at her. She felt her moth water and wanted nothing more than to reach and grab it. When she stopped in a light she grabbed it and felt her pussy twist when she felt its hard caliper and how hot it was. She stroke slowly, like he was doing it but squeezing it a lot more. A loud hunk from the car behind brought her back to reality.

"Please put it away. I promise you will have all the fun you want when we get home." She begged.

She opened the gate of her front yard to park the car. In a hurry she opened front of her house she felt like a teenage girl doing something naughty, like cutting school to meet with a boy. That was kind of what she did, except that she was the professor and she had cancelled both classes and patients in her urge to get laid. "*Wait!*" A *teenager? My daughter will be back from school shortly!*" She thought panicking.

She had been so horny and focused about having a good time that she completely forgot that her teenage daughter would be at home after school already. It was too late to pull back. She thought of going to a hotel instead but Brenda had already seeing her and her boyfriend entering the house. She walked in and tried to think of something, a good explanation of who her lover was that her daughter could buy. She could not say he was a colleague; the age difference was way too big.   It would not have been believable. She thought of saying he was a handyman to help in the garden, but she felt bad saying that. She really liked him and it was low playing on his dark skin to present him as hired labor. Had she known he was a botanist, she would not have felt so bad about it, but all she knew about him was his profile as a patient and his lust as a lover. Yet, she could not say he was her lover. Finally she thought of something half believable. She was going to introduce him as an architecture student who wanted to see the construction of their house. It was as bad a lie as anyone could think but she could not come up with anything better.

However, the Dr. never had to tell the lie. When she tried to explain who her lover was she saw Brenda's jaw drop opened looking at his body and physique. The Dr. looked at him and saw her boyfriend looking at her daughter with the most vulgar expression of lust drawn on his face. Brenda was wearing a tight pink short and tank-tops that stopped just below her breast hanging loosely exposing her flat stomach. She was an early bloomer with well-developed curves, and well-endowed for her age. Her nipples were raised hard in admiration seeing her lover.

It took the Dr. a second to realize what was happening. Her daughter was spellbound admiring the body of the Dr.'s lover and looking at him with the ultimate expression of admiration and awe. Like someone who sees a divine apparition. He, on the other hand, had an expression of predatory lust on his eyes, like a jaguar about to pounce on a helpless Paca. She felt a clash of emotions. He was her lover, she wanted all his lust directed towards her, not any other woman. She felt a rush of jealousy towards the slutty teenager for drawing the attention of her boyfriend. Why she had to wear that immoral outfit when she was at home? Her breasts were large enough that she should wear a bra, even if she was not that old. At the same time her protective mother feelings smothered her. She could not let an adult man anywhere near her teenage daughter. She did realize that the difference in age between her and her lover was far greater than between her lover and her daughter, but still, her daughter was underaged. She could not accept it.

She knew that men with his brain injury often end up as committing sexual assaults, and rapes. Furthermore, she knew about his uncontainable passion. When he took her in her practice, his advance was all but unstoppable. She had wanted him badly and did not resist his charge but had she not wanted him to make love to her, she would not have been able to resist his physical strength in any way or form. There was no way Brenda could resist it. *What have I done? I brought a potential rapist to my house, to my teenage daughter!*" She thought. She had been so horny for him that did not think of anything else. She did not think that her daughter was back from school, and she did not think of his lover as a potential sexual deviant, even if she knew all about his condition.

But this was only the beginning of her problems. She tried to get in the way of the magic ropes holding Brenda to the gaze of the man but her feet did not move. Furthermore, she saw his eyes scrutinizing Brenda's body, exploring the bulge of her daughter's breast and creeping down towards her crotch. That she saw with her eyes but to her surprise she noticed that she could feel on her body a subtle prickle of her skin in the parts where his eyes were exploring her daughter's body. She felt her nipples raise when he looked at her daughter's breast and felt the same sensation traveling towards her pussy as his eyes explored her daughter's exposed navel in his way to her crotch. The Dr. felt her pussy twist and turned and wondered if her daughter's pussy was doing the same as hers. The Dr. tried to move towards them to get in the way but her feet did not move, instead she was shaken with a gasp as her body reacted to the soft pressure of his eyes on Brenda's body.

The Dr. felt to the ground as she was overcome with a more intense wave of lust, and terror, as she saw her daughter slowly inch her steps towards the man. Brenda's eyes moved from his sharp jaw line to his thick neck and chest and the Dr. felt her own mouth filling up with saliva. She crawled a few more steps but was again overcome with such a powerful wave of lust that she had to stop in the ground reaching for her crotch, to appease its restlessness.

What was happening to her? Her scientific mind tried to find an explanation in the middle of her colliding emotions of jealousy, protectiveness, and lust. Why could she not move? Why was she feeling prickles in the parts of Brenda's body where he was looking at? And why was she feeling such uncontrollable lust? She felt anxious, rather, curious as if about to discover something she was longing to know for a long time. Only a few steps separated her beloved daughter from the sexual deviant in front of her. The same distance that separated her lover from that teenager slut who was so hot for him. She saw Brenda put her hands on his chest and take in a deep breath. To her surprise, the Dr. felt warmth on her palms and felt her lungs filling up with his scent.

"Wait! Am I feeling her emotions? Am I feeling what she feels? How is that possible?" She thought. She closed her eyes and saw him right in front of her. She could see his lusty eyes looking at her but instead of making her worry for the sexual predator about to have his way with her daughter, his eyes made her feel warm, wanted, special. She felt excited, adventurous; ready to discover who she was sexually. He brought her closer to him and she looked up to his spellbinding gaze. He lifted her chin and placed his large and warm lips on hers. The Dr. discovered the most special feeling in her entire life. There was nothing else in the world she wanted better than to be his. His tongue found her way in her virgin mouth and her whole body exploded with happiness. Her nipples prickle with anticipation and her pussy was doing summersaults. Her arms reached around him pressing herself against his chest. His smell was so perfect, his arms so strong, she was the happiest girl in the world. Her lover lifted her and she wrapped her legs around him. He pulled up her t-shirt and took in her breast in his mouth like he had done in her practice the first time. His mouth felt warm and special and she felt her nipples aching with a new feeling of pleasure she had never experienced.

The Dr. forced herself to open her eyes and saw from the floor, not three feet from them, her lover holding her daughter up against him sucking feverishly on her left breast. She had her legs wrapped around him, grasping with both hands his thick curls, her back arched backwards, and her face to the heavens with the outermost expression of pleasure in her face. She felt again the conflict of emotions. She felt happy for her daughter discovering so much pleasure, she felt angry that the slut was giving herself to her lover. She felt protective to see the sexual predator taking her daughter, and she felt confused at all the different emotions she was feeling. She tried to say something and drag herself to them but another guttural grunt came out of her throat and she collapse in the floor aroused close to climaxing.

The Dr. could not understand what was happening or how, but she was experiencing the same feeling that her daughter was having. She was terrified of the fact that her daughter was feeling so much lust at her young age. She herself had problems controlling her lust after she had a life of learning about her sex and her body. What would result of her young daughter experiencing the same feelings of lust and desire so intense, so overwhelming? No girl her age should be exposed to these feelings. How could she helped her cope with this experience after it was over? She had done a lot of work to help women deal with the experience after being raped and how to overcome it for the future sex life of the victim. But this was the exact opposite. She was exposed, too early in her life, to such intense experience of lust, how can she transition after this event to a normal life? Was her daughter bound to become a nymphomaniac seeking this intensity of pleasure from now on?

The man walked her to the coach and sat on it with her daughter straddled over him. He pulled out her short and the Dr. saw her daughter cooperate with this maneuver, removing the last piece of clothing protecting her from the man. The next logical step was for him to pull out his member to penetrate her. She could not stop thinking on his member. She had felt it. She knew how hard and how thick it was. She panicked dreading he would pull his member out to consummate the sex act. Then she saw with terror that her daughter reached for his pants. Unbuckled the belt and pants, unzip his zipper pulling down the edge of his underwear, and letting his member come out erect and ready. She felt her mouth overflow with saliva and she no longer knew what was her own lust of that of her daughter's overwhelming her senses.

She had to do something quickly to prevent him from making love to her daughter. She did not know why but if she was feeling what her daughter was feeling, could she move her daughter's body? She realized that when she thought of his cock her daughter reached for it. She closed her eyes thought hard of pushing him away and telling him to stop and to say "no". She was hoping that if she could have her daughter say no, he would stop.

But it did not work. Brenda's arms reach up to his chest as if about to push him away but instead of pushing her nails sank on his chest, her elbows bent at the time she let go a guttural sound, some sort of protestation, as her mouth reached for his chest and bit it.

Her efforts to control Brenda's body had merged with Brenda's own desire and produced a conflicted response. She tried one more time but the results were the same. The Dr. realize that she was also working against her own

41. MERCEDES'S LOVER

Mercedes knew that distance was a bad thing with José Ignacio. . She knew that he slept with other women when she was not around. In particular, she disliked Gabriela the most. She was her major rival. Mercedes decided to cut her employment short so she could come back to her man. She knew she could keep other women at bay, even Gabriela, if she was present but she was uneasy to be far from him for too long. Mercedes knew that she was the one he preferred over any of the others. She knew she gave him the passion and sex that he longed for. She could feel his lust, on the feverishly way in which his hands squeezed her hips, the hunger of his kisses on her neck, the wild thrushes of his cock inside her. She knew to time her breathing with his rhythm in order to be able to breathe. Often, he squeezed her so hard against his chest when he was coming that, at times, she feared he could break her back. But that was all the better, she felt the more special for it, and she knew that he did not feel the same when he made love to others. There is no way the puny little thing of Gabriela could stand it. That was why even though he slept with other ones, she always knew he will come back to her

The day she arrived, they made plans to meet in the herbarium room where she often met with her lover. The very walk to the place, at the end of the afternoon made her horny. It was the time to give herself to the most abandoned passion on the strong arms of her beloved. She had a light blouse with no bra to give him easy access. She wore a small miniskirt, because she knew how much he liked her thighs, but not too small, not to look whorish and make him jealous. That was something else she was no crazy about. She hated that he was so jealous and she always had to be careful not to awaken the monster. It was not fair, he slept with other women whenever he wanted but if she ever gave the impression to flirt with a man, or wore a dress that he did not approve of, she was up to different degrees of punishments.

Sometimes it was as simple as bending her over his lap and giving her a bout of spanking. He was so strong that every spanking really hurt. She could tell he really enjoyed spanking her and it turned him on. He was drawn to her behind and spanking her firm buttocks made him horny which always resulted in love making. The problem was that spanking really rubbed her the wrong way. Painful as the spanking was, her pride hurt even more. It was all the worse when he decided to punish her sexually. Their sex was so special that it hurt her deeply in her heart when he used it to punish her. She hated to be taken in the rear. It was painful enough to be penetrated dry by his monstrous cock in her butthole without any lubrication. But she also felt so insulted, so humiliated. He seemed to have just as much fun fucking her in her rear end but it was such dramatic difference to her. It was such a waste of his delicious orgasm that she liked so much. She viewed herself as equal to any man in the world, but José Ignacio had a way of making her feel inferior. By sleeping with other women, by taking her up her rectum, she got the message that she was inferior to him. Worst of all when he finally came she felt equally relieved, equally special. She loved feeling his pleasure satisfied in her body even if she was not enjoying it. She just loved him that much. She was sure that on time, he will come around and be only hers, when he realized that they were meant for each other.

When Mercedes arrived at the herbarium room he was waiting for her. He hugged her kissed her and pulled out a handkerchief to cover her eyes. Mercedes smiled to the kinky turn getting even hornier in anticipation of what he was going to do to her. He bent her over the desk and pulled over her skirt. He held both her wrist behind her back with one of his powerful hands, and the other one pulled her under wear down. Mercedes prepared herself to imminent penetration. She was used to the rough play. Sometimes he did not bother with foreplay, she was always horny anyway. Plus, he could fuck her forever without coming. It was only when he felt her coming that his orgasm mounted.

Mercedes felt his mouth greedily licking and sucking her upper thigh and his hands squeezing her thigh in both sides feeling it appreciatively, moving them up and down her thigh all the way to her pussy and back down to her knee. He licked the back of her knee so slowly and deliberately that it made her feel currents traveling to her pussy. Mercedes was getting more and more aroused to feel the hunger of his kisses and his greedy hands feeling her thighs so intently. Wait! He was holding her hands behind her back and pinning her to the desk. There was another man licking her buttocks and foundling her thighs. She tensed for a second but soon relaxed. There was nothing she could do. He was in control as usual. She was his for his pleasure and that was the end of it. She wondered who it may be.

Mercedes had always fantasized with having two lovers together. She would never have proposed it to José Ignacio because he was so jealous, that it was sure way of getting herself a long bout of spanking. She felt so lucky that it had been his own initiative! She wanted to ask who it was but she did not dare to say anything so it would not stop. She was going to be double fucked and she was really looking forward to it. That was why the blindfold, so she did not know who had made love to her. Likely it was nobody she knew. If it was an anonymous lover it did not matter. She felt so strongly for him that she did not care who he gave her to. She was his pleasure, whoever he wanted to share her with, she was happy with it. She always relished a good fuck. The only reason she did not fuck estrangers was because of fear to where it may lead. That was a slippery slope that she was afraid of taking. But José Ignacio was uncharged. Because it had been José Ignacio's initiative, he would not accuse her of being a slut; and she could count on him to keep it under control. If she did not know who it was, it was all his doing and she was kept blameless. She fantasized with a well-groomed cute boy, very young, very cute and tender. That was the perfect contrast with José Ignacio's brutal virility.

José Ignacio pulled her upright still holding both her hands behind her and turned her around sitting on the desk and presenting her frontally to her other lover. She felt José Ignacio's member prodding underneath her and moved her waist right to let him come inside. His cock worked his way up in the familiar ground. She was so horny and so wet that she only had to relax a bit and let his lover get inside her. She took in a deep breath and let it go slowly. She heard the other lover echo her breathing as feeling her arousal to see her being impaled. Mercedes felt his mouth suck the crevice of her hip bone and his hands in her thighs and buttock pressed more firmly feeling her flesh taking big lungfuls of her scent by her pussy.

Mercedes wondered if he could also feel the smell of pineapple that José Ignacio claimed she emanated. She could not smell anything and she had never heard that from any of her former lovers. Jose Ignacio opened her shirt exposing her breast. Her second lover climbed up to gobble up her left breast with his hands feeling her trunk and waists, one of them crawling down to her pussy. His hands were tender and soft just like the young man she imagined. He took her breath with one hand and squeezed her other one with his other hand. Jose Ignacio had her both hands held behind her back and his other arm was around her womb, which he always caressed. She took a deep breath to smell her second lover. The air was thick with José Ignacio's musky smell, that turned her on so much, but she could still feel another scent, a sweet delicate smell she did not know.

She felt her second lover caress her lower belly and finger her clit. She felt his mouth hungrily kissing her breast climbing up to her neck with so much lust, so much greed, like someone who has desired her for a long time and finally was having a go at her. No mystery there, she was a very coveted woman for her sensuality. She knew most men in the university wanted a piece of her. She had made sure to show herself well enough for anyone to notice. This one was the lucky one that José Ignacio had consented to share her with him. She was so turned on with José Ignacio's familiar cock inside her, his wall of a chest on her back and her new lover having her with so much hunger. She abandoned herself to their combined lust. He pinned her against José Ignacio, with one delicate hand held her chin and a set of tender lips started kissing her and his gentle tongue got inside her mouth traveling softly through her inner lips. She answered the kiss with her thick sensual lips licking his lips back and making love to his tongue inside her mouth. He was so delicate, his touch so tender, clearly very white, and young. She took another deep breath to drink his scent. A soft smell of Jasmine filled up her lungs and it dawned on her: A woman!

Of course, it made a lot more sense. José Ignacio's jealousy would never allow her to have another man kiss her. A lifelong upbringing in a homophobic society made her react against the thought of being kissed by a woman. She could not help to think that it may be that runty little Gabriela. José Ignacio had on occasions asked to make love to both of them together but it was mostly to annoy her and get her to fight back against him. Yet, there was not much she could do. José Ignacio had both her wrist securely grasped behind her back. His other strong muscular arm secured her around her belly. She was sitting on his lap deeply impaled in his cock. There was not much she could do even if she tried. As usual he was having his way with her. She felt affronted to have Gabriela's tongue inside her mouth. Mercedes could feel that Gabriela's kisses were tender and passionate, like José Ignacio liked it. She felt jealous, and challenged by the thought that Gabriela was such a good kisser. Yet it was Mercedes the one that had is cock inside and she was going to make sure that did not change.

Gabriela was between her open legs. Mercedes felt her nipples in her chest, rubbing with hers as she moved up and down José Ignacio's member. She was naked too! She felt humiliated at not being asked. She was furthered bothered because she could feel Gabriela's breast round and juicy on her breast, and it was clear to her that Gabriela's were bigger. She was angry and wanted to attack her but José Ignacio knew her well, that is why he had her so well immobilized. She bit Gabriela's mouth, who was tenderly kissing hers. She heard a soft little whine. She passed her tongue over Gabriela's trapped lips. They were so soft and tender. Her mouth was small and delicate but her lips felt good in her mouth. No wonder why José Ignacio liked her so much!

Mercedes let go of her mouth and bit her in to the side in her cheek. She wanted to bruise that perfectly nacreous face of her that she envied so much. She was so angry that she felt tears streaming out of her eyes. Gabriela let go another soft whine and her lips now free kissed Mercedes tenderly on her cheek. Mercedes was so angry at her and Gabriela kissed her with so much tenderness. Mercedes let go disconcerted.

Mercedes hated Gabriela because she had taken her boyfriend away from her. But also, she hated her kind. Gabriela was so perfectly pretty, Mercedes always was jealous of women that pretty. Her breasts were larger than hers which also made her unhappy. Mercedes had tasted Gabriela's lips and they were every bit as delicious as they looked. She was a most formidable rival. And here José Ignacio was offering her to taste for the woman she hated the most She just hated to have the gorgeous Gabriela, her only rival, naked with them, when it was her time to be with him. She knew his eyes were on her and that he liked her tiny well-proportioned body. All she could do was to play to her strengths. She knew José Ignacio was a butt man and her behind was far superior than Gabriela's. She had to use it well to make it count. She moved her hips and play along José Ignacio's slow rhythm. There she had a connection that she knew Gabriela could not mess with. She knew she could play her hips game to outperform any woman.

Gabriela went back to kissing and licking her mouth so eagerly, with her full breast pressing against her. Mercedes did not know what to do. Biting her again when she was being so loving seemed unreasonable. Then Mercedes realized that it could not be Gabriela. This woman was far taller than her. Plus, the way this woman was kissing her was something special. No, this woman had a true lust *for her*. There was no way Gabriela would feel that way. Mercedes relaxed a bit to this realization and let José Ignacio work her up and down, and letting the woman do as she pleased with her; relieved that she was the center of both of their lusts. Despite her original reaction to being kissed by a woman she could feel the true desire in her touch and how hungry she was for her. Mercedes could recognize lust and she was feeling it intensely on the lips of her mystery lover. She was sucking her lips like someone who eats a delicious treat. Plus, she really knew how to touch a clit! Mercedes let go of herself and quickly felt galloping to a strong orgasm lead by the combined attention of her two lovers.

When she came, her new lover kissed her tenderly all over her face, her eyes and cheeks while blowing air in her hot skin cover with perspiration. José Ignacio lifted the other woman like a feather and put one of her breast in his mouth. Mercedes had a flash of jealousy that he was sucking another woman's breast, but then she realized that if José Ignacio was going to suck another woman's breast, being between both of them was about the least maddening scenario for that to happen. Plus, this woman had sucked her nipples with such lust and such hunger that it was obvious that it was she, the one the woman wanted. Also, his cock was still inside Mercedes and that made all the difference in her book. In actuality, Mercedes had less to fear than she thought. The main reason that the woman was letting José Ignacio had her breast was to have access to Mercedes, who she had loved platonically for a long time.

Sashawarmas,   by Jorge Bandido

Sandwiched as Mercedes was between them she ended up with the other woman's breast in her face. José Ignacio had in repeated occasions described in thorough detail what it is like to suck a woman's breasts, normally referring to Gabriela's. He regularly had gone to town describing the smell of the skin, the soft consistency the breast, the texture of the nipple and how it changes consistency when aroused. She was still held with her hands behind her and she could feel the smell of her breast. Not having anything else to do she open her mouth and took her nipple in and started sucking it. She felt it grow and hardened and heard her lover moan with pleasure. The woman moaned with pleasure to her treatment.

Mercedes' lover opened her legs and wrapped them around her rubbing herself with Mercedes' hip bone. Mercedes's lover held her face tight to the breast she was sucking and leaned back on the José Ignacio's arm behind her shoulders. She rubbed her clit with long strokes on Mercedes and regaled herself to the two different feeling in her breasts. While José Ignacio's hot mouth was sucking one of her breast hard as if trying to suck her soul through its nipple, Mercedes was doing a soft, rather exploratory recognizance of her other breast.

The woman lowered her face to meet Mercedes' lips. She had felt her lust since the beginning and now Mercedes could feel inside the woman's mouth , her true, absolute love. Shortly after their lips met the woman held Mercedes' face with such tenderness and such love that immediately started coming with an orgasm that made her whole-body spasm as if discharges of current were going by her.

Mercedes knew what a woman's orgasms did to José Ignacio and prepared herself because she knew the ride will become a lot rougher. José Ignacio released her hands and held her by her hips lifting her, and her lover, up and down slowly all the length of his shaft. With her hands free Mercedes uncover her eyes to see who her lover was. Shortly Virginia's face came into focused. A classmate of them, right in front of her, with her hair in disarray, her cheeks pink of arousal, a red bite mark in her left cheek, and her eyes welling up with emotion. Virginia's eyes searched anxious to read into Mercedes' approval or disapproval of her. It took Mercedes a few seconds to recognize Virginia and connect her with the woman that was kissing her mouth so tenderly and that had made love to her with such passion. Virginia's face was astonishingly beautiful. Virginia's perfectly sculpted nose, her thin face, large green eyes and freckly cheeks made for a very beautiful woman; beautiful enough to rival Gabriela herself. She had medium size and well-shaped breasts with the perfect form and large pointy nipples; this Mercedes had experienced well. They were much larger than hers, as she had calculated, far better shaped but

239

she could feel José Ignacio rough hands squeezing hers to the border of
aching, as he always did. Mercedes had always been jealous of women that
pretty since she was little. She felt that men were far more attracted to them
than to her. Every time she saw Virginia in the university she felt that she was
truly beautiful and some part of her was jealous wanting to be a pretty as she
was. Mercedes was reassured by the fact that she was the one moving up and
down as the rhythm of José Ignacio's desire, impaled by his member.
Mercedes simply smiled and Virginia's eyes exploded with tears kissing her
with so much love and so much passion that Mercedes could do nothing but
to reciprocate her kisses.

She hugged her and both merged into a loving hug of passion and
tenderness in equal measure. It was an interesting contrast with the extreme
masculinity of Jose Ignacio body banging her right behind her. Slowly she felt
José Ignacio's rhythm fasten and she braced herself for what was coming. She
turned her head around to kiss him and feel him in her mouth at the peak of
pleasure. They locked up in a full lip kiss and Mercedes was waiting to feel the
final squeeze and painful bite that José Ignacio often delivered when he was
coming, but she felt his lips leave hers and heard a high pitch whine right by
her face. José Ignacio's arms crushed Virginia against Mercedes, and her
against his chest making it hard to breath. Mercedes open her eyes and saw
José Ignacio's mouth locked on Virginia's virginal face biting half her lips and
half her cheek. Virginia's tears streamed down her perfectly smooth, freckly
cheeks, as she whined in pain and surprise. Mercedes grabbed fistfuls of José
Ignacio's hair with both hands and lifted herself drawing his face towards his.
Mercedes feared she was going to break her with his cock as it went inside and
outside her full power. José Ignacio's mouth quickly let go of Virginia's face
and locked on Mercedes' mouth. Then it came Mercedes' time to moan in
pain when he bit her.   It was the price of being José Ignacio's lover.

After the peak of pain his rhythm slowly slowed down, his teeth soften on
her and he finally let go. Mercedes felt Virginia's tender mouth on hers; as if
trying to console her from the pain of José Ignacio's bite. She could feel a bit
of taste of blood in Virginias lower lip where José Ignacio had bitten her.
Mercedes let go of José Ignacio's curls and reached back over her shoulders to
feel José Ignacio's massive shoulders. She inhaled deeply and took in his
musky scent flooding the room. Mercedes felt the flavor of Virginia's mouth
kissing her softly, and again felt aware on her breast pressing on hers,
sandwiched between her delicate feminine presence and the massive wall of
muscular chest impaling her behind. She relaxed between them and was
happy to be there.

Sashawarmas,   by Jorge Bandido

The kiss between Mercedes and Virginia was crashed by José Ignacio's large lips joining them. They kissed together in three directions. There was a contrast between the thin small lips of the white woman and the thick meaty lips of the two brown ones. Virginia felt the rough animalistic kissed from José Ignacio compared with the tender and sensual ones from Mercedes. She exploded with happiness to being accepted among them and finally had had the opportunity to be with the woman she had loved for so long. Mercedes never saw herself as a lesbian. She had an appreciation for a woman's body. She certainly had seen Claudia's body as a threat for her but she had never felt inclined to have sex with one. The time that Claudia was taken in the forest by the mysterious presence, she had been turned on by looking at her being possessed by whatever it was that took her. She had straddled her naked body and she had actually kissed Claudia during her trance but she was mostly looking for José Ignacio whose essence she was sure had been the presence making love to Claudia in the jungle. She never told this to Claudia though. She did not know what she would think, and she herself did not know what to think about that impulse she had had. But now it was different. She had kissed Virginia on her own merit. She had enjoyed her touch, she had felt aroused by her lips and her mouth kissing her. She had enjoyed the feminine feeling of Virginia's kisses. She had given her a long delicious orgasm. There was no way to putting it: she was sexually attracted to Virginia. She was happy that José Ignacio had forced her to this experience because she would have never sought it out herself. Also, his masculine presence in her love making with Virginia had made it easier for her to let herself go. She was not necessarily inclined to seek it anymore but it felt good inside her to know that she had it on her, if she wanted.

42. FAMILY AFFAIRS

Because José Ignacio was now Mercedes' official boyfriend he would go regularly to her house. Mercedes had five younger sisters. The second one, Amanda, was only 11 months younger than Mercedes and looked surprisingly similar to her. They were like twins and a lot of people confused them. They were not only similar in their face but also in the shape of their bodies, their expression, and gestures. When José Ignacio met Amanda, it was unavoidable that he would wonder if she was as good in bed as Mercedes was and since then he desired to have her.

Amanda had a very sad history of relationships, though. She had a boyfriend for many years, a man of means who had his own small airplane and would take her all over the country in wonderful vacations. She was about to get married when a younger brother of her fiancé stabbed him to death 12 times over some inheritance dispute. Amanda was crushed as it is easy to imagine, of losing her partner in such a violent way. In the services for his fiancé she got together with one of his fiancé best friends, another pilot, as both of them were so sad for his passing. Before long they found out that they liked each other and started dating. Everything was ready for them to get married when his plane blew up in the air killing all their passengers. It was probably victim of a political assassination as he flew the plane for some government officials. It is a small wonder that Amanda was traumatized and felt that she was responsible for their deaths. She felt victim of some superstitious fear that she was jinxed and chose not to date anybody else, fearing she could bring death to her next boyfriend. She chose to live without a partner a quiet and calm life.

These tragedies had happened 2 or 3 years before José Ignacio started coming to Mercedes' house regularly. So, Amanda was the maiden sister of the five. The other ones had boyfriends and they all had tempting bodies. Even the baby sister, Trina, who was still a teenager, had a perfect hard body that would make a person sick of lust of only looking at her. Nothing voluptuous, just the perfect shapes, the prominent derriere and the tempting broad hips. No teenager should have such a tempting woman's body, but Trina did. Because Mercedes was so good in bed, José Ignacio wondered if it ran in the family and was always curious about her sisters. Amanda was the main temptation because of how much like Mercedes she looked plus her 3 year long celibacy. José Ignacio figured that she would be pretty horny. She was, after all, Mercedes' sister who was a notch short of a nymphomaniac. Any simple reckoning suggested that Amanda should be easy to get in the sack. When he went there he played his card of amicable, touchy-feely, brother-in-law. Every time he greeted her he hugged Amanda a little too tight and little too long, assessing her reaction to the male contact. She always let him hold her and he could swear she took deep calming breathes when he hugged and held her as if struggling with her own desires.

Amanda was often working in the kitchen of the small apartment, doing the dishes, cooking, or doing laundry, because all the appliances were crammed in together with little room. When he got to the house he wold corner her, holding her from behind touching her and pressing himself against her greeting her. He would kiss her neck, right below her ear holding her in a tight embrace. She reacted to the normal tickling that it produces which led him to turn it into a tickling game reaching for her other side of her neck and sucking her ear lobe restraining her against the sink, pressing himself shamelessly on her behind while his hands reached for her stomach. He had learned this game very well with Maggy and it came naturally to him. Amanda would grab his wrists firmly and open his arms to escape to the side but he could see her aroused cheeks, and dilated pupils showing that she had felt him. It was a barely masked sexual fondling, but he was good at it, and she always seemed to quietly endure it. Sometimes Mercedes saw him from outside the kitchen and because it was so obvious what he was doing, she would shove him out of the kitchen scolding him.

"Respect my sister." She would say as she shoved him out.

No secret there. She knew José Ignacio would fondle and make love with any woman with a hot body that would let him. He even had told her about his curiosity for doing Amanda, if nothing else to get her angry and have some hot angry sex. Amanda was an easy one to get Mercedes pissed because she had been her sister rival all her life, and on top of the jealousy, it triggered her protective instincts because of her misfortune in love affairs. Mercedes wondered if he fondled Amanda just to make her angry or if he actually lusted for Amanda as much as he said. She knew also it did not have to be one or the other. Likely both were true.

As their relationship became more serious, José Ignacio would go more often to her house. His member was hard since the moment he walked through the door in anticipation of hugging and kissing all the sisters but touching Amanda was what got him horniest. When he cornered her against the sink and was rubbing himself on her hard behind, she would move away discretely. If there was nobody in sight he would lock her preventing her from moving and fondled her breast and buttock forcing her to endure all his groping and caresses. She would try to move out but she would not denounce him. Because it always happened she had to know he was going to touch her but she always waited in the kitchen for him to corner her, when she could

243

have avoided it all together by going to her room or greeting him in the living room in front of Mercedes. It occurred to José Ignacio that giving him the chance of feeling her, she also gave herself a chance of being felt!

José Ignacio never knew for sure why Amanda did not tell Mercedes what he did. It is possible she did not want to give Mercedes the bad news that her boyfriend was a womanizer that fondled her sister at any chance he got. He did not know if it was that Amanda liked him groping her, since she would not date, he gave her the only male contact she had had in a long time. On occasions when he got there he could see her nipples hard and erect as if she had been anticipating arousal when she saw him. This, however, was not a sure indication because Mercedes' nipples were hard all the time. It could just be something that ran in the family, which made him all the more curious to taste.

One day Mercedes and José Ignacio were going to Isla de la Plata, a small island off the Ecuadorian cost, a touristic paradise but rather pricy for Ecuadorian standards. They had planned this from a long time and managed to save to what he called: "an early honey moon".

When he got to the door Amanda opened it. "Mercedes is taking a shower." She told him and turned around heading back to the kitchen.

He could see her nipples were not hard when she opened the door, as she was braless. But when he caught up with her in the kitchen her nipples were hard and pointy, piercing her t-shirt "*she was anticipating caresses*" he thought. Plus, she did not give him the regular greeting with a kiss on the cheek that was customary at the door. She was obviously counting with the usual "greeting" in the kitchen. He followed her and kissed her ear lobes, with no disguise. He attached himself to her hips and started rubbing himself in her behind. His hands went from her abdomen, under her shirt, up and up until he cupped both her breast and caressed them lustily. Amanda, stopped doing dishes and held herself at the sink panting letting him feel her up at his leisure . . . and hers.

She turned her face around and presented to him her thick African lips, half parted, with her eyes closed. José Ignacio kissed them with gluttony. Just like Mercedes her lips were large and warm and her tongue was wrestles. As he felt her getting excited he got him member out and put it between her legs. He pulled down her shorts enough to have access and his member slid inside her smoothly, as if it knew the way already. She was Mercedes' sister! Her pussy was deep, broad, and wet; hot and hungry; and as she started moving he felt her pussy twist and turn in all directions. A soft scent of ripe grape started to fill up the environment.

244

Sashawarmas,   by Jorge Bandido

José Ignacio could not but help remembering one of his most daring affairs, the time he made love to Margarita, Gabriela's sister, while he waited for Gabriela. Except that time Gabriela was away. Now he was going after Amanda with Mercedes just across the wall, not 4 feet away from him. The tall window of the bathroom looked towards the kitchen so they could hear Mercedes' shower running, as he banged her sister. They were in the middle of a long kiss when they heard Mercedes turning off the shower.

"Come José Ignacio, come, come that Mercedes is almost done". Amanda whispered to him.

José Ignacio enjoyed making love slowly and tenderly, and he did not feel like ruining that good moment by rushing to an orgasm, so he continued his rhythm with deep thrust and full contact between their bodies pinning her against the sink. Plus, the thoughts of Mercedes finding him making love to Amanda was most arousing to him.

They heard the door of the bathroom open as Mercedes headed to her room to get dressed.

"Hurry up, Jose Ignacio come, come quickly, I beg you, or Mercedes will see us". Amanda whispered at him in deep sense of urgency.

He crossed his arms over her chest with his hands firmly squeezing her breast, securing her against him and continued impaling her, deep and slow; making her face almost reach the wall in front of her with every thrust. Shortly after, they heard Mercedes' step coming out of her bedroom and walking down the hall towards the living room and kitchen area, unaware that José Ignacio was in the house, much less that he was doing her sister.

Amanda was torn inside. She loved the passion of his hug and the strength he was hold her with. But she also was in complete state of desperation now trying to free herself from him and begging him to let her go but her arms were immobilized by her sides; all she could do was to struggles within his embrace. When Mercedes saw them, Amanda was struggling with all her strength trying to free herself from his grip while he had her firmly pinned against the sink skewering her from behind. Mercedes came at him full of anger.

"What are you doing? Let go of my sister you fucking rapist!" She yelled.

She punched and kicked him but the strength of both sisters was no match for his. In fact, it turned him on more to feel Mercedes' rage and Amanda's desperation. Mercedes jumped on his back and cross her arm across his neck in a futile attempt to strangle him. Her useless struggle to free herself

245

and her distress to be seen in the act aroused him all the more and soon he started to come in a delicious orgasm.

"AAAAHHH!" screamed Amanda when he bit her hard on the neck, typical of his intense coming. Mercedes was livid feeling the impotence to protect her sister and taken over by rage that he was enjoying another woman. She felt that his pleasure and his moment of coming was hers and hers alone. Here it was wasted on another woman. As soon as José Ignacio let go of Amanda, she pulled her shorts up and went crying to lock herself in her bedroom. Mercedes continued yelling at the top of her lungs insulting and punching him.

"How can you rape my sister? How can you rape any woman, you fucking pig," she said irate punching and kicking any target she could find in his body.

José Ignacio grabbed her arms, turned her around and in no time had her immobilized; holding her from behind, like he had held Amanda, with both her arms wrapped around her own body and giving her tender kisses in her ear and neck.

"Oh, it was delicious my love. It was like making love to you. She tastes sooo good." He taunted her.

"She is my sister. You are a monster. You raped my sister. You are the worst scum bag I ever met." Mercedes cried out of impotence and anger. "She trusted you, I trusted you coming to my house. How can you do it?"

"It is alright my love, I did not hurt her. I bet you she wanted a good fucking right about now after so long without a man," he said trivializing her pain and Amanda's feelings.

"How could you do that to her? How could you do that to me?" Mercedes said tears streaming out of her eyes.

"Fucking your sister is like fucking you, it all stays in the family," he said pressing her hard against his chest and showering her with kisses.

Mercedes never understood why he would not have enough with just one woman and how he could take a woman against her will. It was just like the time he tried to rape Claudia but this time she had arrived too late. She loved him so much but can she love a rapist? She was torn with her own feelings. It was that same incontrollable lust that took him over when he was loving her that she loved so much, except that he would fuck anything! Why her sister?

Something on the back of her mind bothered her. Claudia had been a collaborating partner at first. It was later when she was rejecting him. Plus she never knew what happened to Claudia in the Igapó. When Claudia woke up after the estrange possession she was confused and even embarrassed as if she had done something shameful. Claudia never mentioned anything and whenever Mercedes said something she acted embarrassed. embarrassed of what? Mercedes did José Ignacio was there when the mysterious entity took her? She had smelled him. Mercedes knew for a fact that José Ignacio magical essence had been there making love to Claudia, Did Claudia know it too? Could Amanda had been part of it too? Clearly, she could not fight off José Ignacio's strength if he wanted to take her. But did she try? She saw her struggling alright, in the end. Somehow, she knew the answer but she could not handle it at that time. She just cried her eyes out held by his strong arms. Raping her sister was another one of his impositions. She could not leave him. Her own pussy ached to have him. She had accepted he slept around but she could not reconcile her love for him with raping a woman, her sister none the less. She just had to make sure he never had a chance to do it again.

José Ignacio on the other hand was in heaven. He had discovered a new dimension to love making. He knew he had desired Amanda for a long time and attributed his feeling of elation to the fulfillment of his wish. Subduing and making love to Amanda while she struggled to free herself was a toxic libation that he did not realize how much he had enjoyed. He was familiar with the struggle stripping a woman that tries to avoid it, but as soon as he penetrated Francia she surrendered. He had never thrust inside a woman that wanted to get free of him. Amanda's final struggle had made his enjoyment gone up 4 folds! He felt so predacious, like a deep calling finally being realized. His euphoria was such that he did not realize that towards the end he had very much raped Amanda. Had he realized that the last minutes of raping Amanda were the ones that made him feel so good, he would have a deep personal crisis. But his dark side was taken too much of a hold on his mind for him to realize that.

43. ALTAR BOY

Arriving to Mónica's house they both got ready to go to the port. Daniela showered and put on the one outfit she had brought. A short yellow miniskirt with a flowing fabric, perfect for spinning while dancing and showing revealing views of her well-formed legs. She also had a light shirt not quite see-through, but it was clear enough to invite staring. She came out of the bathroom fully attired with sandals that strapped around her ankles. Mónica burst out laughing when she saw her.

"Is that how you are going to the port to look for the father of your baby?" she asked in disbelieve. "You are going to find another father for another baby dressed like that!" She told her.

"This is the only outfit I have." Daniela said a bit defensively.

"You are such a slut. You can't go to the port dressed that way." Mónica pointed out. "Here, I have home *honest woman* clothing you can borrow if you want to make any progress at the port."

When Jaime, came to pick them up for their big night, they both were ready. They wore long jeans, covering their legs; even if they were nicely adjusted to their bodies showing their forms, they were nothing scandalous. They both wore closed shirt with short sleeves, nothing too low cut, not too tempting. They drove into the Port Zone and went into one of the most popular bars. Both women were at each side of Jaime. They surely attracted stares but nobody made any attempt to invite them or talk to them as they were clearly with a man; and Jaime was strong and muscular. After the bar tender brought each one a drink, Daniela asked the bartender.

"Do you know José Ignacio Guzman?"

The bar tender looked at her in surprise with a wrinkled brow and after a brief pause he answered.

"Yes, but I have not seen him in a long time".

Do you have any idea where he might be? Or when he is coming back?" Daniela continued.

"No, last that I heard he had joined a tuna fishing ship and was in the shores of Alaska. He must be freezing his Zambo ass right off right about now!" He commented jovially as someone who was not very unhappy the Zambo was not around.

They left and went to another bar. The made similar inquiries but found similar results. The answers were never consistent. Some said he had gone to the Galapagos to serve in a tourist crew as stud for wealthy American women who wanted to hire a man to fuck them, others said he was in a plantation down in Peru, or that he was swallowed by the forest. Another one assured them that he had gone to Colombia through the forest where he had join the Fuerza Armada Revolucionaria de Colombia, FARC, as a guide for their operations. This Daniela felt this could have some truth to it. At least that is the direction she saw him running last, and it matched with the search the guard had unleashed on him after the revolt was controlled. *"Was he involved in some political thing from the beginning?"*

That night as Daniela got ready to sleep on Mónica's coach, Mónica had an idea.

"You know what? Did she not come a week before the revolt to the hospital for some medical attention?" She asked.

"Yes, I treated him myself. Why?" Answered Daniela.

"Well in the admission form there must be some information we can use to find him. Tomorrow we can look up the form and see what we learn."

This was not necessarily proper use of the hospital records but Daniela would take whatever she could. After all, it was Mónica doing the snooping. With a bit of a new hope they went in the morning to the hospital and followed their plan.

"Here this is his address. We can go to his house." indicated Mónica pointing to the form.

Daniela read the address to be sure but not too encouraged. After she read it, she told her

"No, that is where I first looked for him. The landlord does not know any more about him than the rest of the town." She told her.

Then Mónica pointed to the lower part of the form and said. "How about this?"

She was pointing to the line where it read "Place of Birth: Esmeralda". Daniela looked at her blankly not understanding how knowing where he was born could help to find him.

"There is not a good record of babies born in town but the record of the baptism in the church go as far back as the old father has been around. We can find out who his parents are or if he has any relatives. If he does, they can lead us to him" Explained Mónica.

Both nurses arrived at the church shortly after lunch. They took a little time off to run their important errand. The old priest happened to be arriving from the garden and stopped seeing that they were people wanting to talk to him judging for the fact that they did not enter the church via the main door as everyone who wanted to pray did, but instead they stood by the side door where his office and living quarters were.

"How can I help you my daughters? Asked benevolent the old priest.

"We would like to see the baptism records of the church back a few years if that were possible." Answered Mónica. "We want to find someone that fell out of the map." Completed Daniela.

The old man looked at them somewhat surprised. He looked briefly at Mónica but did not give any signs of recognizing her. After all Mónica was not a very practicing person. However, when his eyes stopped on Daniela, his eyes opened in recognition. Daniela did not know if he remembered the believer that came to church regularly or if he remembered the nurse that helped with the recovery actions after the revolt, that he had helped get to Quito asking a favor from a friend. May be both?

"Well the records go back a long time but only those that were baptized in the church." The old man answered turning around to open the door of the building where his office was. "It depends on who you are looking for and why you need to find them?"

"His name is Jose Ignacio Guzman", Daniela answered pleadingly, hoping that he would let her search the records within the reasonable range of dates; guessing the year of his birth.

The priest who had begun to walk into the building stopped and turned around to face her, clearly recognizing the name

"And how do you know him my child." He asked.

Daniela stammered, not knowing how much to disclose: "Err, mmm he, mm". "They are friends and she wants to give him something he lost." Mónica came to her rescue as the old priest invited them in.

However, they were technically in the church and Daniela could not muster the courage to lie in the house of God.

"He is the father of my child Father. I would like to find him so he can meet his son and his son can meet his father," said Daniela coming clean.

250

Sashawarmas,   by Jorge Bandido

The old man's eyebrow raised way up in understanding and nodded in assurance. "Come here, I think I can tell you what I know about him but unfortunately I have not seem him in a while." He said.

This was odd. The Zambo certainly did not come across as the church going kind. How did father Carlos know him by name? Surely, he had a sharp eye and he had recognized her from attending to church the day she came asking for help. But how did he remember his name, and how was he so sure he was no longer around?

The old priest invited them to come into his office, a modest room to the side of the church's main chamber, and sat on his desk. Daniela was confused because instead of reaching for a large book with records of birth and baptism, he sat on his chairs with his hands folded over his lap. Sitting in expectation both nurses looked at the old priest for what the information that he had promised.

"I don't need to look up the records to tell you about him. He was born in this church, actually in this very room," said the priest.

Daniela's eyes welled up with happiness to see that she was going to get, perhaps more information than she ever thought she could get from the mysterious man that was so hermetic in words and had disappeared into thin air the way he did.

"But, how." Asked Mónica a bit confused.

"His mother was entrusted to my care when she was only a teenager. She had served under the care of one of my mentors when I first came from Spain. My mentor died in unfortunate circumstances and I, let's say, inherited her. She was already pregnant with him when she arrived", clarified the old priest fending off any thought anyone could have that he may have let her be knocked up under his watch.

"Where is his mother? Is she still around? Did you meet his father? Do you know where they live? Maybe they can help us find him." Asked Daniela truly interested unable to stop herself from bombarding the priest with questions about the father of her baby.

The old priest was silent for a while looking at the ground deliberating how much to tell her but since she had a good reason to ask what she was asking he decided to give her all the details.

"His mother was a black woman that was given to the protection of my mentor by her mother who claimed that she could not protect her from some male members of her family. Her mother was the daughter of a woman that

251

came from Haiti. She was a Mandingo woman from the Niger river area. People called her 'La Francesa', (The French woman) for her native language. She was some sort of charlatan that talked about spirits and such. It was not quite Voodoo but a something similar, some Santeria of some sort. The young woman was brought up in that environment but against all odds grew up to be a good woman. Her uncle, the brother of the charlatan was quite something different though. That is why her mother gave her to my mentor to keep her safe from her brother. My mentor started a mission that went into Woaorani territory, the first one to ever try such a feat. He brought her with him to the mission. Things went well for a while but after some time, things turned bad. A raid of warriors came in the middle of the night and killed everyone. They spared her, because they were surprised for her color so she was not killed but she was not fully spared." Said the priest pausing and giving time for the obvious to sink in the mind of the nurses, without having to mention things like rape or sexual assault in the church.

"I accepted her in the congregation when none of us knew anything. A few months later she confessed to me that she was pregnant, although I had noticed it for a little while. So, to answer your question my child, I never met José Ignacio's father but I know he was a Woaorani warrior, one of the warriors that burned down the mission, in all likelihood. There is no much of a chance to find him since the Woaoranis are still belligerent in these parts and no one can go to the recesses of the forest where they live". Continued the father as the nurses listened hanging to every word. "As for his mother, she was a good Christian. She loved her baby dearly. She was responsible and a hard worker". The Father paused clutching the cross on his chest, looking down as if pondering how much more he should disclose about the origin of the Zambo. He crossed himself and continued.

"One day when José Ignacio was only 7 or so, she asked me if I would take care of little boy if something were to happened to her. I found it odd but I assured her, of course that if something happened to her, her baby will want for nothing so long as I have any capacity to attend to his needs. The oddest thing is that the same night she disappeared without leaving trace of herself." Clutching again his crucifix, the old priest continued. "Some of the superstitious pagans in town said that she had gone to the forest to live with the forest creatures, but of course that was only superstitions that the spawn out of ignorance and the lack of a true faith. She might have victim of some wild animal in the forest, more likely. The truth is that she never returned."

The old priest turned on his chair and reached for a drawer behind him pulling an old picture.

Sashawarmas,   by Jorge Bandido

"Of course, I kept my word. I raised little José Ignacio as if he were my own son," said the old priest with pride handing the nurses a picture of much younger him in the mass assisted by a very dark, and skinny altar boy. Daniela's heart made a leap to recognize her mysterious Zambo in the face of the dark boy that must have been 7 or 8 years old at the time.

"He was a very good boy. Respectful with the adults, he was quick to learn, smart in school, and good for physical work too. I thought he had a great future until the time that puberty hit. He was transformed. He could only think of girls and spend all his time chasing skirts. He no longer wanted to stay in school or do work around the church. As he turned 14 he was out on his own, working in the farms and abandoned his education. He never came to church after he left. He was nice and respectful with me whenever I ran into him in town. One day it was raining and I had to unload the groceries for the Sunday charity and I was by myself. He saw me from the other side of the plaza and came running to help me. He did not let me get wet and did all the work on his own. He was always grateful with me and called me "Father", like many other people here but we both understood that he meant it more in a paternal sense than in the religious one. I am sad he is no longer around but I have no idea where he might have gone. Knowing him, I cannot be sure he is not in some kind of trouble."

The nurses said goodbye to the caring priest thanking him for the information. He presented Daniela with the picture of the little Zambo so his son will have an image of what his father looked like. It also presented his father as a man of faith, perhaps more than he eventually became, but it would work to seed love for God on Daniela's little boy.

44. A MIRROR OF LOVE

After José Ignacio finished making love to Amanda in front of Mercedes, she thought he had raped her, and for the last part of the act, he may very well have done it. Mercedes was aware that he had sex with Gabriela regularly he figured that what most aggravated her of him raping Amanda was not so much the infidelity but having it done in her house, to her sister, and in front of her. Heck she herself had seen him fondling her in several occasions. But raping her? That was a complete different story. Mercedes was familiar with José Ignacio's approach of fondling, and caressing a woman, even if she did not want to, in order to arouse her and coerce her to agree to have sex. She could not see how fondling a woman long enough against her will was any different than raping her. It did not make it any less of a rape, in her mind, but José Ignacio had a different personal narrative on the matter. He did not tell Mercedes that Amanda had consented to the penetration at first. He wanted to have the door open for future romantic escapades with Amanda and if Mercedes did not distrust her sister, he had a better chance of getting away with it.

"Come, let's go to Isla de Plata as we had been planning all along and have an anticipated honey moon." He told her encouragingly.

She disliked him calling it a Honeymoon, because if anything she wanted in the world was for them to get married but she knew that José Ignacio would never get married. He did not subscribe to the institution of marriage and if she wanted to be with him, they were going to do it in an alternative kind of union. So, the term Honeymoon, rubbed her completely the wrong way. The trip to the island was a romantic escapade and knowing that she was going to have to accept what he had done to her sister, there was no point in cancelling the trip. After all she loved going to be beach with him. They have spent lots of money already in the trip and he pretty much dragged her out of her house to catch a cab to the airport.

The trip was in a small airplane that rocked heavily with the weather. This helped a lot his case because the adrenaline and being scared in the flight helped Mercedes forget the anger from the incident with Amanda more than he would have expected. Upon arrival they checked in the small bed and breakfast were they had booked their stay and went into the bedroom where he made love to Mercedes lovingly. Any relic of anger that Mercedes may had, dissipated in the mist of their pleasure.

"I want us to move in together. I don't want us to live separate anymore." He told Mercedes after they were done.

This was pretty much the strongest declaration of love he had made to her since they had met and Mercedes had hoped to hear these words coming out of his mouth for years. So, this was a close as she ever expected to hear a marriage proposal. However, she did not react with the happiness that she once thought she would have felt. Somehow Mercedes knew there was something else involved.

"OK, when?" but she was clearly waiting for the other shoe to drop.

Moving in with her boyfriend without getting married was not a small leap of faith for Mercedes because her father was extremely old fashion and she always gave Mercedes a hard time when she went out with him since it was obvious they were lovers. To move in with a man without getting married was the extreme of sluttiness in his book. Part of the conservative upbringing of her father and part of jealousy for his daughter having sex with a brown man was enough for Mercedes' father to be right down nasty with her when José Ignacio was involved. So, Mercedes moving in with him out of wed-locks was going to come with a heavy price in the relationship with her dad.

"We can find a place to move in within a month." He told her. "I want Amanda to move in with us too." He completed.

Mercedes felt anger boiling inside her. This is what she feared since she heard the proposal

"I knew you were up to something, you damn pig. You will never lay a finger on my sister again. I will never let you come close to her." She yelled at him in anger, breaking the after-sex embrace that they had.

"Look, if you let me have Amanda moving with us I will never have a reason to sleep with another woman. With you two I will have all what I need in our house and will not cheat on you again." He proposed dropping all pretensions.

Mercedes was livid and looked at him with rage and an expression of complete disapproval.

"I will break clean and for good with Gabriela and will always have either you or Amanda with me all the time." He said trying to sweeten the deal since he knew how much it angered her that he slept with Gabriela at least twice every week. "Having you and your hot sister why would I want another woman? You know that I always will sleep with other women, is it not better if it is your sister? Plus, she needs help, she has been traumatized by her bad luck and being with us will help her break the cycle of sorrow and feel better about herself. May be giving her a few good fucks will jump start her sex life. Maybe she will find a boyfriend down the road and move out. I will not prevent her from getting a boyfriend if that is what she wants." José Ignacio concluded.

"Leave my sister alone. I will never let you rape her again. The only reason you want to move in with me is to have her and that will never happen." She said with determination.

"Look, you know that the natural thing for men is to have several women. That is why no single woman works with me. If we move in together, the three of us, we all will be happy and no woman will get between us." Appealing to her biological side he told her: "That is the natural order in a human society. We are not meant to live in monogamy. Our forbearers had several wives. I will provide for both of you and make both of you happy in bed"

Of course, this was a bold claim. He certainly could make two women happy in bed. If making a living were about hunting and bringing game from the forest, he would have been able to provide for two as well. But in the XXI century western world, being poor and starving as he was, it was clear that they all would have to work to make ends meet.

"Why don't we run it by your sister. She will have her own room. You and I will make love all the time. I will only have her when you are not around AND if she consents. You will be my first, always and forever. Amanda will not have to do anything she does not want. I promise on my soul, I will not force her in any way or form. I am sure that if you say it is Ok, she will not object." He continued.

This Mercedes knew to be true. She had never seen a woman who would not give to his courtship giving enough time. There was something about him that women just could not resist. This made her angrier. How was he so sure Amanda would consent? Had he talked about it with Amanda? Had she consented to make love to him before she arrived? She remembered other time shoving José Ignacio out of the kitchen when he was touching her without her doing much to oppose it. She was angry at herself and very angry at him for being so horny and so promiscuous.

Mercedes was quiet for a few seconds which he took for consent. The very idea of having Amanda and Mercedes in his bed, of having both of them to his pleasure turned him on so much that he was ready to have her again. He kissed her tenderly and pulling her legs apart put himself between her legs. She took him in, wet and well lubricated from their previous love making. Mercedes let him do as he pleased but seem not fully engaged. As he made love to her, Mercedes mustard the strength to vocalize what bothered her.

256

Sashawarmas,   by Jorge Bandido

"I do not want my sister to move in with us. I do not want to share you". However, her claim lost a lot of strength in the middle of her heavy breathing he was extracting from her despite of herself.

After they came they both fell asleep. They revisited the conversation about them moving in together with Amanda but made little progress

"What you want is a harem of women, nobody can have that." She argued.

"Most human cultures have polygynous relationships. The native Indians in the Amazon are a good example of it. It is only in the western civilization that men have only one woman. My grandfather was Woaorani (this much he knew from his mother) it is in my blood. Plus, I do not want a harem, I just want the two of you." He would counter.

"That is obsolete. The world is moving forward." She retorted. "What if I want to have two men?" She added.

That was where she knew she was stepping in dangerous grounds. Mercedes knew well that he could be very violent under jealousy and quickly repented having plaid that card. He held her by her hair and pulled it back down

"You know very well what would happen." He said pulling her head back hard and holding her chin up with strong fingers for having had the very thought of it. Swiftly he put her on her belly and spanked her hard to make his point.

"Sleeping with several men is unnatural. Men have several women, woman have just the one man. It is natural selection. Men that have several wives make more children. It does not work that way with a woman. If a woman sleeps with several men she is just a slut. If you sleep with another man I will beat the living crap of both of you and you know it."

Mercedes knew that it was the end of the story. She did not agree, but it did not matter. Her only consolation was that he needed her consent to have Amanda again. He could spank her all-day long. That was not happening for any reason at all.

45. MERCEDES EXPOSED

Clearly José Ignacio's request was difficult to accept for Mercedes. The idea of having two sisters as his lovers, two Mercedes, had made him delirious. On the one hand his feelings for Mercedes were stronger than ever. For the first time he was talking about settling down with her, instead of having her as his mistress while he looked for somebody else. Her blind acceptance of all his misdemeanors had finally captivated him. It did not matter what he said, what he did, who he slept with, she always accepted it. Even if she did not explicitly condone it, she always forgave it or ignored it. There was a new relationship developing between them. One in which she slowly made progress towards her goal. José Ignacio had given up on the idea of a woman other than Mercedes. He now had accepted to stay with Mercedes permanently and give in to his overwhelming sexual drive and deepest instincts. He no longer tried to mastered it, he instead decided to give himself to it and enjoy the good part of it. Having Amanda with them would continue the unbalance that was secretly taken hold of his desire. His darker side was gaining terrain and his nicer, healthier self, did not realize what he was doing, or what he was losing by taking this path.   He was choosing his own path, a place where he could truly be happy without internal conflicts. If surrendering to his Lust was what it took, so be it.

The fact that he could tell Mercedes everything and always count with 100% acceptance of what he did or said, had become an important hook that lured him to her, beyond her lusty body and her arousing woman's scent. He attributed it to his upbringing. He was always keen to use psychology to understand people behavior. He was brought up by Maggy who eventually became his lover for several years. He viewed the sexual relationship as a simple extension from a maternal relationship. This blind acceptance that he so liked from Mercedes was very much the acceptance that only a mother has towards her child. In Mercedes mind he had raped her sister, yet she was there with him in a paradisiacal island frolicking with him in bed after sex.

Mercedes new about the three circuits mediating partners relationships. Having three different chemicals regulating man and woman relationships was bound to be a mess. With testosterone for sexual drive, dopamine mediating seeking and pleasure, and oxytocin making the final bond. It was easy to see that José Ignacio, who was full of testosterone, was driven to sex with her, then his urges to seek her were obvious too. That was the dopamine acting, he always sought her out. The problem was the he did not seem to get the bonding, like he did not have oxytocin. Finally, some oxytocin, some bonding feelings, had started to kick in. It all just was happening so slowly, sometimes she did not know she would have the endurance. Of course, there was the issue of the brain injury. Was it affecting his capacity to develop the regular circuit that leads to healthy pair bonding? The injury was precisely in the centers of pleasure and pair bonding. That could explain why it was taking so long. But she could not ignore that weird connection he had with the forest. She knew she had smelled him in the forest when Claudia had the trance. She did not know what to make of it though. She was a scientist, but there was this other thing that she felt was very strong, but defied scientific explanation.

They have been saving for quite a while in order to treat themselves to this trip because to visit the island was expensive. So, they were few Ecuadorians. Most people visiting the island were foreigner. There were few American, mostly there were Europeans: French, Germans, Dutch, or some other northern Europeans which language they could not recognize. The beaches were far from the place where people staid, normally isolated from everything, with only boat access. Typically, the boat dropped off the tourist in the beach and came back later to pick them up at the end of the day.

They rented a trip to a one of the beaches and prepared to enjoy their day on the sand. Because they were mostly foreigners it was common to see European women sunbathe topless. While José Ignacio was rubbing sun tan lotion on Mercedes gorgeous body from behind, he pulled out the string that held her top. Mercedes reacted with surprised holding her top in place and looked at him. He looked back into her eyes.

"Take it off. Other women are topless too." He told her.

Mercedes liked the idea. She was kind of bothered that other women were topless and José Ignacio could see their breast but she had to keep her bra on for *enforced* modesty that he imposed on her. When he told her to take off her bra, it was exactly what she wanted to hear. She took a deep breath and slowly lowered her hands letting her top fall exposing her small and perfectly perky breast. Taking off her clothes was a familiar action between them that preceded love making and the very act, the positions of their bodies, was a premonition to their sexual pleasure. They both felt the call but now they were on sight of the rest of the people in the beach. Mercedes was not the only topless woman but her body was far hotter than most. Most European woman felt pretty natural being topless in the beach but it was the first time for Mercedes. Her arousal to see herself exposed for the first time in public made her demeanor look somewhat coy, especially appealing for José Ignacio.

Sashawarmas,   by Jorge Bandido

Once the first novelty of being exposed in front of strangers wore off, Mercedes went back to feel at home. She laid down in a towel and he proceeded to rub sun tan on her. He rubbed her legs and firm thighs all the way to the buttocks much of with was exposed by her tiny bikini. He straddled her and rubbed both his oily hands on her skin. He rubbed her belly, and when he reached her breast, she felt shivers when his hands massaged her breast applying suntan lotion. He was feeling every time more aroused to rub her small perky breast. It was very similar to many preambles to their love making but now they were in front of a few people that were in the beach. Some of them were somewhat indifferent but other seemed to have notice the sexual vibes that they were putting out since they both were feeling far more arousal than it was granted for sun bathing.

After a few minutes he could no longer stand it "Come let's go swimming a little bit." He told her.

She came with him and they both went in the water around waist deep. They squatted in the warm water of the tropical island and enjoyed, the sun, the beach and each other company. A whiff of wind came from Mercedes and brought to him the familiar scent of very ripe pineapple that he knew so well and he knew Mercedes and he were thinking of the same thing. He attracted her gently and kissed her thick lips. She received him wrapping her legs around him kissing him breathing heavily. He pulled out his member and moving the strap of her bikini, opened himself access to her deepest intimacy. His member went in smoothly, very much expected. There must have been 20 people or so in the beach. Mostly adults but there might have been a few kids.

"José Ignacio, they are watching us. I can't pretend!" Mercedes warned him as she was being taking over by pleasure abandoning herself to the sensations.

"Let them be envious." He told her and added: "Right now all men in the beach wish they were between your legs where I am".

"No José Ignacio there are children watching." She protested as she was losing herself in waves of pleasure.

"Is love not beautiful for all ages?" He told her reaching deeper inside her. "You are the Goddess of the beach. You are the warmth; you are the sun that bathes us all. As you make love to me you make love to the beach and to everyone who sees you, to everyone who may join us with a glance and envies savoring your delicious body." He whispered in her ear.

Mercedes was beyond help, she tightened him in a deeper hug pressing her breast on his chest hiding her face of supreme pleasure in his neck biting her lips from the inside to repress the loud moan that was taken her over as she climaxed. There was nothing she could do about her amber light shining off her body. Everybody in the beach felt it even if they did not see it. They all felt the elation of Mercedes' sex.

They came out of the water and laid down on the sand where Mercedes let her body decor the white beach regaling everybody present to the sight of her sensual curves. She was tired of sex, relaxed and fell into a deep sleep. The stares of the onlookers crawled over her body producing a relaxing effect of a sensual massage on her body. José Ignacio had never felt so close to her. He was proud of her beauty, their sensuality and for once he was not jealous of other people looking at her, but all the way around. He had never felt the feeling of love as intense as he was feeling then. Now he did not feel the fear of how intensely he desired her. He had given up to his true nature and had let the Lust guide him and direct his actions. He was finding his own self and was feeling truly happy. This was the sweet part of his desire for her that he really wanted to cultivate.

When the time to leave came he could not get over the idea of changing anything and told her to keep her top off. José Ignacio was proud of the body of his woman and he wanted to show it off. He wanted the world to see the hotness of his female and did not care if other men saw her perfectly round and happy breast. She abided happily excited to the new freedom José Ignacio was granting her. She always liked to show her body the only reason she did not do more was because of fear of being sexually molested if she did that in a regular place. However it was different, the environment of the island was very special and with José Ignacio nearby she had no reason to fear being molested. Of course, when José Ignacio was around she had a good reason to dress modestly, not to incur on his anger. But it was him who requested it and she was happy to be able to exhibit her body as she always wanted.

When the small boat got the port, Mercedes realized that she got more than she bargained for. One thing was the relaxed environment of the beach with a few foreigners used to nudity and another thing was in the main island. Local men in the island certainly had an appreciation for her beautiful shapes but discretion was not a priority for them. Now Mercedes was in a place with far more people, Latino men whose eyes devoured her body with unrestrained lust as she walked by topless. They kept their distance do to the respect that José Ignacio inspired but their eyes were not as respectful. Mercedes looked around and saw that she was the only woman that had neglected to put on her top when she got into port. She found Jose Ignacio reassuring hand holding hers and knew that at least she was not going to be assaulted by the many men that lusted after her.

Sashawarmas,   by Jorge Bandido

They started walking towards the lodge through the many people in the small village. It might have been less than 100 yards but it felt like many miles. Every step they gave she discovered more hungry eyes desiring her breasts, reaching for her crotch, wanting to take her. She squeezed Jose Ignacio's hand and stood closer to his muscular body guard covering her nakedness and part sending a clear message to the onlookers that she was not up for grabs. Her familiar scent of pineapple started permeating her surroundings, even she could smell it now. She had to speed up and get to their lodging as soon as they could before her desire took the better of her. She did not dare to stop to put on her top on because she feared what might happen to her if she stopped what she was doing. She did not trust herself!

She went from being intimidated by the lascivious stares of the people to crave them. She relished on the lust in the eyes of the men looking at her and wished that some of them would venture a grab or cup a feel as they passed by, but she did not dare to invite it. It was just how horny she was feeling. She covered herself with José Ignacio's arm fearing to lose complete control of herself. Finally she could not resist anymore and put one of his arms around her carefully placing his hands squarely on her exposed breast and covered the other one with his trunk. The pressure of his warm palm in her nipple was more than she could stand. She felt her pussy make a summersault and a wave of lust travel through her body making her gasp. José Ignacio held her closer and helped her walk in spite of her buttery knees. Mercedes was panting as if she was having sex and it was clear for everybody what was going on in her body.

As soon as they got inside her room she shoved Jose Ignacio on the bed on his back and pulled his swimming trunks down. She straddled him without losing a beat and impaled herself with a single thrust of her hips. Mercedes fists crisped on Jose Ignacio's chest as she collapsed climaxing over him just after the first thrust. She let out a deep felt groan muffled on Jose Ignacio pectorals when she bit into them spasming over him. Thick drool came out of her mouth with indistinguishable moans of pleasure as she rubbed up and down crawling on Jose Ignacio's body as orgasm after orgasms ran through her body as electrical discharges. He held her face tenderly with one hand and whispered tenderly in her hear.

"Whore, you are such a whore. My beautiful sweet, and beloved whore", he said.

Mercedes paused her hips broad range movement where she was. She was sensitive on that issue. Other times José Ignacio had called her a whore on other occasions when she was wearing something revealing but in those cases there was a recriminatory tone to his words; often also spanking her. This time he was calling her whore lovingly as if it were a pet name. His deep voice melted her heart with tenderness even if he was calling her an ugly name. She barely managed to reply: "Your whore," before she fainted of exhaustion after her serial orgasms.

46. COMPLEMENTARY PROBLEMS

The love between Mercedes and Jose Ignacio was such that it scared him. They were closer than ever. As the passion with Mercedes increased, José Ignacio feared the magnitude that it could develop into a wildfire that could engulf them both. Sometimes it meant making wild love pushing the boundaries of desire, like the vacation in Isla de Plata, and other times it was in the darkest ways, when José Ignacio was seduced by violence and power. His high testosterone that made him so horny all the time had the potential to make it also very violent. With his high testosterone, desire and violence could turn into each other with neck-break speed. Like any drug addiction, the person constantly craves stronger fixed. Both the good and the bad ones were equally intense. He had given up in the idea of finding a soft beautiful love as he once tried with Gabriela and had accepted that sex with Mercedes was his future so he sought to devote his life to it, to do more of it, to make it more intense. He knew he had not hit bottom of her sexuality and feared that he could drown in it. Deep inside, this was the reason he was always jealous of her desires, her deeper sensuality. This was also the reason why he continued to sleep with other women, to keep Mercedes always in the chase of him and seeking him out. This gave him some assurance that he was the one she preferred over all the other admirers. While she was seeking him out, it kept the balance on his favor. His lust for her body was such that he could not fathom what to do if it were not available. If she ever realized how bad he truly needed her, if she ever withheld sex from him, she could use it on her advantage. He could not imagine living in a world without her. They continued to talk about moving in together but none of them would budge in their position. He insisted in bringing Amanda along with them but for Mercedes it was a deal breaker. Clearly, Mercedes' consent was needed for José Ignacio to have any chance of having Amanda again.

In the meantime, José Ignacio continued to be obsessed with the memories of making love to Amanda while she was trying to fight him off. He had taken a drink of the most addictive elixir and could not get off it. On occasions he stopped pondering about his feeling, how much it excited him to forced women to strip, the times he had done it Francia, Claudia, and others. The old conflict about his true nature came back. Was he, deep inside, a rapist? Was that why he enjoyed it so much? Did he have it? Had his father raped his mother? Did he have rapist genes? Could he control them? Or was the neurologist right? Was his brain scar leading him to do all these misdemeanors? When tender love bathed his soul, he was certain he wasn't but on occasions, he got a taste of the other side and felt lost in a deep pit of uncontrollable desire that knew no bottom.

Mercedes herself had quite a bit of baggage from her own family including those that complemented perfectly with his issues. They both were feeding on each other weaknesses and finding a mutual codependence on each other. There is no telling where the situation would have gone were it not for what happened in those days. Dr. Basil, a well-known ethnobotanist, came to Ecuador to study epiphytes. He brought along José Ignacio to the field due to his climbing abilities and knowledge of the local flora. Mercedes came along to help out in logistic and such, but more importantly, to guard him from Dr. Basil students. One of the students that came with Dr. Basil was Kristal. She was an attractive blond of 5'10", 22 years old, she was a boxer, undefeated Golden Globe winner for the last two years. She clearly had not taken many punches in her matches as her nose was pointy and pretty. Since Kristal was happy for being in the tropics, she wore tank tops, shorts to get sun tanned showing up her well proportions arms, washer board abs, and muscular legs which did not make Mercedes very happy because, clearly she got José Ignacio's attention every time she passed by him.

The work in the field went perfectly well. Dr. Basil kept teaching José Ignacio about the chemical compounds present in different plants they ran into, and José Ignacio would reciprocate telling him the different uses that that plant had, for the indigenous people; which often elicit celebrations from the professor. José Ignacio had a natural talent to find plants no one could see, as if he could smell them under places completely out of sight. He knew some of the medical properties of the plants but seemed to have a supernatural capacity to guess them after smelling the plant leaves, or its extract after breaking the leaves off. Dr. Basil was fascinated by the synergy between his thorough knowledge of plant biochemistry and José Ignacio's uncanny, innate ability to guess uses, as if something deep in his mind already knew it all along, and it only needed to be awaken. After a few days Dr. Basil had accomplished pretty much all the goals of the trip, mostly thanks to José Ignacio capacity to climb any tree, monkey style, without ropes or climbing gear. He had climbing gear and knew well how to use it, but he knew it was the time to show off his skills, so he would just climb up the trees 80 or 100 feet of the ground to reach some plant that Dr. Basil had spotted from the ground or just a epiphyte he suspected he would find up in the canopy when nothing could be seen from the forest floor. They had started talking of having José Ignacio go to the US for a PhD in ethnobotany under Dr. Basil's direction, if he only received approval in a grant that he had applied for.

One day after doing the field work, Kristal had taken a few beers and she was standing closer to José Ignacio than it was customary and flirting very openly with him. She would put her hands on his shoulder, or his biceps, and squeezed it appreciative his muscles. It was not uncommon for José Ignacio to be shirtless in the station due to the merciless heat of the forest and his ripped torso always shone with sweat so Kristal was very taken by the sight, and the feeling. Mercedes had been unhappy about her very presence from the beginning and since José Ignacio was such "the dear" of the expedition Mercedes was getting really annoyed to see Kristal flirting with him. She knew that José Ignacio would not skip a bit to sleep with her if was given half a chance. He would not leave Mercedes for Kristal, this Mercedes knew, but it would be just another slut that he bedded and she was really tired of it. When Kristal reached for his abs to feel them, Mercedes lost it and told her in no ambiguous terms to keep the distance from him.

"Get away from my boyfriend, you slut." Mercedes said shoving Krystal away from José Ignacio. It did not matter that Krystal knew no Spanish, the message got to her loud and clear.

In very few seconds José Ignacio remembered that Kristal was a boxer and stood nearly a foot taller than Mercedes, with the associated arm length. She had been drinking and giving Mercedes rudeness she would have every reason to retaliate. He did not move fast enough and Kristal stroke Mercedes in the solar plexus bending her over deprived of air. He reached over to block Kristal throwing his arms around her. Kristal switched instantly from the fighter stand and melted into a pussy cat when she felt his arms around her. She hugged him back and buried her nose on his neck taking air deeply with a low purr of appreciation. José Ignacio felt her breast on his chest and wondered if he had done the right thing holding her. Kristal lowered her hands and grabbed his ass firmly, taunting Mercedes, who was behind him, in case she did not see her kissing him and sucking his neck.

Mercedes took the line the hook and the sinker and came after Kristal like a wounded lioness. She went by him and punched Kristal in the face. He let go of Kristal to control Mercedes. This, he repented almost immediately. As soon as Kristal was free of his arms, she recovered her fierceness. She moved fast like a lightning and before anyone could react she fired a right-left-right combo. Mercedes never saw them coming. All missiles hit the target, left cheek, right cheek, and jaw; and Mercedes dropped to the ground. José Ignacio moved as fast as he could to control Kristal who was decidedly the most dangerous, if not the angriest. Kristal experienced the same transformation from tigress to kitten when his arms were around her. She hugged him, reaching for his behind and licking his neck and moaning to make sure that Mercedes noticed she was collecting her price for her victory in combat. Luckily there were other two people that came to control Mercedes that got up angrier than ever and was ready try another suicidal attack at Kristal. She was angry for being punched, for facing a clearly stronger rival,

266

Krystal was younger and being blond and pretty was precisely the kind of woman Mercedes most dislike. She was also hurt for José Ignacio letting Kristal's fondling, with complete nonchalant in her presence.

José Ignacio dragged Kristal away from the scene to avoid another confrontation and heard Mercedes swear and curse at being restrained. He was burning in lust to see how quickly Kristal turned from wild animal to tender loving kitten in his arms. Her mouth in his neck was sucking intently as if trying to give him a hickey. He was burning feeling her breast on his chest, but Dr. Basil was an admired professor that he hoped would one day invite him for a PhD in the US. He had to show some good manners if it was not too late. He walked her to the bathroom where he told her to just take a cold shower to chill. Kristal took off her shirt showing him her round breast before José Ignacio had a time to close the door. There was nothing that José Ignacio wanted more than to have a good taste of her but he was already in enough hot water with the scene that had taken place and not knowing how Dr. Basil would take it. He took a good, resigned, breathed deeply looking at her naked upper body, and turned around closing the door behind him.

José Ignacio took Mercedes from the other students that were restraining her and brought her to their bedroom. He was so horny that just walking in the bedroom he stripped her to take Mercedes that wounded and resentful let him do her, glad to have, somehow won this stand-off. Mercedes was angry, hurt both in her pride as well as for the punches. Kristal was some 5 years younger than Mercedes, taller, she had larger breasts, and she was feeling really threatened by her presence.

"That bitch wanted to fuck you. There is no respect for other women!" Mercedes said with anger noticing his hickey on his neck, happy to have him inside her. "You are mine, your cock is mine and only mine".

Feeling José Ignacio make love to her, helped her cool down. Mercedes knew José Ignacio was more of a butt person where she was definitely the advantage, but she knew he would gladly "*give her a poke*" like he would shamelessly confess after making love to other women. He promised her he would not let Kristal hit her again.

"You know you are the love of my life." He reassured her knowing that it was all she wanted to hear. It did not escape Mercedes attention that he did not promise he would not have Kristal, however. Because the visitors were schedule to be in the field for another 5 days they had to negotiate some sort of truce or working scenario for them to coexist.

The next day life was uneventful. Mercedes and Kristal ignored each other very actively, which was as much anyone was going to hope at the time.

Sashawarmas,   by Jorge Bandido

In the evening when Kristal was going to bed she announced she wanted to sleep in a hammock that was in the hall. She was not going to sleep the same bedroom where all the other visitors were. José Ignacio seemed to have caught a glimpse of complicity that she directed to him right as she was announcing to the others that she was going to sleep outside. They went to bed shortly after but José Ignacio did not fall sleep. He waited until he heard Mercedes restful respiration of a deep sleep and went out quietly to Kristal's hammock. She received him with a greedy kiss.

"I thought you would never get out of the bed of that bitch". She told him even though it had been only a few minutes since they went to bed.

They made love quietly and he went back to his bed shortly after. He was solicit and loving with Mercedes during the day to give her peace of mind but he repeated the night visits to Kristal all the four remaining nights they were in the field always managing to sneak out of Mercedes bed undetected. In actuality he was burning to tell her about his escapades with Kristal as he did with other women, but he feared that Mercedes could make a scene.

When they came out of the field site, they spend the last night in Coca, small town at the entrance of the rain forest. They all had dinner and said the goodbyes until the next day but it was the last time to do Kristal and José Ignacio did not want to have to be sneaking around. He wanted to spend all night with her and not just do her once. Because all the other were gone to bed, he was no longer worried about scenes. He walked Mercedes to their hotel room.

"I am going to have a drink before I go to bed". He told her.

It was a crude excuse that Mercedes could not possible buy.

"Like hell you are" She told him defiant. "You are going nowhere alone while that cunt is around."

They were having this conversation at the threshold of the hotel room with Mercedes inside and him at the door. When Mercedes made her statement a female voice rang from the hall.

"Who is a cunt?" Kristal asked over hearing their conversation.

Mercedes told her walking towards her and ready for a rematch

"You are a fucking cunt. Stay the hell away from my man."

This time José Ignacio held Mercedes who was the most likely one to start a physical attack that she will eventually lose, and told her to calm down.

268

"Look, you just go to bed and I will be back later ok?" He told her hoping to diffuse tension.

"I don't want that slut around you when I am not there" Protested Mercedes.

Kristal close the door behind her. "Oh, get over it, we have been fucking for a week. And we are going to fuck tonight too whether you like it or not." She taunted Mercedes not helping his plans.

Mercedes roared in anger and charged Kristal who took a step back and was ready for her. But José Ignacio held Mercedes down and laid her on the bed holding both her arms behind her body to immobilize her.

"We are not going to be able to do anything now that Mercedes knows we have to do something if we want to be together." He observed.

"Let's do something then." Kristal said determined.

José Ignacio instructed Kristal to hand him his backpack with the climbing gear. He pulled out a thing cord and tied up Mercedes' arm behind her back. Mercedes tried to resist but she was no match to José Ignacio's strength. Pinning Mercedes down and tying her up was getting him very turned on.

Kristal helped him handing him materials and unhelped him taunting Mercedes. "I love sucking his dick. I am going to eat him all the way".

José Ignacio gagged Mercedes with a t-shirt inside her mouth and secured it with duct tape to keep her quiet. As he saw her angry eyes of helplessness he felt consumed by such incontrollable lust. Mercedes' struggle and frustration was turning him on way too much and unbeknown to him his darkest side was awakening.

"Hey, we can fuck here in front of her so she can see how I make you come." said Kristal reading José Ignacio thoughts and kissing him in the mouth.

It was the ultimate insult to Mercedes, the ultimate humiliation to see José Ignacio fucking her rival and just what José Ignacio was wanting to do the most. José Ignacio always told Mercedes how he fucked other women to annoy her as a show of power. He had asked many times Mercedes to come and see him doing Gabriela but she always refused. Kristal was the woman that had defeated her in a fight and that was taller, and younger than her. Forcing her watch him doing Kristal was the ultimate power game, and he was loving it.

For starters Kristal knelt in the ground and took his cock in her mouth a few inches from Mercedes face. Mercedes was crying of anger and impotence.

After a brief demonstration they laid down in the bed next to the immobilized Mercedes. Mercedes could have closed her eyes but she could not get herself to do it. Watching them was a sick fascination Mercedes could not resist. José Ignacio took Kristal's shirt off and used his teeth to unbuckle her bra. Her round and well-shaped breast were easily twice the size of Mercedes'. He sucked them long and slowly. Kristal's moans of pleasure and Mercedes muffled roars of anger made an arousing contrast for him. He took the rest of the cloth of Kristal and laid on his back with Kristal on top of him. Kristal was also moist with anticipation and took his member with groan of pleasure. Kristal licked his beautiful face as she was sucking it as if it were a breast. Mercedes hit rock bottom, to see her hated rival enjoy his beloved and impale herself with his manhood, giving him pleasure. She knew what it felt, it was her pleasure to feel not Kristal's.

"You are one lucky bitch. He is delicious." Kristal declared breathing heavily.

She felt robbed. As his rhythm accelerated, so did Kriystal's breathing. Kristal's hot body and the feeling of power over Mercedes gave him a telluric orgasm.

"He is the greatest fuck. Isn't he?" Kristal taunted Mercedes laying on him recovering while he kissed and caressed her.

He found so arousing humiliating Mercedes and the inclusion of bondage in their sex games that he wanted to push it farther. He rolled Mercedes on her back and opened her shirt exposing her breast, and kiss them for Kristal to watch.

"Wow, wow, what are you doing" asked Kristal.

"Look, do you want to suck them? It feels good. Let's give her a goof fuck." He invited Kristal.

Mercedes squirmed and groaned in rage to the thought of Kristal kissing her breast.

"Stop." Order Kristal. "I am not going to let you rape her!"

"Oh, come on. It is not like that. I am not raping her. It is Mercedes, she likes all these stuffs." José Ignacio said reaching between Mercedes legs and reaching under her skirt. "Look, it's no big deal. Suck her boob, I swear you will like it."

But Kristal was having none of it. She shoved José Ignacio away from Mercedes and started to untie her.

270

Sashawarmas,   by Jorge Bandido

"One things is having sex with you but I won't let you rape her in my presence. Whatever you do when I am not around it is another thing but being here I cannot let you rape her." Explained Kristal while she released Mercedes' arms.

It was that word again. Why? It did not make sense.

"Come on! It is just a game. Let's give her a good fuck, she likes being fucked. You will like it too. I promise." Insisted José Ignacio not understanding Kristal's determination. "I have fucked her with another girl other times"

As soon as Mercedes' arms were free she pulled out the duct tape from her mouth and turn to punch Kristal. Kristal was on her feet in a flash and stepped back. Mercedes lounged at Kristal just as José Ignacio grabbed her by her waist preventing her to reach her rival.

"I am the one who untied you stupid bitch. He is the one who was going to rape you. I am out of here I don't want anything with you two fucked up people," and slammed the door as she left.

47. DARKNESS AWAKEN

With Mercedes restrained by her waist with her shirt open and her breast bare, her chest heaving with anger, José Ignacio was aroused enough that he could not stand that sight. José Ignacio felt besiege by the strongest feeling of lust he had ever felt. His stare froze in terror looking closely into Mercedes' eyes. Mercedes knew that something was wrong the instant their eyes met. She was expecting to have him fuck her hard, to see him yell at her for not cooperating, even spank her but she was scared to see the terrified look on his face. Jose Ignacio grabbed his arms with both hands crossing his forearms over his chest and managed to fall back on the mattress with a *rictus* of terror frozen on his face.

"Please help me." He pleaded and then in a much deeper voice that contrasted sharply with his expression of ultimate terror he added: "I want to hurt you".

Mercedes felt the hair on the back of her neck stand up in fear to see the contrast between the expression of terror on his face and the deep threatening voice coming from his throat. Tying up Mercedes, humiliating her with Kristal, the prospect of having Kristal rape Mercedes while she was tied up had presented him with the next step on the corruption of his soul and he knew that tasting this drug meant immediate addiction. The air of the forest became very still and the scent of overripe fruit thickened every breath he took. Something in him told him he had to resist it at all cost. Mercedes remembered that weird afternoon at the Igapó. She felt a presence. She felt all her hair of her body stand. She knew she was not alone with José Ignacio in the room. Grabbing his elbows with the opposite hands and asking for help was the only thing he could do to restrain himself and fence off the beast that was possessing him.

Mercedes was scared to see his expression of fear and the most fearless man she had ever met and immediately knew what to do. There were many things she did not know about José Ignacio's darkness and his weird connection to The Lust but she knew how to tame him; she had to make him come. He had fallen backward on the bed and was struggling to hold his own self. He had taken off her underwear when she was tied up so all she had to do was to straddle him and take in his hard member. She took him inside with a single stroke. She took a deep breath and started her unique rhythm and rode him at full gallop with the wild stride of her hips.

"Come on my love, come to me." She pleaded as she grabbed one of his hands and pressed it against her breast. "Take me the way you like it".

Mercedes gasped in pain to feel his herculean hand squeeze her breast as if he wanted to rip it out of her chest.

"Come on baby, fuck me good. I am yours to fuck. Do me hard the way you know how to." Mercedes encouraged him tears streaming freely out of her eyes both in fear for the weird presence taking her lover and the pain of his hand crushing her breast. "Come back to me please. Come to me." She begged.

She held his face in her hands like a person would hold the face of a scared child to give him comfort and kissed his mouth tenderly. She grabbed his other hand and kissed it sucking his pointer as it was his cock. This was part of the sex games they play sometimes before they abandoned themselves to their love. She was trying to do anything that reminded him of the good sex and sweet love they shared. That was the only thing that could fight of the darkness in which he was sinking. He bend the finger and dug his nail inside her gums.

Mercedes gasped with pain but continued riding him with full stroke of her hips. He reached with his ring finger inside the hand that was clutching her breast and dug its nail in her nipple crushing it against his palm. Mercedes was blinded with pain but she knew she could not give up them. She was about to lose him.

She looked at his unseen eyes. Hi eyes had sheer terror, but the deep groan from his voice was downright malignant. The struggle was occurring inside him, away from her reach. Mercedes understood that she could not stop regardless of how much it hurt. Tear were coming out of her eyes as his nail dug deeper in her nipple. Her pussy was the only connection she had with the man she loved and she had to make it count. It was the only way she could tilt the balance between the struggle occurring inside him.

Mercedes felt the taste of blood in her mouth from his nail breaking the soft skin inside her lips. She closed her eyes to better focus all her love on the man that was hurting her. She ignored the excruciating pain from her crushed nipple, held his face in her hands putting her face in contact with his to better give him her most intense feeling of love, and gave her heart and soul to her tormentor.

Mercedes pulled out almost all the way stopping when just the tip of his cock was inside her. Then she moved back and forth fast letting it in and out just one inch 3, 4, 5 times before she shoved it inside herself slowly deliberately the full length until both their pubis touched. She moved it almost all the way out and went down slowly again 3, 4 5 times. Then she went back almost out and repeated the first superficial penetrations 3, 4, 5

273

times. Mercedes alternated the fast superficial and the slow deep penetrations one after the other playing her hips as she only could do it.

With her closed eyes she had the most vivid image of the Igapó in the rain forest. It was the same place where Claudia was taken by the unknown presence. In the pond about waist deep, she saw a young dark-skinned boy of 11 years old or so. He was lanky with long legs, long arms, and coppery dark skin. He did not have the muscular built of her lover but Mercedes could recognize the same face and the same expression of terror. The water of the Igapó was not clear as she recalled it. It was pitch black. It had an unnatural solid darkness. A dense dark mist started raising from it and engulfing the terrified boy that seemingly could not move away from it; his terrified eyes mirroring the eyes of the adult man she was making love to. Mercedes put her heart and soul on her rhythm. She moved herself doing a seductive circle she knew aroused him and made him come and focused all her love on the little boy that was taken by the mist, and in her lover whose face she was kissing with her full lips. The pain of her nipple was unbearable but Mercedes knew he needed her to resist, to bring him back from darkness. That became her only goal in the world.

Finally, the magic rhythm of her hips tipped the balance on her favor. He let go of her lip and wrapped her around in a rib crushing hug. She felt she was going to faint with the pain of his hug, his other nail digging on her nipple to the point of drawing blood, and the brutal bite in her face as his orgasm mounted but she continued her unstoppable rhythm knowingly that it was the only salvation card they both had. She could not breathe and she feared for her ribs but she knew she was close. With great relief she felt him raising his hip to meet hers, the pressure of his bite slowly released and the nail digging in her nipple slowly relinquished. She was happy to see him come, happy her ordeal was over, happy their relationship had survived the test of Kristal, and the weird possession he had experienced. She would let him fuck 20 Kristals if that mean not to risk this again. Heck she would let Kristal fuck her all day long if that was what it took. She was happy to be back to normal as she covered his face with kisses and her most tender love.

274

48. GET BACK ON THE HORSE

Mercedes rolled down from top of a panting José Ignacio when he released her. Her nipple hurt so much that her eyes could not stop streaming tears. Her nipple was swollen and bloody and extremely sensitive. She covered it with her hand to stop the bleeding and was blinded by the pain that the very contact of her hand produced. She laid face down, crying non-stop of happiness to have succeeded in bringing José Ignacio back and tears of pain for the injured nipple. He hugged her from behind kissing and caressing her. Thanking between kisses and declarations of love. He did not realize how much damage he had done to her. When he rolled her over to kiss her mouth, she maintained her hand covering her nipple. Realizing something was up, he removed her hand exposing the swollen and bloody nipple she was trying to hide. José Ignacio felt his heart sink!

He was horrified of what he had done to her during his trance in the struggle with darkness. He recoiled in fear of his own actions. He was ashamed and fearful of himself. He had feared for a long time the intensity of his feelings for Mercedes and how much pleasure he derived from hurting her. Now he had evidence that it was far more than he could control and that he had not begun to discover the depth and intensity that they could reach. His orgasm had been downright fabulous but likely because he was doing such horrible damage to his beloved. It was such a contrast between the devoted love she was giving him and the sadistic pain he was inflicting her. How far was it going to go? What was the next step his darkness would take him to? He remembered what the Dr. had said about his brain injury and addictions. It was just like an addiction to drugs. Well, addiction to drugs do result in seeking of stronger and more addictive drugs all the time. Surely there will be some delicious new discoveries in their good, mutually loving sex, but what would happen the next time the dark monster that he knew lived inside him awakened and wanted to go the next step? Now he knew that there were far more depths than he could fathom and that he was no able to pull out of them by himself. He could not count on Mercedes to bring him back at whatever cost it could take on her. He could not ask Mercedes to do it. It was not right for her.

"I could have really hurt you. I don't want to." He said with tears of sadness coming out of his eyes.

Seeing how contrite he was and fearing he would take a rush decision.

"Oh, come on. You cannot really hurt me. I am tougher than that. I can take your passion however it comes at me. I won't give up on you." She told him fencing off any drastic action.

"I wanted to rape you. I would have done it if Kristal did not stop me. I don't want to be a rapist." José Ignacio argued finally accepting something he had denied in his mind despite all the evidence.

"You were not going to rape me. I wanted it. I want you to fuck me anyway you want, all the time. You know that. I did not want her to touch me and I hate her with all my soul. She is the one who started all this. I wanted you to fuck me tied up as I was." Replied Mercedes trying to ameliorate his fears.

Then José Ignacio said that last words she wanted to hear from him.

"We can't continue being together. We need to separate before it gets worst. I am afraid I can truly hurt you and I cannot control myself."

Mercedes' world felt apart. "No, don't be silly. I am far stronger than you think. I can take it."

Seeing in his eyes a determination she had never seen in them before, when it came to splitting up, Mercedes pleaded. "Please, I would not know what to do without you. I need to have you with me. We belong together and you know it." She was bearing her soul. Her insides actually ached to the thought of not making love to him again.

Seeing his determination Mercedes decided to gamble it all. She reached for his cock and stroked it a couple times to feel it. Seeing that it was still hard and knowing of his endless sex drive she got obsessed with one thought: "*get back on the horse.*" It is a common saying when someone falls of a horse, they need to get back on the horse before fear for the fall sets in. Their last love making had scared José Ignacio. She had to make love to him again having a good experience to erase the scary one he just had had.

"Look, we will move in together as you wanted. I will talk to Amanda. We can convince her to join us. You can seduce her and make love to her." she told him taking his member inside her as she started to make love to him again slowly, softly. "We both will be yours and will make sure to make you happy and you will never feel anything bad. The problem was Kristal, she has anger in her soul. There will not be any bad vibes between us anymore. You will never want to hurt anyone because we will fill you up with the most pure love." Mercedes offered with tear streaming of her eyes.

Sashawarmas,   by Jorge Bandido

José Ignacio was quiet, considering Mercedes' offer. It was precisely what he had been wanting. Up until 30 minutes before, he would have accepted it without hesitation but after seen what he had done in their last love making, he was not sure. The passions that Mercedes inspired him, were just too intense, too much. Like a confluence of two worlds that should never be together and that united are meant to produce unpredictable results. He knew he had to put distance with Mercedes but he lusted for her too much. It felt too good to have her to give it up. But every time he sank deeper into his darkest instincts and he knew Mercedes was the catalyst. He knew he had to stop. He knew that people with the brain injury that he had often end up as sexual predators. That is who he was and he felt there was no point on fighting it off any longer. It dawned on him the certainty of something he had known all along but he kept ignoring it. His mother had been raped and he was the son of a rapist. He had suspected it for a long time but now he got the certainty. Raping was in his genes. If his Lust will always rule him, it was better to give in it in a controlled situation than to try to resist it and snap. Mercedes' skim of having Amanda join them was appealing and it might work. With two women to take care of him he had a better chance to channel his lust into some controllable scenario than going solo. They would flood him with sex and pleasure and it may be just what he needed to ward off the darkness he feared.

Mercedes reached behind her and started massaging his testicles. A treatment she knew always made him come quicker. Mercedes, on her own mind kept repeating to herself: "*Get back on the horse*". She had to have him make love to her tenderly, with love. She had to leave him with a good last impression of true love before he was too far gone. Before the fear of their recent love making sank too deep. "*Get back on the horse. Get back on the horse* " She thought to herself repeatedly as she moved herself slowly up and down his member. Mercedes' eyes had not stopped flowing. First it had been with pain, then with fear, now they were streaming tears of love, of passion. She professed him her undying love and upped the offer.

"Amanda is a real slut. If you think I am a horny, Amanda is a real nymphomaniac." Mercedes continue whispering softly on his ear as she rubbed her breasts on his chest. "When we were younger we always talked about boys. She is ten times hornier than me. You will have a field day fucking her and she will not stop fucking you. When we were in high school, she fucked everything that moved. She was fucking the PE teachers since she was 16 and fucked everyone she ran into until she was 19 when she met Robespierre. You want to fuck a whore? Amanda is your whore. We both will team up to fuck you unconscious."

Sashawarmas,   by Jorge Bandido

The notion of living with both sisters and having his sex cravens satisfied by both women was working the desired effect on his mind and Mercedes' sensual hands stroking him was working well too. She sucked his nipples, licked his skin covered by the musky sweat it always had, and felt a sweet after taste on his skin as if some honeydew covered it. But she was not sure she had convinced him.

"We can invite Virginia too. We all will be yours." Mercedes continue whispering on his ear raising the stakes. Mercedes knew that Virginia had let José Ignacio have her before he orchestrated their encounter. "I will tell Virginia she can have me again but she has to let you put your huge cock inside her first. You can fuck her pretty little ass and then you can watch us make love. We will fuck her the way you both fucked me that time."

Her own words were working on her. As she talked sensually about offering him sex and pleasure, with his cock inside her going in and out, she started feeling the effects of her own sex talk. Reminiscing of the day she had the encounter with Virginia she felt a wave of lust traveling through her body. She kissed his lips tenderly and inhaled deeply his aphrodisiac breath.

Mercedes felt that she was making progress but she knew she could lose him any time if the wrong thought came to his mind, so she wanted to up the stakes some more. Her mind drifted to Claudia and she knew how horny he was for her. She herself thought that Claudia was super hot and thinking of her lesbian encounter with Virginia she thought of Claudia too. Mercedes own thoughts went to the Igapó when Claudia was naked on the sand and she straddled her and kissed her on the sand. She felt her own pussy twist and realized how horny this recollection made her. But she chose not to mention it to José Ignacio. She was sure something mysterious of José Ignacio had been there and she was not sure it was the good side she wanted to bring up. She feared that he might have having the same visions of the Igapó that she had in their last love making so she rushed that thought from her mind.

There was of course a safe image that she could invoke that would always bring José Ignacio into a tender loving frame of mind. She knew it would work but she hated to use it. It felt all wrong as in quite the opposite of what her good judgment told her. She grabbed his curls with both hands and licked all his face like an ice cream. She knew bringing her up will tilt the balance in her favor but she knew it will not be in her benefit to do it. "*Get back on the horse. Get back on the horse.*" She thought to herself and made up her mind. It was about him, not about her.

"We can invite Gabriela to come join us. You can lick her gorgeous face." She whispered on his ear. She hated to plant that image on his mind but she

278

knew it will work. Then switching to his other ear, she added "You can put your huge cock in her beautiful little mouth and have her suck it the way you like it. I will watch how she does it and learn how to put your whole dick in my mouth myself.

Mercedes imagined his cock inside Gabriela's beautiful mouth nearly fully open to accommodate his girth and felt her own mouth fill up with water. She remembered enjoying the filling of Virginia's lips in her mouth thinking that they were Gabriela' and wonder what it would be like to kiss her actual lips.

"We can fuck her together the two of us and sandwich her curvy little body between us." She added and meant to talk about sucking her juicy breast and feeling their pressure against his chest but another wave of lust travel through her body. She realized then that she herself was craven to have her. "We will invite Virginia too to fuck her and between the three of us we will fuck her until she passes out." Mercedes added as she let herself be lost in a shaking body long orgasm panting over him. Her pineapple scent flooded the room and her amber glow shone in the darkest recesses of his soul.

Her magic worked. Her last words and intense orgasm tip the balance. She eased José Ignacio into a smooth, and intense orgasm, all the better to help erase the memories of the last one. She braced for a bite but she only felt long warm loving kisses her lover was giving him during his climax. She was perfectly aware that there was a darkness inside him that she had barely rescued him from. She knew perfectly well that there was a risk that this darkness could one day come back and be beyond their control. She knew her Herculean lover could easy break her in half or snap her neck in an assault of passion. Yet, if she had to go, she could not think of a better way. She rather died in the paroxysm of his passion on the hands of her lover than live one day without him.

Sashawarmas,   by Jorge Bandido

49. A CALL FROM ABOVE

Arriving to Quito, they met with Amanda in private. They invited Amanda to her room and Mercedes was the one to break the news.

"Amanda. José Ignacio and I are moving in together."

Amanda was not surprised since they have been dating for a while and it seemed the next logical step, knowing, as she knew, that José Ignacio was not a person who would get married. Yet, the context of the announcement was unexpected. It was like there was another part of the message. Amanda waited for the next part and Mercedes finished.

"We want you to move in with us". Now Amanda was surprised. She looked nervously from José Ignacio to Mercedes as trying to understand what she had heard.

"Look, I know what happened last time but he promised he would not do anything to you do don't want." Added Mercedes.

Now Amanda was more confused. She had consented to have sex with José Ignacio, if Mercedes knew that it did not make sense what she was saying. The only explanation was that she did not fully know. But what did she mean? José Ignacio came to her rescue hugging Amanda from behind like he had done countless times in the kitchen sink, and reaching for her breast, told her.

"Remember last time?" Amanda covered herself much too aware of Mercedes presence.

Mercedes opened Amanda's arms gently letting José Ignacio reach for Amanda breasts, and looking into her sister's eyes told her.

"He is too horny for me. I need you to help me. I need you to make love to him when I am tired or not around. He will not do anything you don't want but if you let him seduce you, I assure you, you will like it." Upon saying this Mercedes stood up and left complicity: "He is really good. I will let you guys to talk."

Amanda had felt cursed by her bad luck with her lovers. For several years she avoided any romantic involvement with any man. Having been taken by José Ignacio had been a Godsend for her. Amanda has been affected by a poisonous lust for José Ignacio since he made love to her. But Mercedes had changed the rules of visitations so he could not come and take her again. She wanted like nothing else to make a secret appointment with him to get fucked one more time but she did not dare betray her sister. When Mercedes told her

280

that José Ignacio was coming, it had made her aroused in anticipation. If she could sneak a fuck with him every couple years, it was good enough to keep her going. The proposal of being his lover, his second woman as it may be, was more than she could hope for. She recalled the expression *"God may close a door but He always opens a window."* Perhaps she was not meant to be married to a wealthy pilot but God had opened a window for her after closing that door. Being the mistress of her sister's partner was not ideal but it would be far better than the celibacy plan she had for herself.

When Mercedes left the room Amanda asked José Ignacio, who was busy behind her kissing her neck and feeling her breast.

"Does she know?"

"No, she thinks I took you by force all the way." He tranquilized her and laid her on the bed pulling up her t-shirt.

José Ignacio sucked her breast and pulled out her short and in no time was making love to a confused Amanda that, nevertheless acquiesced to his love making. Mercedes came back in the room a while later latter when she calculated they were done. It was flooded with the thick smell of ripe grapes. José Ignacio was naked laying on bed with naked Amanda frolicking after sex. Amanda covered herself when Mercedes walked in. Mercedes smiled and asked rhetorically.

"What did you guys agree upon?"

Amanda had agreed to the idea but she was still confused and shy about facing Mercedes with an answer. Before she could answer José Ignacio's phone rang. He stood up and took up the call, from a foreign number. He went out of the room to take the call. Mercedes heard him speaking in English and had a bit of concern of what it could be. Minutes later José Ignacio walked in the room with a radiant smile.

"It was Dr. Basil. He got the grant! He has invited me to come to the US to do a PhD under his direction!"

Mercedes' heart sank. Her plans of moving in and keeping him was suddenly shaken. It was not like he was leaving her for fear of his feeling and his internal struggle as she feared earlier but leaving the country for a PhD, would still mean separation, except in different terms. Even if they kept a long-distance relationship, that was not what she wanted. She could come to visit when her finances allowed and he could come back too but it was a far cry from living with her beloved, shared or not, as it may be with her sister. If he was alone in the US, he would clearly sleep around. There was that bitch of Kristal and countless more Kristals that will show up on his path. It was definitely a bad thing to have him sleep with others and not her. Just as she felt she was about to succeed in keeping him she saw the providence taking him away from her, nobody knew for how long.

For José Ignacio, it was a one in a life time opportunity. It was what he had dreamed all his life since he realized he wanted to be a botanist. He really liked the idea of living with both sisters but this opportunity was far too good to ignore. It was a Godsend in every way. He knew that their mutual passion with Mercedes could be destructive. He was not a religious man but his catholic upbringing crept in now and then, especially in situations where there were forces beyond his control. Forces beyond his control were precisely that darkness that lead him into the path he feared. The chance to move to the US for such a great professional opportunity was also something he never imagined. He thought "*If God wanted me to separate from Mercedes he could present himself with his mighty power and tell me 'I want you to leave Mercedes.' However, another alternative that God could try would be to send me clear sign of how dangerous our relationship is, and send me an opportunity that I cannot refuse that involved putting distance with Mercedes. Perhaps later, as I mature, I will learn to control my urges and then it will be safer for both to be together.*" José Ignacio was thrilled on the merit of his professional career but also, he was glad that this could mean a distance with the darkness he feared. He had come to realize that the best thing that could happen to both of them was to find different paths, for now.

When José Ignacio informed Mercedes his final resolution of going to the US for his degree, she already knew the answer. She just had to keep at it, loving him, trying to get the opportunity to go with him later. She had to trust the magic hook of her sex on him to buy her a little more time until he came around. But she knew for a fact he will come around. It was just a matter of time. She could move in to the US with him. Maybe she could get a job there and live with him there. As for José Ignacio it did not escape his attention that the US was a far more racist country than Ecuador. The thought of living in a place openly racist towards dark people and foreigners in general did make him a bit uneasy. Yet, it was a wonderful career opportunity and he was never being characterized for being afraid of a big challenge. If racism was a problem, he was willing to weather it for the sake of the other good things he could get professionally.